Y0-BZF-403

THE HELEN KATE FURNESS
FREE LIBRARY
WALLINGFORD, PA 19086

The Devious Debutante

The Devious Debutante

URSULA LECOEUR

Enjoy!

Ursula LeCoeur

The Devious Debutante
Copyright © 2015 Royal Street Publishing

www.ursulalecoeur.com
ursulalecoeur@gmail.com

This book is licensed for personal use only. Please do not participate in or encourage piracy of copyrighted materials in violation of the author's rights.

All rights reserved. In accordance with the U.S. Copyright Act of 1976, the scanning, uploading, and electronic sharing of any part of this book without the permission of the publisher is unlawful piracy and theft of the author's intellectual property. If you would like to use material from the book (other than for review purposes) prior written agreement must be obtained by contacting the authors at ursulalecoeur@gmail.com. Thank you for your support of the author's rights.

ISBN-13: 9780578166698

Publisher's Note
This is a work of fiction. Names, characters, places and incidents either are the product of the author's imagination or are used fictitiously. Any resemblance to actual persons, living or dead, events or locales is entirely coincidental.

To Frank Scully, husband and father, for his untiring support of our romance fiction. Always ready to provide a male point of view, he saved us from many faux pas. His notes in the margin — "A man would never say that"—led us to rewrite more than a few pages of dialogue.

Chapter One

*B*en Merritt scanned the large Collins property. His eyes darted from left to right and back again.

Was that?

It was. A figure appeared in the garden to the left of the enormous stone house. Someone walking fast—actually running. In a skirt.

Watching her race through a line of bushes and across the broad lawn toward the open front gate, he anticipated her path and turned just in time to catch the full brunt of her head and shoulders against his chest. He wrapped his arms around her as she fell backwards from the impact.

Stunned, she wriggled free of his arms, sniffed and brushed her hair off her face, wiping her wet cheeks with the same motion. "I beg your pardon."

Ben bowed and tipped his cap to the most beautiful young lady he'd ever seen. A governess perhaps to the young daughter of Patrick Collins? No, she couldn't be. A man with three sisters, he took in her blue wool coat, fashionably falling to the hips, unbuttoned to reveal the expensive fabric of her dress. The decorative braid, the jet beads were far beyond the means of most employees.

Perhaps an older cousin? He'd been told Patrick Collins had but one child—a daughter, thirteen years of age.

The young lady's head barely reached his shoulders, but she was lusciously proportioned. *Not thirteen.* He'd felt her full breasts against his chest. In the flickering flames from two gaslights mounted on the stone pillars he admired the face of a Madonna: white skin as smooth as alabaster, huge sparkling blue eyes, and a perfectly rosy, pert little mouth. A mouth swollen, cheeks flushed with desire.

"To what do I owe this unexpected honor, Miss?"

"I ... couldn't sleep," she stammered, showing remarkable dignity as she uttered such a bald-faced lie. "I came out for a stroll."

"You seemed to be strolling very rapidly. And at midnight."

"Actually, I prefer a run to a stroll. It's the newest exercise for ladies." She raised her chin. "I'm surprised you don't know that."

"Ah, of course." He met her serious look with equal gravity, pretending as she did that her appearance alone on the street at this hour didn't violate every rule of propriety. "And it's done without a hat or gloves? This new exercise—a run, you call it. Perhaps you'd enjoy a run with me?" He offered his arm. "Or a stroll?"

She studied him under her long, black lashes. Her eyes swept from his laced-up workman's boots and denim pants to his plaid shirt and rough black wool jacket. He cursed silently that he'd not dressed more formally for his watch in this fine neighborhood. She focused a moment on his hair, unfortunately no longer neatly combed after two hours at the docks.

He waited as she hesitated, knowing she calculated her options. She glanced back to the gate through which she'd come. Running away from someone, was she? Not someone all that threatening. Her breathing had calmed. Her clenched fists had relaxed. He saw defiance, not fear, in the straightness of her back.

"It's tempting," she said finally. Raising her blue eyes to his face, she sighed heavily. "But how do I know you're not a scoundrel? There seems to be no shortage of them out and about tonight."

A lover's quarrel, then? He put on his friendliest face and denied her charge. "A scoundrel would not have as warm and friendly a smile as I have."

"I suspect that's what all scoundrels say." With remarkable pluck, she leaned in a little forward to examine him more closely. "And who told you your smile was so friendly?"

He laughed. "Are you disputing my mirror?"

"Perhaps it needs a good dusting." A smile lit her face and her eyes sparkled as she said it. Quick-witted, she was, and flirtatious. She tilted her head just so and a black curl tumbled down her bodice and settled on her right breast.

Seized by a desire stronger than he'd ever felt for a lady he'd known for five minutes—or for a lifetime—his breath quickened. With tingling fingers, he grasped her face and brought his lips to hers. The softness of her cheeks, the warmth of her lips and the rose scent of her hair overcame all logical thought. She didn't move. Neither did he for some moments.

Oh, my. The mirror didn't need dusting whatsoever. The gaslights illuminated his handsome features. Clean shaven with longish straight hair, a high forehead and strong jaw, he stepped back and grinned at her predicament. She liked his kiss and he knew it. In fact, she liked it so much she was breathless, her knees trembling beneath her skirt.

In any case, she couldn't return by way of the garden. Vespasian, with whom she'd just had a disagreement, might be waiting for her at the kitchen door or he might be lying drunk in the bushes.

And, if this man followed her to be sure she were safe and encountered Vespasian ...

He stood a respectful distance away. Was there harm in lingering here to talk with him? But a stranger on the street? Well-spoken but with an accent that revealed Northern roots. And incongruously dressed in workman's clothes? They'd not been introduced. And he'd kissed her. "I believe it would be best to forego my midnight, er ... run ... tonight ... I should go back in the house."

"So you would deny yourself a stroll? And deny me the opportunity to spend more time with the most beautiful woman who's ever run into me?" The left side of his mouth rose in a quirky grin.

She pulled her coat together and buttoned it. She'd had enough foolish gallantry for one evening. "Good night, sir."

He pointed to the front porch. "I'll watch until you're safely inside."

That was the last thing she needed. "I'm sure that isn't necessary. You should be on your way."

He tilted his head toward the gate and walk beyond. "I insist."

To get in the house, Maureen needed to reach for the key above the front door. Problem was, she'd have to stand on something to grab it, which would confirm for the gentleman what he probably already knew: She'd sneaked out to meet a lover.

There was no help for it. She forced her feet to turn and step through the gate. Had he heard her and Vespasian shouting at each other? Had he heard him say he would have her yet? Sound traveled at night. She could feel the man's eyes boring into her back as she made her way slowly up the front walk. She added a little swing to her hips that swayed her skirt from side to side.

Under the porch light, her face flaming with mortification, Maureen dragged a heavy rocking chair across the stone porch, lifted her skirt to mid-calf to climb on it, and balanced rather precariously as she felt along the ledge with one hand while holding on to the door facing with the other. No doubt the gentleman on the sidewalk found this show quite amusing. The key in her grasp, she jumped to the floor, repositioned the chair in its original place and unlocked the door.

Was he still there, really waiting until she was safely inside? Her hand on the doorknob, she paused. She wanted to look back, just a quick glance, but she kept her eyes forward and entered the house.

Pausing in front of the hall mirror, she went hot with embarrassment. She stared at a mass of flyaway curls, sprinkled with bits of broken leaves and grass, which also dotted her overcoat, and skirt of her dress. Without question, the handsome man had noticed. Thank heavens she wasn't likely to see him ever again.

Chapter Two

Maureen tended to run late. Late for meals, late for Mass, late for the dressmaker. She was due at Renee's to decorate for Christmas in less than thirty minutes, and she wasn't even dressed, wasn't finished picking camellias. Noah would have to be a little reckless with the reins to get her down to the French Quarter even remotely on time.

Her hands clipped another branch, carefully making a clean cut and laying the twentieth perfect flower in her basket. She'd had to choose carefully. Some of the petals were brown—her own fault for bruising them when she dashed through these bushes Friday night.

From the arms of Vespasian Colville right into the arms of? She didn't even know his name. Yet she'd fallen asleep that night and the next two thinking about his kiss. Vespasian's kisses tended to be too forceful. But this man—whoever he was—had applied his full lips to hers firmly yet tenderly. She'd never felt anything like it. Even now, her pulse fluttered just thinking of it. And every morning, she woke up to the memory of his intense brown eyes.

Vespasian had not bothered to apologize by note or in person for his outrageous behavior in the garden. When he'd tried to raise her skirt, he'd announced they were betrothed. *Betrothed?* He'd never proposed and if he had, she wouldn't have agreed. She was pleased with herself for resisting his advances Friday night. She'd even kicked him in the shins—hard—before she made her wild dash through the yard to the front gate.

Luz hollered from the kitchen door. "Miss Maureen, you're gonna be late for Miss Renee if you don't get right upstairs and change out of those old clothes!"

She looked down at the faded grey gabardine dress, the muslin apron, the threadbare wool shawl. She grabbed her basket of camellias and clippers, removed her gardening gloves and hurried inside.

As Maureen had hoped, Renee wasn't fazed by her tardiness. A basket of gorgeous white camellias calmed anyone's pique. Renee had married William, Maureen's Irish cousin, last January. Not a year later, the couple had settled into an old home they were slowly refurbishing, with a nursery occupied by six-week-old twins, a boy and a girl. Renee's extensive plans for decorations for her first Christmas in her new home included Maureen as a valuable assistant.

Pine roping, yards of satin ribbon in red and white; pinecones; red and white candles; a half dozen pairs of silver candlesticks covered a small side table in the dining room. A yardstick, wire, brads, a hammer, scissors, clippers, and two aprons lay on a cloth on the main table. A tall ladder leaned against a wall.

"Mantels first?" Maureen asked.

"In both parlors and the dining room. If there's enough roping, and I think there will be, let's hang it with ribbons from the stairs."

The ladies tied their aprons at their necks and waists, then moved the ladder to a spot on the hearth in the dining room. Maureen climbed. "I'll anchor the roping just so, don't you think?" She held a piece in a loop.

"I'll follow you with ribbons and candles. Then, you again, with your camellias. You're the plant lady."

While she worked, Maureen related her meeting with Vespasian, explaining he had some nerve expecting her to kiss him when he hadn't written her in four months. She didn't say he'd had more in mind than kissing. "Imagine. He arrives home from college and expects me to be thrilled to see him."

"Studying too hard to write, was he?"

Maureen laughed. "Vespasian?"

Renee broke into a giggle. Everyone knew book learning was far down the list of Vespasian's charms. *Not that such a list even existed.*

"There's no way I can be polite to Vespasian at his family's *reveillon.*"

"You and your father have accepted the invitation, haven't you? You'd have to break your leg to get out of it."

Imagining she might at least break her ankle if she tumbled off the ladder, Maureen saw herself missing a step, shrieking, hitting the floor. But avoiding Vespasian wasn't worth a broken bone. She'd never experienced one, but she'd heard it hurt and sometimes caused permanent problems. She refused to limp the rest of her life.

Her family never missed the annual Colville *reveillon.* The party after midnight Mass on Christmas Eve often lasted until dawn. With sumptuous food and copious bowls of eggnog, the gathering was the highlight of the holiday season for the French Creoles. Her mother and Helene Colville had enjoyed a friendship closer than some sisters. Even after her mother's death, Maureen and her father continued to attend.

At last year's party, Vespasian had led her into the library. He'd given her a gold and garnet brooch in the shape of a bouquet of roses and had taught her to open her lips for his tongue. Did he have a special gift planned for this holiday? She cringed as she recalled his words in the garden: *We're betrothed.*

Renee chattered on: She'd heard the Colvilles expected sixty guests or more. She had a new dress, purple velvet, she couldn't wait to wear.

The dining room decorated, the pair moved to the back parlor, carrying the small table between them. It took two of them to move the ladder the distance. Renee put a steadying hand on Maureen's arm as she climbed. "There's certain to be a receiving line. You'll have to speak."

Hell. Maureen almost said out loud. Her language—learned at the convent school in Atlanta where the young ladies were far more precocious than in New Orleans—was bound to get her in trouble one day. She pushed Vespasian and his family from her mind and doubled her efforts. They repeated their steps: roping, bows, candles and finally camellias.

Mounting the ladder in the front parlor, Maureen glanced down at Renee. "I trust you won't tell William I was alone with Vespasian."

"Not if I have your assurance that you won't be so foolish again."

"I swear it." With great flair, she put her right hand over her heart. "I won't be in any company with him, much less alone with him."

Men didn't duel these days, at least not legally, but between Cousin William's skill with a pistol and Vespasian's, she'd put her money on Vespasian. Last winter, the visiting Buffalo Bill Wild West Show had actually offered to hire him after he'd shown up several of their sharpshooters at an audition. Indeed, he often said he practiced regularly with a dueling pistol and a sword—preparing for the day when he'd be called out to the Oaks by an irate father, brother or husband.

She told herself his boasting was nothing more than a joke, even though she'd heard rumors that Vespasian was intimate with a number of married ladies. Add to that, her beau—that is, her *former* beau—was said to spend a good many evenings on Gallatine Street where men enjoyed every carnal pleasure.

More than a year ago, Maureen's best friend, Carine Bouchard, had overheard her parents discussing the young man's exploits, and had repeated every word to Maureen. Yet she'd still continued to see him until he left for Spring Hill College in Mobile in September.

"Mardi Gras balls will begin before long," Renee said with a conspiratorial lilt in her voice. "I think it's high time you meet some other gentlemen."

Maureen jumped from the ladder's second rung to the marble hearth. "I don't care if I *ever* meet another gentleman as long as I live." The smack of her shoes added emphasis.

"I'm sorry to hear that, Cousin."

She whirled at the sound of William's voice from the hall. He and—oh, my—the tall, dark-haired stranger, walked into the parlor. The brick wall, dressed in a black pinstriped suit, nodded slightly in her direction. Her skin went hot and her heart beat faster than a sparrow's.

The slap of leather soles resounded on the hearth. Over it, Ben heard every word. He recognized her voice and despite his training, stared at the young lady, the very governess—no, William called her his cousin moments ago—who'd plagued his sleep for the last three nights.

William introduced his wife, a beautiful woman herself, then his magnificent relative. "May I present my cousin, Miss Maureen Collins, daughter of Patrick Collins."

Ben hoped his polite smile masked his confusion. He'd been given incorrect information about the Collins family. Supposedly the one daughter had lived with an unnamed aunt in Atlanta for a time after her mother's death, but now resided in New Orleans. *Not Thirteen.*

He delighted in watching the porcelain complexion of Miss Collins turn from a delicate pink to a warmer rose to almost

fuchsia in a full blush. He locked his eyes on hers, large sapphire
pools in a delicate face, with a small turned-up nose and pouty
sensuous lips. Voluminous black curls fell past her shoulders where
they met a cook's white apron, now scattered with pine needles
and sap. Was this woman always covered in foliage? She held clippers, which she transferred to her left hand before greeting him.
He inhaled sharply and bowed to her. "Delighted, Miss Collins."

His gaze moved upward from her ankles to her plum skirt of
tiered ruffles beneath her apron to her well-rounded hips, slim
waist, full breasts and startled expression, which he found adorable.
She bit her lower lip, struggled to alter her face into a socially
correct smile, and murmured how pleased she was to meet him.
He enjoyed watching her squirm. He could easily imagine her
underneath him, thrashing with need.

Madame Collins, removing her apron and gloves, took her
place on the settee and suggested he sit down. "You, too, Maureen."
She gestured to two chairs on either side of the glowing fire. "It's
time for a rest."

Ben waved an arm toward the mantel. "You mustn't stop on
my account."

"I won't," the gorgeous creature said. Turning her back on
him, she took her time placing flowers artfully.

What an incredible turn of events. Maureen Collins. A stunning young lady, more beautiful this evening than she'd been with
a tear-stained face at midnight on St. Charles Avenue.

"May I help? I've been known to assist my mother and sisters
with holiday trimmings." He marched forward and picked up a
length of pine roping from the carpet.

She faced him and their eyes met. Mesmerized, he couldn't
speak. Only vaguely aware of anyone else in the room, he
heard Madame Collins tell Maureen he was a new attorney at
Mermentau & Plemer, now handling the Collins account. "Did
your father tell you he'd hired a new attorney?"

"Papa mentioned it. He thinks attorneys are a dull lot, a necessary evil."

Ben smirked at the insult, amused that she chose to offend rather than befriend the man who'd seen her out alone at midnight. Who'd kissed her inappropriately, yet had received no objection from her. He whispered for her ears only. "Do you agree with your father?"

She fastened her eyes on his. "No, I don't happen to agree. After all, attorneys are known to be discreet regarding their clients' affairs. Isn't that so, Mr. Merritt?"

How amusing to quote her father and then dismiss his ideas in the next sentence. He wanted to laugh, but managed to tame his reaction. "As discreet as the dead, Miss Collins, but not nearly as lifeless."

Her eyes sparkled. "That remains to be seen."

Drawing a little closer to the lovely young lady, he breathed in the pine scent mingled with the roses of her perfume. "What's next?"

She tilted her head toward the hall and the staircase. "Renee wants the banisters decorated."

"First, a little drink," William commanded as he crossed the room with a tray. The ladies took sherry glasses. Ben scooped up a glass of whiskey. William settled on the sofa beside Renee. Maureen motioned to Ben to follow her. *Anytime, Miss.*

Ben lifted the ladder in one hand and carried his drink in the other into the hall. After positioning the ladder so he could reach the highest banister on the staircase, he turned to her. "If you don't mind, may I remove my coat?"

She nodded, then licked her lower lip. My God, was it a nervous habit or a deliberate flirtation?

"Shall we begin at the top, Miss Collins?"

"I'm led to believe that's what most men prefer." As she ascended the stairs, she removed her work gloves and dropped them on the steps.

His whiskey in hand, he climbed until his face was level with her breasts. Her scent, her heat, engulfed him. He was so aroused he reached out and grabbed a banister with his left hand to steady himself.

She pointed to the mahogany railing. He held the pine roping against the wood. She tied it in place, brushing the back of his hand with her fingers. He sucked in a breath and nearly toppled to the floor.

"Done," she whispered, leaning closer, her breasts nearly touching his cheek. He dismounted, moved the ladder and climbed again. Aware that she studied him carefully, he tried to affect a calm demeanor. Surprised by his reaction to her—a heart thumping like a school boy's—he fell back on his training. He slowed the pace of his movements as he lifted his drink from the top rung of the ladder, took a healthy swallow and returned it. He held another loop of pine on the railing. The wire touched his hand, but her fingers did not. *Inadvertent, then, last time.*

William ambled into the hall to hand him a second drink. "My cousin's hobby is growing exotic plants and flowers."

"You consider it just a hobby, William?"

Her cousin rolled his eyes and Ben guessed this was familiar territory. "What do you cultivate, Miss Collins?" *That is, besides a rapid heartbeat, sweaty palms, and a painful erection?*

"White camellias imported from Japan. I picked the blooms on the mantels from my bushes." A brisk answer, a touch defensive. He forced himself to look away from her breasts and into her bright eyes as she continued with an earnest explanation, outlining her intention to graft cuttings from red camellias to white bushes.

In the parlor, William murmured to his wife.

Ben had never in his life felt drawn to a woman as he did to her. Every new thing he noticed about her shocked him with its beauty and perfection. Her hands, her face, even a shoulder beckoned as appealing destinations for his hands. He was almost grateful for the mundane rhythm of decorating. He concentrated on descending the ladder, moving it and climbing again. She walked down another two steps.

William returned to the hallway. Maybe he had picked up on the charged atmosphere. Ben's mind grew cloudier by the moment. "There's a rumor someone is giving Maureen a greenhouse for Christmas, a perfect place to perform her experiments."

Had William said a greenhouse? "How wonderful," he mumbled, his eyes shifting to the man at the foot of the ladder. What was going on here? He turned back to her. "I'd be honored, Miss Collins, to have a tour of your conservatory."

She issued no invitation. She said she had not been allowed inside yet. Was there not a greenhouse? Had he heard incorrectly? He'd seen her on the street, clearly running away from a suitor she'd sneaked out to meet. She'd allowed his kiss, and damn her, until this moment she'd flirted unmercifully.

Putting that together with her diatribe against all gentlemen, he concluded Maureen Collins had thrown over her previous beau. Or had he thrown her over, although he couldn't imagine that? Would she welcome a formal call later this week, after Christmas?

Maureen leaned over the railing, shamelessly examining his broad, muscular shoulders. He hoisted the ladder as if it were a child's toy. He wore a single-breasted burgundy waistcoat, starched white shirt and cream bow tie. His slender waist suggested he wore stays as some vain men were doing these days, aping the ladies with their tight mid-sections. No, not possible, she decided as quickly as she'd entertained the thought. Mr. Merritt moved freely, turning his body on the ladder to face her, to grab a banister or to swivel back to speak with William.

Her eyes traveled to his long legs. He wore expertly tailored trousers in the new narrower style, which revealed—she shouldn't look, but she couldn't help noticing—the man's arousal. She breathed a whiff of citrus, a light lime aroma with a hint of bay leaves and cloves, on his clothing that mingled pleasantly with the scent of the pine roping.

Mr. Merritt pushed his dark brown hair back with a quick motion of long fingers while his playful brown eyes darted from her to the pine roping. He was checking, she thought, to be sure he was impressing her—which he was. At ease on the ladder, he took sips of whiskey, put his glass down, picked it up again. All normal actions, but so graceful, especially while balancing a good twenty feet in the air.

When she brushed his fingers, she heard him suck in his breath; saw a light pinking on his cheeks. But she dare not do it again. Dutifully, she clipped wire and twisted it until he stood on the floor, she on the second step, her hands securing the last wire in place.

"Mr. Merritt is joining us for supper. You must stay, Maureen," Renee called from the parlor. "We'll make a pleasant foursome."

Her flesh on fire, she couldn't imagine sitting down to eat with this man. Her hands would shake, her mouth so dry, she wouldn't be able to swallow a morsel. "That sounds lovely, but I have another engagement. I better get home."

"We'll do it another time. I'll hold you both to it," Renee answered.

Resting both hands on the railing, Maureen called back: "We're just finished here."

Mr. Merritt slid his hands along the slick wood to touch hers. "We're just beginning."

Had he whispered "just beginning"? Her heart raced.

She couldn't see Renee or William, which meant Mr. Merritt's body blocked their view of her. Her face warmed.

The brick wall lifted her right hand and brought it to his mouth. Bending low, his eyes meeting hers, he put his lips on the tip of her index finger, then sucked it deeper into his mouth.

She held her breath. No man, even Vespasian, had ever done such a thing.

He gave her finger a gentle bite, then released her skin above the knuckle, then the forefinger and finally the fingernail. He leaned closer. "Your secret is safe with me."

Yes, she'd been indiscreet. But he was hiding something, too. Flecks of green and gold lit his brown eyes, a feature she'd missed in the dim light on the street last week.

She licked her lower lip. "And yours with me, sir."

Chapter Three

*H*er skirts held up to her calves, Maureen bounded down the steps and into the dining room, hoping to catch her father before he left for work. She found him with a cup of coffee in one hand, the *Daily Picayune* in the other. Kissing his cheek, she put a hand on his shoulder, a feeble attempt to hold him in his chair. She thought it absurd that he stood every time she entered or left a room. Despite her protests, he rose and held her chair. He was old fashioned. There was no cure for it.

She didn't mind humoring him. He was so distinguished, she supposed he could be forgiven for his refusal to join the modern age. His white hair and sun-darkened complexion accentuated the brilliant blue of his eyes, making his appearance more striking than it had been years ago. Sure, he'd thickened around the middle some-what during the years she was in Atlanta after her mother's death—he was fifty-five now, after all—but his tailor fit his suits beautifully.

"You're looking cheerful this morning," he declared, his voice barely muffled by the paper. "I suppose the decorations at William's home surpass those in the St. Charles Hotel."

The compliment pleased her, but she didn't take total credit. "Renee has quite a talent for the task, but I will say the white camellias from our garden were the finishing touch." She poured a half-cup of coffee from one pot, warm cream from a second, added two lumps of sugar and stirred.

Julia glided in and placed a plate of ham, grits and poached eggs in front of her, then cleared her father's bare plate away.

Maureen continued. "We did such a good job together, your new attorney—what's his name? Meridith?"

"Merritt."

"That's it. Mr. Merritt suggested Renee and I could hire ourselves out as decorators."

He harrumphed, his face more than half-hidden by his paper. "No daughter of mine will hire herself out. *Ever.*"

She took a forkful of egg yolk, mixed it with some grits and put it in her mouth. She let his words hang in the air.

"I met Merritt only briefly," he continued. "William's been dealing with him, having him look over all our contracts. Handsome young man. Well-spoken. But he has no business encouraging you to hire yourself out."

She sipped coffee before asking a favor of him. "Would you please bring home a ledger and a few notebooks from the office? I'd like to record my expenses in the greenhouse and I think I should take notes on my plant experiments."

His white eyebrows arched. "I don't quite see the need for a ledger."

She tilted her head sideways, a move she'd used to great effect on her father for years. "We've talked about my grafting experiments, Papa. If they work, I might sell some of my new camellias."

He pursed his lips, let the paper fall from his hands to the table. "No daughter of mine will sell flowers," he snapped. "You're not in trade."

His firm voice signaled the end of the discussion, but she pressed on. "But, Papa—"

"You will *not* sell flowers."

She pushed her bottom lip out in a pout. Juvenile, yes, but it often worked with him. Today he didn't seem to notice.

"I had the greenhouse built for you to pursue your hobby. A hobby and *only* a hobby."

He picked up his cup, finished off the contents and placed it back in the saucer with a clatter.

"I've ordered two red *camellia japonicas* from a nursery in Savannah," Maureen went on. "They're quite expensive and I want to record my costs."

He waved his hand in a dismissive gesture. "Not a bad idea. But I won't bring home ledgers from the factorage for your personal use. I don't allow employees to take such items and I don't either. We record all our expenses, including notebooks, ink, all those supplies. Why not stop by Seebolds today and buy whatever you need with your allowance?"

His expression softened a bit. "And while you're in town, go by Desselle Millinery and order some hats. I love to see you in a new hat. You had a meeting with Frau Kohlmeyer last night and ordered dresses, didn't you?"

"Several day dresses, a suit, and two ball gowns."

During the dressmaker's visit, she'd thought of no one but Benjamin Merritt. What would he think of each of the fabric swatches, each dress design? She didn't know him well enough to predict his color preferences, but she knew from the way his eyes followed her, he would like anything that showed off her figure.

"Surely you need some new hats to match."

Hats. Of course. That's what she was supposed to do. Buy hats and shoes. Spend her time with dressmakers. Her job was to look pretty until some fine man, preferably with a large income, offered to marry her. Then that man—her husband—would control her—or try to.

An image of Mr. Merritt flashed through her mind.

Her father reached out and gave her shoulder a little squeeze. "You're a beautiful young lady, looking more like your mother every day."

Maureen saw her mother's face every time she looked in the mirror, but damn it—and she could use the phrase silently as often as she liked—she was *not* her mother. Her mother's life had revolved around her husband, her daughter, her clothes, her house, her garden and her parties, in that order. That's all women were allowed to do in past generations. She wanted more than that. She wanted to accomplish something herself. The idea of grafting camellias to create more camellias to enjoy—and just maybe to sell to other ladies—intrigued her.

She spread fig preserves liberally on a corn muffin and ate the entire thing. *You'll change your mind, Papa, when you see how beautiful these plants are.* Out loud, she affected submission. "I believe I'll ask Noah to drive me to Desselle's. If I order some new hats today, they'll be ready by Mardi Gras."

"Buy anything you like." He wiped his mouth and dropped the napkin on the table.

Her father had never questioned her mother's expenditures on dozens of dresses, dozens of hats, dozens of pairs of shoes. Maureen, too, had been dressed in the latest fashions all her life. How could she complain? Thousands of young ladies in New Orleans would trade places with her in a heartbeat.

"Big meeting this afternoon to discuss a shipping contract with William and Mr. Merritt," he murmured as he pushed his chair in to the table.

"What time is that?" She hoped her voice sounded casual in a just-making-polite-conversation sort of way.

"Three. Why do you ask?"

She felt her face warm. "You'll be home for supper then?"

"I expect a tense meeting, but I should hope it won't last all afternoon." With that, he bowed toward her, said good day and left the room.

She repeated the name Merritt softly, liking the way her lips moved when she said it. "Merritt. Mer-rit." Then she took a second cup of coffee into the parlor and penned a note to Elise Bouchard.

The minute Elise sat down in the carriage opposite her, Maureen announced she had a plan.

"Stop right there." Holding up a hand, her friend rattled on. "I'm afraid to hear it. I'm sure I already know what it is: a new scheme to see Vespasian. Oh, I should have known better than to believe your note that we were going shopping!"

Elise huffed and crossed her arms over her chest. "You're true to your nickname, all right, Maureen Collins. Did you know everyone called you the *devious debutante* last year when you had your season?"

Maureen laughed softly. "I knew. I believe Vespasian coined the term for me."

Elise stared out the carriage window. "He did. It wasn't very kind of him."

"It didn't bother me then and it still doesn't. If any of you young ladies had lived with my aunt for three years, you'd have learned to be devious, too. I was nearly a prisoner in her house."

Elise patted her arm. "It must have been a nightmare, but you're back in New Orleans where you don't have to worry much about your reputation because your father's so rich. But I can't afford to risk *mine*. I just think Carine is right. You shouldn't waste your time on that rake Colville."

Elise went on for so long that Maureen gave up the idea of revealing her idea concerning an entirely different gentleman. Finally, she ended Elise's monologue with one sentence: "I don't care if I ever see Vespasian Colville again."

The young lady had a repertoire of gasps: surprise, disbelief, disapproval. This was the first variety. "You don't mean it!"

"He's such a child."

Elise drew her hand to her throat with another gasp. The second variety. "He's a gorgeous young man and you know it. I hear he's home from Spring Hill. You've seen him?"

Maureen smoothed her skirt and placed her purse beside her on the seat before answering. "We met in my garden Friday night. He was drunk. I'm so tired of that."

"Alone?" The third—a gasp of disapproval—escaped Elise's lips.

Maureen closed her eyes and nodded.

"You shouldn't have been alone. But ... but ... Carine will be glad to hear that you've come to your senses." She looked at her half boots firmly planted on the carriage floor. Her head tilted up just a trifle. "That is, if what you say is indeed true," she mumbled.

"I should have listened to Carine's misgivings about the man all last spring and summer," Maureen said. "Do tell your sister I'm through with him."

Elise raised her head to meet Maureen's gaze directly. "I know she'll be pleased." Then a frown wrinkled her forehead as if her expression finally caught up with her mind. "It's so sudden. Are you certain? Really certain?"

Maureen recalled Benjamin Merritt's lips around her finger. A suck. A nibble. Her tingling skin. His lime scent, the warmth of his breath. Her shiver. "I'm positive."

Elise giggled. "Am I to guess who the next gentleman is?"

Ignoring the question, Maureen distracted Elise with a stop at Seebolds on Canal for ledgers and notebooks. She made her selections quickly, but Elise looked at pale blue stationery, then pink, then yellow, and finally came back to blue with matching envelopes.

At Desselle's, the pair examined fabric swatches, trims and sketches of Renee's newest designs. Maureen ordered two hats: a plum felt with a low crown and a wide brim and a smaller green velvet hat with a rolled brim, trimmed with peacock feathers.

Elise agonized over her choice. Hats were far more challenging than stationery. Finally she selected a black felt with a wide brim trimmed in jet beads. Rather funereal, Maureen thought, but didn't say it. Hat two, a boater style in burgundy felt with velvet ribbon a shade lighter, matched the wool coat she wore today. Maureen lavished praise on it, noting how becoming it would be with her blond curls and bright green eyes.

While Michelle D'Artois, Renee's assistant, took Elise's deposit and wrote out a receipt, Renee motioned Maureen into the workroom, a slight smile playing on her lips. "I happen to know Mr. Merritt often has coffee at Café Du Monde in the mid-afternoon."

"Ahh. How good to know," Maureen whispered back. Coffee was far preferable to her original plan—dropping by the factorage to see her father at three o'clock.

Out on the banquette—New Orleans' name for a sidewalk— she grabbed Elise's arm, pretending a sudden inspiration. "I think we should have a coffee before we go home. What do you say?"

Elise's brow knit in confusion. As the youngest of the Bouchard sisters, Elise always did what her mother, her father or two older sisters suggested. Anna, the oldest girl—a know-it-all—had married last year. A good match to a plantation owner who was actually only a few years older than she. The middle girl, Carine, exactly Maureen's age and her best friend until the set-to over Vespasian, possessed a strong set of likes and dislikes and preferred a planned day from which she never strayed. Elise, one year younger, had few thoughts of her own, and Maureen suspected she could lead the girl through the gates of hell with no great difficulty.

"I suppose," Elise said slowly. "That does seem like a wonderful idea for a chilly afternoon."

At the busy café, Maureen scanned the sprawling slate patio where dozens of round metal tables accommodated a large crowd. No Benjamin Merritt. Disappointed, she forced a bright smile and selected a table at the banquette's edge so as not to miss him if he walked by.

In minutes, a white-coated waiter took their order for café au lait and beignets and delivered these in less time than it took the ladies to remove their gloves and put them in their purses. Maureen stirred sugar into her coffee and tried to calm her mounting excitement. Afternoon encompassed a long expanse of time. His meeting at the factorage was at three. It was two-thirty now. He'd come by any minute or he wouldn't come for hours. She'd have to be mighty inventive to keep Elise here the rest of the afternoon.

Nibbling her beignet, sipping her coffee, she watched the crowd over her cup's rim. She inhaled sharply when she caught sight of him, a head taller than most. She began to sputter, then cough.

Without a word, Elise shoved a glass of water toward her and she drank quickly. Maureen gained control of her breath and smiled when he was close enough to know she intended her show of dimples just for him. "Mr. Merritt, it's so good to see you this afternoon."

He stopped, locked eyes with her, tipped his hat and bowed slightly. "Miss Collins. What a pleasant surprise."

She held her breath as he bowed a second time.

"Elise, may I present Mr. Benjamin Merritt, a new attorney in town? Mr. Merritt, my very good friend, Elise Bouchard."

"So pleased to make your acquaintance." He bowed to Elise.

When he looked up, Maureen licked her bottom lip. "Would you like to join us for a coffee?"

"I'd love nothing better, Miss Collins, but I'm rushing to a meeting," he replied. "Perhaps another time. Have a wonderful afternoon, ladies."

With a graceful pivot, he stepped into the street, signaled for a cab and disappeared inside the vehicle.

Elise sighed and leaned forward across the little table. "Maureen Collins, I understand why you think Vespasian is a child."

Elise wasn't as dim as she pretended.

Chapter Four

William led Ben into the office where he shook hands with Patrick Collins. The two young men settled into green leather chairs opposite his desk. Ben had met the man once, the first day he came to this office, but he'd paid little attention to his features. His bright blue eyes resembled Miss Maureen's. In his mind, Ben heard her voice: "Papa thinks attorneys are a dull lot, a necessary evil."

After hours reading the tedious contract, Ben thought himself damned indispensable to the welfare of Collins Factorage, but the older man's manner was brusque, his forbearance written on his face. "I believe William called this meeting to discuss Imperial Shipping's offer."

Ben spoke up. "I would advise you to reject it, sir."

Collins pursed his lips and narrowed his eyes. "That's not what I wanted to hear," he said, an unmistakable edge to his voice.

Red-faced, white-haired, Collins had been in the business a long time. If Ben read his tone correctly, the man thought this a minor decision.

"Imperial Shipping is relatively new; I suspect that's one of your objections, Merritt, but the way I see it, its managers are smart enough to undercut the competition. It's a great offer."

Ben conceded that point. "I understand Imperial Shipping always bids below its competitors."

Collins glanced over to his nephew. "So, why not sign? Give me some very good reasons, William. I know you're against this, too."

William looked at Ben. "The low price makes me think there's something underhanded. How can Imperial ship cotton from New Orleans to Liverpool for so little money? Is that your objection, too, Merritt?"

"That and something far more serious." Ben cleared his throat. "Shipping contracts generally contain what's called a General Average Clause, which ensures that, in the event the crew has to toss part of the cargo overboard in order to save the ship, any losses are shared by *all* the owners of the cargo onboard. Shared in proportion to their financial share. If Collins Factorage has only fifty percent of the cargo space on a particular vessel and the ship is lost at sea, or its cargo is jettisoned to save the ship, your loss is averaged with the other parties in this shared venture."

His explanation irritated Collins. "I'm familiar with typical shipping arrangements."

"I'm sure you are—both of you." Ben paused for a moment, sliding his eyes from one to the other. "This contract"—he handed his copy across the desk—"omits that General Average Clause. It's an egregious error. Has to be deliberate."

William's face reddened as he grasped the ramifications. Ben was sure Collins understood, too, but the older man's expression didn't change.

"So without this clause," William said slowly, "if the cargo dumped at sea happened to be our cotton, the factorage would lose every penny?"

Nodding, Ben answered. "I admit I may be overly suspicious here, but my job is to look for ways one company can cheat another. If you sign this contract, the law can't help you get satisfaction from the shipping company or the owners of other cargo aboard."

Ben knew Collins had already made up his mind. Nothing he'd said had altered the man's original opinion, but he continued his argument. "It's a huge gamble, gentlemen." He paused. "It's my understanding that Imperial Shipping made this offer to you. I believe they're hoping you'll sign without noticing the lack of the clause."

Collins snorted. "You think it's a deliberate attempt to make us vulnerable, Merritt?"

"I do, sir." He kept his eyes fastened on the man. "It opens up the possibility of—I'll be blunt—deliberate destruction of a shipper's property."

"Oh my God," Collins muttered. "You really are a Philadelphia lawyer."

Keeping his face neutral, Ben mused over the phrase. Was this an insult or a compliment? A 'Philadelphia lawyer' could mean the most crooked lawyer you could hire or the most competent one. Ben opted for the latter definition.

"Trained to look at every detail, sir." He pressed on. "I'm thinking planned piracy. If brigands board a ship at sea and remove your cotton, the law cannot protect your interests."

"Pirates?" Collins exploded. He stood and stomped about behind his desk for a moment, then sat again and leaned forward across the expanse of mahogany. "You're worried about *pirates*, Merritt?"

Adopting a dispassionate, totally rational tone in contrast to Collins' anger, Ben explained. "Planned piracy would explain the low price. Imperial then sells the stolen cotton on the open market, getting paid to ship it while also reaping rewards from its sale."

Collins' face turned a deeper red and he slammed a fist on the desktop. "Is that what you believe? *That's* the extent of your faith in the integrity of English businessmen?"

Ben held firm. "As your attorney, sir, I cannot allow you to depend on notions of integrity. You must have the law as a fallback."

His position stated and defended, he relaxed against the back of his chair and watched his clients exchange a look. Neither spoke for some moments.

William's eyes narrowed as he addressed his uncle. "Given what Merritt has suggested, I think we should have him draw up a new contract. I'll telegraph Imperial and say we're adding a General Average Clause."

Collins rubbed a finger across his upper lip. "I think we should accept it today—right now—by telegraph—exactly as it is."

"With all due respect, sir, I think that's unwise," Ben reiterated.

William agreed. "I don't see how a few weeks to redo the contract can hurt. Then we'll have the protection we need."

Apparently lost in thought, Collins stared past Ben and William, through the glass windows of his office, into the huge room beyond—the cotton grading room with its long table and skylights. A few moments later, he shifted his glare from William back to Ben.

"I've noticed through the years that young men take fewer risks than older men. A cotton factor takes risks all day, every day. It's the business, plain and simple. I appreciate your advice, both of you, but I will sign the contract and take my chances. Our profits will be huge."

"As you wish, sir." Ben stood and shook hands with both men. If he read William correctly, he was unhappy with his uncle's choice, as he himself was. He'd hoped to save the firm from a huge mistake and be praised later for it. Defeated, Ben wished them both a Merry Christmas and exited quickly.

On the stairs, he mulled over the elder Collins' rejection of his own well-reasoned arguments. Was Imperial offering a cut-rate to the city's largest cotton factor in order to begin a smuggling operation from England or the West Indies to New Orleans?

Probably not. Every shipper wasn't a smuggler, he reminded himself, especially one as prosperous as Collins Factorage. The firm made a fortune doing legitimate business. Yes, he'd been told that Collins—the largest shipper in the city—was the number one suspect in the city's smuggling operations, but his surveillance to date had turned up nothing but one gorgeous lady out for a midnight stroll.

Walking back to his office—where the attorneys were to share some Christmas cheer this afternoon—he heard Miss Maureen's lilting Southern accent in his head. She spoke quite distinctly, but elongated her vowels so her beautiful eyes became beautiful "ahs" and her smile, pronounced "smahl," lit up the room around her.

What in the world had possessed him to kiss her? He'd never taken advantage of a woman out alone at night—not a governess, a housemaid, or a lady. He'd been trained to control his emotions, yet he'd momentarily lost his mind. And nearly his footing yesterday.

My God, her tongue on her lush lower lip—which she repeated more times than he could count—had intoxicated him. When she brushed her fingers against his, he'd nearly catapulted off the ladder.

Christmas Eve, a holiday, dawned sunny, but cold. Ben donned a heavy overcoat, hat and gloves and began a search for a *camellia japonica*. The flower shops in the French Quarter remained open until noon, but none sold the flower he sought.

The proprietor of Belle Fleur on Chartres Street suggested he try the docks. "You'll want to find a ship from China called the *Hailong Hao*."

"The *Sea Dragon*?"

"You speak Chinese?"

"A few words."

"The captain's name is Kwan. He speaks fine English. It's expensive buying direct from the ships, though."

What did cost matter if a camellia produced dimples on Miss Maureen's cheeks? What could be better to win her heart than the gift of the exotic flower she needed to begin her experiments? What's more, if a camellia ensured his welcome for multiple visits to the Collins home, how easy it would be to investigate the lord of the manor.

Was he losing his mind? Here he was, taking his precious time, looking for a plant he couldn't describe. Anyone could sell him anything green with flowers. He wouldn't know the difference. He should be sleeping instead. In truth, one week of his double duty had exhausted him more than he'd expected it would.

By day, his job as an attorney specializing in admiralty law for a prominent local firm demanded his full attention. By night, his role as an investigator for the U.S. Customs Service, a branch of the U.S. Treasury Department, required surveillance of the docks as well as suspects' homes and clubs. His orders were straightforward: Find opium smugglers, arrest them, confiscate the drugs. For seven days, his telegrams to D.C. to Samuel Carleton, the man in charge of all territory east of the Mississippi, had reported no progress.

Buttoning his overcoat against the chill and pushing his bowler hat lower lest the wind from the river carry it off, he wandered the levee. Stretching for eighteen miles, the harbor moored as many as a thousand ships on any given day. Tug boats, fishing boats and banana boats dominated the area where he began his search. In the next mile, he came upon an array of paddle-wheel packet boats. The railroads had taken passengers from the large, elaborate steamboats on the Mississippi, but cargo and those needing to save money still filled the smaller paddle-wheelers.

He asked several times where to find larger vessels, specifically the *Hailong Hao*, and was told repeatedly to keep on going. Finally, in the distance, his eyes found the larger, ocean-going steamships flying flags from countries around the globe. Walking rapidly, he scanned the names on the sides of one ship after another. He saw countless hulls painted with names for birds, for cities, and for mythological creatures before he spotted the Chinese characters he sought.

Along his path, four stevedores, each twice his size, sat atop sugar barrels sharing a bottle of spirits. He guessed from their blond hair and fair skin they were German and their response to his questions in their language proved him right. Yes, they knew about the ship just up the quay, which came from Hong Kong, via Cape Horn, arriving two months or so ago. From New Orleans, one man offered, the captain made trips to Jamaica every other week. Ben slipped them a few coins and moved on.

The gangplank swayed in the wind and he held to the rope railing on his climb. When his feet found the firm deck, he stood for a moment, unsure which way to turn. Plants in clay pots lined every available space from the ship's railings to the center mast. Above the deck an ingeniously designed series of awnings could be raised or lowered with ropes and pulleys to shield the plants from sun or bad weather.

The variety stunned him. Palm trees fifteen to twenty feet; hydrangeas, wisteria and azaleas not yet in bloom; ferns so large they looked capable of devouring any botanist who dared approach them. He called for the captain and heard a rustling in the bushes. A figure emerged from behind a tall, lush fern, the branches of which stretched wide like a banana tree's.

"I'm Captain Kwan. How may I help you?" He spoke in clipped sentences in good English with the British accent common in a generation of Chinese from the Canton area, which the British had controlled for so many years. The captain wore his long black hair in a queue, sported a mustache and beard and wore the baggy trousers typical of Oriental seamen.

"Good afternoon, Captain. My name is Andrew Franklin," he said, using the alias printed on his credentials that identified him as Plant Inspector, U.S. Customs Service. "I'm searching for a particular plant and have been told by the proprietor of a florist shop on Royal Street that I might find it on a Chinese ship."

"A plant?" The man spread his arms wide in a gesture that took in the pots surrounding him. "There are hundreds right on this ship."

"I'm looking for a *camellia japonica*, specifically a red *camellia japonica*," Ben explained. "Do you have such a plant?"

The captain's eyes took in his clothing from his hat to his boots before he spoke. "I believe I understand what you want." The man shifted his eyes to the quay for a moment and then back to him. "Come out of the cold."

He followed Captain Kwan into a cabin where a pot-bellied stove actually made him uncomfortably warm in his coat. He unbuttoned it, and, at the captain's suggestion, sat in one of two pine chairs pulled up to a round table.

"A brandy, sir? To chase away the chill."

He'd intended a quick exchange, but he was cold and a drink promised to do more than warm him. It was Christmas Eve, after all, and a brandy presented a companionable way to spend the next twenty minutes or so negotiating his purchase. "Brandy, thank you."

The captain opened a cabinet, removed a bottle and glass and poured a generous portion. "I'm just back from Jamaica. I have a few red *camellia japonicas* that might interest you. "

Ben took a swallow. The brandy cut a rivulet down his throat and warmed him.

Captain Kwan sat opposite him. "You desire the best stock, the finest plant?"

He nodded. Miss Maureen was the most beautiful female he'd ever met. He felt his blood warm just thinking of her body. Perhaps it was loneliness, perhaps it was the brandy, but he was convinced only the finest plant on this ship was suitable for her.

"I have two types of *camellia japonica*. Do you want one with fragrant roots?"

Grinning, Ben took a large gulp of his drink. "I'll admit I know nothing about plants, sir. Are these fragrant roots better?"

The captain chuckled. "The plant is healthy if the roots are fragrant. They bring peace to those who own such a plant."

He could accept that fragrant roots meant a plant was healthy. But peace to the owner? He supposed Miss Maureen would understand. If a flower brought her happiness, it brought a certain peace, too.

"Fragrant roots, then. As long as the plant is beautiful. It's a gift for a beautiful lady."

"Oh yes! Many ladies appreciate!"

Miss Maureen wasn't like most ladies. She intended to take this plant and experiment with it in order to produce more of the species more quickly than nature strictly allowed. The very idea fascinated him. Everything about her fascinated him. He didn't think it possible to explain any of this to the ship's captain.

The man stood. "One moment." As he stepped through the door, a gust of wind ruffled the papers on the desk against the back wall and chilled Ben enough that he pulled his coat closed. He'd just finished his brandy when the captain carried in a remarkable bush. Roughly eighteen inches high, it burst with blooms from its top to its lowest branches. Blood red with bright yellow stamens, some of the flowers measured at least three inches in diameter. He knew his face betrayed his delight and he'd admitted he knew nothing. He was resigned to pay dearly. "That's exactly what the lady wants. And what is the price, Captain?"

Captain Kwan pulled on his beard for some moments, then lifted his head to stare at the ceiling. At length, he met Ben's eyes. "A fine shrub like this is five American dollars"

Ben fell back against the hard chair. "My God, man." Did the captain think him an absolute fool, besotted by love? He feared he might be besotted by love—more accurately, lust—but not to the point of stupidity. "For five dollars, I could feed a family for two weeks. We're talking about a flowering shrub."

"One that comes from thousands of miles away. A beautiful plant that will transport your lady friend as she's never been in her life."

Transport her? To where exactly? Make her over into the botanist she longed to be? Perhaps. He outlined the plant's future for the captain. "The lady's going to cut off the branches and graft them to other bushes, red camellia branches to white camellias. She's going to cut the bush in half for all I know."

Captain Kwan's eyes widened, but in the end he shrugged again. "I cannot go lower for such a shrub. Perhaps you would like something other than a red *camellia japonica*? It is sad to destroy something with such exquisite qualities." He waved his hand in the direction of the door. "I have many, many other plants."

"How does four dollars sound?"

The captain stood. His dark eyes flashed. "You insult my product?" he hissed. "I assure you it is the finest available. Five dollars is the price for one red *camellia japonica*." He crossed his arms and looked down at Ben. "You cannot do better."

Guessing the price quoted was two or three times what a *camellia japonica* should cost, Ben capitulated. He opened his wallet and counted the dollars into the captain's hand. As he did, it occurred to him the lady might kill the camellia with her experiments and want another. "If the lady is happy with this plant, do you have more just like it?"

"She will be happy and you will want more."

Ben nodded and started to rise, but the captain restrained him with a light touch on his forearm. "If you plan to be a repeat customer, Mr. Franklin, we should seal our deal with a pipe."

An opium pipe? Ben hadn't expected such an offer while buying a camellia, but he'd been told time and again in training that if invited to smoke, he must accept. So he followed the captain across the room, ducked his head to pass through a doorway and then down three steps into a tiny space furnished with two upholstered benches bolted to the floor. A small table, also secured to the floor, held a burning oil lamp, a long ivory pipe with a bowl that resembled a barnacle attached to it, a long needle and a dish of dark brown paste.

He breathed in a faintly sweet aroma, the same odor he remembered from the opium dens in New York, where he went with his friends from time to time in order to see them home later. He'd never smoked opium and didn't want to now. In fact, he desperately wanted to be at home, nodding off with a good book in front of a fire.

Ben stared at the pipe and accoutrements. The challenge here: to remain unaffected, to pretend enjoyment, to take short puffs and stay in control.

The captain, already recumbent on one bench, motioned Ben to take the other. Fascinated, he removed his coat and reclined. His eyes followed his host's motions.

Twisting the blunt needle in the paste in the dish, he gathered a pea-sized amount of what resembled resin. He held it over the oil lamp until it swelled to ten times its original size and changed color from dark brown to golden brown. Next, he smeared the opium on the bowl of the pipe, swirling the substance with the needle, like he was pulling taffy, until it formed a neat ball. Holding the bowl over the flame again, he pushed the ball into the pipe with the needle and handed it to Ben.

Tightening his lips around it, Ben inhaled. The captain took the pipe from him and smoked. He prepared another pipe more rapidly and Ben took it again.

Chapter Five

Ben's body grew warm. He lay down and melted into the soft couch. Aware that his breathing had slowed and the muscles in his arms no longer functioned, he didn't believe he could lift the pipe again to his lips, or draw on it. When the captain offered it, he shook his head slowly, his neck turning one way and another.

How marvelous, the way the human neck swiveled. Lying on his side, he stared at Captain Kwan for a few moments, then closed his eyes. Comfortable. He felt more than comfortable. He was overwhelmed with serenity, optimism, affection for the entire world. No yesterday, no tomorrow, no three years ago, no six months hence.

He floated. Warm, soothing water surrounded him, bright green water covering his entire body. Clouds of purple, white, and gold swirled above him. He began to swim—effortlessly—his arms and legs cutting through the water, propelling him forward at an incredible speed. Had he just swum five hundred meters in a race? Impossible. His heart beat slowly, so very slowly. Ben pulled himself from the pool, lay on his stomach, smiling uncertainly. What had he won? He couldn't move a muscle, couldn't stand to receive his trophy, but he was elated, happier than he'd ever been.

Hours passed. Or not so many hours, he wasn't sure. But he had a sudden desire to breathe fresh air. Captain Kwan held his arm to guide him up the steps from the little room, through the larger room with a blast of warm air from the stove, and outside to the cold and dark—very cold and dark—ship's deck. The captain handed him his coat and hat, which he put on, then his purchase, which he gripped to his chest, and escorted him down the gangplank.

The New Orleans levee bobbed up and down like a floating dock. It should not be moving under his feet, should it? He clutched the red camellia tighter. He waved good-bye to the captain, then attempted to walk purposely away from the *Hailong Hao.*

He hadn't taken more than a dozen steps, his mouth impossibly dry, his tongue coated with the taste of onions and chewing tobacco, when his stomach revolted. He put the plant on the ground, turned away, sank to his knees and retched until his stomach muscles ached.

Finally, the sickness passed, he wiped his mouth with his handkerchief, grasped the camellia, rose to his feet. His whole body ached. Fog crawled forward like an advancing army, coming straight toward him from the river. A flame protruded from the side of a building up ahead. As he drew closer, he made out a torch lighting the peeling paint on the sign: Sugar Park Tavern. He needed to get his bearings. He wanted a beer, something cold and liquid before he walked further. He stumbled toward it and pushed open the oak door. The room was darker than the captain's cabin, but a roaring fire in the fireplace made it toasty. The place was busy with sailors, far from home during the holidays.

"Evenin', *guvner*," came the voice behind the bar.

Ben nodded, his eyes sweeping the place. One table between two wooden, high-backed benches in the corner remained empty. He placed the camellia on the seat and slid into the booth beside it. He ordered a beer from a half-clad young woman, who appeared beside him in seconds. She leaned forward and lit a candle on his table.

He wanted to sleep forever, to put his head down on the table and lose consciousness. But the tavern was loud and anger flashed through him. Who talked when he wanted to sleep? How could they be so obnoxious? The conversation from the booth behind him burst into his consciousness.

"There's gold to be made, a lot of gold, Smiley."

"Don't care." A beer mug clunked hard on the table.

"I need your help."

"I ain't in this one, Timmie. I'm a thief, but I ain't no kidnapper an' I sure as hell ain't no murderer."

"Nobody's gettin' murdered."

Ben would get no sleep here. Thieves and murderers. He drained his mug, but it did little to ease his thirst. He signaled the barmaid and she brought him another. As he sipped, his thoughts, real thoughts, circled in his mind. The plant he'd bought—a *camellia japonica* for five dollars—sat beside him, his only companion on Christmas Eve. What he must do is stand up and walk out of here. He should find a cab and go to Maureen's house.

The server's breasts overflowed from the top of her dress as she put the third mug in front of him. No, he couldn't let Maureen see him like this. He wanted to kiss her again. This time Maureen would lean down over him. Her abundant breasts—two round handfuls of flesh—would burst from her bodice as her lips met his.

The words of the two men continued while Ben slaked his thirst. Had he heard the name Collins? Or was it only in his mind? Maureen Collins—her name, her face, her body, her laugh, her voice—were in his heart and mind all day and half the night.

The first man—the one who needed help—repeated his words: "Nobody's gettin' murdered, Smiley, at least not the Collins lass."

Ben put his mug carefully on the table, pressed his back against the hard boards on the bench and strained to hear more, but the men's voices were too low.

Feet shuffled, the booth creaked as the two men rose. Ben turned toward them. Two knit-capped heads, rough work clothes and rubber boots lumbered past. No faces.

He stood. Unsteady on his feet, Ben fished more than enough money for his three beers from his pocket and plunked it on the table. He cradled the flowerpot in the crook of his arm and concentrated on placing one foot in front of the other as he left the Sugar Park Tavern. He always took his friends home in a cab after they smoked. That's what he needed right now.

A cab.

Ben gave the driver a large tip and wished him a Merry Christmas. He made his way through the courtyard, unlocked the door to his cottage, placed the precious red camellia on his desk, collapsed on his bed and slept.

When he woke, the opium no longer clouded his mind, but his stomach felt uneasy. Shaky, hungry and cold, he removed his topcoat, suit and shirt, found his wool bathrobe and tied it tightly around his waist. In his sitting room, he threw logs on the warm coals and the resulting blaze warmed him. The mantel clock said two a.m. It was Christmas morning. Why not celebrate?

He guessed he had slept for hours on the cushioned bench in the ship's cabin because his vivid dreams had lasted an eternity. He had won a swim meet, and after that, he had drunk a few beers in a dark tavern with the camellia beside him. All the while, voices had plagued him, two men planning a robbery; gold to be made, one had promised the other. Or was it a kidnapping or a murder? They were loud at first and then quiet. That's all he remembered.

He lit a festive red candle he'd bought only yesterday, opened a bottle of claret and poured himself a glass. He didn't know the remedy for overindulging in opium, but he well knew it for liquor—the hair of the dog. He took a few gulps of wine and felt better. In the icebox, he found some cooked sausages and a hard loaf of bread—leftovers from a day or two ago. While he warmed the meat in a frying pan, he drained his wine glass. Sitting down at a small table by the fire, he tried the sausages with the mustard his sister, Letitia, had sent from England. He washed down two with more wine, but, apart from the pungent mustard, they were fairly tasteless.

In a few hours, the Irish cook at his family home in Philadelphia would rise to prepare the stuffing for the turkey. She'd have the bird in the oven by six a.m. so it would be succulent and ready by noon. His mother always had a crowd of guests ranging in age from infants to elderly. He could almost smell the fare that would soon be on the table. The buttered rutabaga, mashed potatoes drenched in gravy, slices of turkey, green peas, creamed onions. And the finish? Apple pie with crumb topping.

Ben had never been so lonely in his life. He pushed his own meal aside, unlocked the central drawer of his desk and retrieved his grandfather's journal. He needed to remind himself what in God's name he was doing in New Orleans. He opened the leather–bound volume, the contents of which had horrified him at the age of twelve.

A knock on his door startled him. Who could it be at this hour? Lord, but he was jumpy. He rose, opened it a crack and found the smiling face of Samuel Carleton, his mentor at the Treasury Department.

"I was in the area and thought I'd stop by to wish you Merry Christmas. How are you?"

Ben shook the man's hand, flung the door wide and motioned him inside. "I'll be honest." He ran his fingers through his hair and grimaced. "Not good at this moment."

Carleton removed his bowler hat and coat, walked to the fire and warmed his hands. The clean-shaven Negro with a handsome face, kind brown eyes and a soft voice had trained Ben for six months. He'd dropped by for a report. "You're mingling with the right crowd?"

Ben threw himself in an armchair and nodded to Carleton to do the same, but he continued to stand.

"I'm not sure. A sea captain shared his pipe with me after some high-level negotiations over the price of a *camellia japonica.*" He pointed to the plant on his desk.

Carleton's eyebrows shot up. "Hmm. You're not here to buy camellias. It's opium that we're after. Do you have some brandy?"

"I do. Can I get you a glass?"

"Yes, and another for you. Brandy might clear your head. I've always found it effective after opium."

Ben served them and they sat in front of the fire.

"My credentials and badge as a plant inspector looking for beetles and diseases are excellent. It's just as you told me. Large numbers of plants fill the decks of many of the ships along the levee."

"We're not so dumb in Washington." Carleton took a sip of his brandy and smiled. Carleton had been the first of his race to graduate from West Point. After graduation, he served in the Indian Territory where he witnessed untold brutality on both sides. The man's expertise extended to tracking human and beast, as well as launching and retreating from attacks in the wilderness. And then there were his town smarts. He could pick a door lock or a safe in seconds, or kill a man with a shot straight through the heart with a rifle or pistol.

"Plants are said to calm sailors who don't see a scrap of land for weeks," he said.

"The camellia's a gift for Patrick Collins' daughter, and by the way, she's not thirteen. More like eighteen." He almost said beautiful, but stopped himself. "She has a new greenhouse and wants to try to graft camellias. I can get close to Patrick Collins through her, I believe."

"Were our notes on him more accurate, I hope?"

"Confident, decisive, the biggest shipper from this port. A very wealthy man." Ben explained that Collins had chosen to ship the cotton harvest next fall with Imperial Shipping Company out of London, the firm that happened to own the *Hailong Hao,* with a Chinese captain who smoked opium. "Collins was adamant about his decision."

Carleton began to chuckle. "So you've impressed Collins with your legal skills?"

"The man can be pig-headed."

Carleton interrupted his thoughts. "Feeling better?"

"Thank you. You know, I actually am."

"How are you doing socially?"

"Two invitations for New Year's Eve parties. And I've joined one of their parading krewes, Proteus."

"Just keep to a strict training regimen. I've bought you a membership in the New Orleans Athletic Club."

Ben welcomed a place to exercise, especially to swim. He'd met quite a few gentlemen who were members. "I understand they employ excellent trainers."

"Use them. You never know when you'll need the skills I've taught you."

Ben changed the subject. "Do you want to see what they call Collins Castle? It's an easy walk from here."

Carleton was eager, so Ben dressed quickly and they were out the door. The brisk night air drove the misery from his body. They walked down St. Charles Avenue enjoying each other's company, not mentioning opium once.

Ben stopped in front of the gate—the gate from which the gorgeous daughter had emerged. "Here we are. As I said great wealth, but in good taste." *And a daughter so beautiful and charming ...*

"And the daughter Maureen grows the camellias?" Carleton gestured to the line of flowering bushes that lined the side yard.

"She does."

"I don't need to tell you to keep her at a distance. Just enough contact to get the information you want."

"That's exactly what I intend."

Chapter Six

The splendor of midnight Mass at St. Louis Cathedral didn't put Maureen in a spiritual frame of mind. She wanted to feel holy, her thoughts lifted to heaven, but instead examined Renee's new purple velvet dress. A gorgeous shade with lace and gold braid at the waist and cuffs, it fit her slender post-babe body as if Frau Kohlmeyer had stitched it right on her skin this afternoon. Her hat, also purple velvet, featured a narrow rim with a crown that rose four or five inches high. What facing—buckram, perhaps—did Renee use to give the hat its shape?

Dozens of candles blazed from the marble altar as the bishop and six priests in gold-embroidered white vestments paraded down the center aisle accompanied by a legion of altar boys carrying censors, clanking them as they went. A cloud of incense rose over Maureen's head. She breathed deeply. The organ music and choir's voices reverberated off the walls and ceiling, penetrating her body until she felt the thunder of *Adeste Fidelis* in her chest.

Pray. She prayed for her dead mother to guide her; she prayed Benjamin Merritt would walk into the church, stand in the back for a moment and recognize her in the crowd. But she already knew he wouldn't. His family lived in Philadelphia. No doubt he'd taken the train north for the holidays. Or perhaps, heaven forbid, he was a Protestant. Her father would never approve. Approve of what? She'd seen the man only three times, if she counted the night outside her gate, which she did. She liked him, but she wasn't going to marry him. He could be a Protestant if he chose.

She forced herself to say three Hail Marys, then turned around and scanned the church behind her. The gentleman wasn't here.

One of the bishop's concelebrants approached the lectern to read the epistle. Grateful to sit, she glanced toward her father and saw his eyes focused on Renee's aunt, Sophie O'Brien. Was he admiring her hat, her shoulders, the nape of her neck? Or perhaps he was looking at her ears and the dainty pearl earrings that hung from them? He'd been seeing her—taking her to dinner, squiring her to balls and card parties—for more than a year now.

She wasn't jealous of his attentions to Sophie; in fact, the sooner he married the better. A wife was certain to diminish the time he expended questioning and watching his daughter's every move. Oh, dear. She bowed her head. *That sounds so selfish, God.* She truly wanted her father to be happy. And she wanted to be happy, too.

Where was Benjamin Merritt right this minute? The one man who made her breath catch, her body tingle, her spirit hum. She pictured Benjamin's face on the body of the bishop, saw his hand brush his hair back from his forehead. No, it was the bishop removing his miter. When she stood for the gospel, she glanced once more around the church. Disappointed again, she forced herself to listen. The gospel began with the genealogy of Jesus. Since Jesus wasn't born in New Orleans and she knew none of these families—*Solomon begot Roboam, Roboam begot Abia*—she turned her attention to the Colvilles in the second pew.

Damn him, Vespasian had trimmed his dark hair off his collar, an improvement. He stood far taller than his father or older brother, Emile—at least a head taller—with longer arms and legs. His long delicate fingers rested lightly on the back of the pew on either side of his thighs as he listened, head slightly tilted, to the gospel. He seemed attentive, but she noticed that he swayed slightly. How many parties had he already attended? She suspected he had plans for an outing in the early hours of the morning after he performed host duties at his family's *reveillon*.

Vespasian's mother, Helene, a stunning beauty, stood beside her husband. Her velvet suit was a lovely green. Not forest green, but a little lighter. The fitted suit jacket with pleats falling across her hips flattered her. Had she really told Vespasian he and Maureen were betrothed? *Stop it. Stop it. This is Christmas Mass.*

The rustle of silk skirts as the other worshippers sat down for the sermon cued her to do likewise. Delivered in French, it meant little to her. Her mind turned to food. The vigil of a holy day was nothing short of torture. In her father's strict household a day of fast and abstinence translated to black coffee—no cream or sugar—and toast without butter or preserves for breakfast. They skipped the noon meal completely. Supper this evening consisted of a small piece of fish and a bit of rice without gravy. No wine, sherry, whiskey or brandy. Nothing between meals except water. Her stomach rumbled.

Enduring High Mass on an empty stomach wearing a tight corset demanded every ounce of strength. She prayed for her deceased mother during the consecration, remembering to thank God for a myriad of things, for life first of all, for a good mother and father who had doted on her. At last, the procession up to communion began. The tiny piece of bread would taste mighty good right now and offer a bit of nourishment. In fact, wasn't there a saint who lived on nothing but daily communion for years?

Kneeling at the altar rail, she felt certain Vespasian was admiring her hair, her hips and her derriere. She put out her tongue for the wafer, drew it back into her mouth and let it soften for a few seconds, then swallowed it whole. The nuns had said it was sacrilegious to chew Jesus. When she stood and turned around, she kept her eyes on her hands meeting at her waist in prayer. She didn't favor Vespasian with even a glance.

In the receiving line at the Colville home, Maureen managed polite kisses on the cheeks of Monsieur and Madame Colville and Emile, their older son, but when she reached Vespasian, she pursed her lips and offered him a slight bow of her head .

"Good to see you, Missy." He leaned forward, his mouth within an inch of her ear. "Alone later, I hope?"

She'd rehearsed a remark for him, something to deliver in the hearing of others, to welcome him home from college. But when he called her Missy, and suggested a rendezvous, she turned her body sideways with a murmur. "I'm afraid I don't share your enthusiasm, sir."

Vespasian laughed loudly.

William led Renee and Maureen into the dining room. "I thought Renee might perish from hunger during Mass," he remarked to Maureen.

Renee patted her husband's hand. "I was perilously close."

Maureen, starving herself, stepped back and motioned to Renee to go ahead in the buffet line. "You first. There's plenty to satisfy a mother of twins. And the rest of us, too. " She waved a hand toward the dinner.

The banquet table, at least sixteen feet long, sagged in the center under the weight of the magnificent feast. She picked up a Haviland china plate with a delicate pink rose pattern, and followed Renee.

William joined a group at a smaller table in the corner where several servants shucked oysters as quickly as the men filled their plates. She'd heard jokes about oysters increasing men's sexual stamina for so long that at age fourteen she'd asked Vespasian for an explanation. She felt color rise to her cheeks just thinking about it. After a full description of the male member's function, he'd noted that virile men had no need of such aids as oysters. Perhaps. But only men gathered at that table. Not a lady partook.

She thought organ meat as vile as oysters, so she hurried past the sweetbreads, and studied other offerings. Sliced turkey, lamb, duck, venison, quail and goose covered large silver platters. Centered among these the *daube glacé*, sliced beef in a jellied red wine sauce, attracted her notice and she served herself some. She added a helping of cheese soufflé, a spoonful of cheese grits, and two fluffy biscuits to her plate. She gazed at bowls of yams encrusted in a brown sugar glaze, potatoes Lyonnaise, and asparagus in Hollandaise sauce. She took a small serving of each, but stopped short at the eggplant fritters.

No matter the occasion, the Colvilles always served these, one of Vespasian's favorites. The site of a fritter on her plate or its taste in her mouth was certain to conjure up memories of good times with the rake. She preferred to remain angry with him through the evening.

Plate in hand, she turned away from the table and nearly slammed into Madame Colville, who stood directly behind her. The lady grasped her arm and led her into the ballroom where at least two dozen white-clothed tables glittering with candles awaited hungry diners. "Sit, my dear, I'd like to talk."

Putting her plate carefully on the table between linen napkin and silver knife, fork and spoon, Maureen sank into a chair. "It all looks so delicious." Her mouth watered, but she couldn't wolf down food in front of her hostess who had no plate. "Won't you have something to eat, Madame Colville?"

"Maureen, dear, I couldn't help but notice your lack of warmth in greeting Vespasian this evening. No kiss for my boy? No laughter at his jokes?"

What in the world? Was Madame Colville the go-between? Maureen plastered a smile on her face. If Vespasian wanted to talk with her, he'd have to come speak to her himself. "We haven't had an opportunity to become reacquainted since he returned."

She looked up at the lady's lovely brown hair, always fashioned in a chignon at the nape of her neck. It contrasted with her green velvet hat perched at a jaunty angle over one eye. Two peacock feathers took flight from it into the air. "Your hat is most becoming, Madame."

Madame Colville accepted the compliment with a nod, but her attention went to the nearest waiter, whom she waved to the table. "Have some eggnog, dear." They each took a cup from the tray and drank. The eggs and cream did little to alter the power of the whiskey; it burned her throat, but miraculously she didn't choke. The Colvilles always served strong spirits; their Christmas drink was no exception.

Madame Colville drank again and Maureen did likewise. On an empty stomach, she knew she shouldn't. Lest her head fall with an undignified splatter into her plate, she had to end this discussion quickly. "You wish to talk, Madame?"

This time the lady didn't pause for eggnog, but Maureen took another swallow. "Vespasian isn't returning to Spring Hill. He's taking a job in New Orleans."

Dizzy already, Maureen put her cup down with care, placing it just so above her plate. "You and he will have more time together—time to court properly."

Oh, my. The last thing in the world she wanted right now was Vespasian courting her. But that was most definitely not the proper thing to say to the gentleman's mother. She threw the phrase back in a polite question. "To court?"

Madame Colville's face lit up with a genuine smile. "I hope you and Vespasian will marry within the year."

Maureen felt her mouth drop open.

The lady arched both eyebrows. "Is that presumptuous of me, dear?"

Unable to compose a thought in her brain, much less speak distinctly, Maureen mumbled, "We're not suited."

"Did you say not suited? Oh, child, you're perfectly suited." She covered Maureen's hand with hers. "It was your mother's fondest wish—and mine—that you and Vespasian marry when you grew up."

"We're betrothed. My mother says so." The words echoed in her head. A year ago she wouldn't have wished for anything more wonderful than marrying her childhood friend. Tonight, her legs trembled under the table. She swallowed, not sure she could speak. Finally, she whispered: "I never knew that."

"Your mother and I planned it the day you were born—one year and one week after Vespasian's birth." Madame Colville's tone was matter of fact. She might have been ordering new upholstery fabric for the furniture or a new walking dress. "I visited the minute I heard she'd delivered. She held you in her arms and said, 'She'll be Vespasian's wife at eighteen. Do you agree?'"

Maureen shook her head, but Madame Colville had turned to signal for more eggnog. This was 1885—1886, next week. Not 1800. Did a young lady have no say in the choice of her husband in these modern times?

"I agreed to your mother's suggestion immediately," she continued.

With a shaking hand, Maureen grasped another cup and drank more of the frothy liquid. Her hostess stood abruptly, leaned over and whispered in her ear. "I know you will want to do your duty to your mother's memory. You wouldn't want to disappoint her." Raising her eyes toward the ceiling, Madame Colville placed a hand at her throat. "I miss her so and I look forward to welcoming you as my daughter."

She glided away, stopping here and there to greet other guests with a Merry Christmas, followed by compliments on a gown or hat to one lady after another. Alone at the table, Maureen glanced down at her plate. Her stomach churned. She feared she might be sick on the ballroom's parquet floor. Snapping her head around, she searched for her father and Aunt Sophie. Vespasian leaned against the pocket door separating the dining room and ballroom. He leered at her, then turned away.

Her head throbbed. The room began to spin. Perhaps a broken ankle would have been preferable to this. She'd been a fool not to stage a fall from the ladder and manage a simulated sprain, at the very least. Benjamin Merritt would have arrived to see her stretched out on the couch instead of stamping her foot. But then he wouldn't have helped her decorate the banisters and she'd have missed the sight of his broad shoulders, the touch of his hand as she twisted the wires, the stirring in her belly his lime scent inspired and, dear Lord, the nibble of her finger.

Her own mother had arranged her marriage? Eighteen years ago? Perhaps. But surely, if she were alive today she wouldn't pair her with the handsome but thoughtless Vespasian. *Thoughtless.* Not just inconsiderate, but without a mature thought in his head. Her mother wouldn't insist on a marriage between her only daughter and a man she didn't love.

Bridget Collins had possessed enormous common sense. She always knew what to do, what to say in every situation. What Maureen wouldn't give for her mother to sweep into the ballroom, sit at the table, pat her hand and tell her she'd take care of this issue with Helene Colville. Oh, how she longed to talk with her now. How sad she was that her mother, dead more than five years, couldn't guide her through the labyrinthine path of courtship. When tears began to trickle down her cheeks, she staunched them with a linen napkin.

Maureen stood. Cautiously, she took a few steps, balancing as best she could. She dared not run for fear she might fall. She just wanted to reach the ladies retiring room before she made a fool of herself by vomiting on her party shoes. How much eggnog had she drunk?

No one could force her to marry Vespasian Colville. Not her father, not the gentleman himself, and certainly not his mother.

She zigzagged among the partiers past a table of desserts against the ballroom wall. The Carlotte Russe, fruitcake, crystallized fruits, bread pudding and caramel custard—all treats Maureen loved—turned her stomach. She ran from the room.

In the carriage, she took deep breaths, hoping to get home before she vomited. Little traffic detained them at close to three in the morning. She trained her eyes on the passing scenery to distract herself.

Was that Ben Merritt walking down St. Charles Avenue, not two blocks from her house?

She pulled the window curtain back a little farther. By God, it was. Dressed in a fine suit, overcoat and bowler hat, he strode along, keeping pace with and speaking with an equally well-dressed Negro. How very odd.

Chapter Seven

*L*uz never minced words. "Lord, girl, you looks like something a cat wouldn't drag in." She crossed the room and put a tray on the table beside Maureen's bed. "I knew you was bad last night, but you's worse today. I done brought you tea and dry toast."

Turning to the dresser, Luz picked up a mirror and handed it over.

"Oh," Maureen whimpered. She examined her swollen eyelids, her red nose, her lips drawn tight, her hair knotted from a sleepless night. "I can't let Papa see me like this."

"Luz'll make you all right."

It took more than an hour. The tea and toast settled her stomach. Cold compresses reduced the swelling skin around her eyes; a curling iron tamed the hair framing her face; a dab from the rouge pot put roses on her cheeks. Finally, Luz slipped her new Christmas dress over her head and began buttoning it up the back. The red velvet with Alancon lace at the neckline and cuffs brought a smile to her face.

The chimes on nearby churches announced the noon hour as Maureen descended the stairs. The dining room empty, she tried the back parlor and found her father sipping a glass of sherry by the fire.

Luz's work didn't fool the man.

"My heavens, lass, what on earth is the matter?" He rose quickly and came to her, circling her shoulders with his strong arms and kissing her on the cheek.

She didn't want to cry, but one look at the tender concern on his face, and she sobbed into his jacket. "I drank eggnog on an empty stomach and was too sick to stay another minute at the *reveillon.* Noah brought me home and Luz put me straight to bed." *Where she hadn't slept for one minute all night.*

Her father walked her to a chair by the fire and handed her his handkerchief. "Everyone expressed sorrow that you were taken ill. Vespasian promised to call today to check on you."

She sank into the chair. "How kind," she muttered more into the handkerchief than to him.

"Christmas is difficult without your mother, I know." He took a chair just opposite hers, leaned forward and patted her hand.

"I'm not upset about Mother." She was. "It's not that I don't miss her." She did. What she couldn't believe was the decision her mother had made for her. She had made plans for a newborn without knowing her personality, her talents, her desires.

"You won't." She stopped, glanced up at her father and tried again. "Madame Colville talked to me last night."

He raised an eyebrow.

"Do you intend to *make* me marry Vespasian Colville?"

His eyes flashed; he sprang from his chair and began to pace. *God help her. It was true.* All night, she'd hoped the lady had allowed her own desires to reinvent the past. *The mothers had made a pact. And her father knew it.*

"Madame Colville said she and Mother agreed to it when we were infants." She paused to take a deep breath. "She wants us to marry within the year."

Her father took a sip of sherry, put his glass down on the mantel between the sprigs of holly and camellias, then lowered his eyes to hers. "She and Bridget talked of it for years. I don't know what Bridget would say now, but I believe Helene thinks you'd be good for Vespasian."

"He *wouldn't* be good for me." New tears stung her eyes and she made use of her father's handkerchief again. She glanced sideways and saw his expression remained grim.

He faced the fire. "Most fathers would have forced a marriage between you and Colville last November after your crazy stunt—spending a night at his house."

Maureen bit her lip to keep from objecting yet again that nothing happened between them. She regretted that night more than anything she'd ever done in her life. He hadn't forced the marriage because he thought them too young. She'd heard her father say it many times.

Much more important, what did he think *today?* She took a deep breath and waited.

Sighing loudly, he turned back to her. "I believed you when you said you remained chaste, that Colville had been a perfect gentleman."

"It's true, Papa," she whispered.

His jaw tightened for a moment and then he went on. "Reason two was my reluctance to tie you down to a young man who is so immature. He can be an amiable fellow, but I worry there are few truly sensible thoughts in his head."

Maureen squelched a laugh at her father's accurate assessment. "You're right, Papa. There are none. Sensible thoughts, that is."

He paced between the chair where she sat and the sofa across the room. "His father is one of my oldest friends and clients. Emile Colville hired me as his broker when I was just a new Irish in town with a broken-down cotton factorage."

Maureen interrupted. "I've grown up a great deal in the last year and the trouble is, Vespasian hasn't. Will you tell Monsieur and Madame Colville we're *not* betrothed?"

He rubbed his finger across his mustache. "I'll tell the Colvilles the betrothal was a wish shared by two women who loved each other as sisters."

"Thank you, Papa. Thank you."

Thank heavens.

"Since you're at the age when it's time to choose a husband," he said, clearly thinking out loud, "I'll suggest to the Colvilles that you and Vespasian begin to court."

She gasped, but he held up a silencing hand. "You spent all last year mooning over him. William and I sat through supper after supper during which you talked of nothing but the young man's charms. It was your season and you didn't look at another man, much as we both urged you to."

She felt her chin tremble, and gritted her teeth to prevent it. She couldn't deny it. She'd been insufferable in her praises of Vespasian.

Clasping his hands behind him, her father stood directly in front of her chair for a few moments, then continued his pacing. "Henceforth, you must think of the young man as a potential husband and give him the opportunity to prove himself worthy. He won your heart once." He shrugged. "Apparently he lost it while he was away."

She crossed her arms over her chest and stared at the carpet. "He thinks only of himself."

"Immaturity he'll outgrow in time."

How much time was she supposed to give him? And how about his advances on her virtue in the garden Friday evening? If she mentioned it—which she certainly couldn't—what excuse would her father offer for that behavior?

"Vespasian drinks way too much and he visits Gallatine Street—often."

His steps stilled. She glanced up, but his back was to her. "Both will stop when he begins working," he said gruffly. "I've given him a job at the factorage."

"You have?" With a shout, she jumped to her feet. "I've been begging you to hire me for the last year, and you offered Vespasian a job?"

He sighed loudly. "No daughter of mine—"

"I know, I know." She thought about saying it—*will work for a living*, but didn't. He crossed back to her, motioned for her to sit again and took the chair opposite.

In a softer voice, he continued. "His father is my largest client. He asked me to find something for him. He starts Monday. I intend to work him to death and see what he's made of."

Maureen dabbed at a new flow of tears. "I don't love him."

"That's not what it looked like to me. And William, Renee, the Bouchard sisters." He reached out and patted her hand. "You might not love him, lass, but you've been friends your whole lives. That's not a bad way to start a marriage. He's from a fine Creole family on both sides. He's a member of one of the wealthiest families in the state. He can keep you in fine style." He gestured toward her new dress. "That's very becoming, by the way. I want you to give Vespasian a chance to win your heart."

She vowed silently, right then and there, to do the opposite. With a pleasant smile, she promised her father she'd give Vespasian a chance. "For you, Papa, I will allow him to call on me."

Never, never would she marry him. Not when men like Benjamin Merritt roamed the city.

And roam, he did. What in the world was he doing strolling near her house last night?

She closed her eyes, trying to understand why she'd just agreed to let Vespasian court her.

Last fall when she returned from Atlanta—from exile with her aunt as she referred to it—she thought Vespasian the finest man on earth. Tall, handsome, full of fun. They went to balls, to concerts, to the opera, in well-chaperoned groups. When they sneaked time alone, they flirted and kissed.

Those few months with Vespasian, she'd given zero thought to marriage, while lost in the excitement of being in love. At Vespasian's suggestion, she'd agreed to spend the night with him. But when she arrived at his house, the idea of making love terrified her. He'd not forced himself on her. They'd continued to see each other—through her season, and all summer.

Then he left for four months. An eternity. When he didn't answer her letters, she began to doubt his love. She no longer watched the mail. She no longer wrote to him. He ceased to be the center of her universe. She replanted her mother's garden, planned some plant experiments and designed her greenhouse.

Her greenhouse.

"Papa," she said with a sly smile. "With all this serious talk, have you forgotten it's Christmas afternoon?"

"Oh!" He feigned surprise. "So it is."

She raced down the hall ahead of him.

In her mother's sunroom, he caught up with her. "Close your eyes, take my hand."

He led her through French doors and down three steps. "Now walk straight ahead. Two steps, maybe three. All right, take a look."

Opening her eyes, Maureen swirled in a circle, trying to take it all in at once—the arch of the glass ceiling, the glass walls, the workbench and shelves above it. The afternoon sun shone through glass walls on three sides. The peaked glass roof rose twenty feet, high enough to grow trees if she wished. Tropical plants would thrive here, even in the dreariest winter weather.

"I'm speechless—it's spectacular!" She'd worked on the plans with the architect, but the finished room surpassed her expectations. She ran her hand around the rim of a large copper sink with hot and cold running water. She walked the length of a twelve-foot workbench, admiring its stone top. She opened several drawers positioned at one end and glanced at the shelves supported by iron posts embedded in the ground. Multiple drains positioned at intervals dotted the slate floor. Her heart thumped as she ran her hand through the soft granules filling the sand table where she would nurture seeds and tender shoots.

Spinning around again, she noticed a dark green iron table and four chairs, positioned to offer both a view of the garden outside and the greenhouse plants. "For coffee and even meals? It's more than I ever dreamed of. Thank you, Papa."

She leaped to hug him and when she pulled away, his eyes were wet with tears.

His hand swept the room's expanse. "Guy and I weren't sure where you wanted the plants. Ask him to help you move them about as you decide where they look best. Some are too heavy for you. And maybe me." He put a hand to his back and made a face.

"You didn't strain your back?"

"I was careful," he said with a smile. "I'm pleased you like the finished product."

"Like it? I love it!" Unable to suppress her delight, Maureen chattered about her plans as she circled the room again, stopping now and then to speak directly to a plant. In another moment, she whirled around to face him. "Forgive me. I'm just so pleased." She hugged him again. "But your patience must be wearing thin. I have a special gift for you, too."

Her father's eyes glistened with tears again when he opened the box containing a gold watch fob. His old one, a gift from her mother, had broken not two weeks ago, its links worn thin from years of use. He declared the new fob the handsomest he'd ever seen and attached his watch quickly. They enjoyed a glass of sherry together beside the Christmas tree and then ate a simple late luncheon of leek soup, sliced ham and biscuits.

Not long after, her father excused himself to rest before Christmas dinner at Renee and William's house, a celebration with Renee's family—including Sophie.

Maureen hadn't a thought for napping. Rushing back to the greenhouse, she donned an apron and set to work adjusting plants. She shifted her tropical ferns to the darkest side, shaded from the west sun by the house. She transferred her trowels, gardening gloves, clippers and some of her flower pots from the cabinet in the sunroom to the workbench. All the while, she hummed happily, refusing to let Madame Colville's wishes or her father's or Vespasian's, for that matter, dampen her mood. She would allow him to call on her—but only with her father as chaperone. What better way to give the appearance of a smoothly running courtship?

Marriage within the year? No, Madame Colville. Not to your son.

Another man occupied her mind. A lawyer, of all things. *The necessary evil.* She giggled at the thought.

Chapter Eight

Maureen woke with a bad cold on New Year's Eve. She spent the day in bed, but by evening decided the humid air in the greenhouse would do her good. The air and hot tea. Her hands encircled a cup, warming her tingling skin, as she sat on a stool at the workbench, staring at Ben's gift, a large *Camilla Japonica* with more bright red blossoms than she could count.

She plucked the card from a branch and reread it for the tenth time.

> *Dear Miss Collins,*
> *Captain Kwan of the Hailong Hao (the Sea Dragon) assured me this is one of the finest camellias in the world. He claims even its roots are fragrant. He promises many hours of enjoyment from their aroma in the New Year.*
> *Your devoted servant, Ben Merritt*

Holding the stationary to her face, she tried to breathe in the man's familiar citrus scent. Her stuffy nose made it impossible. Did he dab cologne directly on his note just as she always perfumed any letters to men? Did gentlemen do that sort of thing?

Ben's words on the card nestled in the lovely plant Noah had found on the front porch this morning puzzled her. Fragrant roots? Camellias didn't have fragrant roots. Even their flowers weren't fragrant.

She put on her leather gardening gloves, softened the soil with water, ran a trowel around the inside to loosen the roots and laid the pot on its side. Gently grabbing the shrub's trunk, she pulled.

A tin box tumbled onto the bench. She pushed it aside for the moment, leaned into the roots and sniffed.

Dirt.

Much as she loved the rich familiar odor of dark, rich soil, she wouldn't use the word *fragrant* to describe it. Or maybe she just wasn't smelling accurately tonight? She did have a horrible head cold, after all.

Had Captain Kwan taken Ben for a fool? She wondered how much he'd paid for a camellia with fragrant roots. She dropped the plant into a larger pot, carefully troweled additional soil around the sides and on top, patted it down with her hands and then watered it. She addressed the shrub while she tended to it. "Your roots, dear camellia, don't smell particularly sweet, but your blossoms are gorgeous."

She reached for the tin. The Chinese lettering meant nothing to her. Plants from American nurseries often came with a sample of the company's fertilizer, though she'd never seen it tucked in the roots. She paused for a moment to blow her nose, then pried the lid off the box.

Pine resin? That's what it looked like. She pinched off a little. Sticky, too. Her gloved thumb and index finger pasted together, she brought her hand to her nose. From what she could tell, the substance had a pleasant smell, not unlike fresh cream. She formed it into a small ball and set it aside.

With a shrug, she rolled eleven more balls the size of green peas and lined them up along the workbench. Ordinarily, she used a nitrogen powder mixed with water to fertilize her camellias. Instead, she placed three brown balls on the soil of each of three white camellias, labeled White A, White B, White C, and three balls on her new red one, labeled Red A. Pulling out her notebook, she noted the date, time and the words "Chinese fertilizer" next to each plant name.

While dressing for New Year's Eve, Ben contemplated the idea of love as opposed to lust. Maureen's constant intrusion into Ben's thoughts forced him to consider whether he suffered from love rather than mere lust. Or if it were possible to suffer from both simultaneously. His experience with women wasn't vast, but when he had bedded a woman, he'd never given serious thought to her after the fact.

What did his persistent memory of Maureen's face and figure mean? He told himself he was too young—twenty-eight—and too committed to his mission—to contemplate love and its next step with a lady—marriage. When he decided to settle down, he'd always thought he'd choose one of his sister Letitia's friends. They were constantly in and out of his family's house and he felt comfortable with them. One of these days, he'd court one and marry her.

He went dutifully to two New Year's parties in order to meet as many New Orleanians as possible in the shortest amount of time. His law school friend Paul Hebert and his family hosted an annual event, beginning at eight o'clock. Iced champagne in silver goblets and food harvested from the Gulf including shrimp, raw oysters and all sorts of crab confections led him to stay longer than he intended.

A number of unattached young ladies buzzed about. But idle talk with these beautifully dressed women made him long to see Maureen, to smell her rose-scented hair and hear her laugh. As he thanked Monsieur and Madame Herbert for inviting him, he hoped Maureen and her father might be guests at the next party— the Mermentaus' annual event.

Again, he met with disappointment. No sign of Maureen or her father. He forced himself to meet every gentleman there and encouraged these males to introduce him to their female relatives. He danced with a few of these ladies, then thanked Monsieur and Madame Mermentau for a wonderful evening. Dashing out into the rain, he soon secured the services of a man driving a buggy pulled by one horse. On a rainy holiday night, it was a lucky find even though the open vehicle with a leather bonnet only partially covered him, leaving him with wet legs and feet in short order.

He had thought the camellia's presence on Maureen's front porch might have elicited a response this morning. A thank-you note, an invitation to call on her—something. His only sure bet was to call on her at home. When the Collins house came into view, his watch read quarter to eleven, far beyond the acceptable hour to call. A surprise visit, even to her greenhouse where Maureen said she often worked late, would astound her father if he ever found out. Bad manners, yes, but this meeting might provide an opportunity to steal another kiss. And, he reminded himself, it might further his investigation.

Apparently another gentleman intended a late call. When Ben caught sight of a man jumping down from a cabriolet parked across the street, he signaled his driver to stop. He climbed out and stepped into the shadows. He recognized Vespasian Colville— introduced to him at the factorage—rushing across the street and through the front gate.

Colville didn't follow the walkway to the front door, but slinked into the camellia bushes—the ones Maureen had run through the first night he saw her. He understood the man was welcome in this home. Hell, the two had grown up together, he'd learned. Why was he sneaking about?

Heavy rain blew sideways as Ben darted through the gate and into the bushes. Soaked through from his overcoat to his limp dress shirt, he dogged Colville's steps, hiding in the shadow of one tree and then another. When he rounded the edge of the house, he faced a blaze of light from the greenhouse and dove to the grass, landing in a mud puddle at the base of a sweet olive tree. The golden orb of light turned the trees and bushes beside the path to the door into a patch of broad daylight. His breathing quickened. Maureen must be working tonight.

Colville banged on the door with the flat of his hand. Crouching low, Ben scurried among the bushes until he knelt behind a large azalea. Its branches hid him completely, and best of all, he could see Maureen through the rain-streaked glass. She sat at a round iron table, drinking from a teacup.

A knock on the door startled her. Who in the world was in her garden on New Year's Eve? Could it be Ben to see how his gift was doing? No one had told her about her plant until she came downstairs for tea in late afternoon. Surely he wondered that she'd not sent a thank-you message immediately.

She turned toward the knock and her heart sank. Vespasian bowed with a flourish.

Two nights ago, he'd stopped by without an invitation and asked her to marry him, but without the traditional kneeling on one knee. In Vespasian's inimitable way, he'd sworn he couldn't live without her and simply told her marriage was their destiny. She'd demurred, explaining she'd been stunned by the revelation of their mothers' pact. She'd told him in no uncertain terms she'd need to think about it for a *long, long* time.

Was he here so soon to try to convince her to change her mind?

She unlocked the door and opened it an inch. "You risk your death from a cold just being near me." Her voice surprised her. She'd heard croaking frogs sound better.

He shrugged. "New Orleans is out celebrating the New Year and you in bed with a cold. I'll risk it. At least your father thinks you're in bed."

She motioned him inside, keeping her voice to a whisper because it didn't hurt as much that way. "You saw my father at Sophie's party?"

"At work today. I work these days at the factorage. You know that."

She sat and pointed to the chair opposite her. "I'm having hot tea." She paused to wipe her nose with a lace handkerchief. "Would you like a cup?"

He shook his head vigorously. "Can you name a gentleman who'd want a cup of tea to ring in the New Year?"

She tilted her head toward the sunroom. "On the table, you'll find whiskey and glasses. Do help yourself."

Returning with a full glass of whiskey as well as the decanter in hand, he stood still in the room's center. "It's magnificent, Maureen, it truly is." He walked through the aisles created by scores of potted plants and finally bent his head back to stare at the glass roof. "I know you'll enjoy playing here with your plants."

"Don't, Vespie. I'm *not* playing and you know it."

Chuckling, he walked to the workbench and gestured toward the red camellia. "Merritt's gift?"

"How did you know?"

"I guessed. No, actually I heard it was left on your porch this morning."

She wasn't going to pretend the new gentleman in town had not impressed her with the camellia. Or ask the source of Vespie's information. "It's beautiful, isn't it?"

Joining him at the workbench, she explained her intentions. "I'll cut off a few limbs from the red plant and graft them to these plants." She motioned to the white camellias.

She began to cough, returned to her teacup and took a gulp.

He stood beside her and poured another glass of whiskey. "Let's drink to your experiments."

She raised her teacup and touched it to his glass. "But not too much"—he held one pointed finger up as if to scold her—"I started at your papa's office party around four, but I'm not drinking to excess tonight. I'm a working man these days."

"It's quite a change for you." She coughed softly into her handkerchief again and sat down at the table. "How is it at the factorage?"

Grimacing, he sat, muttering that the iron chair wasn't designed for comfort. He met her gaze. "The factorage is work, which I believe by definition is dull. That cousin of yours—William—is as hard driving as I expect I'll find Satan in hell."

"You know this is a slow time? Harvest is over." In spite of her sniffles, her headache, chills and fever, Maureen couldn't help smiling at the thought of Vespasian actually doing work.

"That young assistant, Fabre, keeps telling me how lucky I am to get 'broken in'—I don't like the horse term—when it's not harvest." He sighed, shook his head, finished his drink and poured another.

"It's not the best way to use your talents. A clerk? Can't you talk your father out of the idea?"

He took several swallows of whiskey and continued. "Father said it was Collins Factorage or the U.S. Army. Fighting Indians. Can you imagine? No one should be fighting Indians in the first place and I certainly know it's not something *I'm* interested in doing."

She leaned forward. "To your future at the factorage, then." She moved her cup to his in another toast.

His emerald green eyes sparkled. He periodically pushed his hair off his face with a sweeping hand from forehead to crown. She loved his hair and had sometimes run her own fingers through it. A soldier? Actually with his height and trim figure, he would look dashing in a uniform. She pushed that thought from her mind.

"I'm glad you came by, Vespie. We should talk."

He groaned. "When a lady says that, a man is always doomed."

"Tomorrow begins a new year." She convulsed with a sudden, racking cough. Her throat burned, her eyes watered and she gasped for breath as she tried to bring it under control.

Vespasian dashed for the sunroom. "I'm mixing a cough syrup for you right this minute. Is Julia here?

"Night off with Guy," she sputtered. "Noah's with Papa."

Damn it to hell. She smiled at Colville. Let him in. Even seemed glad to see him. He disappeared, returned with a glass and a decanter. Colville walked up and down the aisles, then wandered over to the workbench.

Of course he would pretend an interest in her plants. He gestured to the red camellia and to some smaller pots holding white camellias beside it. She went to the bench, touched a blossom on his gift and pantomimed the cutting of the branches.

Good God. He couldn't see every gesture her hands made, but it appeared the plant that cost five dollars was going to be dismembered tonight or tomorrow. Maureen returned to the table; eventually Colville joined her. Every few minutes, her handkerchief went to her face. Her nose, her eyes, her mouth? Was she crying? Suffering from the toothache? A head cold? The lady must have a bad cold. Not surprising considering she gallivanted about in her garden at night and sat outside in blustery weather at the Café du Monde by day.

Colville laughed often as he entertained her. He drank down his whiskey and helped himself to a third glass. What Ben wouldn't do to change places with him. The greenhouse would be warm, the whiskey bracing and Maureen's smile heavenly.

Wet through and chilled, he knew he should leave. The drenching wasn't worth it when he couldn't hear the conversation. But he didn't. Damn it, Maureen's shoulders shook with laughter once or twice when Colville raised his eyebrows in mock horror or gestured wildly. When she leaned forward in a coughing fit, Colville jumped to his feet and darted from the room. Ready to run toward her, Ben held his own breath until her spasm ended.

Vespasian returned with a tray containing a spoon, a lemon, a sharp knife, a jar of honey, and a glass, and Maureen nodded in gratitude. He mixed a cough syrup at her table. Whiskey, a few spoons of honey and a squeeze of lemon. She opened her mouth for the concoction and he ladled three spoonfuls onto her tongue. The honey coated her throat, soothing it. "Thank you."

"Stuff works every time." He laid the spoon on the table by the glass. "I made enough to last all night. Take it up to bed with you. Better now?"

She was. Vespie could be kind. Tonight, he knew just what she needed and took care of her. But on plenty of occasions, she'd seen him think only of himself. And he was such a child in his pursuit of pleasure. She couldn't picture them married. Ben Merritt had nothing to do with her decision, she told herself. She spoke in a whisper: "I think we both realize that the fun we've had together in the past year was a childish infatuation."

He drained his glass. "I hope to make it a grown-up infatuation."

She shook her head. "I'm sorry I encouraged your romantic intentions."

"I don't blame you for that. You returned from your Atlanta exile and here I was—all grown up, devilishly handsome, irresistible—let's see, a very good kisser." He paused to pour another glass from the decanter.

"Yes to all that." She sighed heavily. "And a year ago, I didn't know what I wanted. I was young and silly."

"And now you do? Does this Merritt fellow have anything to do with it?"

She met his eyes. "I hardly know the man. There's so much I want to do before I marry. I want to develop and sell new plants."

He came to stand beside her chair. When she looked up, she saw Ben Merritt's face atop Vespasian's shoulders.

He put his glass on the table, locked his hands behind his back and began to pace, his head bent, his eyes focused on his boots. He looked terribly serious.

"To be perfectly honest, Vespie," she continued. "I want to be your friend, not—not your wife."

He turned abruptly, glared at her for a moment, then laughed loudly. "Friends? I believe that means we don't kiss or do anything else involving our bodies?"

"Exactly. A Platonic relationship."

He gave her a quizzical look.

"Plato," she emphasized the name. "Greek philosopher."

"I've managed to fail philosophy more times than I can count."

"He believed men and women could be friends without a romantic or physical relationship."

"Idiot." He shrugged. "Friends? Not possible. During both my waking moments and my sleeping ones, I think of some of our past actions and I know I'll never be able to get you out of my mind."

He resumed his pacing, traveling the length of the greenhouse while she waited. He strode back to her, looked down and spoke in the most serious tone Maureen had ever heard come from his mouth:

"My mother is impatient to announce our engagement, but I'm not. I can wait until you're ready. Assuming, that is, it's not a decade or two hence."

He wandered to the workbench, glancing at the white camellias, then fixed his eyes on the new red one. He frowned. "What's this stuff that looks like peas in the soil?"

Maureen joined him. "That?" She pointed. "A new fertilizer came in a tin in the roots of the plant."

A dark expression crossed his face. He asked if she still had the tin.

"Right here." She pulled open the top drawer. "What's wrong?"

His eyes fell on the Chinese lettering. "That's not fertilizer."

She frowned. "Well, then, what is it?"

"It's opium."

She put her hands on her hips as she shook her head. "It can't be. That's absurd. Nurseries often give away packets of fertilizer with plants."

"Trust me. That's opium. People smoke it in pipes."

"Are you saying opium would be a good fertilizer?"

"I don't know about that." He gestured to the tin and the plant. "But it's a good hiding place—in tin boxes in the roots of plants—if you want to smuggle it."

"Why would anyone want to smuggle opium into the country? I can buy it at the Royal Street Pharmacy."

"The cost has gone up, practically doubled in the last year."

Her sore throat no longer made her speechless. Her mind whirled. Opium smuggling? Ben couldn't know anything about it. He just bought a plant for her.

"I'd take it off the plants and put it back in the tin. Wear gloves when you handle it."

Voices in the front hallway startled her. "That's Julia and Guy. Go."

Maureen ran to the door, opened it and gestured for him to hurry.

"Your beau Merritt must be a smuggler," he announced as he strode toward her, showing no urgency.

Her insides roiled. She struggled to keep her composure. "Vespie, I don't believe Mr. Merritt's a smuggler. And even if I did, it wouldn't change my mind about you and me."

He smirked. "Oh, you're always changing your mind, Missy."

Ben held his breath. Maureen opened the door and motioned to Colville to leave. She looked straight at the azalea bush he'd chosen as his hideout.

Colville, his face grim, said a few parting words. The meeting ended unhappily for him, which brought a smile to Ben's lips. The young man stepped through the door, then raced around the side of the house, not being nearly as careful in the retreat as he had been in the advance.

Turning his gaze to Maureen, Ben fought the impulse to rush in and hug her, mop her brow with a cold rag, take her to her bed and hold her until she fell asleep. With a sad face, she locked the door and returned the key to a drawer in the workbench. She put on her gloves, picked at the camellias, as if removing something—pests, maybe?—and dropped these one by one into a small box. She put it in the same drawer with her door key.

Her hair was tied back with a ribbon; she wore a gray house-dress with some age to it and her nose was almost as red as the *Camellia Japonica's* blooms. She turned off the gas lamp above the bench and another over her round table before disappearing up the brick steps.

God help him. As sick as she was, she looked beautiful.

Ben retraced his own steps among the bushes and trees, careful to stay in the shadows until he arrived at the street. Colville's cabriolet was gone, so he went straight out the front gate. Walking down St. Charles Avenue toward his waiting driver, he stared at the gas lanterns on the front of an approaching vehicle.

Too late, he recognized the Collins carriage. Dropping his head, he turned his coat collar up and shifted his body sideways as if tilting away from the rain and wind. Even so, his gut told him Patrick Collins saw him skulking away from the house.

Chapter Nine

*H*er heart filled with nervous elation, Maureen entered the foyer of the Odd Fellows Hall, confident she'd be in Ben's arms for a waltz within the hour. Her father escorted her on one arm, Sophie on the other. The three made their way to the coat check where ladies eyed each other's gowns and gentlemen eyed the ladies' *decolletage*.

Generally she loved nothing better than comparing her ball gown with other ladies' attire and admiring the handsome men in full *costume de rigueur*—a black tailcoat and a white tie. Tonight she felt decidedly different. Gowns and handsome men didn't interest her. She looked for one man. She ached to see Ben in formal attire, clothes that made the homeliest man presentable and a handsome man irresistible.

She scanned the hall a third time and her face warmed with something like humiliation. He wasn't here. How could he not attend the first ball of the season? And if he were here, how could he not wait in the lobby for a glimpse of her? She knew from Renee, who knew from William, that Ben had been invited to the Twelfth Night Revelers Ball by Pierre Hebert, Paul's father. And she knew he'd accepted. Maybe he was just running late. Maybe he was already in the main ballroom. He *had* to come.

They had corresponded all week. She'd sent a thank-you note New Year's Day; he'd answered with a request to call on her. Her cough was worse, her fever high and as much as she wanted to see him, she didn't want him to see her looking her worst. She'd put him off with a flirty response that she was saving her strength to dance with him.

What would she say when he arrived? When his hand felt warm on the small of her back, when he led her in a waltz, her favorite dance, would she look into his eyes and tell him she found opium in the roots of the plant he gave her? Or would it be her secret—hers and Vespasian's?

At the same time, how could she not tell him? He certainly didn't realize what he'd bought from the captain of the *Sea Dragon*. If he knew, he never would have given it to her. Did he think she smoked? Did he smoke and hope to convince her opium was a pleasant diversion? Did hard-working respectable attorneys smoke opium? She didn't know. She would ask around. She would find a book on opium. But tonight, she forced the question from her mind.

With a polite smile, she removed her black velvet cloak, revealing the silk lining that matched her pink and black plaid silk gown.

Sophie leaned in and whispered. "I was a little nervous when Renee told me you were having a dress made up in *plaid* silk." The lady's eyes took in the low-cut square neckline, cap sleeves and narrow ruched skirt. "I admit I just couldn't imagine it, but it's gorgeous."

Sophie nodded her head in the direction of Aisling Moreau, one of the city's wealthiest and most fashionably dressed ladies. Aisling and the three ladies surrounding her were all openly gaping at Maureen's dress.

"You're setting a new style," Sophie continued, her eyes glittering. "Frau Kohlmeyer will have a dozen orders for similar dresses tomorrow."

Maureen acknowledged the compliment and responded in kind, only half her attention on the conversation. "Renee's idea.

The lining of the cloak and the evening bag." She raised her arm to show off a matching plaid silk bag dangling from her wrist. "She ordered this as a surprise for me." They turned away from the gawking group. "And you look spectacular, Sophie. I love the plum silk. I'm betting the dress is also Renee's design?"

Sophie nodded. "Made more beautiful by your father's Christmas gift." She touched her fingers to the gold and pearl necklace from which a large amethyst pendant hung.

Maureen had seen it in the jeweler's box, but on the lady's neck it sparkled with every move she made. Her father joined them, circled Sophie's waist with his arm—a gesture she thought quite intimate for a couple not officially engaged—and suggested they all go inside. They climbed the grand staircase to the second-floor. The ballroom's enormous size and its high-ceiling dome resplendent with gas-lit chandeliers had thrilled Maureen when she came out at this ball last year.

Tonight, its luster dimmed. Elise Bouchard caught her eye, greeted her and whispered how surprised she was that Mr. Merritt was tardy for his first Mardi Gras ball. "He'll be here," Maureen promised. "And he'll dance with you, Carine, and me."

Madame and Monsieur Colville, Vespasian a step behind, approached the Collins table. Madame Colville greeted Maureen with a kiss on each cheek, and complimented her gown. "Vespasian mentioned what a terrible cold and cough you suffered last week. I do hope you're feeling well enough to begin the Mardi Gras season."

Maureen drew in a breath. Surely he didn't tell his mother he'd called on her on New Year's Eve? "Thank you, quite well tonight," she murmured.

Vespasian looked over his mother's shoulder. His sly smile told her he'd not reported that her answer to his proposal had been a firm no.

He edged to her side as his mother drifted away. "Do save a waltz for me tonight, will you?" But his eyes left hers—to rest longer than was polite on a young lady halfway across the room. He nodded his head in the direction of his gaze. "Know her?"

Admiring another lady while he talked with her? She'd have been furious a year ago. Not now. Her eyes, too, swept the ballroom every few minutes looking for a different partner, and every time her eyes came up empty, her heart sank another degree like a barometer before a storm.

Maureen turned as discreetly as possible to glimpse the woman who'd caught Vespasian's eye. "Knew her at Ursuline. Suzette Juneau."

"Married?"

"I believe she married an older man by the name of St. Aubin, but I'm not positive." Although Maureen prided herself on knowing just about everyone in society, she'd lost track of Suzette. "She was a boarder from Baton Rouge, a year ahead of me." It would actually be good, she realized, if Vespasian entertained another love interest. She smiled up at him. "For you," she said under her breath, "I'll find out what I can."

"I'd be forever grateful," he murmured. "And don't forget that waltz, Missy." Then he excused himself.

Her father, Sophie, William, Renee, and Maureen sat in a semi-circle—in that order—facing the dance floor. Renee looked lovely in a purple silk dress. Her diamond necklace, a gift from William on the day after the twins were born, twinkled in the light from the candelabra on the table.

Although the conversation was lively, Maureen felt hollow in her gorgeous new gown. The two ladies beside her wore jewels given to them by doting gentlemen. The gold necklace Maureen wore, beautiful as it was, had belonged to her mother. Feeling out of place with two couples so obviously in love, she once again cast her eyes about the room.

How could Ben do this to her? When he *did* show up, she would act a little cold, she decided. And she'd make him apologize ardently before she agreed to a dance.

Ben had it on good authority—Paul Hebert, a New Orleans native—that everyone in the city celebrated Twelfth Night. Those who didn't go to the Revelers Ball hosted smaller parties or went out to restaurants or bars to start the Mardi Gras season with good food and good spirits. He didn't expect to find a soul working late at Collins Factorage.

Though he felt ridiculous in his formal wear, he entered the main unlocked door of the building housing the firm's offices and climbed the stairs to the third floor. His skill at picking locks allowed easy access into the outer office. He took a quick look through clerks' desks and found nothing more than correspondence with clients.

He picked the lock on William's desk. Nothing. He knew where Vespasian sat and couldn't resist a glance at his unlocked drawer. A copy of *The Mascot*, the city's weekly gossip rag, and a few copies of transcribed correspondence. Clearly the man did little work.

Next he tackled the lock on the door of Patrick Collins' private office and later the one on his file cabinet. The safe in the corner offered a greater challenge, but in ten minutes he'd opened that, too, and quickly examined the account books. Not a number out of order. He was discouraged, but not particularly surprised. What man left evidence of smuggling operations in his legitimate place of business?

He'd have to break into the Collins home—a task he didn't look forward to. Or maybe during a call on Maureen, he could excuse himself, sneak into Collins' library and look through his desk. *No. Too risky.*

Disappointed that he'd found nothing and irritated that he now ran the risk of being late for the ball, Ben decided to pay a quick call on Captain Kwan. Was he a smuggler? The fact that he smoked opium on board was no great indicator either way. Buying and smoking opium were legal in the United States. But bringing pounds of it into the country without paying duty on it was decidedly not. The *Hailong Hao* made frequent trips to Jamaica where a buyer could pick up opium from a variety of sea captains. Tonight he intended to try to make a large buy from Kwan. *Free of the import duty.*

Hebert's description of Twelfth Night applied to the levee as well. Commerce was at a standstill. No dock workers milled about. Even the colorful lanterns on the foreign ships were dark. This opportunity wasn't likely to present itself anytime soon. He walked up the gangplank and peered into the ship's cabin. Dark.

He picked the lock and went in. He lit a succession of matches. A desk in the main room housed maps and Chinese ledgers. Dozens of plants now cluttered the cabin floor. In the smaller room, he opened drawers in a bureau, but saw only a few pipes and a small amount of opium. If the man smuggled the substance, he disposed of it the minute he came into port.

On the way out in the dark, he banged his shin into a heavy flowerpot. Refusing to howl like he wished, he hobbled out, relocked the door and left the ship.

His duty done for the night, he turned his thoughts to his first Mardi Gras ball. According to Hebert, the Odd Fellows Hall boasted the finest dance floor in the country. In his short time here, Ben had noticed that New Orleanians always spoke in superlatives. Antoine's was the finest restaurant in the world; the Fairgrounds was the fastest horse track in the world; Gulf shrimp were the tastiest in the world; coffee with chicory the richest in the world.

It amused him that many citizens who spoke this way had never left the banks of the Mississippi.

But, maybe it was true. Maybe all these things *were* the best in the world. He was fast falling in love with the city and the variety of its inhabitants. So what if its people prized all these attractions and overpraised them? They found enjoyment in life itself. The New Year's parties he'd attended had been lavish entertainments. He couldn't imagine what he would witness at Mardi Gras.

Would Maureen wear her hair up or down? Up, no doubt, because ladies somehow thought they looked more beautiful that way. In reality, men—he, anyway—preferred long, silky hair down a lady's back and shoulders.

Her gown? He'd spent many a wistful moment thinking what her breasts might look like spilling from the top of a ball gown. Her ivory complexion and neck held a promise of more luscious white skin below, tipped with rosy pink buds. My God, what was he thinking? He wasn't looking for a wife. Maureen's role lay in helping him get to know her father and cousin better, as well as other members of society.

Colville would attend the ball tonight, too, but he didn't let that sour his mood. She couldn't possibly enjoy his company. Or only in small doses. Maureen was too intelligent and too passionate about botany to be attracted to an idle man about town who Ben had heard left college to pursue what? A clerk's job at Collins Factorage? Absinthe? Married women?

His heavy wool coat covered his tailcoat, but his top hat and silver-topped walking stick lent him a certain foppish air. From the corner of his eye, he saw two men approach from his left, gaining ground on him fast. His breathing quickened, the muscles in his arms tightened, he fisted his gloved hands. He looked an easy mark, but he was anything but. In fact, he was eager to show these characters all he knew. He'd studied judo under Carleton for six months.

On the dock ahead, sugar barrels and burlap sacks lined the path in front of him. They obstructed his route, forcing him to walk a little to the left, closer to the men. Their footsteps thudded on the wooden dock. He smelled liquor and sweat, heard mumbled speech. *That's right, Smiley... We'll take care of it ...*

As they neared him, one man reached out and knocked his top hat to the ground. Hoping they were just out to have a little fun in their drunken state, Ben stopped, turned and looked each in the face. One was more than six feet tall and heavy, the other a head shorter. Carleton's wisdom ran through his mind. *When outnumbered, go for the strongest opponent first. Knock him out or kill him and the weak ones will run away. If you can't knock out the big guy, knocking out the weaker men isn't going to do you a damn bit of good anyway.*

Two against one and these two possessed the blind strength of drunks. Ben had been taught that his mind was his best weapon. He said politely, "Fine evening, isn't it?"

Neither answered. Twisting his body a little sideways, Ben bent, pretending to retrieve his hat near his feet. The smaller man sprang onto his back, but Ben was ready. Rising, he slammed an elbow into the man's stomach, knocking him away. Cursing and bent double in pain, the man backed off.

Pivoting, Ben faced the taller man and waited for him to make the first move. As he stepped forward, Ben gave him a solid kick to the ankle of the leg supporting his weight. Confusion on his face, he fell to the ground with a groan.

The fight had just begun. The first man, recovered now, charged at him, his fists in front of his face. Ben dodged to his left, then brought his walking stick down on the back of his opponent's head. He fell at Ben's feet. *Not exactly proper judo, but a victory.* Ben's eyes remained on his bleeding skull a split-second too long while he wondered if he'd killed him.

When he turned, the other man, about his own height, landed a hard fist in his left eye. Pain shot through his head. Blinded, he raised his left arm to block anyone coming from that side. Instead, the man came straight in, which allowed Ben to use a basic throw. He grabbed his arms, planted one foot on his stomach and used his powerful thigh muscles to support him as he sank into a squat. The guy flew over his shoulder and splashed face first into the water. *Fabulous.* He hadn't realized they were that close to the dock's edge.

He retrieved his top hat and, with his hand so close to his foot, removed his knife from its sheath. *Just let anyone try to approach him again.* Armed now, Ben felt a moment of pride that he'd defended himself so well. His head pounding, his left eye swollen and useless, he didn't see a small barrel sailing toward his head until the last moment. He ducked just in time, but lost his balance and fell to his knees.

A third man, out of nowhere, dove on him, knocking him to his back. Ben held his knife in a firm grip. Thrusting it into his attacker' arm, he sliced from his elbow to his wrist, going deep through his clothes and into his flesh. Screaming, his opponent rolled off him and ran, clutching his arm.

Chapter Ten

Sipping champagne, Maureen trained her eyes on the young ladies who paraded out on their fathers' arms to be presented to society. Dressed in white gowns of silk and satin trimmed in sequins, pearls and lace, each curtsied to the crowd in turn. Renee and Sophie nodded to each other and murmured comments. Maureen did her best to add a remark here and there.

Following a Twelfth Night tradition that went back to Roman times when slaves hid a bean in a cake and the finder was king for the day, the eight young ladies approached the center of the ballroom. Each took one-eighth piece of a king cake and bit into it carefully, hoping to find a gold locket, an exquisite stand-in for a bean. That lucky lady became queen of the ball and the other seven her maids.

Last year, Maureen had been quite hungry and had chomped down on the gold locket, almost swallowing it. She recalled her magical night as queen, Vespasian hovering near her, taking her on the dance floor more times than she could count. She had been thrilled at the touch of his hand on the small of her back as they waltzed. She was sure she was in love.

Tonight, she felt bitterly disappointed as the presentations ended and the dancing began. Paul Hebert offered his hand for a dance, which she accepted though she hadn't the heart for it. While her feet moved in rhythm to the music, she alternated between anger that Ben would disregard an invitation and—suddenly—worry that only something very serious would prevent his attendance. She pushed the thought aside.

Vespasian partnered her next, but while he held Maureen in his arms, his eyes followed Suzette. The lady—blond, quite tall and married—resembled Aisling Moreau, with whom Vespasian had also danced. One more reason why he and she didn't suit. Vespasian found tall, blond ladies more appealing than petite, dark-haired ones. She hoped Madame Colville noticed her son's taste.

Another excruciating hour passed. She shared two more dances with men she termed unmemorable partners. Then Vespasian returned to waltz with her. He pulled her close and she made no move to stop him. When the music ended, Vespasian suggested a turn on the terrace for old time's sake. She agreed, not even bothering to glance back at the ballroom's entrance.

He grabbed two glasses of champagne from a waiter and handed one to her as they headed for the exit. He walked her to the far corner of the stone porch and leaned on the rail. "If I may confide in you now that we're friends, I must tell you—I trust you won't be jealous—that I'm madly in love for the first time in my life."

She did feel a twinge. The first time in his life? "Jealous? Don't be foolish. Friends aren't jealous of their friends' attachments."

"This friend," he pointed to his chest, "isn't jealous of yours." He paused. "I know you're positively miserable because the gentleman you're looking for hasn't arrived."

"Is it that obvious?" She sighed heavily. "I wanted to dance with him. But maybe he doesn't know how. Could that be it? Would a man stay away because he can't dance?"

"I wouldn't. I'd make damn sure I learned before the ball."

She sipped her wine. It was true. Vespasian would have hired a dance teacher the moment he received the invitation. Ben struck her as far more cautious, a man who might think dancing frivolous.

But also a man who would come to the ball and not hesitate to say he didn't dance.

Maybe Ben had left town suddenly. Maybe she'd never see him again. But in any case, she knew Vespasian—now in love, he claimed—was no longer in her future.

She chose her words carefully. "I want to hear about your new love, but first, will you do me a favor?"

"I'm always delighted to accommodate a lady."

She hesitated. "Will you agree not to ever speak of our past—as a couple, I mean?"

"Ahhh. I see." His face lit up in a knowing smile. "Those were some good times."

She clung to the thin railing with her free hand, while her other clutched the stem of her glass with tensed fingers. "I'm thinking specifically of the night we spent together in your library last year." She paused to catch her breath. "And our recent meeting in my garden."

"I believe I had overindulged on both occasions. I'm a bit foggy on the details."

"We kissed."

He raised one eyebrow. "Foggy or no, I remember a bit more than that."

"Promise me you'll never tell a soul—and that includes Ben Merritt—about either incident."

He patted her on the shoulder as if she were a child. "You have my word as a gentleman."

"Thank you," she whispered. She suspected her face must resemble the red blossoms on the camellia bush Ben had given her, but even though she'd never been more embarrassed, she felt pleased she had gained what she wanted—Vespasian's promise that their past was past.

They clinked glasses and sipped.

"And may I ask something in return for my silence?"

Her stomach clenched. "Blackmail?" She spoke too loudly and several young ladies turned from their escorts and stared for a moment.

She leaned in. "I haven't any money to speak of," she whispered. "Not serious money. I can't pay you to be quiet."

He chuckled. "Oh, my dear, Maureen. Nothing so terrible as that."

She let out the breath she'd been holding. "What then?"

"I want your help in wooing the lady of my dreams."

That, she hadn't expected. "If you're speaking of Suzette ..."

"Who else? Of course I am."

She turned to him, shocked. "But she's married! I confirmed it."

"Yes, well." He waved a hand.

Maureen seized his forearm. "Listen to me, Vespie. She's not a lady to trifle with considering the man she's married to."

In the dim light, his face was as serious as she'd ever seen it. "But I'm in love with her," he said.

"You'd never laid eyes on her until tonight!"

He gazed into the garden. "What does that matter?"

She believed if a group of sword-wielding pirates carried her away at this moment, he wouldn't even notice her absence.

"She's as beautiful as a forest nymph, a Greek goddess, an Indian princess."

Maureen reached out, touched his cheek and turned his face to hers. "She's married."

"Forgive me for admitting this, but that hasn't stopped me in the past."

She felt her cheeks grow warm as she stared into his eyes. So the rumors about Vespasian were true. He had just confessed to adultery. Would he be faithful to her if they were forced to marry? She didn't dare ask him. "Vespie, her husband's a tyrant. From what I hear, he's known for his terrible temper. He's more than capable of killing you. You can't even think about—"

Vespasian interrupted. "I'll gladly risk my life for her."

"She's already taken."

"Against her will, I'm sure. She's twenty, married to a man fifty-five, sixty, something like that. A bald, bespectacled, corpulent oaf. Did you *see* him?"

She bowed her head and murmured. "I did."

"Can you imagine the horror of having that man in your bed?"

Maureen couldn't, but she felt certain this affair would end in disaster for Vespasian. "Suzette married him," she insisted. "Maybe she loves him."

"I don't believe that for a second. Help me, Maureen." His voice had grown hoarse. "In return for my silence ..."

She glared at him. "You wouldn't."

He raised an eyebrow. "Call on her. Get her out of the house and I'll meet you somewhere. Anywhere. A favor for my silence."

She nodded stiffly. With a satisfied smile, Vespasian took her arm and led her back into the ballroom. She was amused when Madame Colville caught her eye and nodded with genuine approval. What would the lady say if she knew they had been on the terrace plotting her son's affair with Suzette St. Aubin?

Vespasian returned her to the Collins table and held her chair just as Ben Merritt came to stand at her side.

"Good evening, Miss Collins," he said with a bow. He nodded to Vespasian. "Colville. I see I've arrived just in time to enjoy a dance."

Startled, Maureen stared at Ben's swollen eye while she nodded a greeting to him. What a dashing figure he cut in his formal clothes. But what nerve to walk in more than three hours late sporting a hideous injury that turned a deeper purple while she watched. Quickly, he proceeded with the customary ritual of bowing to the ladies and shaking the gentlemen's hands. No one said a word about his eye as they greeted him. When he turned again to her, she gave him her dimpled smile.

"May I have the pleasure of this dance, Miss Collins?"

"I'd be delighted." She put her arm through his and held her breath until they stepped a few feet away. "I should be polite and ignore your swollen eye as everyone else has," she whispered, "but I'm too curious. What in the world happened to you?"

"I ran into my closet door. I was hurrying to dress, it was dark and I slammed into it …"

She laughed out loud. "Oh, please. Surely you can be more inventive than that."

He leaned toward her, placing his lips close to her ear. "Let's leave it at that. I'd rather you not know."

A shiver ran up her spine as his breath tickled her ear. "You're right. I'd rather not know."

The music began. His hand warmed her back as he led her in a perfectly executed waltz.

And she had wondered if he knew how to dance! A waltz often made her dizzy, but she believed it was her partner producing that effect tonight. She wanted to close the distance between them, to press her chest against his in a very improper manner, to kiss him right here on the dance floor in an even more improper manner. "I intended to scold you when you arrived, but I don't have the heart." She looked straight at his eye. "Does it hurt much?"

His quirky grin covered his face. "Not while I'm with you."

"I'm assuming you've used the accepted remedies, ice alternating with a piece of raw beef to bring the swelling down?"

"I have. Is the botanist also a medical doctor?" She laughed again while he spun her around. "It'll be better tomorrow," he said with a finality that meant subject closed. He moved his hand up and down her back, making her breath quicken. "I love your plaid dress and you look beautiful in it. You're the loveliest woman at the ball."

As the music stopped, the urge to kiss him overwhelmed her. She stared at his lips, barely breathing. Then she licked her bottom lip.

"That did it," he whispered. "I'd like to find a dark terrace fast. Can you lead me to one?"

She could. In minutes, they moved outside and stood at the same railing where she'd been with Vespasian not a half-hour earlier.

"I promised Elise that you'd dance with her and her sister Carine."

"Not before I kiss you." He glanced around at other couples surrounding them. "I believe it's permissible, isn't it?"

His lips met hers. She opened her mouth and he deepened the kiss. Her knees went soft as he wrapped both his arms around her and pulled her closer. She broke off the kiss. "I could do this forever, but I think we may be overzealous. People are staring."

"I believe your greenhouse might be a better place?"

"It could be. Please come by soon and I'll give you a dose of Collins tonic. It's the ideal remedy for all aches and pains."

After a waltz, the orchestra always seemed to play country dances, which involved a great deal of moving from partner to partner. These were lively and particularly good for couples just getting acquainted. Maureen made certain Ben took Elise and then Carine to the dance floor. With the next waltz, she made herself available only to him.

When she and Ben returned to the Collins table, William bluntly asked Ben what happened to his eye.

"It's a long story. I had to go to the docks on an errand. A few ruffians attacked me. Trying to steal my wallet." He shrugged. "I fought them off with no problem."

Her father warned Ben that the docks weren't a friendly place by day or night. "Lots of illegal goings on, I'm afraid."

Maureen bit her lower lip. *Such as smuggling opium?*

Chapter Eleven

ear Mr. Merritt,
As I suggested last night, I have just the cure for your injured eye.
At your earliest convenience, I hope you'll come by for a dose of Collins
tonic, which heals all wounds.

Sincerely,
Maureen Collins

Her perfumed note in hand, Maureen asked Guy to have it delivered right away, and went straight to the dining room for a cup of coffee, the newspaper and a cornbread muffin.

She continued to feel as euphoric as she had last night when Ben appeared unexpectedly at her side. One look at him made her heart race. One touch shattered her calm demeanor. One kiss weakened her knees. One waltz with him? She'd struggled not to swoon in his arms. She had extinguished her gaslight after three, but her mind replayed every moment of her dances with Ben over and over for at least another hour.

As she drank her coffee, she muttered to herself that Ben Merritt could *not* be an opium smuggler. True, the tin she thought contained fertilizer held opium. And didn't Vespasian have a gleam in his eye when he proclaimed Ben a smuggler? He had wanted to shock her, to make her question the background and integrity of the new man about town, the man who'd caught her notice.

But what opium smuggler would leave the smuggled product *in* the plant? Then again, what respectable attorney—who was supposed to be at a ball—would go on a stroll on the levee late at night?

What was Ben doing on the levee? There to watch for smugglers? Or there to meet his smuggling cronies? His knowledge of shipping companies and the laws of the high seas would make him an ideal partner in such an operation.

The night they met, Ben wore laborer's clothes. Days later, when he'd been introduced to her as her father's attorney, she'd been so relieved that he would keep her nighttime stroll a secret— and frankly so smitten with him—that she'd struck his own odd appearance at midnight from her mind.

He'd been watching her house that night. She was sure of it. And he'd been watching it again early Christmas morning when he was there with the Negro, both dressed as gentlemen. There was absolutely no logical explanation for his presence there either time—and on foot. Why, Why? She had to learn the secret that lay beneath his handsome exterior.

She flipped quickly through the pages of the *Daily Picayune*. When it came to Louisiana politics or world news, she read the headlines only. The society pages were of more interest because they focused on people she actually knew. She always read "Society Bee." Her heart sank as her eyes rested on familiar names.

Sophia O'Brien looked lovely in a shimmering purple silk gown at the Revelers Ball last night. The gold and amethyst bauble around her neck? Said to be a Christmas gift from Patrick Collins, who seems to be at her side every minute these days. Do we hear wedding bells?

Certainly they'll tinkle soon for Patrick's daughter, Maureen, and the dashing Vespasian Colville. He gave her quite a rush at the season's first ball. She had no rest between sets. The moment she sat down, he took her to the dance floor. The next step? To the altar.

She took the next section of the paper to her greenhouse and spread it out on the workbench. She intended to mix fertilizer for the ferns today, but an editorial bemoaning the use of opium in New Orleans caught her eye.

OPIUM: A PREVENTABLE SCOURGE ON CITY

Ships from the Orient dock at the levee and bring in beautiful goods: fine china in fantastical designs, exquisite painted screens, silks of the finest texture, teas of many varieties and even flowering shrubs. But one item accompanying these imports that we don't need in New Orleans is opium.

The number of vessels and the frequency of landings by Chinese ships have increased the pounds of opium imported here to an astounding level. And with this comes an increase in the number of opium dens, those hell holes where unfortunate addicts clamor for a puff on the opium pipe.

We know that in the second district alone, more than ten of these dens exist. Many young gentlemen and even ladies from fine families find the allure of the opium den too enticing to resist. It's a sad fact that both possessing opium and smoking the substance are legal in the United States of America. However, the City Council of New Orleans would do well to outlaw opium dens, which are dens of debauchery and depravity, and save its fine citizens from this vice.

She'd never thought of the harm that came to American citizens from importing opium. Or from the proliferation of these dens. It hadn't occurred to her that the imported Canton china they used at the Collins dinner table, the silk fabrics she bought to be made into ball gowns, the delicious tea she drank almost daily all increased the number of Chinese ships that came into New Orleans and surely increased the opium trade as well. She felt a little guilty that she loved and used Chinese products. She glanced at the camellia. Ben's gift had come from a Chinese ship and no doubt cost a fortune. Perhaps she'd be wise to learn more about grafting before she began slicing off its branches.

What a vision. Was that Maureen Collins at a table across the room or was he hallucinating? This was no phantasm. She sat in the Tulane University library, her maid beside her, both partially hidden by a stack of books.

As he watched, Maureen ran her tongue across her bottom lip as her pencil raced across the page of her notebook. Dear God, her lips were cherry red, and her tongue—which flirted constantly with her bottom lip—made him hard with desire. He wanted to kiss her this minute more than he wanted to do anything else in this world. Vowing he wouldn't leave this library until he contrived to get her alone, he continued to stare at her for some minutes, but Maureen never looked his way.

The librarian noticed him, however, and motioned him to the counter.

"I'd like to have a key to a study room, please. My firm has library access."

She flinched at the sight of his eye, a gruesome combination of yellow, green, and purple. "Of course, sir." She shoved a ledger across the desk. "Sign in with your name and firm, please." She handed him a key. "You'll find these rooms up two flights to your left."

"Thank you, Madame. I see my secretary"—he nodded his head toward Maureen—"is already here. Thank you."

Key in hand, he walked down the aisle between tables, his heart beating faster, his desire quickening his steps. At last Maureen glanced up and saw him. Her face lit up in a broad smile, but she recoiled slightly as he came closer. One delicate hand clutched at her high-necked dress.

He grinned down at her, crinkling the skin, pulling painfully in the corner of his sore eye.

"Mr. Merritt."

"Good afternoon, Miss Collins."

He bowed to her and to Luz when Maureen introduced her—Luz Bichet—as her invaluable assistant. Luz's eyes widened at his appearance. With a disapproving shake of her head, she returned to reading a book on camellias.

"Thank you for your note and invitation," he said.

Her eyes locked on his swollen one. "I'm so sorry about your mishap with the closet door. I do like that excuse more than robbers on the levee. Does it hurt terribly?" She winced in imagined pain.

"Not unless I smile." He chuckled softly. "Seeing you can't help but bring a smile to my face, but I'll gladly endure the pain."

"I'm reading about grafting camellias," she whispered. "It's fascinating and I'm eager to follow the steps here."

The page open on the table in front of her contained a color plate of a field of opium poppies. He ignored the alarm bell in his head. "If you'll follow me, Miss Collins, I'll show you more volumes on flowers—in the stacks."

A look of surprise crossed her face. "I didn't know anyone could go back there."

He opened his palm and her eyes flicked from the key to his face. It was all he could do not to grab her shoulders and yank her to him right there in the reading room.

She stood and told Luz she'd just be a few minutes.

"The firm pays for library privileges," he murmured. He held the door to the stacks open and followed her in. "Single-file, straight back to the stairs," he said softly.

Maureen didn't hesitate; in fact, she walked faster now that they were alone in a dimly lit corridor, floor-to-ceiling bookshelves on both sides of them.

"Oh, my," she said, stopping in front of an iron staircase that spiraled upward. "There are more books up there?"

He dangled the key. "Thousands." She flushed crimson. Did she understand he wasn't interested in books? As he took her hand, he became keenly aware of how soft and delicate it was. He felt his own pulse jump. "I'll lead."

His hand locked in hers, he started up the steps.

"Don't look back," she whispered. "I have to hike up my skirt or I'll break my neck."

"Don't break your neck."

She giggled.

He dared not turn. If he saw her ankles and so much as a hint of her calves, he'd want to kiss her on the landing. What was he doing taking her to a private room? She'd baldly lied to him not five minutes ago. She hadn't been reading up on camellias. She was doing research on opium, no doubt for her father.

Ludicrous. From what he understood, extracting opium from flowers was a time-consuming, difficult process. She'd need many acres to make it pay. And many, many workers. Hell, the family probably owned fields of cotton or sugar cane. He knew Patrick Collins employed Chinese workers on the docks. Why not grow opium poppies?

Stop it. Maureen was a refined young lady studying camellias.

On the third floor, they found the section on the flowers of Asia. Maureen beamed with delight. She selected four books she wanted to examine more closely. One contained beautiful color prints of many varieties.

"Come," he said. "There are study rooms over here."

The room matching his key number was a little smaller and more intimate than Ben had expected. He wondered if Maureen felt uncomfortable. He got his answer when she, nearer to the door, pushed it closed.

Maureen sat and flipped through the book of prints, murmuring now and then. Ben sat beside her, feigning interest, but Maureen's nearness and the smell of her perfume held him spellbound.

"I believe I must kiss you," he said, struggling to keep his voice calm. "That is, if my visage isn't too horrible to behold, may I kiss you, Miss Collins?"

Her mischievous smile gave him permission. "Please call me Maureen. I believe we're on a first-name basis."

"Indeed we are, Maureen." His hands went around her waist and he bent his head, enjoying the sweet scent of roses emanating from her hair and skin. He brushed her lips with his, a mere touch. He ran his own tongue across her slightly parted lips—first the lower, then the upper. She raised her hands, circled his neck and pulled him closer. Her body scorched his, heating his chest as she leaned into him.

She opened her mouth.

When his tongue touched hers, he felt her tremble. She sucked playfully. He thrust in deeper and she sucked harder. Again and again. When he retreated, she advanced, her tongue on his. He slid his hands from her waist to her hips, but her corset's stays were an impenetrable barrier.

"Oh, my," she panted between kisses.

"Forgive me." He tried to quirk his eyebrow to make it a question, but it hurt like hell. "Am I am too bold?"

Tilting her head, Maureen flipped her hair to fall down her back. She stood and moved toward the door, Ben right behind her. She licked her lower lip. "Perhaps; perhaps not. I'll find my way downstairs."

With that, she was gone. He sat for a few minutes and took deep breaths to calm down. What was wrong with him? He'd truly lost his mind. She was as beautiful as a Renaissance Madonna— that was the comparison his mind always conjured—with her oval porcelain face, small nose, pert little mouth and the most gorgeous eyes he'd ever seen. Deep blue sapphire. And her hair! Like silk, it fell in curls past her shoulders.

He'd been around many beautiful ladies and never felt this kind of maddening lust. He'd come to the city for one purpose. He could not see Maureen Collins at all. He could not think about her. A visit to Gallatine Street, where gentlemen paid for their pleasures, didn't interest him.

Remembering why he'd come to the library in the first place, he went down to the second floor and selected the law volume he needed. A good ten minutes later, he entered the reading room.

Maureen, her head in a book once again, sat beside Luz. Her flushed face told him what he already knew. She'd enjoyed their passionate interlude as much as he.

He strode up to her and asked if she'd like to take some of her volumes home. In a demure voice, she said she'd be most grateful, then dropped her pencil and flexed her right hand's lovely long fingers. "My hand's cramped from taking notes."

Once outside, Ben handed Maureen into her carriage and then carefully placed the three books—all on camellias—in her hands. "You have two weeks with these."

"This is a huge help to me."

"I put your name on the firm's list of users. You may check out books on *camellias* any time you like." He emphasized the word.

Her eyes lit up in that way that made them seem to have a bright light behind them. "That's wonderful. Thank you, Mr. Merritt. I think I'll lock myself in the greenhouse and get to work on my plants right now."

Luz rolled her eyes. "You're not locking yourself in no green-house, Miss Maureen."

Ben laughed. "You tell her, Luz."

"What would Mr. Vespasian do without you?"

Ben saw a flicker of annoyance cross Maureen's face. She faked a little cough and recovered quickly. "Maybe I'll lock myself in for just a half-day at a time."

"I believe that's a much better idea, Miss Collins. I agree with Luz. You shouldn't deny the gentlemen of New Orleans the plea-sure of your company."

Not twenty minutes ago, he'd resolved not to see her, but he couldn't help himself. "I believe you promised me some Collins tonic to mend my injury." He motioned to his eye. "May I call on you tomorrow evening?"

She murmured an assent.

His gaze followed her carriage as it disappeared down Dryades Street. He walked toward Canal where he hailed a cab. One thing was certain: Colville, damn him, had taught the young lady to kiss.

Chapter Twelve

The moment she arrived home, Maureen changed into her old gray gabardine gown, made herself a pot of tea and took it to the greenhouse. Sitting at her table, she selected *Practical Camellia Culture*, which had diagrams with its explanation on grafting. She couldn't underline in the library book, so she took notes, including sketching the branches of the plants she intended to use.

Why had Ben suggested tomorrow night? She wanted to see him tonight, especially after their kisses. Kisses? Could she call them kisses? She couldn't think about them without a delightful shiver running up her spine. Those moments in the library with Ben were the closest she'd ever come to heaven. It had been bliss: the tightening of her stomach when she lifted her skirt to follow him up the stairs, the catch in her breath when he led her inside the small, dark room. Opening her mouth for his kiss when he teased with his tongue, finding his tongue with hers.

Perhaps she should have played innocent, as innocent as she'd been when Vespasian first taught her to kiss like that. She could have let Ben believe she knew nothing about men—or kisses. What's more—she cringed thinking about it—Luz had purposely named "Mr. Vespasian" as a man who'd miss her if she locked herself in her greenhouse.

She refocused on the camellia book in a vain attempt to get Ben out of her mind. She learned grafting was the fastest technique for propagating new plants. She was determined to learn how to do it. Furthermore, she defied the author's suggestion that a smart grower would graft an *alba plena*, a beautiful white variety that grew in her own yard, onto the red *Adolphe Audusson,* which Ben had given her. She intended to do the exact opposite—red onto white.

She wanted to see what would happen, a thought she'd been harboring since she'd asked her father to build her a greenhouse. And she had to admit she wanted to impress Ben Merritt. She wanted him to see that she was a real scientist—a modern woman who used her mind.

Four white camellias lined the workbench. She looked them over carefully, picked the healthiest one, and spoke to it. "You're first, my dear plant. You're going to grow up to be something other than a white camellia. You're going to have red blooms in a year."

Guy interrupted with a message, inviting her to Sophie's for dinner tonight. Her father's note explained that Sophie's son, Sean, had received a half dozen ducks as a gift from a friend who hunted daily this time of year. Sophie had been obliged to take several so they wouldn't go to waste. "Renee and William will be there," her father wrote, "and Sophie begs you to join us. What do you say?"

Maureen pictured cozy fires blazing in both parlors and the dining room. Estelle's roast duck with peach sauce, served over rice, her delicious dinner rolls. Maybe even bread pudding with whiskey sauce for dessert. But she didn't think she could stomach another night surrounded by so many loving couples. She pulled good stationery from the workbench drawer, where she kept a few sheets, and answered quickly that she was exhausted after last night's ball and thought it best to stay home and rest so her cold would not come back.

Around six o'clock, she took a quick supper break in the dining room alone and then went back to work. To graft properly, she must make exact cuts in the stems of two plants and fit them together. She'd never been particularly nimble with her fingers. The Ursuline nuns had despaired of teaching her to crochet, knit or embroider. Was she out of her mind to think she could do a graft?

With a pair of sharp clippers she removed the branches of the first white plant, making sloping cuts. With a knife she trimmed these smooth. She then made a half-inch vertical incision into the side of the trunk.

From the red camellia, she clipped a three-inch branch, laid it on the bench and cut a wedge at the tip of it. With a small knife, she held the slit in the trunk of the white plant open, and inserted the stem of the red bush. Holding the branch and trunk together with one hand, she bound the two pieces tightly together with cord, winding it several times. She followed that with a pinch of wet clay, which she molded over the joined bushes. She hoped her humid, warm greenhouse would stimulate growth.

Five minutes later, Vespasian knocked at the greenhouse door. She fetched the decanter of whiskey and a glass from the sunroom and suggested he sit with her. He poured and took a long swallow.

Leaning toward her, he kissed her cheek, then raised an eyebrow. "Why so happy tonight?"

Her face grew warm.

"Oh, God. Don't tell me you've decided to accept my marriage proposal. I know you find me overwhelmingly charming, and I am moved, I truly am." He paused and laid his right hand on his heart. "But my dear, as much as I hate to dash your dreams of happiness, I'm afraid I must tell you it is too late. My heart is taken."

Sipping her sherry, Maureen waited for him to finish his little drama. "And is Suzette St. Aubin aware she's stolen your heart?"

"She must suspect."

"I would guess so." Not an hour ago, she'd had a note from Elise Bouchard with the news that Vespasian had called on Suzette that afternoon. "You've called on her ..."

"Your spies are well informed."

She shrugged. "New Orleans is a small town."

He chuckled and finished off his first drink. "So you know I called on Suzette today. Is there anyone in New Orleans who doesn't know Ben Merritt is mad for you?"

To hide her discomfort, Maureen rose and poured herself a glass of sherry. "And what makes you think that?" she asked casually.

"Any gentleman brave enough to go down to the docks after dark to buy a camellia bush for a lady is either a damn fool or besotted by love. Merritt's no fool." He took a drink of his whiskey.

Maureen gasped. "Is *that* why he went to the docks last night? To buy me a camellia?"

"According to Paul Hebert. I ran into him on Royal Street this morning."

That sort of gossip among men worried her. Vespasian could ruin her reputation with an offhand remark. What if he told a few cronies at the Boston Club or in the Proteus krewe that last fall she'd sneaked out and spent the night in his library drinking wine with him? If such a tale floated about New Orleans, she'd lose Ben. He was a gentleman. He'd not be interested in a lady with such a past.

She had no one to blame but herself. Not only had she met Vespasian and gone to his house, she'd talked non-stop with her friends about her desire for him. She was mortified when she recalled her talk with Renee last year. She had said she wasn't sure she ever wanted to marry, but was certain she did want a man— Vespasian, in particular—in her bed.

Right now, she wanted a different man in her bed. And maybe she wanted to marry him.

"… wedding bells," Vespasian said.

"Pardon me?"

"A little distracted, are you?" He frowned. "I said my mother was thrilled to read 'Society Bee' in the paper this morning. I quote, 'Do I hear wedding bells between Maureen Collins'—and how did the author of that fine column phrase it?—'the dashing Colville'"

Maureen grimaced. "I thought she'd be pleased by the gossip, though I don't believe the writer could have been at the ball. How could anyone have missed you mooning over Suzette St. Aubin?"

"Agreed," he drawled. "And how could anyone have missed your misery when you checked the door every other minute for Merritt?"

She felt her face flush in embarrassment and she raised her glass to hide it. "Don't you think it's dishonest to let your mother think we plan to marry?"

He shook his head. "As long as we both know there are no wedding bells in our future, I don't think it hurts to let her think it while we pursue other interests."

"Are you sure about Suzette now that you've actually spent time with her? Are you really in love?"

"Today I had a precious fifteen minutes alone with her." He dropped his head back and stared at the stars through the glass roof. "She's as graceful as a gazelle, scampering over a moonlit desert."

She glared at him. "You never said anything like that to me."

"For heaven's sakes, Maureen." He ran a hand through his hair in exasperation. "Help me. Take her shopping at Desselle Millinery. I'll wait at Lanoux's next door. We'll stage a surprise encounter."

"Oh, I don't know."

His face fell, reminding her of arguments when they were children. He was so expressive. She always knew what he was thinking. And right now, he was suffering. What was the harm in a chance meeting between Vespasian and Suzette at a hat shop? Especially when she herself could lose Ben if he knew of her past.

Vespasian would give her his right arm if she needed help. She truly believed that. He asked very little in return for his silence. He showed all the symptoms of being in love, and people in love—as she well knew—went to great lengths to win the object of their desire.

"Oh, all right," she said softly. "I'll set it up as soon as possible. I'll let you know when." She paused, calculating. "But can you do me a favor?"'

He shrugged. "You owe *me*, remember?"

She waved a hand to hush him. "I need a book on opium. Maybe a medical text about the drug's effects and cures for addiction."

Vespasian rolled his eyes. "So now your beau is a helpless addict as opposed to a villainous smuggler?"

"Vespie," she warned. "I just want to learn more about it, just as you want to learn more about Suzette."

"Always reading ..." he mused. "What I want to learn about Suzette doesn't come from a book."

She started to interrupt, but he held up his hand to stop her.

"Fine. Nobody will believe I'm buying a book. I don't think I've bought a book in my life, but for you, I'll do it."

Chapter Thirteen

Ben sat beside Maureen, his thigh touching her plum skirt. The outer flounces of the soft wool did little to insulate him from her heat. He longed to clutch the wool in his hands.

Her father and Sophie O'Brien were at the room's opposite end—the back parlor—just the two of them, playing cards. Their laughter, but not their conversation, reached his ears. Confident they couldn't see his hands, he ran his thumb back and forth across the back of her hand. He liked feeling those fragile bones and the dips in the valleys between them.

Maureen caught his fingers in hers and squeezed. Her touch sent his mind straight to the day he'd seen her at William and Renee's home. Her flirtatious words and outlandish actions had captivated him. In response, his behavior could only be termed outrageous. Playing with her hand, sucking on her finger was so unlike him. Damn it. He'd never felt such an attraction to a woman.

But coming between them was Vespasian Colville. Surely he'd taught her to flirt, to kiss, to moan appreciatively as she melted into his chest. Just thinking of the man caused his insides to twist. What else had he taught her? Jealousy was an emotion he'd never experienced—not over a woman, anyway. There was a time in school when another student's excellent term paper drew the teacher's praise and his did not.

Taking a drink of Collins whiskey, the tonic she'd promised would soothe his swollen eye, he breathed in her scent, felt the enjoyable burn of the straight spirits in his throat and stared into her sapphire eyes. "Have you been back to the Tulane Library for more books?"

She laughed. "I read fast, but not that fast. It was only yesterday." She tilted her head up and licked her bottom lip. "But I've given the library a great deal of thought."

God, there it was again. That bottom lip. Did she know what that did to him? He smiled as well as he could with his black eye. "As have I."

Her acceptance of his tongue had stunned him. But he was determined not to repeat it tonight. He needed to keep his mission in the forefront of his mind. He leaned closer to her, so close he smelled the sherry on her breath. His mouth came dangerously close to brushing her ear.

"I believe I owe you an apology for being too forward."

Her coy smile seemed to suggest she might actually think he had not gone far enough. Had he or hadn't he? Quickly, he turned the conversation to her books. "I would be happy to escort you and Luz to the library again ... for more books if you need them."

"Thank you," she murmured. "Perhaps next week."

Could he wait a week to kiss her again? "At your request, Maureen."

Her eyes twinkled. "I believe I should tell you what I *learned* from the books you checked out for me."

He watched her lips part, then touch her sherry glass as she took a sip. Gazing at her mouth aroused him and he found it difficult to concentrate on her descriptions of grafting the red camellia to the white rootstock.

A gorgeous young lady, Maureen would have attracted his notice if she had sat quietly on a toadstool by the side of the road. But when she talked excitedly about her favorite subject, her eyes danced, her face glowed and her lovely hands swirled in front of her as she gestured to illustrate a point. When she flicked her curls off her left breast and onto her back with a toss of her head, his eyes went to her shirtwaist, specifically to the perfect mound of plum-colored wool.

"I'd love to see what you've done. And the greenhouse, too. I've not seen it."

Her cheeks dimpled. "The grafted plants?"

"Would your father allow us to slip into the greenhouse for a moment?" He raised his healthy eyebrow.

"I'll convince him." She jumped up from the sofa.

He stood when she did, but he deliberately turned away from her, crossed to the fireplace and stared into the flames rather than watch her hips as she walked into the front parlor. He took a few deep breaths and was ready to face her when he heard her voice: "Papa said five minutes; I said fifteen and we ..."

"Settled on ten," he finished. With a smile, he offered her his arm and they hurried from the room, down the hall, through her mother's sunroom and down the steps into the warm glass house.

He whistled in awe. "I had no idea. It's a tropical forest." Ben stood still for a moment, then turned in circles, taking it all in. The scent of earth, the moisture, the smell of citrus engulfed him. Her father had given them ten minutes. He'd be delighted to spend the rest of his life here with her.

She pulled on his hand, bringing him to the workbench. One glance at the four new grafts she'd completed—the branches of the red camellia jutting out as they did from the trunks of four whites—undid his self-control. He put a hand on each of her upper arms and held her still. As he bent his head to place his lips on hers, he moved his hands to the side of her face. Now that he was alone with her, he convinced himself that a deep kiss would not imperil his mission. He felt her jaw tremble, but this time she didn't open her mouth to him. He broke away and began again, this time licking her bottom lip slowly, then her upper until her lips parted. But just slightly.

His tongue barred, Ben wondered why she held back, why she wasn't willing to repeat yesterday's luscious kisses. Her erratic breathing told him she wanted to. Her lips pressed hard against his and when he stilled for a moment, she followed his lead and licked his lower lip, then his upper before pulling her head back. "We're almost out of time."

He groaned. "Can't we push your father's limits a little?"

"Just long enough to show you my grafts." She stepped to the side and pointed to the camellias. His eyes descended from the grafted joint to the small beads arranged carefully around the base of two plants. And his heart skipped several beats.

Oh, my God. Opium. The fragrant roots that would give his lady many hours of pleasure. The exorbitant price. Captain Kwan Wei smuggled opium!

Ben clenched his teeth, then turned his gaze quickly from the grafted camellias to her face. She was looking at him closely, one eyebrow raised almost tauntingly.

Maureen's throat tightened. She could barely breathe. Ben had failed her test. The polite smile he wore plastered on his face made her sick to her stomach. Straining to sound nonchalant, she spoke the sentence she'd rehearsed all afternoon: "I found the most amazing fertilizer tucked in the roots when I transplanted your camellia." She motioned to the small balls on the soil.

He tilted his head sideways and frowned. "I wasn't told free fertilizer came with the plant. Where did you find it?"

How far was he going to extend this charade? "In a little tin hidden in the roots," she said, pointing to a container covered with Chinese writing. It lay on the workbench where she'd deliberately placed it.

He picked it up, studied it, then shrugged. "It's Greek to me. Captain Kwan Wei—the man I bought this from—seemed to be a plant lover. I bet this works well, that it's made just for camellias."

Maureen struggled not to roll her eyes. He placed the tin back on the bench and smiled, the uninjured half of his face cooperating, the other half painfully stiff, it seemed to her. "Is it—the fertilizer, I mean—a good one?

She looked up, trying to read his thoughts. "I can't possibly tell yet. I put it on only two plants. It'll take a week or two to know its effects." She paused to let him speak, but he didn't. "We better go back." She gave his arm a little push toward the door. His muscles were as hard as granite. How could she forget? The brick wall.

"If I may, I'd like to visit often to look in on the progress of all this." He waved his hand toward the camellias.

She nodded graciously. "You're welcome any time."

"Actually, I'm lying."

She swiveled to face him and held her breath. He would tell her. This minute.

"I'd like to visit the greenhouse to see *you*. I care about the plants only because *you* do."

She let out her breath slowly. Not trusting herself to speak for fear her voice might tremble, or she might begin to cry, she turned away and ran up the steps to the sunroom, Ben at her heels. She rushed down the hall to the parlor and collapsed on the sofa. "I believe we made it in time, Papa," she called out.

Her father addressed Ben. "Are you impressed, Merritt?"

"I should say so, sir. Your daughter's skills are apparent." He sat down beside her again and took up his drink.

Her heart pounded. Ben knew opium when he saw it. Yet he said nothing. He didn't warn her not to touch it with bare hands, didn't say he wasn't sure what it would do to plants—all comments Vespasian made. What was he hiding? He'd given her the plant. He'd bought the plant at a great cost, she presumed. Why did he pretend not to know what it was?

Needing fortification, Maureen finished her sherry. She could barely keep up with the conversation as doubts flooded her mind. He sat so close, his lime scent engulfed her. She took a breath and swallowed. His smell intoxicated her.

Had she read the situation wrong? Perhaps Ben really didn't recognize opium when he saw it. Attorneys were a dull lot, after all. Had the man spent so much time in libraries he'd missed the she-nanigans other young gentlemen pursued—drinking, gambling, smoking opium, and whoring? Just as the newspaper editorial said, opium dens existed right in this city. Surely New York City contained its share. She would have thought a young man about town would be doing that sort of thing—at least occasionally. She wasn't surprised Vespasian knew exactly what the substance was. She, herself, hadn't the faintest notion it wasn't fertilizer. Could Ben Merritt be as naïve as she?

But she *hadn't* read the situation wrong. The moment he saw those beads, he had clenched his jaw. Almost imperceptible, he had ground his teeth together for a split second, and she'd seen the move-ment of the skin of his cheek as the muscle tightened beneath it.

He knew, he knew, he knew.

Perhaps he'd hoped she would admit she knew it was opium, just as she hoped *he* would. Her instinct was to confront him here and now. She usually said exactly what was on her mind. Subtlety had never been her strong card. She bit her lip. She wanted another glass of sherry, but she didn't want to prolong the visit.

Ben went on and on, attempting to entertain her with his expe-riences as a new recruit to Proteus. "I'm still a little hesitant about wearing a costume and parading through the streets on a float."

"Most gentlemen enjoy it immensely. I know I'd love it. It seems to me there are a lot of experiences—and substances—gentlemen enjoy that some women wouldn't even recognize."

His perplexed look amused her. He was working so hard to pretend he didn't know what she spoke of. He cleared his throat. "I suspect they'll let women on Mardi Gras floats before too many more years."

She decided to taunt him. She tossed her hair over her shoulder and whispered. "Maybe I could sneak onto your float. What do you think?"

"I think I'd enjoy your company much more than the company of the males on board."

She gave him her dimpled smile. "In that case, I'll have a costume made directly."

"Unfortunately, I can't tell you how to dress. As you know, the theme is a closely guarded secret." He became so serious, she supposed he actually believed she intended to join him on the float. "It's so closely guarded I don't even know." He took a large swallow of whiskey. "They've taken my measurements and I have to endure a fitting sometime soon, but I'm told I'll be blindfolded. I won't know until I arrive to dress for the parade what my costume is."

"I'm only teasing." She gave him a dismissive wave. "Actually, I've already ordered my costume. I'm going to be a pirate."

"A pirate? Or a pirate's lady?"

"A pirate. You inspired it with your idea that pirates might steal cargo from Imperial Shipping. I'll be in men's clothes all day until the ball that evening. It's the only day of the year that it's legal in this city for women to dress as men. I intend to take advantage of it. I'll be a wild man of the sea, feared by all."

He laughed but she could tell it pulled painfully at his injured eye. "I believe you instill fear in men's hearts when you're dressed in silks and lace."

"Afraid of soft fabrics?" She forced a little giggle. "Why is that?"

He lowered his voice, making her strain to hear. "I'm terrified right now that you're going to make me wait for days or, heaven forbid, a week or more before you'll allow me to kiss you again."

Days? A week or more? She'd never allow him to kiss her again. And that thought made her heart break. She wanted to kiss him again; she wanted to melt against his strong chest; she wanted to let her knees go weak. She wanted to feel that delicious ache between her legs she'd experienced in the library. Her voice came out rather stern. "It doesn't hurt a gentleman to wait for a lady's affections."

He grinned. "I disagree." He paused for a moment, his eyes locking with hers. "Will you set a date for our next visit? Tomorrow? The day after tomorrow?"

She was more tempted than she'd ever been in her life. Could she be falling in love with a smuggler? She fell back on the years of training in the social graces that enabled her to put people off if need be, even a man who fascinated her.

"I'm quite busy this week. I have calls to make, a tea party to plan, appointments with my dressmaker and a whole greenhouse to tend ..."

"I will await your command, Maureen." He rose, glanced back at her father, and whispered. "A lovely hand is all I can hope to kiss at this moment."

She nodded and lifted hers.

Taking it, Ben bent low and closed his lips over the end of her index finger. Her breath caught in her throat. He sucked her finger into his mouth, gave it a gentle bite.

She snatched her hand away.

Chapter Fourteen

The day dawned dreary, but Maureen had made a promise to Vespasian. Dutifully, she climbed the steps of Suzette St. Aubin's home on Chartres Street. Not to call on a former classmate, new to town, would be rude. Wouldn't it?

She rapped on the door and handed her calling card to an elderly butler, who glowered at her with piercing light gray eyes and told her to remain in the doorway. Remain in the doorway! Where was this man from? In New Orleans, people's servants didn't leave guests standing on the steps. Leaning forward, Maureen heard a woman's voice ask who was there, but couldn't understand his answer. In minutes the white-haired servant returned, gave her a half-hearted bow and asked her to follow him. He turned and glided soundlessly down the hall.

She had no time to take in the furnishings beyond the Persian carpet at her feet before Suzette rushed out to greet her. A hostess generally waited for her guests to be escorted into her drawing room, but nothing appeared to be typical in this house.

Suzette clasped both her hands in a genuine show of affection. "It's been ages and ages, Maureen. It's so good of you to call."

"I've come to welcome you to the city. I caught a glimpse of you at the Revelers Ball last week and learned that you and Monsieur St. Aubin had settled into a home here."

Maureen handed her coat to the butler, who accepted it with a frown. She followed Suzette into the parlor and they each took a chair in front of the fire.

The proximity gave her an opportunity to study the young woman, who had blossomed with age. Maureen remembered her as a skinny girl with long blond braids. But that had been four years ago. At the ball, she'd not given her much attention. Every time Vespasian had stared in her direction, Maureen had turned away.

Today, a pale green wool dress with a high crocheted collar and cuffs set off her tall, willowy figure. Her hair, pinned up in a stylish chignon, reminded Maureen of corn silk. A pale yellow, it glistened even in the parlor's dim light. Her delicate white skin looked as though it never saw the sun. Her eyes—the very same deep green of emeralds in the window of A. B. Griswold Jewelers on Canal Street—told an unhappy tale. They'd seen a good cry not minutes ago.

Very sorry she'd dropped in without an advance note, Maureen apologized for intruding.

"Not at all." Suzette dabbed at her eyes with a lace handkerchief that she twisted in her hands. I suffer from a sensitivity to pollens and ... such," she said vaguely.

"How terrible. I have an affection for flowering plants. I would be unable to endure it if I ..." Halfway through her sentence, she noticed a vase of white chrysanthemums and red holly berries on the marble-topped table beside the sofa. "... couldn't have cut flowers in the house at all times."

Suzette blushed, then stammered. "I see you've ... caught me in a lie about my tears."

Maureen said nothing.

The lady sniffled into her handkerchief. "Would you like a sherry? I'll ring for some." Jumping to her feet, she pulled the bell cord.

Maureen wouldn't turn down sherry anytime, especially not right now. It was cold in here, for one thing. The fire sputtered with little flames and little heat. And Suzette seemed so distraught she feared some terrible tragedy had befallen the household and she'd walked right into it.

Suzette wandered to the fireplace and stood for a moment with her back to her. "I have no one I'm able to speak with plainly." She whirled around to face her. "May I?"

Maureen nodded jerkily, well aware that she was the last person on earth this lady should take into her confidence. At best, she was performing a social duty. At worst, she was hoping to manipulate Suzette into meeting Vespasian in order to save her own reputation. And for what? To win the love of Ben Merritt, an opium smuggler! For certain, she wasn't here as Suzette's friend.

The sullen butler, whose mere presence added a chill to the atmosphere, placed a silver tray on the table. It contained two glasses of sherry, two linen napkins, two china plates and a third plate heaped with cheese straws. Suzette handed her a glass, napkin and plate and held the cheese straws out to her. Maureen took three because she loved them and she was hungry. While she nibbled, her hostess took several sips of sherry.

Seeming to gain both energy and courage from her drink, Suzette leaned forward and whispered, "Monsieur Leveque, the butler, watches me every minute. I'm miserable in this house. When I'm in the country, at Monsieur St. Aubin's plantation, my family is nearby. My three sisters and my mother visit often or I go see them. Here ..." she stopped and shuddered. She tilted her head toward the open door. "He leaves for several days when the coffee ships come in, every few weeks. That's my only freedom."

From her chair, Maureen could see the butler lurking in the hall.

"New Orleans is a desolate place if you're alone," Suzette continued in a whisper. "There is gaiety everywhere around you, but it doesn't include you."

Maureen's heart filled with pity and she reached out to grasp Suzette's hands. "Oh, you mustn't think you're alone. It's a new year and time for a new social flurry." She told her most of the young ladies she knew at Ursuline remained in town. She began with the Bouchard sisters and ended with Regina Zervigon while Suzette nodded and murmured that she knew this one or that.

"I'm having a tea party next week in my new greenhouse. You must come. It's Wednesday the 20th of January. Some of the ladies have married as you have, some have children already. They will all welcome you back. It will be great fun."

The suggestion brought a half-smile to Suzette's face. "That's very kind to include me."

In the next moment, Maureen imagined an even grander event—an evening soirée to which she'd invite gentlemen, but when she broached the idea, Suzette's face darkened and she said tersely she'd rather have ladies only. "Monsieur St. Aubin spends most of his time at the plantation in the country ... or in the West Indies. He wouldn't be here to escort me."

Maureen covered her mouth in surprise. "You don't go out alone for an evening if you wish?"

Suzette took a fortifying drink of her sherry and said her husband didn't permit it. Maureen enjoyed some quick gulps of her own, not entirely sure whether or not she wanted Suzette to elaborate.

"He's very jealous. I suppose because he's ... well, he's quite old and I'm very young." She paused for a moment. "If he's not with me, I'm permitted only to go to the opera in the evenings."

And she thought her father was overprotective! Suzette might as well have bars on the windows. Murmuring she understood, which she didn't, Maureen made more suggestions. "How about shopping or dinner with me at a restaurant? Are you allowed to go to the theater? And the tea party? Surely you can come to my tea party."

"Your tea party, yes, and dinner with a group of ladies." She bit her lower lip and frowned, then leaned forward again.

Suzette's voice fell so low, Maureen scooted to the chair's edge and angled her head closer, nearly sliding off the tapestry upholstery.

"Shopping, not at the moment, I'm afraid. Monsieur St. Aubin was furious with me for overspending my account. My account at Collins Factorage. He received a letter from a clerk, Vespasian Colville ..."

Maureen gasped. "Vespasian?"

"You know him?"

"Since childhood. Our mothers were close friends. Last season he was gracious enough to escort me and the Bouchard sisters to various social events when I returned from Atlanta." She explained quickly that after her mother's death, she'd lived with her aunt for several years. "Vespasian works at Collins Factorage; he's an assistant to my cousin, William Collins."

Suzette raised a hand to her cheek, as if anticipating a blush. "I shouldn't tell you, but Mr. Colville called on me last week. Told my butler he was my cousin." She smiled, the sly smile of a married lady smitten with another man.

"How clever of him," Maureen replied, pretending surprise. Vespasian could charm the skin off a snake. But how had he managed to manipulate that odd butler?

Suzette went on. "St. Aubin left Tuesday morning. I expect he may be gone a week or two"

"Then I must get you out of this house. It's not healthy to stay in here cooped up."

Maureen was growing increasingly tense. A more sterile place she'd never seen. The flowers and the fire were the only bright spots in the tomb-like interior. The curtains were drawn to block out light. No books or newspapers offered a diversion. Matching lamps sat on matching mahogany marble-topped tables. The globes of light did nothing to relieve the gloom. Dark paintings hung so straight she suspected the maids set a level on the frames daily after dusting.

She needed to complete her errand here and return to the sunshine and fresh air. More importantly, she wanted to embark on her other undertaking of the day.

Suddenly she pretended to have an inspiration and stood up. "I best be going. But why not meet me at Desselle Millinery on Saturday?"

Suzette opened her mouth—to object, Maureen supposed.

"You don't have to *buy* anything. It's fun to look at the copies of *Godey's Lady's Book* and the latest issues of *Harper's Bazar* and discuss the newest fashions. I could treat you to a coffee at the Café du Monde afterwards. What do you think?"

Suzette hesitated, then her face softened and she sat up a little straighter. "I'll do it. That's perfectly acceptable to meet another lady and go shopping, isn't it?"

Maureen moved toward the doorway and reached up to adjust her hat. "It's settled then. Shall we meet at Desselle's at quarter past eleven or shall I stop by here and pick you up? I have a carriage and driver."

Suzette gestured to the hallway. "Monsieur Leveque serves as a driver for me. I'll meet you."

How convenient that the butler accompanied Suzette when she left the house. She might as well be chained in the attic. It wouldn't be easy for Vespasian to get to know this lady. Not for lack of desire, but opportunity.

Maureen's next stop was Desselle Millinery. She breezed in the front door and announced to a startled Renee that she was on her way to buy another red camellia at the docks.

Renee looked up from her sketchbook and leaped to her feet.

"I'll be in no danger," Maureen called back over her shoulder as she rushed into the workroom. "I told Noah I'd be an hour or more with you."

Renee caught up with her and seized her elbow. "Maureen Collins, have you lost your mind?"

She shrugged. "It's broad daylight. I'm not going at night like *Ben*, I mean Mr. Merritt, did."

Renee's eyebrows arched. "Maybe you don't know the whole story about that night."

Annoyed that Renee knew something she didn't, she halted. "What do you mean?"

"Oh, dear." Renee, looking sheepish, explained that Ben had been attacked by three men. "If Ben weren't such a good fighter, he ..."

"He could have been killed." Maureen shuddered. Her voice dropped lower. "And I understand he was at the docks to buy me another camellia. I heard that from Vespie, who heard it from George Hebert."

"And *you* could be killed yourself even in broad daylight at the docks."

"Ben should have told me what really happened," she said petulantly.

"Please, Maureen, don't even think about it. It's dangerous."

Nodding solemnly, Maureen agreed. In less than two weeks, she'd made two promises to Renee. One, she wasn't to be alone with Vespasian—a vow she'd already broken twice—and two, she wasn't to go to the docks alone—a vow she wasn't likely to keep either.

Although thermometers told a different story, Ben swore it was colder in New Orleans than in Philadelphia or New York. It wasn't the temperature in degrees; it was the persistent humidity that made winter in this city so miserable. The houses, offices and shops, designed to combat the heat, were drafty and high-ceilinged. Even when it wasn't raining, a thick fog settled over the city at nightfall. The afternoon after he called on Maureen, the damp lodged in his bones as he walked to Belle Fleur. The fog was so thick, he wanted to clear a path by putting out both hands to separate it as he would a curtain. Adding to the dampness, the wind off the river blew constantly.

The weather complemented his dark mood. No way around it, he'd made a terrible mistake with Maureen. He had sat beside her in her parlor, knowing he'd lied to her—which had become instinct as a result of his rigorous training: *Never tell what you know. Your job is to gain information, not reveal it.*

Problem was, Maureen recognized the opium herself and knew he had lied! He was sure of it. Now there was nothing real between them, nothing honest. He had held her hand and made stilted conversation. The heat between them had gone icy long before he closed his lips over her finger.

Belle Fleur, the flower shop in the French Quarter that had directed him to the *Hailong Hao*, looked ready to close when he peered in. Monsieur Gaudet, whom he'd met on his first visit, stood alone at the counter. Two weeks ago there had been a female assistant in the back room. Gaudet had gone to great pains to shield her from any discussion of camellias. He'd ushered Ben to the window, away from her hearing, before he'd suggested he try a specific Chinese ship for the plant. As he stepped into the shop tonight, Ben saw the female clerk was absent. He greeted the shopkeeper, guessing the man didn't recognize him. He was wrong.

"Were you successful, sir, in your quest for a *camellia japonica*?"

"I'm surprised you remembered," Ben said.

The clerk nervously fingered his mustache. "I don't often have requests for a flowering shrub. What can I help you with this evening, sir?"

Ben scanned the shop quickly. He didn't know the names of many flowers, but he recognized a vast array of roses. "I'll have a dozen roses, please."

"Lovely choice. These were unloaded from a Cuban ship this morning. A bouquet in a vase, sir?"

"No, no. Mix up the colors. Red, white, pink, yellow. Three of each. Just wrap them in paper, please," he said. Then he went to the door, locked it, and turned the sign to FERME. "It's closing time, no?"

As he expected, Gaudet's eyes went wide with fright.

Ben watched the shopkeeper as he, with visibly shaking hands, counted out twelve roses from the vases that lined his shelves, and disappeared into his back room with them. Soundlessly, Ben followed. He waited until the small wiry man wrapped the roses in tissue paper. Then he leaped, circled his neck with his left arm and pulled him tight against him.

"Whaaat?" Gaudet made a wheezing sound as he tried to speak.

"I don't want to hurt you, Gaudet; I just need information."

The tendons on the man's neck stood out; Ben could feel his accelerating pulse beneath his forearm. His voice trembled as he asked again what Ben wanted.

"You sent me to find a Chinese ship and Captain Kwan."

Gaudet squirmed and Ben tightened his arm on his neck. "The Chinese captain ..."

Coughing, Gaudet tried to speak. "You're choking me."

Ben eased up.

"He ... sells ... plants."

"And in the *roots* of the plants?" Ben demanded.

The man tried to shake his head; he mumbled again that he knew nothing. The man's breath came in gasps; sweat beaded on his chin and dripped on Ben's topcoat. "The lady I presented with the camellia found a tin of opium tucked in the roots."

"O ... pi ... um?" Gaudet strung the word out to three syllables.

"Don't play games with me," Ben snapped. "Captain Kwan smuggles opium in the roots of camellias."

Gaudet disengaged Ben's arm with both his hands. "Wha ... at?"

Ben stepped back. "Now tell me what you know."

His victim swallowed hard. Ben turned him so they were face to face. The florist's body was backed up against his workbench. Sweat covered his brow, the top of his lip and his chin. Frozen in place, his face pale, the terrified man wasn't going to move.

Stepping back again, Ben gave him more space.

He began haltingly. "I know ... the captain brings camellias ... from the West Indies ... maybe Cuba or Jamaica, I'm not sure." His next words came in a rush. "He comes to port every few weeks and brings back hundreds. Exactly like I told you. I thought he would have what you wanted."

"A man can make an awful lot of money on opium if he doesn't pay the proper import duties. You warned me the camellia would be expensive. And you didn't know why?"

Gaudet's voice dropped to a raspy whisper. "Captain Kwan tried to sell me his shrubs months ago. I deal only in cut flowers. He suggested a high price and I told him I didn't want them, and wouldn't pay that much if I did." Gaudet stammered on. "I had no idea. How the hell did I know he sold opium?"

The man knew nothing. Dozens of Chinese captains on the docks sold plants. Gaudet had simply directed him to a captain whose name popped into his mind. "Do you know anyone else who sells camellias with what Captain Kwan called 'fragrant' roots?"

"There's another man—he tried to sell me bushes at high prices. I have no idea if he hides opium in them."

Ben waited while Gaudet straightened his jacket and waistcoat and then crossed his arms on his chest. "What's his name?"

"Vito Mendoza."

"Where do I find him?"

"Runs Lafitte Nursery over on Bayou St. John at the end of Esplanade. Sells potted plants, seed packs and bulbs. I hear he always keeps some exotics from the Orient with very high prices. He tried to sell me camellias once, just like Captain Kwan." He shrugged. "Very high prices, so ... perhaps." He shrugged.

"Thank you, Monsieur Gaudet. What do I owe you for the roses?"

Gaudet rubbed his hand across his neck, reaching under his cravat to massage it. He shook his head. "Please, just go."

Ben picked the bundle off the counter and put two dollars down—an exorbitant price for a dozen roses. "For your help."

Roses in hand, he let himself out and signaled for a cab. He'd met his sister, Letitia, three hours ago at the docks, escorted her to the St. Charles Hotel and left her to rest. He stopped there to deliver the roses and pick her up for dinner. His mission to Lafitte Nursery would have to wait until tomorrow.

Chapter Fifteen

ate the next afternoon after work, and free from Letitia this evening, Ben hailed a cab for Bayou St. John. The driver said he knew the area well, but scratched his head when Ben said Lafitte Nursery. "Ain't no place I know by that name. Lafitte? Like the pirate? Some say he ain't dead, but I never woulda thought he'd open a nursery."

"He's long dead. It's nonsense to think otherwise."

The man shrugged. "Some say he ain't."

Ben pushed the remark aside with a command to hurry. The carriage cut through the French Quarter to Esplanade, turned left and picked up speed on the divided roadway. He observed block after block of large, beautiful homes, lights glittering in the windows on both sides of the avenue, but he knew in another half mile, the landscape would become rural.

Although he'd lived in the city a short time, he understood legends died hard here. The past was present to many folks. They talked about the "War of Northern Aggression" as if General Lee had surrendered last week. And they told tales of people long dead as if they'd spoken to them yesterday. He looked forward to meeting this Vito Mendoza, owner of Lafitte Nursery. Probably thought he was Jean Lafitte himself.

The fine homes gave way to pastures and barns, the paved road turned to oyster shells. He was a little embarrassed that he'd held Monsieur Gaudet's neck in a near death grip, but he was pleased with what he'd learned. He expected in the next few minutes to meet the second opium smuggler in New Orleans. He'd learned from the customs office that these operations necessarily required many people, but there was typically an inner circle and a leader. So the question remained: Who was running the show? Patrick Collins? Captain Kwan? Señor Mendoza?

The carriage slowed. "Keep your eyes peeled, sir, we's about at the bayou," the driver shouted. In minutes, the carriage stopped at the water's edge. To his right loomed a large frame building. A few lights shone from the second-story windows, but otherwise the place was dark. He could make out a sign above the door, but only because the letters were large and written in purple paint on what was once a white building: Lafitte Nursery.

He bounded from the door and handed the driver a dollar. "There's plenty more if you wait for me. I'm buying plants and I'll need a ride back."

The man told his horse to take it easy and took a sip from a bottle he kept on the seat beside him. Ben focused for a moment on the shoreline, and listened to the peaceful sound of lapping water against the dock. He spotted a few pirogues lit with lanterns drifting down the bayou. Burlap sacks covered the cargo onboard. A man in each boat rowed lazily or stood and pushed a pole into the water to move his goods.

At the sight, Ben felt both fueled with passion for his endeavor and overwhelmed at the scope of his responsibilities. There was no way in hell to stop anyone from smuggling anything they wanted into this city. The waterways, the huge lake, the many islands in the Gulf and the enormous length of the river made controlling smuggling just about impossible. You'd need a garrison of customs officers stationed every half-mile along every waterway to maintain any kind of control in Southern Louisiana.

He rapped on the double front door. He suspected its peeling paint kept society ladies, who weren't likely customers anyway, far away from here. If even a fraction of the plants housed here contained opium in their roots, Vito Mendoza did very well for himself.

He heard heavy footsteps. The door creaked open and a black-bearded, black-haired man with a sun-red complexion peered out at him. "What do you want?" the deep voice snarled.

"You Mendoza?"

"Maybe, maybe not."

"Andrew Franklin, sir." The man didn't step from the doorway and Ben stood stock still. "I'm looking for some *camellia japonicas*. I bought one from Captain Kwan last week. I've heard you sell them, and other exotic plants."

"I 'spect you didn't hear it from Kwan."

"I didn't." Ben chuckled. "A competitor, I suppose?"

Stoney silence greeted the question. The man looked him over, then finally backed up and motioned him in. Gigantic was the only word in Ben's vocabulary to describe him. He towered over him by nearly a head, and Ben was tall enough himself to often be the tallest gentleman in a saloon or a church or a ballroom. And by God, the man had heft as well as height. Big-boned and stout besides, he resembled a monster from a fairy tale. Ben suspected Mendoza could strangle him with one hand if he wished. He wondered briefly if bullets from the gun he carried under his coat could fell this man.

"I want something exotic to please a lady. I was thinking *camellias*, but what else do you have? Can you show me some plants?"

"Follow me." Holding a lantern high, he tromped off and Ben kept pace. In the shadows were bins, which he guessed held seed packs and bulbs. The room smelled of flowers and rich earth with a hint of animal manure. A steep flight of stairs in the room's center groaned under the giant's weight. Ben deliberately didn't put his weight on any of the same pine planks as Mendoza, but stayed respectfully behind him.

"I've got camellias, but I also sell roses." He stopped at the top of the steps and waited for Ben to complete the climb. "Tea-scented roses from China ..."

"Do these have ... I believe the term I'm looking for is ... fragrant roots? She particularly enjoys the roots ... smelling the roots." The man must think him out of his mind! Smelling the roots? He hoped to God Mendoza dealt opium. If not, he'd probably just toss him from a window—a second-floor window—for wasting his time.

The giant nodded thoughtfully. "I understand perfectly what the lady needs. These tea roses rival the *camellia japonica* in their colors. Look at these." Mendoza pointed to a half dozen pots of roses, profuse with blooms, both ivory and pink. The lighting on the second floor couldn't be called good, but he could see perfect blooms of delicate color. "Roses are a much better choice than camellias. Stronger in their scent."

"Really?" Ben shrugged. "I know very little. As I said, I'm buying for a lady."

He held a pot up, grazing Ben's nose with a bloom. Ben sniffed and a pleasant scent filled his nostrils. "The roots then are fragrant?"

"Without a doubt." He gestured to the plants again. "You can't go wrong with a tea rose imported from China."

"How much do they cost?"

"Can you put a price on making a lady happy?"

Ben laughed out loud. What a salesman this man was. "We both know a lady's happiness is priceless, he agreed. "If I bought four, could you offer a discount?"

Mendoza shook his boulder-like skull. "I couldn't, not for the quality of my product."

That was a familiar line. "Six dollars each," Mendoza continued. "That's the price."

He'd brought plenty of cash. "That's high," Ben said, pretending to be surprised. He pursed his lips for effect. "I'll take two white and two pink. I need your assurance that she'll find these ... intoxicating."

"I'm certain of it."

Mendoza put the pots on a small cart, which he rolled to a dumb waiter at the back of the room. Ben waited, watching him rather than following. He preferred to stay near the stairs, his only escape route.

Back downstairs, Ben counted out twenty-four dollars.

"Thank you, sir," Mendoza said cordially. "I'll help you carry them to your carriage."

"Thank you. If she likes these, I'm sure I'll be back."

Ben picked up two pots, Mendoza took two and they walked side by side down the oyster-shell path to the cab. When Ben approached, the sleeping driver raised his head and sat up straighter on his bench.

"Well, lookie there. They is bee-u-tiful!"

He asked Mendoza to hand his pots to the driver. He put the other two on the seat of the cab and climbed in beside them. He'd just spent a fortune for rose bushes containing opium. He had no doubt that's what Mendoza had just sold him. He needed a witness to corroborate what was in the roots—and that would be the cab driver. The man seemed a pleasant sort. Surely he'd assist for the right amount of money.

At his lodging, it took under fifteen minutes to unearth the tins of opium. He opened each tin and had the man smell it. Then he wrote out a simple description stating that each rose with a tin of opium in its roots came from Lafitte Nursery on Bayou St. John on Wednesday, January 13, 1886. The driver scratched his name, John Flanagan, to the affidavit, as well as the address of the company that employed him.

Chapter Sixteen

On Saturday morning, Maureen settled into one of the comfortable pink silk-upholstered chairs at the counter in Desselle Millinery and began to page through the latest issue of *Godey's Lady's Book*. Ordinarily this was one of her favorite pastimes, talking about the newest fashions from Paris with Renee and her assistant, Michelle D'Artois. Today, she struggled to concentrate on the colorful plates in the magazine. Her eyes drifted to the door that divided the hat shop from Lanoux Haberdashery. Surely Vespasian, who had distinctly said he'd be there at eleven o'clock, would appear any minute.

When Maureen heard the door of Lanoux's shop open and the words of greeting from the tall, shadowy figure visible through the curtain, she sighed. Thank heavens he made it before Suzette.

How had she gotten herself involved in this charade? She buried her head in the magazine until Vespasian peered through the adjoining door and spoke in honeyed tones.

"I thought I saw the lovely Maureen Collins through the veil here"—he gestured toward the curtain—"and I'm thrilled. The moment I finish my business with Monsieur Lanoux, I'll join you and help you select some fashionable hats."

"That would be lovely, Mr. Colville," she called back.

Michelle looked up from a tray of feathers she was showing a customer and nodded to the gentleman before he closed the door once again. The lady made her selection, paid and left the shop. Michelle tidied up, putting the trim boxes back in the chifforobes behind the counter. "That Mr. Colville," she remarked, "is such a handsome gentleman, isn't he, Miss Maureen?"

"And something of a rascal."

"Ah," Michelle said knowingly. "There ought to be a law against *that* particular combination."

Maureen giggled and turned another page. Vespasian could be vain and selfish, had a propensity to drink too much and would probably make a terrible husband, but his love of life charmed everyone he met. Fearless and curious, he led his friends to great adventures. He thought nothing of hanging a hammock under the pier at Grand Isle. He was the first to jump into the Gulf in February, pass out shots of absinthe before Easter Mass, race carriages down St. Charles after midnight.

She knew she didn't want to marry her lifelong friend. Yet here she was, about to hand her mother's choice for her husband over to another woman, a married woman. And what was she trading it for? A devilishly handsome attorney, who had a propensity to lurk about her family home and didn't mind lying to her about opium? A chance at love?

Her stomach cramped at the idea, but she worked at calming herself by turning the pages faster. Would a man complete college, go to law school, acquire a good position with a prominent firm and then risk losing his job and going to jail just to make money through smuggling? His clothing and manners told her his family had enjoyed wealth and privilege for several generations. It just didn't add up.

The shop door clanged. Out of the corner of her eye, Maureen saw Michelle glance up and smile warmly.

"Madame St. Aubin!" She greeted the new customer happily. "I'm so glad to see you. May I help you with something today?"

Suzette greeted Maureen with a kiss on each cheek, then turned back. "No, thank you, Miss Michelle. I'm only here to look."

Michelle came over and deposited a pile of ladies magazines on Suzette's lap. "Here's the latest from Paris and New York. Be sure to look at the color plates in the front of the last few *Godey's* issues. Miss Renee and I were saying just the other day that plaid of all kinds has taken over the world."

Maureen saw a flash of blue and green plaid as Suzette unbuttoned her cape and placed it carefully over the chair beside her. Her hat was navy blue velvet, not unlike the one Maureen wore. A little different shade of blue. Velvet flowers trimmed Maureen's hat, a Desselle Millinery original William had bought her a little over a year ago. Blue and green peacock feathers adorned Suzette's hat.

Michelle stepped into the workroom, leaving them alone, just as Vespasian opened the door. "Miss Maureen ... oh ... what a surprise, Madame St. Aubin."

Suzette stiffened at the sound of his voice. Then, with a big smile, she gushed, "Cousin Colville, so good to see you."

Maureen noted the twinkle in her eyes as Vespasian bounded across the distance separating them. He kissed her on each cheek, then turned his attention to Maureen. As he kissed her cheeks, he mouthed, "Thank you," then sank into a chair beside Suzette.

Maureen nodded and spoke to Suzette pleasantly. "I happen to know your *Cousin* has marvelous taste. She couldn't resist emphasizing the word. "As you know, we've been friends since—"

"You were born," he interrupted, leaning across Suzette to pat Maureen's arm. "I've been told I behaved very badly at your Christening because my mother held you for a few moments. I threw such a tantrum I had to be removed from the church."

While the ladies laughed, Michelle appeared with a tray holding glasses and a decanter of sherry and invited them to help themselves, then retreated again to the back room. Vespasian poured and sipped the sherry slowly, just as the ladies did. He pointed to one gown after another, noting that the dresses showed the models' necks, but he deplored the gathers of fabric across the bodices, which he said would not be to any gentleman's liking as they concealed a lady's figure.

Maureen watched the folly unfold. She saw Suzette's eyes stray from Vespasian's shoulders to his waistcoat and finally to his trousers where they rested for a few moments.

"I think ladies' fashions are often designed to conceal the body," Suzette purred, "whereas men's fashions tend to accentuate the masculine anatomy, don't you agree, Cousin?"

Vespasian spoke in Suzette's ear—something about anatomy— and slipped his arm around her waist. Maureen rolled her eyes. The heat between these two warmed the room. She tried to fill the silence with an explanation of *ruching,* that gathering of fabric Vespasian didn't like, but the couple preferred to stare into each other's eyes rather than listen to her. She launched into a discourse on fabrics for ball gowns, particularly Chinese silk, and noticed Suzette growing increasingly anxious.

A few minutes later, the lady lurched to her feet. "I think I must be going. Monsieur Leveque is waiting, and I've been away from home for some time."

"I must escort you, Madame St. Aubin—Cousin, I mean."

Good heavens, Vespasian needed to get this straight. Cousins used first names, not *Madame* or *Monsieur.* He had to address her as *cousin.*

"That wouldn't be a good idea, Cousin. I came alone and should leave alone," Suzette said, a slight tremor in her voice.

Maureen put on a bright face. "Why not send Monsieur Leveque home and we'll all walk together?" She stacked the magazines and rose with the two of them as they said their goodbyes to Michelle. Once outside, she, herself, marched up to the St. Aubin carriage and explained to Leveque that she would see that Suzette returned home at a reasonable hour. He glared at her, but without a word, urged the horse onward.

She turned back to the couple. "It's settled. Why don't we go to Antoine's? I didn't eat breakfast and I'm famished. What do you think, Suzette? Monsieur St. Aubin's away, isn't he?"

"That sounds … I don't know." She glanced at Vespasian.

"Lovely," he said.

Maureen winked at him, but he didn't even notice. His face shone with the golden light of love, an expression she'd never seen on him before. It gave her pause. At the same time, she felt a little piqued that Vespasian made no acknowledgement of her ingenious effort to arrange a meal together. With her as their chaperone, her charges would visit in a setting so respectable no one in the dining room would ever think they were anything more than three friends enjoying lunch.

Vespasian trotted along like a happy dog. And Suzette? She flushed with happiness.

At Antoine's, Andre, her father's usual waiter, escorted the threesome to a table in the main dining room. Maureen sat, looked straight ahead and there, not ten feet away, Ben Merritt and a young lady lingered over coffee and bread pudding. For a moment, her heart stopped dead. But the cooing conversation between Vespasian and Suzette was so insufferable she didn't hesitate to study the couple across the room. The lady's dark hair and eyes and her tall, lean body left no doubt in Maureen's mind she was the sister Ben had mentioned, the one who was interested in culinary history.

Ben nodded his head toward Maureen. She smiled until her dimples showed while her stomach flip-flopped. My word, he was handsome. His eyelid and the skin surrounding it had turned yellow and the puffiness had abated. Her heart swelled.

Andre appeared beside her. She let him and her guests know this was to go on her father's bill, then ordered a bottle of claret and suggested they select appetizers. Vespasian chose a half-dozen raw oysters; the ladies, turtle soup. As Andre turned away, Maureen brought her gaze to Ben's broad shoulders.

She wished they could be alone at a table together in the dark. No Vespasian. No sister. And above all, no Suzette. She longed to watch up close as he lifted a spoon of bread pudding to his mouth. She wanted to see his tongue slip out now and then to lick the whiskey sauce. She sighed out loud. The next time she had an opportunity to kiss him, she would allow deep kisses. But she had vowed never to kiss him again.

She sipped her claret and enjoyed being in the magnificent dining room of the city's most famous restaurant. She loved the tall, lace-curtained windows facing St. Louis Street and its gas-lit globes suspended from the ceiling that cast a gentle light on the diners beneath them. Maureen's mother used to say that every lady looked her loveliest under Antoine's golden orbs.

Same for gentlemen. Ben's dark hair shone in the reflected light. Maureen stared at him from time to time. Laughter and constant conversation indicated he and his sister enjoyed a comfortable rapport.

At her own table, the palpable ardor made her uneasy. The tablecloths draped to the floor. Perhaps the pair touched toes underneath it? Did Vespasian remove a shoe and run his foot up Suzette's shin? Up to her thigh? Did he have his stocking foot between her legs? Suzette's face colored again and again and she giggled like a schoolgirl.

On most occasions, Maureen wouldn't have hesitated to interrupt her companions and insert herself into the conversation. She didn't like being ignored. But today, she played the adult in charge, remaining largely mute, hoping Ben saw with his own eyes that Vespasian's interest focused on only one lady at the table—Suzette.

Ben signed his check and stood. She tilted her head slightly, an invitation to stop at the table to speak.

"Miss Collins, so good to see you."

She lifted her eyes. He stood over her, the corners of his mouth turning up in a smile. "May I present my sister Letitia?"

Vespasian leaped to his feet and the introductions went around the table. Maureen's first thought was to throw herself into Ben's arms, but she had to remain seated and satisfy herself by staring into his eyes. After the requisite chat about the weather, he offered his arm to Letitia and they glided away.

Andre rushed over to the table, refilled all three wine glasses and asked if Maureen would like a second bottle for the table. She would. The food arrived and Maureen ate without enjoying the delicacies before her.

"I see we share an affinity for beef and Bearnaise sauce, Cousin," Vespasian said as soon as Andre served the couple's identical meals. Maureen's grilled lamb chops with fresh mushrooms didn't merit a remark.

The constant "Cousin," and "Do you agree, Cousin?" grated on Maureen's nerves. What had she done? These two were going to be inseparable for the rest of the season and maybe beyond— that is, until Monsieur St. Aubin challenged Vespasian to a duel and one killed the other. She pierced a slice of lamb, added a smidgen of her favorite, pommes de terre au gratin, an irresistible blend of cheese, cream, butter and potatoes, and slid the fork in her mouth.

The couple embarked on a dangerous game with this ridiculous cousin story. On the other hand, Suzette's husband had come from Martinique in the West Indies just two years prior. With no history in the state, he couldn't possibly know all his wife's cousins. As long as they were discreet, and the young lady didn't get with child by Vespasian, who would be the wiser? But Maureen's food went tasteless in her mouth. She had a premonition this alliance would end tragically.

Suddenly anxious for Vespasian, she took a sip of wine and turned toward Suzette. "I'm curious. Just how are you and Vespasian related?"

Suzette gazed at the ceiling for a moment. "It's on my mother's side and your mother's side, isn't that right, Cousin?" she asked, turning to Vespasian.

Heavens, Maureen thought. This will be a disaster. Suzette has no story ready.

Ever quick, Vespasian jumped in. "It's complicated, I assure you, Maureen, due to the fact that my mother's grandfather married three times."

"Your great grandfather?" Maureen clarified.

"Indeed, yes, my great grandfather. Three wives." He dramatically held up three fingers. "Each wife died in childbirth. One of those wives' first cousins—and I can't remember her name—is Suzette's great grandmother on her mother's side."

"Close ties, I see." Maureen met both their eyes to be sure they were catching her warning. "I believe knowing who one's relatives are, is of utmost importance." She arched her eyebrows. "This being New Orleans, you never know when someone might ask."

"You've always been interested in genealogy, Maureen," Vespasian said with a grateful glance at her. "You're quite right that my dear cousin and I should make a study of this and learn more about the relationship between us." Suzette colored as Vespasian boldly reached across the expanse of white linen to cover her hand with his. "The important thing is that our family is reunited, don't you agree, Cousin?"

Chapter Seventeen

After the luncheon, Ben couldn't keep from smiling on the carriage ride home. Just the sight of Maureens's lips had sent his heart racing. He had dragged out dessert until Letitia's summaries of the lectures she attended in London forced him to concentrate on cheese-making and not love-making.

The threesome at the nearby table had fascinated him. The blond lady had clearly cast a spell on Colville. He stared into her eyes while she leaned toward him and fluttered her eyelashes at his every word. If Maureen remained interested in Colville, he didn't share her affection. Not anymore.

"How charming!" Letitia exclaimed when he opened the door to the garconniere and ushered her in. "You have your books, a fireplace, comfortable chairs, a desk."

"The oldest male child is given his own quarters, where he's allowed to entertain women. I suppose the custom would horrify the British."

"It feels male here. Like a cozy gentlemen's club."

He watched her gaze travel to the pots of roses lined up beside his desk.

"Horticulture, Ben? I had no idea you were interested in roses. The ones you gave me are still lovely. And these?"

"They're a gift for a friend, a New Orleans lady who has a beautiful garden."

"Miss Maureen?" She sat in one of his chairs and removed her gloves. "Build up the fire, will you, and then tell me all about her."

Ben threw a few logs in the grate. Straightening from the hearth, he stepped to his bookcase, removed Merriam's *An American Dictionary* and Charles Dickens' *Our Mutual Friend* and retrieved a bottle of whiskey, and two glasses.

She frowned. "Why hide it?'

"Habit. I used to keep a bottle in my bedroom years ago, hiding it from mother and father and you, actually."

She laughed. "Me?"

He shrugged as he poured two tumblers of straight whiskey. "You were too young."

He knew she was bursting with curiosity, but she took the glass from him without a word. Only her left hand drumming on the arm of her chair betrayed her impatience. Six years younger than he, Letitia had followed in Ben's footsteps in both academic and athletic pursuits, and she had bested him at many that he cared about. She'd mastered Greek, Latin, philosophy and calculus, rode horses and bicycles, played lawn tennis and even swam. She drank whiskey straight. Add to all that, he thought she was beautiful with her dark hair, large brown eyes and lovely figure.

She took a tentative sip. "That's very good."

"It's Collins Irish Whiskey."

"Miss Maureen's family?"

He nodded as he slouched in a chair opposite, then took a long swallow himself while he mulled over how much to tell. He shouldn't reveal anything, but she was his sister and he trusted her.

"I bought these four bushes at a nursery the other day"—he motioned to them—"and found opium concealed in the roots."

"Opium?" Her shriek startled him. "Please tell me you haven't started smoking that vile stuff. Are you selling it? Oh my God, like Grandfather?"

"No," he said, taking a quick drink. "I'm on the government's side."

"So was he. The British crown supported the lucrative opium trade."

"I work for the U.S. Customs Service."

Speechless for a moment, Letitia simply stared at him, then brought her glass to her mouth and drank. When she spoke, she jumped to the accurate conclusion. "You were roped into this by Daniel Manning, the Treasury Secretary, weren't you?"

"Let's not bring his name into it."

She rolled her eyes. "All right. We'll call him just another friend of Father's."

He didn't reply and she continued. "The last time this *friend* and his wife came to dinner, he told us the treasury is losing a great deal of revenue because of opium smuggling."

Ben nodded. "He told me the same. There's still Civil War debt to pay off, but increasing the import duty on opium from six dollars a pound to ten dollars a pound last year hasn't helped much."

She held up her hand. "You're going to tell me *legal* imports have dropped."

"Precipitously, yet opium dens and smokers have increased across the country."

She grimaced. "It's dangerous, isn't it? What you're doing? You found opium in these roses. The person who sold you those roses probably followed you home. Maybe he'll decide to kill you!"

"Why in the world would he do that?" He flashed her his reassuring smile. "On the contrary, he's hoping I'm pleased with his product and will want to buy more in the future." Glass in hand, he stood and paced. "I haven't been in the city long and I've already learned that two smugglers bring in opium in the roots of plants. I found an eighth of a pound in each of the roses."

She finished her drink. "I did wonder why you chose a law firm in New Orleans."

"It's one of three big smuggling ports. New York and San Francisco are the others."

"Does Father know you're doing this?"

"I suspect so and I pray Mother doesn't." He bent down, grabbed the poker and stirred the glowing logs.

Her eyes came together in a profound frown. "But why?"

Without a word, Ben unlocked his desk drawer and pulled out a brown leather-bound volume, cracked and worn. "Grandfather's journal. I found it in a trunk in the attic when I was twelve. Listen." He sat beside the fire and read aloud:

September 6, 1842

Now that the Chinese have surrendered and this war—what they are calling the Opium War—is over, I believe there is more opportunity than ever to reap great profits in the opium trade. I put the blame for all that has happened in the last three years at the feet of the Chinese Emperor.

The Chinese population craved the fine opium from the fields of India. British sea captains, including Weckford and me, brought it from Indian ports to Canton, where British merchants sold it to eager buyers. I cannot reiterate enough that the Chinese were ravenous for opium. All went well and we made money until the Emperor attempted to outlaw the substance. When the trade continued unabated, he sent his minions to destroy 20,000 chests of opium owned by British merchants.

Did he not realize our Queen would send ships and troops to avenge the destruction of British property as well as protect the right to free trade? Did he not think we could whip him with superior arms and superior numbers of men? The Chinese will now pay millions of pounds in reparation to our merchants for the destroyed opium. What's more, they must open more ports to trade.

He glanced up to see Letitia's pale face and wide eyes. "There's more. Bear with me."

Weckford and I have purchased a second clipper ship, which we've named Lucretia, *in honor of my beloved wife. (Weckford finally relented on the name after I regaled him with stories of the many ways my dear wife made me the luckiest man on earth.) With two ships, we will earn twice the profit. I have agreed to captain the* Lucretia *to transport opium from India to Canton. With the silver we earn on opium sales, we will purchase tea, silk and porcelain, which Weckford will transport to England where all these goods are in great demand. (On his first trip, I intend to send* Lucretia *a set of china from Canton to placate her in my absence.)*

Along with those goods, Weckford will take some of the opium home so apothecaries and doctors can administer it to those who need to relieve pain of body or mind in the British Isles. It gets weary, always weighing the good and the bad, but opium offers a patient many benefits. Indeed it is Lucretia's conscience, not my own, which sometimes gnaws at me. I foolishly wrote her of the ravaged, permanently slumberous creatures addicted to this smoke. I know she won't approve of our expanded enterprise.

Though Weckford assures me this trade is good for the British Empire as well as good for us personally, it is not without risks. Typhoons and pirates are constant threats. God forbid I lose my life at this business before I see Lucretia's face again! But I must spend at least one more year in the East before I sell the ship and return to my dear wife and the countryside of Devon. The more opium I bring to Canton and sell, the faster I will return to my wife and my country.

Letitia shook her head. "He stayed more than another year, didn't he?"

"Until the second opium war began in 1856. When he returned to England he lived on his fortune, never worked again."

"Mother was twenty by that time. He missed her childhood."

"The day I read the journal I went to Grandmother. She told me about his nightmares, the atrocities he witnessed during the first Opium War. Since that day, I've felt guilty that the family's great wealth was earned through human suffering."

She waved her empty glass and he poured them each a refill.

He went on. "At Columbia I researched details of the Opium Wars. I read about the attack on Amoy where British soldiers broke into every house and destroyed everything inside, in what their commander later wrote was 'a wanton waste of valuable property.'"

"The British love understatement."

"Then there was the massacre at Chin-kiang-fu, the last battle of the war. Casualties during the assault on the city were light on both sides, but when the British took control, they found dead bodies in every house, including women and children. Many Manchu had killed their families and then committed suicide, believing that preferable to falling into the hands of the British monster." He paused. "Grandfather had one interest—huge profits. The men who are smuggling opium into the country today are no better. It's my mission to stop them."

Letitia stared into the fire. Neither broke the silence for some time.

Ben ran a hand through his hair. "I'm troubled. I suspect Miss Maureen's father and possibly she, too, might be involved."

Letitia sat in stunned silence while he explained about the contract with Imperial Shipping, Maureen's library book open to a page on growing opium. He struggled on.

"The problem is ..."

His sister finished for him: "You've developed an attachment to the daughter?"

He grimaced. "Which is why I need to get an answer to my questions and resolve this issue as soon as possible."

Chapter Eighteen

A week later, Ben felt relief when he saw Letitia off on a steamer for Baton Rouge. She would be away for a week, visiting a college friend and gathering recipes for a Southern cookbook. Without his sister to distract him, Ben threw himself into his law practice by day and into his mission by night.

After eight hours at Mermentau and Plemer, which included contracts and meetings with Collins Factorage and half a dozen other clients, he took an early evening walk along the docks. He recorded the names of ships, captains, crews, and owners. He flashed his government badge and inspected plants. Sometimes he even used a magnifying glass on the underside of leaves—looking for pests—to establish his *bona fides*.

He ended each discussion with an offer to buy plants. He asked for fragrant roots or sweet roots or both, but captain after captain met his inquiry with odd stares. Whatever the cost, whatever they sold, Ben bought. Pots of geraniums, chrysanthemums, China asters, lobelias, petunias, baby's breath, dahlias, bleeding heart and sweet alyssum. Then he returned to his cottage and dug up the roots to check for opium. Night after night, he came up empty-handed.

By ten p.m., he changed into rough worker's clothes and returned to the docks. He watched for anything out of the ordinary, but witnessed little activity, even at the *Hailong Hao*. An occasional buyer slipped off the ship with a plant or two during the late hours. But Captain Kwan seemed to prefer to brashly peddle his goods during daylight. Perhaps he saved his evenings for indulging in his opium habit—which, Ben reminded himself—wasn't illegal.

Ben made two white camellia purchases one afternoon himself, two days apart, paying the outrageous five dollars per plant. Both contained opium tins in the roots. And he never walked by the ship during business hours that he didn't see a well-dressed gentleman stepping from the ship clutching a flower pot. He wasn't naïve enough to think the gentlemen of New Orleans were suddenly adopting gardening as a hobby. The smuggled opium from the *Hailong Hao* was the city's open secret.

Once he watched from a distance as three men moved azaleas, camellias and myriad ferns into two mule carts. He followed on foot easily enough as the ornery beasts meandered down the levee to Canal Street. They traveled up Canal, took a left at Elk Place and ended at Tulane Avenue. They unloaded at four opium dens in the same block. Opium purveyors purchasing a large number of plants? Did that not awaken the suspicion of law enforcement?

Not here. Carelton had confided that Captain Perry McCorkle, captain of the New Orleans police, made no attempt to track down smugglers. He'd told Carleton plainly he had trouble enough catching thieves and murderers and didn't worry what came into port.

Twice when Ben left the firm to visit the Tulane Library, he followed delivery carts to several respected apothecaries in the French Quarter and Uptown. He visited these, asked for advice on a nagging headache and the proprietors invariably suggested laudanum, the mixture of opium and alcohol, said to relieve just about any ailment. His mother had spooned it down his throat a few times when he had a bad cough. The reddish-brown liquid tasted bitter, but as he recalled, it cured him by putting him into a deep sleep. Every merchant he spoke with bemoaned the higher import duties, which made laudanum more expensive, a terrible burden, they all said, on the poorer classes.

Ben's schedule of work plus two trips to the docks every twenty-four hours exhausted him. He rarely turned out his light before midnight. Every morning before work, he found a messenger on Jackson Avenue and sent Maureen the best plants he'd purchased the day before. He hadn't the strength to be clever in his notes so he often scribbled what he thought inane, barely satisfactory. "More beautiful flowers for a beautiful lady." The others he sent to Charity Hospital to brighten the spirits of patients in the wards there.

The flowers, he hoped, made up for his absence, which he explained with excuses of burdensome work at the law office. The flowers seemed to be having a salubrious effect on her. He wanted her to think of him, only him, in her greenhouse no matter which way she turned. He hadn't seen her since the disastrous night when he'd recognized the opium on her plant and didn't acknowledge it. She knew he was a liar and she was right. But, damn it, she was hiding something, too. He wanted to be with her, but first he had to know the truth.

Her thank-you notes, waiting for him every evening, made him feverish with desire. He could picture her writing them, her hair covering her bodice, her toss of her head, the flip of her hand to throw the hair off and reveal the curve of her bosom. He thought perhaps she wrote them early in the morning in her dressing gown or in nothing more than a sheer nightgown. That image often entertained him for many minutes before he pushed it aside.

His absence clearly perplexed her. Her notes became more and more suggestive. On Thursday, his flowers produced quite a response:

Among the flowers you sent today, the polygonum orientale *took my breath away. The clusters of purple flowers hang in graceful tendrils. And the fragrance is quite sweet. This generally blooms in the fall. Where did you ever find one with such abundant blossoms this time of year?*

I'm guessing you know the plant's popular name is Kiss Me Over the Garden Gate.

What I wonder, Mr. Merritt, is this: How is a lady to do any kissing without the presence of a certain gentleman?

He could not see her. To see her and not be able to have her would drive him stark, raving mad. He couldn't look at her bosom, her hips, her lovely derriere and not want her desperately.

And he couldn't have her.

He had broken into her father's office, into his files. And he still harbored plans to sneak into her house at his earliest opportunity. He'd go through Patrick Collins' library, through his bedroom. He'd turn the place upside down if necessary.

What's more, Imperial Shipping owned the *Hailong Hao*. Ben thought it highly unlikely that Captain Kwan undertook his smuggling operations without the company's knowledge. The connection bolstered his belief that Patrick Collins signed a contract with that company in order to give the shipping line easy access to the port of New Orleans. Would he have to arrest her father, testify at his trial? Would he have to endure the hatred in Maureen's eyes when her father was led off to jail?

Just thinking about her heated his body into a fever, but his attraction went far beyond physical passion. Images of her talking and laughing—her dimples, her sparking blue eyes—played in his mind. Her enthusiasm was contagious. Around her, he grew more animated. No matter how much he fought it, no matter how much he pretended his interest was driven by his investigation, he knew she drew him to her with an irresistible force. He wanted to bed her. But more important still, he wanted to spend every minute with her, possibly for the rest of his life.

On Thursday evening, Ben steered Paul Hebert to the St. Charles Hotel bar. When his friend remarked that he looked tired,

Ben mentioned the punishing work for Collins Factorage and his exasperation with Patrick Collins' refusal to heed his advice on the Imperial Shipping contract.

Over his second whiskey, Hebert expanded on the details of Patrick Collins' past. Collins had arrived in New Orleans a month after the Confederacy surrendered at Appomattox. Young, industrious, with plenty of capital, he bought an abandoned factorage, run into the ground by a man who padded his bales, cheating both planters and mills. "Eventually, the man committed suicide," Hebert continued. "Patrick bought the business from his widow. And I'll say this about it, he paid handsomely for it. He didn't talk her down even though the warehouses were dilapidated. From day one, he paid decent wages to the Negroes and the Chinese who worked on the docks and in his warehouses."

Ben stifled a cough. "Chinese?"

"After the war, many planters imported Chinese laborers to take the place of slaves on the cotton and sugar plantations. Collins hired plenty of them, but paid fairly, which most people didn't—and still don't."

Pretending surprise, Ben drew Hebert out further. "You have a large Chinese population? I didn't realize. Is there a Chinatown like in New York?"

His friend nodded. "And the opium dens that come with it. In fact, maybe tonight ... are you interested?"

"I'm not a smoker, but," he paused, "why not?"

Their tour began only a few blocks from the hotel on Gallatine Street. Pool halls, beer brothels, cabarets, and oyster bars attracted sailors, gamblers, whorers and drunkards who—according to Hebert—partied from dusk to dawn.

During the night hours, the police stayed clear. "Not even murder will bring Captain McCorkle down here before dawn," Hebert joked. Ben made a show of moving his wallet to his inside overcoat pocket while he gazed at a group of approaching women who, due to their height, he assumed were men dressed as women. They, like most of the other pedestrians on this street, were foxed. The crowd swayed as it moved down the banquette.

They stopped in a dancehall where Ben drank three straight whiskeys in rapid succession while a troupe of women in very short skirts and very low-cut bodices did a New Orleans version of a Parisian can-can. He thought only a small section of their anatomy was left to the imagination. When the dancers, who wore no drawers, kicked up their legs, the men had a clear view of a rainbow of pubic hair. Blond, brunette, red and all shades in between. The sight aroused him, but not enough to seek solace in the arms of a dancer, when, between sets, they trolled the bar looking for business.

Ben had often accompanied Hebert and other young blades to opium dens in New York and was eager to take in the local scene. They took a cab to the eleven hundred block of Tulane Avenue—the center of Chinatown, said Hebert—and the exact place where Ben had seen the mule cart deliver dozens of flowering plants. The den occupied the back room of a Chinese laundry that also housed a bar and a small store.

Bunks lined the back room. Ben declined to partake, but Hebert paid twenty-five cents, entered and lay down between two gentlemen in cravats, waistcoats and jackets. Opposite the well-dressed, people of all sorts sprawled across the beds. Dark-skinned and light, male and female, some dressed as laborers, waiters, washerwomen and vegetable vendors. He counted at least a dozen people, including Hebert. Rich or poor, everyone sought a few hours of release from their problems. At twenty-five cents per pipe, the proprietor earned quite a sum, especially if he bought the cheaper, smuggled opium.

He watched Hebert put the pipe to his lips and shut his eyes. The sweet smell of the smoke nauseated him. He remained in the room just long enough to watch Hebert take a second turn with the pipe, then retreated to the store to wait. He browsed the fireworks, embroidered slippers, straw hats and shelf after shelf of soap, figurines, flags and other packaged products. He assumed most were food, though in truth, they could contain anything. He could read very little Chinese.

Sitting at the bar, Ben drank another whiskey. Several sailors came in, their conversations drifted from English to French to Spanish to Chinese and back again. He asked a few questions and learned they were from the *Hailong Hao*. Captain Kwan's employees enjoyed whiskey and rum and went in and out of the back room. His glass empty, Ben checked his watch. Hebert's visit had lasted almost two hours now, plenty of time in his opinion. Ready for bed, he pulled his friend up by his coat collar and dragged him out.

After Ben dropped Hebert, he ruminated during the cab ride to his cottage. He'd uncovered two certain smugglers—obviously rivals. Kwan bought his opium out of the country, probably in Jamaica. But where did Vito Mendoza, the bigger dealer, get his supply? Patrick Collins perhaps. Or someone who possessed equal financial resources?

Every morning Guy brought beautiful flowers to Maureen in the dining room or to the greenhouse. The notes were identical day after day. Lovely flowers … beautiful flowers … gorgeous flowers and then the line: for a lovely … beautiful … gorgeous lady— whatever the adjective of the day was.

Yet he didn't come to see her. She wanted to see his handsome face, feel his warm hand in hers. Kiss him. She tried to fathom why he chose certain flowers. She owned several gardening books that explained the significance of gifts of flowers. Camellias were supposed to indicate admiration; asters, love; baby's breath, everlasting love. But then there was the pot of bachelor buttons, symbols of celibacy. Surely he wasn't telling her that either of them should be celibate. If so, she'd certainly misread his kisses.

Again and again, she asked herself why the man bought all these flowers, but every time she examined the roots and saw the disturbed soil, she forced herself to confront the truth. Ben was an opium fiend, who smoked—she didn't know—did these people smoke several times a day?

Did his addiction explain the rest of his bizarre behavior? She'd read that opium fiends frequently stole in order to buy their drug. Had Ben watched the Collins house at midnight because they were rich? From her home, he could steal silver, jewelry and money to support his habit. The question remained: Could she love an opium addict? Did she love Ben in spite of his addiction?

She did.

Chapter Nineteen

*L*uz often complained that she went off half-cocked instead of thinking things through, but Maureen deemed ten minutes sufficient to determine her course of action. From the greenhouse, she slipped down the hall in her stocking feet, took a coat and hat from the hall closet and hid them in the greenhouse.

Next, she went to her room, took thirty dollars and a pair of gloves from her bureau drawer, and tucked them into her dress pocket. Finally, she found Luz in the kitchen with Julia and told them she was going to spend the afternoon with her plants and wasn't to be disturbed.

She left by the greenhouse door, walked out the side gate. In minutes she hailed a cab on St. Charles Avenue and headed downtown.

Her mouth grew dry and her stomach grew squeamish as she neared the docks, but she hoped to prove that all Captain Kwan's plants with so-called "fragrant roots" contained a tin of opium. Then she'd know for sure that Ben's interest was opium. It wouldn't exactly *confirm* his addiction or smuggling, though she couldn't imagine why he would buy tin after tin of opium if he didn't either use it or sell it.

She paid the driver, asked him to wait and marched swiftly toward the *Hailong Hao*. A few sailors tossed whistles and catcalls her way, but she didn't let it bother her. As she drew near the ship, she caught sight of a large man in a heavy brown overcoat a good twenty feet beyond the gangplank, heading away from the boat. He glanced over his shoulder, but his hat was pulled low and she couldn't make out his features. She started to call out to him, to ask if Captain Kwan were available, but he frightened her, even at a distance. He seemed in a hurry and for all she knew, he might not have been on the ship at all.

Sea gulls circled overhead squawking frantically. She glanced up and shuddered. The leaden sky warned of an approaching storm. Perhaps she'd been hasty to travel all the way to the docks without so much as looking at the sky.

She took a deep breath and put her foot on the gangplank. She grasped the rope railing with her right hand while holding her dress with her left and climbed the steep incline in record time.

The beauty of the flowers, shrubs and trees on the deck surprised her. Citrus trees, all varieties of ferns, camellias, azaleas, roses, and Chinese wisteria covered the open area.

"Captain Kwan?" she called. "Are you here, sir? I'd like to buy some plants."

She called his name a second time. She couldn't imagine that he left the plank down when he wasn't aboard. Even at sensible nursery prices, the deck housed a fortune. She jumped when she heard a wooden door slam to her right and swiveled in that direction. "Captain Kwan?" she called again. "I'd like to talk with you!"

Again, nothing. She tapped her foot impatiently. In the few minutes since she'd come aboard, the wind had picked up. The door banged again. Moving cautiously toward the sound, she looked back over her shoulder. Two motley cats tore at a fish head on the rough-hewn wooden dock. The cabin door opened and closed with each gust of wind.

A chill ran up her spine. A gangplank down, but no one here to guard these plants? Scarcely able to breathe, feeling her heart beating wildly, Maureen tiptoed between the branches of two rubber trees and spotted a window. Taking one last look over her shoulder and seeing no one, she peered cautiously into the gloom. As her eyes adjusted, she made out a table in the room's center with two overturned chairs beside it and another doorway along the far wall. There'd been a struggle of some kind here.

"Captain Kwan?" she shouted.

In the pit of her stomach, she knew she wouldn't get an answer. Something was terribly wrong. A sensible lady would just turn around, walk back down the gangplank to the levee and find her cab. But a sensible lady wouldn't be here in the first place.

The captain might be hurt. He might be ill. She swallowed hard and pushed open the door. The smell hit her first—the hot, coppery, meaty smell of spilled blood. She gagged and, as she pressed her hand over her mouth in horror, her eyes flew to a knife lying in a pool of blood on the floor. "Jesus, Mary, and Joseph," she murmured. She tiptoed forward until she stood in the doorway to the second room.

Captain Kwan lay on his back in a widening puddle of blood. His brown eyes bulged with horror. His neck, cut from side to side, looked as though he'd tied a red ribbon there. Her stomach lurched as she noticed his blood was approaching her walking boot. She stifled a scream. Turning, she ran through the door, nearly tripped over the knife in the outer room and came outdoors where she took a gulp of fresh air. Slamming the door behind her, she hurried through the forest of greenery to the gangplank.

She took two steps down the plank and thought better of it. She'd come for a plant. She had to take one or she'd never know about the opium. Turning around, she glanced at six or seven azaleas—the plants closest to her. Would God punish her for stealing? No matter. She picked up the worst looking plant, a scraggly white azalea worth no more than a dollar—unless it contained a tin of opium, the so-called "fragrant roots."

Grasping the clay pot in her left hand, she caught up a bit of her skirt and coat with her right, bunched it into a grabbable mass and tucked the fabric between the plant and her body. She hoped she'd make it down the gangplank without stumbling. Her hand shook as she gripped the rope; her legs trembled. The wind was growing stronger; a few drops of rain hit her face. The walk to the dock seemed the longest in her life, but at last she put her feet on firm ground.

Retracing her steps along the levee, she passed two sailors, but thought better of sounding the alarm. If she saw a policeman, that would be different, but the levee was largely deserted, everyone taking cover from the impending storm.

The cab, thank God, remained exactly where she'd disembarked. The driver jumped down and took the azalea from her arm.

"That didn't take long, Missy. Let me help you."

He put the plant on the floor and held her arm while she climbed into the seat, then asked where she'd like to go.

Home? Did she want to go there and throw herself on her bed to weep? Desselle Millinery? She could confess all to Renee. No. She needed to see her father. He'd send for Captain McCorkle. Captain Kwan's gray face and bloody neck flashed in her mind and she closed her eyes for a moment while she caught her breath.

"Where to, Missy?"

The driver's foot on the step, he was ready to hop into position above the passenger compartment. In a voice that sounded remarkably like her own, she asked him to take her to Collins Factorage.

The ride lasted an eternity. Her thoughts raced from the dead captain to his murderer. Was he killed for his opium? Hundreds of plants covered the deck. If all those contained opium in the roots, they were worth a fortune.

What would Ben think? He'd bought plants from the captain. Should she send him a message from the factorage, letting him know the news? For the umpteenth time, she went over the details in her mind. If Ben were a smuggler, he would have known the opium tin was in the first camellia and would have removed it before he gave it to her. Just as he did with his last presents—the roses, geraniums, the *polygonum orientale*. An addict? Surely that was better than being a smuggler.

Fingers fumbling with her coins, she gave the driver a generous tip. Flowerpot clutched to her side, she took small steps across the sidewalk to the front door of the office building. Generally a doorman handled the heavy glass door, but he wasn't here at this moment. She shoved her right shoulder against the door and slipped through.

"Miss Collins, what a delightful surprise."

She knew the voice and tried to smile as she looked into Ben Merritt's face. He trotted down the central staircase opposite the front door. But at the sight of her, his mouth opened in confusion. "Good heavens, you look like you've seen a ghost!"

At his words, her composure shattered and, much to her mortification, she began to sob. "Oh, Ben ..."

At her side in a bound, he took the azalea from her arm and guided her with a firm hand around her waist to a sofa on the left side of the marble-floored lobby. Tears wet her cheeks, which she tried to brush away with her hands. "The most awful thing ..."

He sank to the sofa beside her, putting a strong hand around her shoulders. "Whatever's wrong, Maureen? You're shaking. What is it?"

"Captain Kwan ..."

"You've been to the ship?" He motioned to the bush he'd placed on the floor at his feet. "You bought an azalea from Captain Kwan?"

"I saw him. I found him ..." She covered her mouth to keep from gagging and closed her eyes, then forced herself to form the words. "He's dead."

At first, she saw her distress and confusion reflected in his deep brown eyes. Then his face softened and he shook his head. "Captain Kwan smokes … he smokes opium. Perhaps he was in a stupor that you mistook …"

"No. I saw him. His throat …" She put her hand to her own neck. "Was cut." She dragged a finger of her right hand across her high collar, from left to right.

Ben's eyes widened with horror. "My God … but how? When?" He pursed his lips, and she could see his mind racing. Even so, he hugged her to him and patted her back. Feeling warm and safe in his arms, she tucked her face against his neck and breathed in his lime and bay leaf scent until she felt her trembling lessen. When she pulled away, he handed her a handkerchief and she wiped her face.

"I … came here to tell Papa …" She paused to take a deep breath. "He'll report it to Captain McCorkle."

"You've had a terrible shock. Are you able to walk up to the office?"

She nodded. He grasped her hand and raised her to her feet, then bent over for a moment and retrieved the plant. He offered his arm. She tottered and leaned on him heavily. If she let herself recall the surprised look on the captain's face, the horrible gash on his throat, she feared she might be sick. She forced herself to think of something pleasant; the first thing that came to mind was the red camellia on her workbench.

Ben put a steadying arm around her waist and she wasn't sure if her heart raced because she'd seen a dead man or because a very alive one was so close. They turned right on the second floor, took a few steps to the smaller, functional stairwell from the second to third floor and climbed. At the door to the factorage office, he put his hand over hers resting on his arm. Its warmth comforted her as he led her through the main room. She nodded to Fabre, whom she'd met many times, and to a few others she knew. She caught sight of Vespasian hunched over his desk. Neither he nor William even noticed her.

Ben ushered her into her father's office without a knock. "Mr. Collins, I came upon your daughter in the lobby. She's quite distraught."

Her father raised his head from the papers on his desk. He leaped to his feet. Maureen didn't believe she'd ever seen him move so fast.

"What's happened?" He rushed around his desk, opened his arms. Maureen fell against his chest. She heard Ben say that he would leave them alone, but not to hesitate to contact him if he could be of any help.

Then she fainted.

On the street, Ben found a cab and asked for a ride to the docks, to the specific cross street where the Chinese ship was moored.

"Popular place this afternoon," the driver muttered. "You off to buy plants, too? Seems like everyone in the city's gone mad for plants these last weeks."

Ben softened his face into a smile. "I hear there's a new shipment."

He waited on the dock until Captain McCorkle arrived— only twenty minutes later. He introduced himself, showed him his false credentials naming him a plant inspector from the U.S. Customs Service. He explained he was in town inspecting plants on ships, that many ships brought diseased or exotic plants into the country, which was illegal.

McCorkle, clearly not pleased to have him show up, told him he could board the ship if he wished, but not to touch anything.

As the older man investigated the scene, his actions fascinated Ben, who was eager to see what an experienced officer thought pertinent. The man wasted no time in the first room. He glanced at the overturned chairs, the bloody footprints across the floorboards heading away from the back room, instructed the two officers who accompanied him to collect the knife that lay on the floor and to search the room for anything unusual.

McCorkle made straight for the body. Ben followed, bracing himself. He'd stood at the bedside of dying elder relatives, but he'd never seen a murdered human being. The amount of blood shocked him. The very couch where Ben had stretched out to smoke with him last week was soaked with blood. Captain Kwan lay on the floor beside it, his pale face contorted in fear, his right hand clutching his neck just below the gash. Blood coated his entire shirtfront. There were splashes on the walls and across the wooden floor. His dead eyes stared at the ceiling like fish eyes.

Ben pursed his lips and breathed through his nose in quick deep gasps to keep from retching, but McCorkle seemed undisturbed. He felt the face and wrist of Captain Kwan and declared he'd been dead for just a few hours.

"Not cold. No *rigor mortis* as yet, Mr. Merritt. Murdered this afternoon. Broad daylight."

He motioned to the blood on the floor and rendered a conclusion.

"The murderer attacked from behind and cut his throat." He pulled at his own mustache as he spoke. "I'd say the perpetrator stood just about where you're standing, Mr. Merritt. It seems after he sliced Captain Kwan's throat, he lifted him to the bed here …" He faced the body again. "And then the captain tumbled to the floor …where he bled to death."

Ben thought Captain McCorkle's assumption correct but remained silent. "As he fled, the murderer dropped his knife in the outer room," McCorkle continued. "He didn't waste time stopping to pick it up." He turned, stepped over the pooled blood and barked orders to the two policemen in the other room. "Get in here, wrap the body and take it away in the wagon."

My God, what a horrible job that would be. Ben wondered how often these men saw this sort of death, carried away a corpse, and then went home to supper with their wives and children.

McCorkle examined the two pipes, the lamp, a bowl of opium pellets on the table between the couches. "A Chinese man is always an opium smoker," he declared. "Why do you think he's trying to bring exotic plants into New Orleans?"

"If I may say, sir, I've been making inquiries for several weeks."

The captain acknowledged this with a raised eyebrow. Ben explained. "I heard from a florist on Canal Street that Captain Kwan sold camellias and other flowering plants—all legal and healthy. But he also sold exotic plants to collectors at very high prices."

McCorkle pursed his lips into a thin line. "The deck is full of plants. There must be a few hundred. How many of these are illegal?"

"I couldn't say exactly. Maybe half are illegal. I was planning a raid with customs officers in the next day or so."

Captain McCorkle sighed heavily. "Plants? You're concerned about plants? This is the most idiotic thing I've ever heard. Do you really think this fellow was murdered over plants?"

"We've had a problem in America for more than fifty years," Ben said in a grave voice. "A fungus, *phytophthora cinnamoni*, wiped out the American chestnut tree. Got into the roots of the trees back in the 1830s. Rotted the roots. It's a huge loss."

McCorkle shook his head while a deep frown grooved his forehead. "You're one of those Washington boys coming down here to tell us how to run our port?"

"No sir. I inspect plants for diseases and pests, that's all I do. Aphids, bagworms, Japanese beetles, spider mites." He leaned toward him in a conspiratorial stance. "You see, there are wealthy people who want the most exotic shrub or tree they can get. They don't care what it costs. Frankly they don't care that they may infect and kill every tree or shrub in the country."

"And some of these are right here on this ship?"

Ben made an all-encompassing wave. "I see *camellia japonicas, cameillia reticulata, rhododendron* ...," he said, exhausting his knowledge of plants in seconds. "All fine to import." He scanned the deck looking for the unusual. A few Latin phrases popped into his mind. "That one." He pointed to a tree five feet high. "That's an *ale iacta est florissimo,* here's an *aut viam inveniam aut faciam*—very rare and costly—and near the railing, a *floralux et veritas.* Importing any of those is against the law."

Ben stepped aside so the two officers could maneuver the pallet to carry Captain Kwan's body through the doorway.

"If I may make a suggestion, sir. It might be advisable to station several men here overnight. I'd be happy to volunteer as part of the watch."

The older man scowled. Ben knew from Carleton to expect little or no help from this man. But he forged ahead. "This shipment is worth a lot of money. The killer may come back to steal many of these plants."

McCorkle fixed him with a stare. Ben met his eyes with an equally hard gaze.

"I'll handle this, Mr. Merritt. This is a murder investigation, not a fungal detection project and I'll deal with it as I see fit."

He descended the gangplank, then shot Ben one final contemptuous glance.

"In the morning."

Chapter Twenty

Her father sent Maureen home in a cab with a note instructing Luz how to care for her. He ordered two glasses of milk punch, heavily fortified with brandy. After drinking those, she was to lie down on the sofa in the upstairs ladies sitting room and wait for his arrival. Falling quickly into a fitful sleep, she dreamed she was tumbling down a slippery gangplank into the murky river below, while Captain Kwan's contorted face looked on from above.

She woke, disoriented, to the sound of heavy footsteps storming up the stairs.

"Papa?" She raised herself on her elbows.

One glance at his face told her she was in for the lecture of her life. She sat up quickly and trained her eyes on her shoes until he ordered her to look at him.

"I'm sorry you saw what you did. You've seen more than many men ever see, except those who served in the war. McCorkle sent a note. It's exactly as you said. But ..." He pointed a finger at her and his voice quivered with rage. "I can't believe that my own daughter had no more sense than to go to the docks and board a foreign ship ..."

She mumbled, "I shouldn't have."

"You could have been killed!" he thundered. "Suppose you had come up the gangplank just as the killer ran away. What do you think would have happened?"

"I would have been hurt?" she croaked.

"Hurt? You'd have been pushed into the river."

"I can swim," she said, defiance creeping into her voice.

He slammed his palm against his forehead and began to pace. "For God's sake! He'd have knocked you out or strangled you before he shoved you in the water. It was stupid, irresponsible … I'm so furious I'm …"

She interrupted. "Mr. Merritt went several times to the ship to buy plants from Cap …"

"Merritt is an idiot," he barked.

She sucked in her breath. "An idiot?" She repeated his words with a shaking voice.

Her father glared at her, then shook his head sadly. "He's put crazy ideas into your mind. Running off to the docks for plants! What would your mother say?"

Maureen wasn't going to let him use *that* old tactic. "It was *my* idea, not his." She didn't add that it was perfectly reasonable for an intelligent woman to investigate the activities of the man she was falling in love with. She *knew* Ben wasn't an idiot. And she kept her suspicions about what he was to herself.

She went on. "The plants are spectacular. You should have seen some of the species Captain Kwan had on his deck. Hundreds, I'd guess."

He wrung his hands in frustration. "This fixation of yours on plants is clouding your judgment about other aspects of your life." He stared at her for some moments. "There's something odd about Mr. Merritt," he said softly. "He's a bright enough young man, I suppose, but he's always skulking around the docks."

She crossed her arms over her chest. "You spend a great deal of time yourself at the docks."

"I have legitimate business there," he shot back, "and, frankly, I'm not sure he does."

Maureen's chest twisted with anguish. Her father, astute in all business matters, had put her deepest fear into words. Ben Merritt was somehow entangled in the opium trade. At the least, he was an opium addict. She'd joked with him at their first meeting, suggesting he might be a scoundrel. Was he? Could her father see something about him she was too besotted to see?

"I'm sorry I ever allowed him to call on you," he said bitterly.

Speechless for a moment, she grasped for a mental list of Ben's virtues. Tall, good-looking, witty, he was the man who made her insides tumble. But she well knew these weren't virtues. "He's a good ..." Her voice cracked; she swallowed. "... attorney, isn't he?"

"I believe so. But I've seen him prowling around this house late at night, too."

"I've seen him ... at the house only once ... I believe. You were here."

Her father looked disappointed in her—that she would lie to him. "I saw Merritt New Year's Eve," he continued. "He was walking down St. Charles—in our block—when I came home. He turned his head away, hoping I wouldn't recognize him. Did he visit you that night?"

Numbed by her father's revelation, she shook her head. "I was sick. Remember? I didn't see Mr. Merritt that night." How ironic that Vespasian, the man who had wanted to bed her for more than a year, had visited alone with her for at least an hour in her greenhouse, yet her father's concerns focused on Ben. Had Ben been outside watching her with Vespasian? Goosebumps rose on her arms.

"You're not to see Ben Merritt again."

She bit her lower lip hard enough to draw blood; she winced at the pain and taste of it. "But, Papa, you told me Christmas day that I could ... I could see young men and make my own choice. Choose my own husband ..."

His voice lowered to a deep, forbidding tone. "You can, among the rest of the men in this world. Just not that one."

Maureen stood and narrowed her eyes.

He took in her expression but remained unmoved. "Once again, I'm disappointed by your judgment. I can't believe you think he's husband material."

At one time, she had hoped precisely that, but now? "I'm not saying I want to marry him, but I enjoy ... I enjoy his company." She swiveled to face him, her voice shrill. "He's far more interesting than Vespasian Colville!"

"Vespasian's a Southerner. Ben Merritt's a Yankee. That alone makes him untrustworthy."

"Papa," she shouted, "the war ended *twenty* years ago!"

His eyes met hers. She'd never seen a colder look in them. "You have no idea the cruelty exhibited by Yankee soldiers."

"Ben ... Mr. Merritt didn't fight ... and neither did you!"

"You're not to see him. Is that clear?"

"You're being unreasonable ..."

"Go to your room, Maureen, right this minute. It's hard for me to even look at you. Julia will bring you supper." He stalked to the hearth and stared at the fire, his back to her.

She made for the door on weak legs. "I don't want any supper." He didn't react so she walked slowly from the room, her feet unsteady from too much brandy. She wove her way down the hall, slammed her bedroom door and threw herself on her bed.

Ben had been outside their house on New Year's Eve? But why? She pushed the question aside. If Ben had watched her with Vespasian, he'd have seen nothing more than two friends talking.

Her father infuriated her. The war, Yankees! How absurd. My God, suppose she'd fallen in love with a Frenchman or a Spaniard? Ben was an American from a fine Philadelphia family. Her father could order her around all he liked. She didn't have to obey him. She'd sneak out; she'd sneak Ben in. Maybe she'd just throw herself at him, despite what her father said. She closed her eyes and pictured the scene until Julia interrupted with the supper tray.

Ben took a cab to the Collins house, arriving just at nightfall. Guy answered the bell and explained that Miss Maureen was indisposed and wasn't receiving visitors. The man was noticeably cold. Disappointed, Ben left his card.

He'd expected Maureen to be disturbed by her experience, but he'd hoped she'd welcome his company. She was certain to dig up the azalea first thing tomorrow. She'd find more of the so-called fertilizer and she knew what it was.

Yet he'd pretended ignorance. For the hundredth time, he regretted not telling her it was opium the night he first saw it on her plant. He wanted to be honest with her. He couldn't hope to have any sort of romance if he continued lying. Romance? She was a tool in his mission. The lines from Sir Walter Scott came into his head: "Oh, what a tangled web we weave. When first we practice to deceive!"

At his lodging, he changed quickly into dark wool sailors' pants and shirt, concealed his pistol in his heavy outer jacket, his knife in his lace-up work boot. With a close-fitting workman's cap hiding his hair, he walked several blocks to the corner of Jackson and St. Charles before he signaled another cab and ordered it to the levee. He foresaw an unpleasant, even dangerous night ahead. He expected several officers aboard the ship and the entrance barred. His head down, he shuffled down the dock, an empty beer bottle he'd picked up a block back, in his hand. A few drunk sailors milled about, but no one paid him any mind.

As he neared the ship, he felt lucky for the first time since he'd seen Maureen run through her gate and into his arms. The gangplank was down, just as Captain Kwan always left it, a perfect invitation to anyone who wished to board and steal opium tonight. Thirty feet from the ship, he sank to the ground and propped his back against a sugar barrel. He peered around it and saw one lantern glowing in the cabin on the *Hailong Hao* deck. He listened for footsteps and heard only the sound of the boat slapping in the water, the ropes straining against the poles that tied the ship in place. Was it possible McCorkle had left no one on guard?

He didn't think the man so careless that he'd leave the ship unguarded, yet by God, he had! Did it mean that he, too, was involved? Had he been paid off—as was common—to give the smugglers *carte blanche*? McCorkle probably received a plump payment every few weeks or months. Ben pulled out his pocket watch and kept time. Ten minutes passed, fifteen, and not a human sound came from the ship.

Taking a deep breath, he crept to the base of the plank and crouched in the darkness while he removed his boots. He tied the laces together and hung them over his shoulder. He listened again for footsteps and heard none, counted to sixty and made his move. Grabbing the rope railings with two hands, he ran up the plank and softly made his way to a hedge of large azalea bushes and slipped behind them. Ben scanned the deck and chose the first lifeboat in the line that hung just off the side of the ship. He raised the tarpaulin covering it, slid inside and pulled it back over him.

The lifeboat smelled of dust and mildew, enough to make Ben struggle to keep from coughing. He shut his mouth and took careful breaths through his nose. Feeling in the darkness, he put his boots back on, but the cold still numbed his feet. Even encased in leather gloves, his hands soon lost all feeling. At least it wasn't raining. With any luck, he'd be able to hear the conversation of anyone who boarded the ship.

Time passed at an agonizing crawl. Ben couldn't see his watch and dared not raise the tarpaulin to let in enough light to take a look. He knew if the men found him, they'd try to kill him.

Although he'd held his own on Twelfth Night, he wasn't eager to fight a crowd.

At last, he heard footsteps thudding against the wooden plank. Then he heard two squabbling voices.

"Shut your mouth, both of you." The authoritative voice was an older man's, a little reedy, and tense.

Ben brought his face to the edge of the covering, straining to hear more. Three distinct voices. Could there be only three? Not necessarily. Mentally, Ben scrolled the tenets of his training and began to think he'd acted hastily. He hadn't told a soul where he was going, hadn't written a note of explanation to Letitia or Hebert in case he didn't return in the morning.

One of the men grumbled about the cold. The second man's voice—agreeing with every word the reedy voice put forth—was familiar, but Ben couldn't place it. He'd met a lot of people in New Orleans and most had seemed highly respectable. And yet, he knew it was often the respectable men who were the money makers behind schemes such as smuggling. Which is why he hadn't yet ruled out Patrick Collins.

A moment later the reedy voice ordered the men on. "Get it done, Vito. It'll be dawn before we're through at the rate you're going." Vito Mendoza? The big curly haired man who sold him the roses at the nursery on Bayou St. John? Tall and solid, the nurseryman would be a formidable foe, not one Ben cared to oppose.

He sat still listening while pots scraped the wooden deck as they dragged them from one place to another. Trowels clinked against these, clods of dirt hit the deck. An occasional groan accompanied by footsteps indicated a man stood and pulled a large root-bound plant from its pot. A muffled thud, the tin of opium landing on something soft, a burlap sack perhaps. The threesome started working close to him, digging up the tins from the plants near his lifeboat while he lay barely breathing a few feet away.

After listening to them for what seemed like hours, Ben was stiff from sitting in the same position. When he shifted his weight to get comfortable, the chains holding his boat strained.

Mendoza whispered, "What was that? That sound?"

"I thought it came from over there," the weather-grumbler said.

Ben held his breath as footsteps came closer. He dared not move. A creaking sound came from the boat moored next to the *Hailong Hao*.

"It's just the boats shifting in the water," the reedy voice barked. "Come on. Let's get this over with."

Soon they moved on. They worked for several more hours. He was trapped until the three men left the ship with their treasure.

"That about does it," reedy voice said. "Leveque, check around the bow to make sure we didn't miss any pots. You got that?"

Two sets of feet moved away from Ben toward the bow. Another set lumbered down the gangplank. When the pair met, Ben heard the one called Leveque say they had it all. "Let's get out of here. We've put in a hard night for Benoit. It's time to get paid and have a drink."

"I'm for that."

Ben was for that, too. He didn't know when he'd been colder. His back ached and his thighs cramped. He lifted the tarpaulin and raised his eyes above the lifeboat's gunnels. He watched Mendoza grab the rope railing and swing to the dock with a few steps. The man called Leveque took his time descending. Crouching, Ben moved to the cover of the azaleas and from these, he crawled quietly, one plant to another, until he dared raise up to see over the ship's side.

By that time, the men were long gone. No doubt they cut between two sugar warehouses, slipped by the cotton press building a block away and found a waiting carriage. He could guess their destination, so he caught a cab and went straight down Esplanade to Bayou St. John.

He offered the driver a handsome fee to sit there for a few minutes. He guessed the thieves—Mendoza, Leveque and a third man—were inside the nursery. A pirogue was tied to the wharf on the bayou. He could see by the light of a lantern in the canoe that a young Negro boy waited there. The oldest man—the reedy voice—at least sixty and rail thin—came out the front door, limped down the path to the wharf and climbed aboard.

"A good night's work, Percy." The voice carried on the breeze to Ben's carriage. "Take me home, please."

"Sho nuff, Mister."

Ben gave his driver another coin and asked him to wait another fifteen minutes. The time was nearly up when the one called Leveque came out and climbed in a carriage. Ben had his driver follow him into the French Quarter where he slipped through the alley between two fine looking three-story houses on Chartres Street.

Chapter Twenty-One

Emerging from the bushes in the side yard, Ben saw a light in Maureen's window and let the absurd idea in his head gather substance and direct his body to the base of the trellis below her balcony. The lattice was sturdy; the vine on it without thorns. He climbed to the second floor swiftly and vaulted over the iron railing.

He felt an overwhelming need to see her and comfort her. He knew she couldn't be able to sleep tonight after seeing the captain's sliced throat. As always, he told himself the mission guided his decision. He needed to talk with her. The sooner he questioned her, the more likely she was to remember details. He had arrived at the ship quite a bit after Maureen. She might have seen something he missed.

Two sets of French doors opened to the narrow stone porch where he stood. Curtains blocked one completely, but on the other, fabric covered only one of the double glass-paned doors. Its mate afforded him a clear view of Maureen's room.

Ben peered in. Two gaslights, one on a bedside table, another on her dressing table cast a soft glow over the room. Purple wisteria on a pale yellow background papered the walls. On the far wall to his right, a four-poster bed held nothing but rumpled sheets and a bedspread. It was after four in the morning, yet she was not in bed.

Two doors led from the room. He guessed the one directly opposite his window went to a hall, the other, on the wall to his left, to a bathroom. Against that wall were a dressing table and mirror, and a low-back Chintz-upholstered chair positioned in front of it.

Where was she?

The door to his left opened. Maureen walked into the room wearing nothing but a sheer nightgown and a V-necked white dressing gown. She looked like an angel, albeit a sad one. Her little bare feet made a quick turn and she walked out of his view and then returned, her thin robe billowing out to reveal her trim figure through her nightgown.

Her breasts, freed from a corset, were fuller than they appeared in clothing. Her tiny waist accentuated her hips and he glimpsed a black triangle of hair between her legs. He felt his trousers grow tight. She turned abruptly and the cloth clung to her shapely bottom. Ben grew more aroused.

She flopped into her dresser chair not three feet from his window. To avoid her seeing him, he stepped back a little, barely keeping her left side in his sight. Her ankle-length nightclothes, gathered up past her knees, revealed her shapely calf. Transfixed, he stared as Maureen gazed into the mirror. When she pulled the clip from her hair, it fell in tangles to her shoulders, some cascading down her front, covering both breasts.

His breathing quickened as she picked up a hair brush and slowly brushed from her crown to the tips of her curls. Using her left hand, she held sections of hair at chin level and brushed the ends vigorously. The curls bounced back. Her dainty arms, visible through the thin fabric of the long sleeves, worked furiously at her task. Each movement she made, the merest flick of her wrist, filled him with the desire to know more about her, to be part of the scene, to be welcome there.

Placing the brush on the dressing table, she slumped against the back of her chair and closed her red, puffy eyes. She stood, walked back to the side of the bed and paused for a moment. The high bed hid her now from the waist down. When she untied her dressing gown, it gaped, allowing him a view of her breasts and nipples through the thinner fabric beneath. She tugged at each sleeve and the robe slipped from her shoulders. She tossed it at the foot of the bed.

He couldn't wait another second. He pushed open the French door from the balcony and stepped inside.

"My God, Ben!" Maureen squeaked. "What are you doing here?" She lunged for her robe and clutched it to her chest. Her knees went weak. Mesmerized, she watched him shut the door behind him, a finger on his lips.

"Shhh. I had to see you."

Barely breathing, she didn't move—not to step forward or back—as he walked across the carpet and stopped at the bedside. An expanse of green satin quilt separated them.

"I knew you'd be upset, probably couldn't sleep."

This man her father didn't want her to see any longer had come to be sure she was all right. She wanted to rush into his arms, but she waited for a signal from him. She swallowed and tried to speak. "I ..." Tears filled her eyes and threatened to overflow. She bit her trembling lower lip.

He motioned her toward the foot of the bed and tiptoed to meet her. He stretched out his arms. "Let me hold you."

She buried her head against his chest. His strong arms circled her and just held her tight. He asked her to tell him everything. If she talked about it, she'd feel better, he said. Grateful to shed her terrible burden, she whispered her tale—from the big, tall stranger she'd seen near the ship to her shaky ascent up the gangplank. She admitted she was uneasy when no one answered her calls, but she thought the captain might be ill and need help, so she went in the cabin.

"Chairs were overturned, so I looked into the next room." She choked on the words. His lips pressed a kiss on the top of her head as he put a handkerchief in her hand. She sniffled. Ben didn't smell like himself. No lime scent tonight. His rough wool coat scratched her cheek. She pulled back.

"Where have you been? In these clothes?" She held the coat's collar in her fingers. She recognized them as the clothes he wore the night she met him.

"The docks. I went to the ship to look around." He shrugged. "I thought of Captain Kwan as a friend."

Her stomach clenched. Just as her father said. Skulking around the docks. Surely he didn't think she believed the Chinese sea captain was a *friend* of his? Who was this man who stood in her bedroom? She wanted to trust him, but she knew she shouldn't.

"You better go. Someone might hear us. If Papa found you here ..."

"You invited me to kiss you over the garden gate."

Had she really written something so inane? And to a man she barely knew? She waved her hand toward her bed. "This is hardly the garden gate. You should go." She turned and took two steps toward the head of the bed. A floorboard creaked in the hallway outside. His head snapped in that direction. He stood as still as a statue; she guessed he didn't breathe.

She mouthed the words: THE DOOR IS LOCKED.

He nodded slightly, but otherwise remained immobile.

Cocking her head, she listened for the slightest movement. She heard women's soft-soled slippers against the steps to the third floor. Julia or Luz going up to bed. Peculiar that one of them was up at this hour, but perhaps she had wanted a bite to eat and had gone down to the kitchen. The hall went silent once again.

Ben turned now to face her and whispered: "I'm happy you lock your bedroom door and not your balcony door." His mouth curled up unevenly in the quirky smile she loved. Whoever Ben was, whatever his past or present, she was happy he was with her right now. The fact was, she didn't want to be alone.

"I came by earlier, but Guy said you weren't receiving."

"Papa sent me to my room."

His eyes flicked to the tray on a side table. "Did you drink some sherry? Something to calm you?"

"Milk punch when I came home. Julia brought a nightcap, but I didn't touch it."

He came to her side of the bed, pulled the covers back and told her to sit. He picked up the glass, sniffed it and held it out to her.

"Brandy. I'm not going to leave until you drink this. It'll help you sleep."

Her hand trembled when she took the glass and brought it to her lips. It burned her throat as she swallowed. She nearly choked, but she drank it down in five gulps.

"You want me to go, I see."

She couldn't help smiling at his joke. The straight brandy had immediate effects. She now controlled the tremble in her hands. Her stomach settled.

He fluffed the pillow. "Lie down."

She tucked her feet under the covers, turned on her side to face him and let her head drop onto the pillow. "Stay with me."

He pulled the covers up over her shoulder, the very opposite of what his body told him to do. He'd been stiff since he walked in the room. He wanted to tear her nightgown off and make love to her. Instead they talked quietly and just as he'd hoped, Maureen had seen something he hadn't.

The big, tall man she'd told him about must have been Mendoza, very likely the murderer. He'd killed his principal rival in the opium smuggling trade. Now most of the illegal opium in the city would pass through Lafitte Nursery. He felt pleased with himself for following his instinct, coming here and climbing that trellis.

But, dear Lord, she'd had a close call. If she'd arrived a few minutes earlier—he couldn't allow himself to think what might have happened. As he watched her eyes shut, he examined his motives more carefully.

Apart from her father's likely involvement, apart from her role as a tool in his investigation, apart from his mission in New Orleans, Maureen Collins had enticed him more than any woman he'd ever met. Her body made him feverish; her mind fascinated him. Tonight, she'd let him comfort her, let him tuck her into bed. She trusted him enough to be alone in her bedroom with him.

Her eyes fluttered and finally closed. He'd stay just a minute until her breathing slowed in deep sleep. Perhaps if he lay down beside her, she'd feel safer. He removed his coat and boots. If he lay on top of the bedspread, he'd be cold, so he climbed beneath it. On his side, he shifted his body against hers, snuggling his chest to her back. His nose in her hair, he inhaled the scent of roses and put his arm across her body at the waist. It took every ounce of his willpower not to press his hard ridge against her bottom. Some night, he'd lie with her that way. Some night soon.

The light softly angling through the French windows woke Ben. His arm remained tucked around Maureen's waist, but his manhood and legs now fit tight against her bottom and thighs. Aroused, he wanted nothing more than to remain exactly as he was. But the insistent sun demanded action. He slipped his arm away and turned onto his back.

Startled awake, Maureen stammered. "My God, Ben!"

He crooked his mouth in a smile. She looked beautiful with her tousled hair, her cheeks rosy with sleep.

She sat up in bed. "I dreamed you came in my bedroom. But you're really here."

"I believe it's time to go." He leaped from the bed. In less than a minute, he'd slipped on his boots and coat and left by the French doors.

Chapter Twenty-Two

*B*ack at home, Ben slept until a runner woke him in the early afternoon with a note in a fragrant, cream-colored envelope. Recognizing Maureen's handwriting, he questioned him. *Had he received it directly from the lady?* No. *Did he see the lady peering from a window or from the hallway?* No. The runner's answers disappointed.

He threw a log on the still-hot coals, sat down and tore open her note. He fisted his hand in anger as he read that Patrick Collins had forbidden her to see him any longer. She enumerated several reasons including her father spotting him in front of the Collins house on New Year's Eve to his lurking around the docks at night to buy plants from the Chinese sea captain.

He believes you encouraged me to go to the docks by myself, which he thinks was irresponsible. (I know it never occurred to you that I'd undertake such an adventure alone, but he believes you led me to my near death.)

Despite my father's misgivings, I'm inviting you to visit on Tuesday evening. He departs on the eight o'clock train to spend a week in Boston.

Only Saturday now, was he to wait three days to see her again? What were the real reasons Patrick Collins didn't want him to court his daughter? He was a gentleman of good family, with a well-respected profession.

Could the man know he'd been in his office, in his file cabinet? *Impossible.* Perhaps he was offended yesterday when he left

Maureen in his office and didn't stand about outside and wait to see if he could assist in any way. *Damn.* He'd blundered there. A Southern gentleman would never have left a young lady in distress—even in the care of her father—but he'd had no choice. He'd had to get to the *Hailong Hao* as fast as he could.

In the kitchen, he made a pot of coffee and standing over the stove, enjoyed those first swallows. After a few gulps, he crunched the note into a ball, walked into the living room and tossed her note into the fire.

Maureen was willing—more than willing from her tone—to disobey her father's order. So was he.

Maureen tried to concentrate on the task at hand—watering the ferns, but Ben filled her mind. After he'd made his exit from her bed, she'd gone to the balcony and watched him slink—it was a slinking movement—around the corner of the house. She suspected he left the property through the side gate that opened onto another street.

She had slipped back between the sheets and daydreamed about his handsome face, his warm eyes, his powerful shoulders. Countless times, she'd relived the moment she'd drifted off to sleep with his arm across her waist.

When she came down to breakfast, Julia said her father had left for the office. He often worked for a few hours on Saturday morning to catch up on paperwork, but obviously he'd gone early to avoid her today. Just as well. Her father wasn't likely to change his mind and admit he'd misjudged Ben. She didn't expect him to rescind his order regarding him.

Guy interrupted her watering to announce she had a visitor. Ben? He wouldn't dare. Not after receiving her note.

"It's Madame Suzette St. Aubin."

"Please show her in. I'll receive her here."

Maureen wore a pinafore apron of coarse cotton over a plain blue serge dress. Why not let Suzette see the real Maureen Collins, the day after the worst day of her life? No, she corrected herself. The day her mother died had been the worst day in her life. Yesterday was the second worst day. She pulled her hair back in a ribbon off her face, and used a rag to wipe the smudges of soil off her cheeks.

Waiting in the greenhouse, Maureen came forward as her visitor reached the bottom step and kissed both her cheeks. "I'm so glad to see you. Please sit down. Would you like coffee or tea?"

Suzette took a chair at the table. "Nothing, thank you."

Her trembling voice wasn't much above a whisper. Her swollen eyes indicated she'd been crying. Perhaps all morning.

"Whatever's wrong? Would you like a glass of sherry?" Maureen tilted her eyes skyward where the clouds formed a gray blanket, matching her mood. "It's such a dreary afternoon."

"Please, yes." Suzette took a handkerchief from her handbag and dabbed at the tears spilling down her cheeks. "I shouldn't tell you or anybody—my mother says a good wife never reveals secrets about her marriage—but my husband threatened me last night."

Maureen held up her hand. "Don't say another word."

Rushing into the sunroom, she fetched a decanter of sherry and two glasses. She handed Suzette a full glass and suggested she take a few swallows and calm down before she spoke. While Suzette followed her directions, Maureen poured herself a glass and settled into another chair at the table.

"I'm happy to listen, but it's fine if you'd like to just sit here in this beautiful room and have some sherry. You don't have to tell me anything."

But Suzette did. Between sobs, she revealed that she and her husband had argued about his trip to Jamaica. "He returned from the country last night and left again this morning. I'm hurt he hasn't taken me with him to Jamaica. We've been married for more than a year; he travels all the time, and half the time I don't know where he is. But I've never been anywhere. I'd like to go to Jamaica."

"I'd love to go, too. The island is covered with tropical plants." Maureen shrugged. "Perhaps he believes the accommodations on the voyage would be too rough on you?"

Suzette sniffled into her handkerchief. "When I said I'd like to go with him, he went into a rage. He threw a vase of flowers at the fireplace and smashed it."

Maureen felt her mouth drop open in surprise. "Oh, dear, that's ..." She couldn't find the right word for it.

"And then ... then he said I wasn't to ever mention traveling with him again." Suzette took a quick breath. "He said my job was to stay in New Orleans and wait for him."

Frankly, that didn't seem such a horrible fate. What lady wanted to sail off to Jamaica with a man three times her age?

"I'm sure you'll miss him," she said soothingly, "but I'll see to it that you get out and about."

"He doesn't want me to associate with forward-thinking women," she murmured.

Maureen's fingers clutched the stem of her glass with such force she was surprised it didn't shatter. "What a horrid man!" she exploded. "What a horrid husband!"

Suzette's eyes bulged at her outburst.

Maureen slapped her hand over her mouth. "I'm sorry. I'm so sorry. Forgive me. I shouldn't have said that."

Suzette began to giggle. "It's all right. He *is* horrid."

Maureen searched her brain for the right words before she spoke. "Horrid may be too strong an adjective. But he is old-fashioned in his thinking. Renee and I—and Letitia Merritt with her plans to write a cookbook; and Carine Bouchard, she's writing a novel—I hope we all fill your head with ideas of women's independence. This is 1886, after all."

"I'm terrified that he … that he will be very harsh with me if he finds out I've seen you."

Terrified? Not exactly. Suzette sat sipping sherry in her greenhouse and her face looked brighter by the minute. Maureen knew a few ways around foolish fathers. Surely foolish husbands couldn't be any more difficult.

"He'll be hundreds of miles away. How will he know what you do?"

Suzette shivered and pulled her coat tighter about her. She took another swallow of sherry. "I've told you the butler Leveque spies on me. He'll give Monsieur St. Aubin a full accounting."

"The butler can't watch your every move. There are disguises, a change of clothes here and there. Doesn't he go away himself now and then?"

She reached out and grabbed Maureen's wrist. "Yes, he does. It just so happens Leveque's leaving tomorrow on one of his errands for my husband, and I can easily sneak away."

Maureen patted her on the back. "We're going to have some fun, I promise. Let's go sit by the fire." With that, she led her guest into her mother's sunroom. Maureen sat on the sofa.

Suzette faced her, but kept her hands behind her, very close to the fire screen. They were silent for a few moments until Suzette sat beside Maureen and spoke softly. "Perhaps I could stay with you for a while, and I must talk to you about … about Vespasian."

Maureen had expected Vespasian's name would be the first word out of Suzette's mouth when she saw her swollen eyes, but she hadn't expected to have a house guest foisted on her.

"He's a charming cousin, isn't he?"

Maureen couldn't let that pass without comment. "Suzette, we both know Vespasian Colville is *not* your cousin. He used that ruse to meet you, to allow you to receive him at your home."

"I know that, but Mr. Leveque, the butler, and my horrid husband, don't."

Maureen nodded. "And there's no harm in cousins seeing each other socially, is that the idea?"

Their glasses were empty, so Maureen filled them both.

"Monsieur St. Aubin has given me permission to see Cousin Vespasian in our home and to allow him to escort me to social events. He mentioned the opera and Mardi Gras balls ..."

Dumbfounded by that revelation, Maureen clarified her understanding. "Your husband allows you to see Vespasian?"

"Who is my cousin," she said with a sly grin.

Not dumb at all, this one.

"Monsieur St. Aubin is allowing Vespasian to ... to." She stopped herself before the word *seduce* crossed her lips, "... court you?"

"He's not courting me."

"Call it what you like. Vespasian says he wants to marry you!"

Suzette's eyes widened at the thought, resembling a child anticipating a sweet treat after dinner.

"Do you think so?" She blushed. She was even prettier when her cheeks took on a little pink. "Do you think he might love me?"

Maureen stood, walked quickly to the hearth, grabbed a log from the brass bucket and threw it on the fire. It caught immediately. She'd watched her father and her cousin William take such actions to delay their response in conversations. It worked well. She warmed her hands over the exuberant flames for a few moments, then turned to face her guest.

Suzette's eyes met Maureen's. "I've never felt this way about a man."

"Suzette, I must tell you." No, that was the wrong thing to say. She took a deep breath, then tried again. "I assume your marriage to Monsieur St. Aubin is not a love match, but I believe what you're feeling for Vespasian is passion, not love. Vespasian's told me he feels … he feels a similar passion for you."

"And if we pretend to be cousins …"

Exasperated, Maureen threw up her hands. "Pretending to be cousins—or even if you were actual cousins—doesn't change anything. What if your husband discovers your deceit? What you're contemplating is quite different than sneaking out to have tea with forward-thinking ladies."

Suzette began to sob uncontrollably. Maureen sat beside her and patted her hand but she was growing a little irritated with her guest and the situation. What had she done? She had helped the pair spend time together. Just once. And no more.

It took a long time for Suzette's tears to subside.

"You're quite upset. Why don't you stretch out on the sofa here? I'll get a blanket and you can rest. You need to calm down before you go home."

"That's very sweet, Maureen. Perhaps … perhaps I will lie down." With that, Suzette slipped off her shoes, lay on her side on the sofa and brought her feet under her skirts. When Maureen returned and placed the cover over her, Suzette, already drowsy, whispered a thank you and shut her eyes.

Her guest asleep, Maureen went back to the greenhouse. She put on her gloves and apron and began digging up the white azalea bush she'd stolen yesterday from the *Hailong Hao*. In minutes, she found a tin of opium in the roots. She crept into the sunroom to see that Suzette's eyes were still closed, then returned to her task. She opened the tin to be certain. Yes, it was the same sticky brown substance she'd found in the camellia. After replacing the top, she hid it under some fabric scraps beside the first tin.

Ben, Ben, what is going on?

All Captain Kwan's plants must have opium tins buried in the roots. It seemed Ben bought plants, removed the opium, smoked it, and then gave her the plants. There was no other explanation.

Her mind jumped from Ben's opium addiction to her father's distrust of him, to Vespasian whom she was supposed to be giving every opportunity to woo her. But Vespasian loved Suzette whose husband threw vases when she asked to go with him on a trip. What would the man do when he caught his wife in Vespasian's arms?

Maureen came to a snap decision. If she allowed Suzette to spend the week with her while her father went to Boston, while both her husband and the cheerless butler were working elsewhere, Suzette might blossom into a more joyful woman. In the meantime, Maureen could try to talk some sense into her regarding her affection for Vespasian.

Chapter Twenty-Three

On Tuesday morning early, Maureen kissed her father good-bye, promised to take care of the household and let out a sigh as she watched the carriage turn out the front gate. She wouldn't see him tonight as he intended to go straight to the station following work. Not ten minutes after seeing her father off, she received a note and laughed out loud as she read:

Dear Maureen, The train leaves the station in twelve more hours. On Tuesday night, I arrive bearing flowers. Your servant, Ben

Running up to her sitting room, she placed it in her lap desk with Ben's other notes—two on Saturday, four on Sunday, and four on Monday, in which he humorously counted down the hours until her father's departure.

When Suzette arrived with her lady's maid, Alice, Maureen gave her an hour to settle into her room and then suggested she help her in the greenhouse. They planted seeds in the sandbox, trimmed ferns, and fertilized elephant ears. Her houseguest seemed particularly eager to follow the progress of the grafted camellias. All were thriving. A callus had formed on the stems at the graft sites and the leaves on the shoots protruding from the white root stems were still green, a very good sign.

Suzette squealed with delight when Guy brought in a passion flower and placed it in the center of the workbench. Quite large, its vines wrapped around two bamboo poles that stood at least five feet tall. Its innumerable white flowers with purple filaments enthralled her. The note snuggled between the vines said simply: *See you very soon.*

Suzette was convinced Mr. Merritt sent it to convey his passion. Maureen hoped so, but she explained quite a different reason for the plant's name to her guest. "It reminded missionaries in America in the 1500s of Christ's passion. Each flower's crown resembled the crown of thorns. The five stamens symbolized the five wounds of Christ. The ten petals were the faithful apostles, excluding Judas, the betrayer, and Peter, the first pope."

Suzette giggled. "Oh, honestly. Mr. Merritt doesn't know all that. I tell you, he means the flower to symbolize his passion." She smiled slyly.

Passion. Maureen wanted to experience passion with Ben. She recalled the pressure of his chest against her back, the strength of his arm across her waist, the night he slept beside her. He had climbed the balcony to her room, not to seduce her but to comfort her. For the first time in her life, she realized there was something *more* than passion. She knew Ben was a man who understood that need.

"Why don't I leave you alone with him? He's so handsome." Suzette sighed. "I'll go to my room the minute he arrives. I suspect without me, you and he will find plenty to entertain you."

Caught in her reverie, Maureen nodded. She felt her face grow hot and could barely speak. "Don't put ideas in my head."

"I suspect they were already there—in his head at least, if not in yours."

"I think it'd be better if you read in the back parlor while I visit with Mr. Merritt in the front room. Papa wouldn't approve of anything else."

In fact, her father wouldn't approve of Ben being in the house at all.

"Oh, please, Maureen! Trust me, you don't want to do your father's bidding when it comes to suitors. My father laid down the law that I was to marry St. Aubin and I agreed to marriage too quickly." Suzette picked up the watering can and approached the ferns. "Much too quickly."

Maureen truly wished Suzette would stop revealing every thought that drifted through her head. These personal discussions made her uncomfortable.

Distracted, Suzette drowned a maidenhair fern in a rush of water. "I have a rich husband. I have a big house and servants, but he's stingy with me."

Oh, heavens. More complaints. "You're always so stylish," Maureen said quickly.

"I have accounts, but I can't overspend them."

"There's nothing unusual about that," Maureen answered, adopting the soothing voice that she realized she was always using with this woman. "I can't overspend the budget set by my father either." Actually she had signed for amounts far over the limit many times since she'd returned from Atlanta. He'd never scolded her. Once or twice he'd suggested she be "sensible in her purchases." That was all.

"And if you do, does he … does your father scream and throw objects at you and forbid you to shop for a month?"

Maureen turned from the workbench and faced Suzette. "My father's never thrown anything at me in my life. Or at my mother, I'm sure."

Suzette's lips trembled. "When he's angry, Monsieur throws whatever he has in his hand. A book, a candlestick, a wine glass. A full bottle of wine once."

Maureen gasped loudly. *How did she live with him?* No wonder the poor woman couldn't get through a conversation without crying.

Shrugging, Suzette continued. "He's often angry. It seems I never please him. He wants me to look beautiful, my hair dressed just so, my dresses perfect. But how can I when he curtails my purchases?" She pulled a handkerchief from her pocket and sighed. "You know, it's not easy looking your best on a small budget."

Was this woman out of her mind? Her husband threw objects at her—objects that might injure her terribly—yet she focused on looking good on a limited budget?

Crossing the room, she patted Suzette on the shoulder and took up the fashion problem—much easier to deal with than a violent husband. "Monsieur St. Aubin sounds completely unreasonable. And a Frenchman, too. He should know that a lady needs both time and money to look beautiful."

Like all refined ladies, Maureen never discussed her clothing allowance with anyone, not even the Bouchards. And she wouldn't dare ask what Suzette's husband allowed her to spend. Monsieur St. Aubin appeared to be rich—he imported coffee from Jamaica, he had a sugar plantation up the river—and their New Orleans house was beautifully furnished. Perhaps he was heavily in debt. Maybe he couldn't pay his wife's bills in a timely manner. That might explain his stinginess.

What a fool he was. In Maureen's experience—from what she'd observed in Atlanta and New Orleans—an older man with a beautiful young wife generally indulged her every whim to keep her happy.

"Let's finish with the watering." She pointed to the next two pots and watched the amount of water Suzette poured on each.

As she tilted the watering can, Suzette spoke softly. "I believe I'd like to go to bed with Vespasian."

Good God! They'd had this discussion not three days ago! To be fair, Maureen herself had said nearly those exact words to Renee Desselle almost a year ago, about the very same man. It was that same idea that led her to spend a night in Vespasian's company, however chaste it turned out to be.

"You're a married lady, Suzette," Maureen began. "You must think this through before you act. You must wait … until, until. Well, if you love Vespasian and he loves you, you must leave your husband and marry him."

Suzette shook her head slowly. "I can't leave him."

"It's not as unusual as it once was for a wife to leave a husband."

She pursed her lips. "I've not had his child, Maureen, but not for lack of trying. He comes to my bed every night when he's home."

Maureen didn't need to hear these details. She was fast losing her patience and they were less than one full day into their week together.

"A consummated Catholic marriage is binding forever," Suzette whispered. She raised her handkerchief to her eyes and this time tears overflowed.

"Now, now." Maureen patted her shoulder. "How about a cup of tea? Julia brought it in some time ago. I'll pour. Come over to the table."

Continuing to cry, she joined Maureen, who dutifully poured her a cup and pushed it toward her. "There are cheese straws and sugar cookies here. Would you like something?"

Not looking up, Suzette lifted her teacup just as Maureen moved the plate. The plate sent the cup flying into Suzette's lap. She clutched at it, saving it from rolling and smashing on the floor. The tea left a large stain spreading across the front of her gray wool skirt.

Maureen jumped up, a napkin in her hand, and dabbed at the skirt. "You're not burned, are you?"

"I'm all right; it's thick wool. I'm sorry, I'm just not myself." She began a new round of sobbing.

"Luz is very good at removing any sort of stain. She'll show Alice how she does it. I'll lend you a dry skirt."

"Thank you. I'll change and then rest for a while."

Maureen led her upstairs, took a skirt from her own wardrobe—her favorite plum skirt that she'd worn when she and Ben decorated Renee's house. She brought it to Suzette's room. "Don't you have a shirtwaist to go with it?" Suzette asked.

Surprised, Maureen went to her wardrobe again and plucked out three more shirtwaists to lend to Suzette. Then, glad to be alone for a while, she returned to the greenhouse. She glanced at her watch. Nearing three o'clock. Five more hours before Ben arrived, bearing flowers. Surely he'd be prompt.

Unfortunately, the clanging bell on the front porch at eight signaled not Ben's arrival, but Vespasian's. The threesome shared drinks and conversation for at least an hour. Maureen grew restless with the small talk. The "Cousin this, Cousin that" became so tiresome she was ready to scream, just as she had been at Antoine's.

Excusing herself, she settled on a sofa in the front room to read, leaving the pair in the back parlor. In thirty minutes, she hadn't turned a page of her book. Her emotions ranged from annoyed to angry to worried. Did Ben forget? He couldn't possibly have. Did he stay late at the office? If so, the least he could do was send a note to her. Or had Ben had an accident on the docks again? Was he so foolish as to roam that area of town after dark to find a new plant for her again? Opium for himself?

Each time she looked up from her book, Suzette and Vespasian were gazing into each other's eyes and whispering back and forth. Occasionally a giggle reached her ears.

Ben Merritt was far handsomer, far more mature and serious. But Vespasian, fun-loving and glib, could cast a spell on women with his smile and his kisses. But what sort of husband would Vespasian be? If somehow Suzette were able to divorce Monsieur St. Aubin and marry him, would Vespasian make her happy? Would he grow tired of her and take a mistress? Poor Suzette. Maureen feared there would be no happy ending to this particular love story.

At nine-thirty, Vespasian excused himself, saying he was exhausted from work and had an early appointment tomorrow. He gave each lady a kiss on the hand, and took his leave.

The minute the door shut, Maureen turned to Suzette. "Shall we go to bed? I have a slight headache."

"I do hope Mr. Merritt hasn't taken ill," Suzette said as they climbed the stairs.

The comment galled Maureen no end. Was Suzette genuinely worried about Ben? Was it a deliberate barb to hurt her? Suzette, a married woman, enjoyed an attentive beau. Maureen, single and available, sat alone all evening.

"I suspect Mr. Merritt was delayed at work. They're quite demanding at his firm. I'm sure I'll hear from him in the morning." She said a quick goodnight in the upstairs hall and went to her room.

Ben was aware that the hour was growing late, but he forced himself to be patient with the tailor who was fitting him for his Mardi Gras costume. Blindfolded so he couldn't see the fabric or the design—or his watch—he stood in his long johns as the tailor pinned material together at his shoulders, under his arms and at his waist. But when the man knelt at groin level and began pulling and pinning cloth between his legs, he lost all control.

"Damn it! Am I being clad in a diaper? What on earth?"

"Stop complaining, Ben. You're one of the fruits ..."

"A fruit?" he shouted. "A fruit, Captain?"

"That's correct, sir," the tailor said amiably while the Captain, the honorary name given to the leader of the Mardi Gras krewe, laughed uproariously. "The costume buttons at the crotch, sir. I do beg your pardon. Be still."

Ben locked his legs in a wide stance and didn't move a muscle while the Captain placed a glass of whiskey in his hand and reminded him he might happily drink his fill while the tailor worked. His lower body immobile, Ben moved his hand to his mouth, and swallowed two glasses of straight whiskey before the fitting ended.

He stepped from his costume, and allowed the Captain to lead him by the hand into the dressing room where he removed his blindfold. At last, Ben donned his street clothes.

He had not seen Maureen for four days. Tonight, he'd planned to ask Suzette to leave them alone. No suitor, however ardent, could come calling at ten o'clock. He didn't knock on the front door. Neither did he sneak through the side yard as he had done the time he spied on Maureen and Vespasian.

Tonight, carrying a large *jasminum nudiflorum* in a heavy pot, he strode around the side of the house, straight across the lawn—avoiding the bushes in fact—and straight up to the greenhouse door. A gaslight at the kitchen door illuminated the path. He was surprised to see the greenhouse and the sunroom dark. He'd hoped to find her there, but he supposed Maureen had darkened the house and retired to teach him a not-subtle lesson in the consequences of tardiness.

He knew she left a key under a flowerpot by the backdoor so the gardener could come in and out for fertilizer, watering cans and such. He could let himself in and put the plant on the workbench. Or he could leave it outdoors. He'd been told the plant was winter hardy by a nurseryman north of the city—a man who didn't put opium in the roots. He could attach a note and go home.

Ben placed the heavy bush on the ground and lifted the overturned flowerpot. No key.

He put his forehead on the glass and peered in. He thought he saw movement in the shadows. Did the huge elephant ears in the back of the room sway? No breeze in Maureen's sanctuary stirred the plants' leaves; birds and insects didn't land on delicate stems, causing them to dip with their weight. The stillness contributed to her room's charm.

Focusing on the elephant ears, Ben made out a man's shoulders—shoulders clad only in a white shirt—through the green fronds. He couldn't see anything more—not his head, which was hidden by the foliage—or the rest of his body. From the height of the shoulders, the body was kneeling on the floor.

Straining to see more, he watched a lady's delicate fingers reach up and grasp the white cloth of the male's shoulder. A bit of plum ruffled skirt floated upward among the giant deep green leaves.

He knew that skirt. It was Maureen's.

Chapter Twenty-Four

*B*lind with rage, Ben gripped the doorknob and pushed hard. The lock popped and the door swung open.

The shoulders, the skirt again. A man in a white linen shirt lifted Maureen's skirt. He ran down the aisle toward the couple. It seemed he watched the scene from some distant height, looking down on himself as he rushed toward people who thought they were sharing a private moment.

His shouts echoed off the glass walls and roof. "How dare you touch her!"

A woman screamed. Not Maureen. In his confusion, Ben took two more steps, saw Colville's face turn upward in horror. He tried to cover his partner with his body, but Ben grabbed his shirt collar and yanked him backwards, exposing the lady, whose wide green eyes stared up in surprise. Wearing nothing but Maureen's plum skirt, Suzette lay on her back, her arms crossed to cover her bare breasts.

Colville elbowed Ben in the chest, taking his breath away. He returned the blow with a slam into his rival's jaw, then swiveled away from the couple, so his back was to them.

"Madame St. Aubin, Colville, I apologize for the intrusion."

"Good God, Merritt. Can't a gentleman and lady have privacy without some lunatic attacking them?"

"I came to see Maureen," Ben said as if that were sufficient explanation for entering a dark greenhouse after ten o'clock.

He heard scuffling and presumed the pair was on their feet and clothed. Colville snarled. "The front door of the home is the generally accepted portal when calling on a lady."

His voice managed to convey both disappointment in his interrupted assignation and utter disgust that another male would be so inconsiderate.

"So it is, Colville," Ben snapped. "And if I'm not mistaken, the generally accepted venue for adultery is the male's or female's bedchamber, not the floor in a friend's greenhouse."

"Please go, Merritt, before you wake the household."

"Go to hell, Colville," he hissed. "I'm not leaving until I see Maureen."

"Maureen went to bed with a headache some time ago." Suzette's calm voice indicated no embarrassment. The three might be sitting together in the parlor.

"Maureen left you two alone in her greenhouse? I don't believe that."

Just then a light went on in the sunroom. Maureen called out: "Who's there? What's going on in here?"

"Miss Maureen," Ben yelled. "I'm here to see you." He stalked toward her, flicking an elephant ear from his path.

"I heard voices."

The sight of her standing in the sunroom's doorway, pulling her dressing gown close about her and knotting it under her breasts made him want her more than he thought possible. He stared. Maureen locked eyes with him for a second.

He waved his arm, motioning to the couple behind him. "You did hear voices."

Her mouth dropped open in surprise as she took in the lovers. He hoped they'd arranged their clothes properly at this point.

Bounding down the steps, she stopped beside Ben, and glared at them.

"What are you two doing here? Suzette, I thought you went to bed …"

Ben turned. Suzette's blouse was on, even buttoned up the front, but her hairpins were long gone and her mussed hair hung in matted strands past her shoulders. Colville wore his coat, but his cravat dangled from his pocket and the top two buttons of his trousers remained unfastened.

"I can't believe it!" Maureen's voice conveyed her fury. "I trusted you to visit each other—*in my presence.*"

Ben admired her raised voice as she emphasized each word.

"Vespasian, I trusted you to … to meet with Suzette, but not to …" She stopped.

A smirk on his face, Colville came forward, leading Suzette by the hand. "What did you think we were going to do together? Play another hand of whist? Have another glass of sherry in the front parlor?"

Maureen bit her lower lip. "I thought … I thought it was harmless when I allowed this meeting tonight. I was your chaperone. But you lied to me and played me for a fool."

Colville rolled his eyes, then spoke as someone might to a child. "Suzette is a married lady …"

"Which is precisely my point!" Maureen shouted. "You know what, Vespie? You're going to get yourself killed and when that day comes, you're going to deserve it."

Colville laughed. Totally love-stuck, Suzette stood quietly, her eyes fixed with adoration on her man.

Maureen dropped her voice. "How could you? This is my house. And this is my special room. My greenhouse. Here of all places? You're despicable." She looked like she was about to strike him.

Unmoved, Colville turned away and faced Suzette. He ran his fingers down her cheek before he glanced toward Maureen again. "I believe I made my intentions regarding Suzette clear to you. And you *do* owe me, remember?" He raised an imperious eyebrow.

The man had nerve. What could Maureen possibly owe him? His blood boiling, Ben stepped in front of Maureen, separating the two.

"Leave it there, Colville," he ordered. "And get out right now." He nodded at the door to the garden.

Colville moved that way, bringing Suzette with him. Ben grabbed her arm. "You, Madame, go straight up to your bedroom. You and your hostess will discuss this further in the morning."

Suzette looked up at Colville.

"Do as he says."

She stomped from the room, not looking back. Colville exited through the greenhouse door.

Maureen and Ben remained side by side as if they still faced the other couple.

"She's wearing your skirt." Ben bit off the words.

"I lent it to her."

"When I saw his shoulders and the hem of your skirt, I ... I would have killed him."

"Vespasian came calling, but left almost an hour ago. Suzette and I went up to bed."

"So you thought."

"The absolute audacity," she muttered.

He put his hands on her shoulders and turned her to face him. With his thumb, he touched her cheek. When she didn't flinch or step back, he pushed her hair away from her face, tucking it behind her ears. "I'm so sorry I was late. I needed to see you."

She nodded. The only light came through the glass roof from the moon, from the gaslight outside by the kitchen door and one lamp in the sunroom. Maureen's pale skin glowed and her eyes sparkled as brilliantly as the stars above. Her dressing gown, a paisley wool of gold, pink and turquoise, fell to her ankles, but it revealed every curve of her body.

"I have a surprise for you. Don't move." He raced to the door, returned with the winter jasmine and placed it on the workbench.

"It's beautiful." She touched several of the small yellow flowers and a genuine smile turned the corners of her lips up. "You're spoiling me shamelessly. I know it's a jasmine. What kind exactly?"

"My source tells me the genus is *Jasminum*." He spelled out the species n-u-d-i-f-l-o-r-u-m. "It'll climb on a trellis ten feet high. You can plant it anywhere outside and it'll grow and flower all winter."

She smiled now until her dimples showed. Her cheeks turned pink. "Perhaps we could visit for a few minutes."

Ben offered his arm and led her back up the brick stairs. She paused to lock the adjoining door to the greenhouse behind them.

Without asking, she poured them each a glass of Collins whiskey while admitting she was disappointed in Suzette. When she sat on the sofa, he joined her. His thigh touched hers. And she wore no layers of petticoats.

"Her husband and her butler believe she and Vespasian are cousins," she went on, "so Suzette's allowed to see him."

"How'd you get involved?"

Maureen looked away and focused on the base of her crystal glass. In law school, he'd studied evasive techniques among men and women being questioned about crimes. Maureen wanted to avoid this discussion.

Ben didn't want her to have her way just now. He repeated his question, changing the how to why.

Words tumbled from her lips. "I felt sorry for Suzette. Her husband gives her very little freedom."

"You should send her packing tomorrow." His tone sounded harsher than he intended. Maureen said nothing. He took a gulp of whiskey.

"Why did Colville say you owed him?"

Maureen wasn't surprised by his question. From the moment Vespasian uttered the words, she knew Ben would ask.

"An old childhood game. We used to race each other in the country—horse races—and whoever lost had to do a favor for the winner. Last time we raced," she paused for a moment to think through her story, "it must have been four or five years ago, Vespie won. So ..."

Ben frowned. "He still thinks you owe him a favor?"

"I suppose," she said airily.

They both raised their glasses to their lips. She couldn't tell Ben the truth. She wanted to. Oh, heavens, she'd like nothing better than to blurt out the details of her night in Vespasian's library, her need to keep Vespasian quiet because she loved *him*—Ben Merritt.

"A favor such as arranging a time and place to bed Suzette?"

"I ... I ..." She stopped. She couldn't defend herself, couldn't tell him she was blackmailed. "I like her. I like Suzette, and I believe Vespie truly loves her." She focused her eyes on her pink cloth slippers and could feel him watching her intently. Did he think he could pry open her skull and discover her thoughts merely by staring? "Suzette's husband is horrid," she murmured.

"From what I understand, he's a vicious man."

His words startled her. "Suzette says that, but how would *you* know?"

He adopted the matter-of-fact tone she'd noticed he always used when discussing his work. "St. Aubin has a reputation of being unusually cruel to his crew. He owns several ships and his captains follow his orders to beat his sailors for minor infractions. Which is why I'm worried that you're involved with this despot and his wife. It's not safe. If you really care about Vespasian ..."

Her eyes stung with tears, but she blinked them away. "I didn't, Ben, I didn't get involved. Vespie asked me to …"

"Don't call him Vespie," he snapped. "*Please*."

"He asked me to arrange meetings so he could get to know Suzette."

Slapping both hands against his thighs, Ben laughed. "Are you that naïve? There's only one reason a man like Colville wants to be with a woman."

She bit her lower lip to stop it from trembling. He handed her his handkerchief. She dried her cheeks and held on to it, clenching her hand around it.

"Vespie … Vespasian has been a good friend to me my whole life."

He rolled his eyes. "All the more reason to tell him you don't want any part of it. If Suzette's a friend of yours, you should be thinking about her, too." He ran his hand through his hair. "I think you should warn Vespasian about St. Aubin. He might have him killed. And God knows what he might do to his wife."

Ben's words chilled her blood. She'd initially agreed to Vespasian's scheme because she wanted Ben to think her an innocent young lady and love her. Because she loved him. She should tell him, she should.

His icy tone broke into her thoughts. "Was it Colville who taught you to kiss?"

Maureen's face grew hot. Ben had been a far better kissing instructor than Vespasian ever had. "I believe it was you who taught me everything I know, Mr. Merritt."

"I wish that were so," he shot back.

"And who taught you your skills, Mr. Merritt?"

A scowl on his face, he stood, bowed slightly and spoke in a very controlled voice. "I believe it's time to say good-night."

Chapter Twenty-Five

She couldn't let Ben go. Jumping off the sofa, Maureen flew past him, turned and blocked the door. Lifting her chin, she stiffened her back, and folded her arms across her chest.

"You're right. Deep down I knew Vespie might try to seduce her, but she's an adult and so is he. Who are you to tell me what's moral or not? You're not exactly an exemplar of all that's good and holy yourself."

His eyes met hers in a cold stare.

"Why didn't you tell me I'd spread opium on my camellias? Why'd you pretend it was fertilizer?"

He bristled with indignation. "The brown beads? They weren't fertilizer?"

She sniffed. "I know a lie when I hear it, Mr. Merritt. Vespie— and I'll call him Vespie if I like—told me it was opium. When I showed him the tin I found in the roots, he said you were probably an opium smuggler."

Ben's jaw clenched, his face turned stern. "I'm *not* an opium smuggler." He spat out the words as if he'd eaten a piece of rotten fish.

"I figured that much out by myself, Mr. Merritt. A smuggler wouldn't have given me a camellia with opium in the roots. So I've had no choice but to conclude you're an opium addict."

She paused for a moment to search his face, but he remained studiously impassive. "Once you knew Captain Kwan was a smuggler—because I showed you the opium on my plant—you had a supplier for your habit. For weeks, you've been buying plants and digging the opium from the roots before you gave them to me."

"I've done no such thing."

"Don't," she retorted. "Do you think I didn't realize you'd tampered with the rose roots? Or the geraniums, asters, bachelor's buttons? Every plant since the first camellia."

He met her eyes. "I'm afraid I can't comment."

She dropped her voice very low; he responded by leaning forward, closer to her, almost bringing his ear to her lips.

"Please tell me what—" She stopped in mid-sentence. His lime scent distracted her. She wanted to ask a dozen questions, but she didn't.

He pursed his lips together for a moment. "I swear to you. I'm not a smuggler and I'm not an addict. That's all I can tell you."

She couldn't bear it. "Well, I need more." *He couldn't tell her?* Why not? He was a scoundrel after all, and yet she loved him. Her heart dropped. How had this happened to her? Tears rolled down her cheeks and tasted salty in her mouth. She wiped her face with his handkerchief again.

"You must trust me."

"Trust you?" Swallowing hard, she managed to whisper. "Then you have to trust me. Vespie and I are friends. *Nothing* more."

They glared at each other.

In the dim light, her eyes pooling with tears were the deepest blue he'd ever seen. He knew he shouldn't kiss her, but he couldn't stop himself. He put his hands on her cheeks and brought her face closer. When he pressed his lips to hers, he breathed in the smell of roses in her hair and on her skin. He was lost. He planted kisses on her eyelids, her earlobes and finally returned to her mouth. He ran his hands up and down her back, then gripped her waist. "Come."

Never loosening his hold, he stepped backwards and her feet followed. She smiled shyly as they inched across the room until the sofa pressed against the back of his legs. He sat and pulled her into his lap. "I have to kiss you again."

Her lips parted, welcoming his tongue. She toyed with it as she'd done in the library. He didn't care at this moment who'd taught her to do that. He didn't care that she was lying to him. He'd been a saint in her bedroom the other night, but not tonight. Not tonight.

He paused now and then to ask if she liked a particular kiss, if she liked a slow, teasing kiss or a hard one. Did she like him to blow on her earlobe or lick it? Did she enjoy a nibble on her neck? She giggled between her answers.

He shifted so they lay facing each other, her back to the velvet upholstery, his to the room. "I'm about to fall off," he said softly. "One false move and I'll be on the floor."

That brought a dimple-cheeked smile. He dropped a kiss on her forehead.

"There's a solution to our dilemma. Will you straddle me?"

"I ..."

"I take your hesitation as a no." He slipped onto the floor and knelt beside her. Gently he moved her body onto her back in the center of the sofa, then lay on top of her, resting most of his weight on his elbows. "Is that better?"

He suggested she kiss him anywhere she chose. She put her lips to his, enjoying the taste of whiskey, the smell of lime, the scent she'd loved since the first night she met him. Maureen explored his mouth with her tongue and delighted in the moans she elicited from him. He dropped his body lower on hers. His arousal pressed hard against her belly for a few moments and she felt pleased with herself for eliciting such a reaction. But when he slid lower against her tender folds, she gasped.

"Ben!"

"Ssh. Does it feel good?"

It did. Oh, dear, it felt wonderful. She wanted him closer still. Grasping the hems of her robe and gown, she tugged them up to her waist and spread her legs, cradling him between them. No drawers, no petticoat or nightgown.

She bent one knee and then the other. His hard ridge fit against the most sensitive spot on her body. His wool trousers rubbed against her. Feeling wanton, she wrapped her legs around his waist, pulling him tighter against her.

"I'm not wearing drawers ..."

"And no corset."

They laughed together. His fingers opened her robe and danced under the crocheted bodice of her nightgown, inching down the slope of her breast until he touched a bare nipple. She jumped. He lifted his hand.

"Let me try that again. I think you'll like it."

She thrust her chest upward and pulled the fabric off her shoulders.

"How gorgeous!" His eyes gleamed as he lowered his mouth to her left nipple, licking, nibbling, rolling his tongue across it. His hot lips heated her whole body as they closed around one breast and then the other. Her breathing came in pants.

The front door opened and closed with a slam. A man's boots thundered on the hall's wood floor.

She froze, but Ben jumped to his feet, pulled her to a sitting position, and whirled to face the door as her father entered.

"Maureen Collins!" His shout shook the window panes. "What in God's name?"

"Papa!" she shrieked. "You're home!"

No one spoke for a second. Ben, flushed to the roots of his hair, held a book at his waist. Her face so hot it could only be beet red, she clutched the top of her robe closed as if her life depended on it.

Her father's face terrified her. His eyes protruded, his nostrils flared, his mouth contorted in a snarl. He turned to Ben. "Get out, Merritt."

She'd never heard such an angry roar from his father's lips.

"Mr. Collins, sir." Ben bowed. "I'd like to ask …"

Her father's breath came in convulsive spits and starts. "Don't say another word," he ground out.

Ben continued anyway. "I'd like to ask you for your daughter's hand in marriage."

Seething, her father hissed. "Get out now."

Ben didn't move.

"Now, Merritt," he bellowed.

"I want your assurance you won't hurt Maureen."

That did it. His eyes bored into Ben's. "Sir, your insolence magnifies my displeasure at finding you here with my daughter." He waved his arm in Maureen's direction. "My daughter who's not dressed to receive anyone."

Ben nodded. "A prowler disturbed Colville in the greenhouse moments ago …"

"Frankly, sir, I'm not interested in stories." He motioned him toward the hall. Ben bowed to her and slipped out. She listened to the men's steps as they walked toward the front door. Ben spoke loudly enough for her to hear. "I've asked Maureen to marry me. She said yes."

He hadn't, but if he had, she would have said yes. Ben knew it. She loved Ben Merritt. And he must love her, right? For certain, they both loved what they were doing together when her father arrived home.

"She's engaged to Colville," her father spit out. "And if you ever darken my door again, I'll have you arrested or I'll kill you with my bare hands."

The front door slammed and the boots hit the floorboards in a rapid march. For a brief moment, she thought of running through the greenhouse and out the back door. She must sit still and hear her father's lecture. But she would never marry Vespasian. She and Ben would marry—no matter what her father said.

Too frightened to cry, Maureen bit her lip and raised her eyes to her father's face when he entered.

"It's difficult to speak to you right now, Maureen." He maintained better control of his emotions and his voice without Ben in the room. His eyes pierced her for a moment and then turned away in disgust. She'd disappointed him more terribly than she'd ever done before. He'd caught her in her dressing gown alone with a man.

"Don't say a word. Don't interrupt me. I won't listen to any excuse for this behavior."

She swallowed hard and nodded.

"You've willfully disobeyed my orders since Christmas Day." He held up his fingers and counted off her offenses. "One, you promised you would give Vespasian a chance to court you and prove his worth. I've seen no evidence of it. Quite the contrary. Two, after your adventure at the docks, I forbade you to see Ben Merritt. And what happens? The train is delayed and then canceled. I come home and find him in my house with my daughter."

"He didn't ..." She hesitated, took a breath, and got the words out. "We didn't do anything improper, Papa." Even as she spoke she felt the heat rise from her neck and spread up her cheeks to her forehead.

Her father took a deep breath. "I've heard that from you before. And I don't believe you."

She swallowed before she could speak. "He asked me to marry him. I love him. He loves me."

He ignored her. "You will marry Vespasian Colville in the spring. It's nearly Mardi Gras. You can't marry during Lent. I'll post a letter to Helene and Emile in the morning and suggest the first Saturday in May for your wedding. The weather should be perfect by then."

"Papa, you can't."

His narrowed eyes turned back to her. "I'm your father. I can and I will."

"I don't love Vespasian."

"That's no longer important," he snapped. After a few moments of silence, he went on. "I admit that I'm at a loss in these matters without your mother, but I've given you free rein and now, lass, I will not stand by and have you compromised by some slick Philadelphia lawyer. It's my duty as your father to see you make a good match."

"Vespasian isn't ..."

"Silence!"

She fixed her eyes on her slippers. Her father stared into the fire. "What would your mother think? Frankly, I'm afraid she might consider you a disgrace to all the women in your family. Vespasian will love you and support you in fine style."

Her heart thudding in her chest, her cheeks burning, Maureen hadn't the energy to fight him. She didn't pout. Didn't cry. She wanted to run away to her room, but wasn't sure she could even stand.

"I'm leaving tomorrow morning for Boston. I expect you to follow my wishes. Vespasian will call every evening for supper. Start shopping for a trousseau. Now go to bed."

With trembling legs, she climbed the stairs. She stopped in the upstairs sitting room for a few moments, picked up her lap desk, poured herself a glass of whiskey and went to her room. She felt relieved when she locked the door.

Maybe she wasn't alone? Could she hope? She went to the balcony, hung over the railing and scanned the landscape. No sign of Ben. Sad initially that she didn't find him in the wisteria bush, she thought better of it right away. Ben was too smart to climb in her window tonight. If her father caught him doing that, he might kill him. In her life, she'd never seen the man so angry, so out of control.

Sipping the whiskey, she pulled a sheet of paper from her desk, dipped her pen in the ink bottle and wrote quickly:

My dearest Ben,

It breaks my heart to tell you the outcome of tonight's events. My father is writing the Colvilles this very minute to set a date of Saturday, May 1st for my wedding to Vespasian. My intended groom will be as distraught as I am that my father is insisting this long-ago pact be honored.

Your explanation that we had a mutual agreement to wed, though intended I know, to make me appear less wanton in my father's eyes, did not achieve your goal. He said I must marry quickly before I lose my reputation.

He leaves tomorrow for Boston. I'm to shop for a trousseau while he is away. I will comply with his orders in that regard. However, I do not intend to marry Vespasian in May any more than he intends to marry me. It would be wretched to wed when our hearts belong to others.

I will go mad not seeing you this week, but I suggest we abide by my father's rules for the next seven days. I dare not disobey him while he's away. I'm sure he will have my Cousin William, Renee, Luz, Julia, Guy, and even Noah check up on me.

All my love,
Maureen

Chapter Twenty-Six

*S*uzette, sitting on the sofa, sobbed and buried her head in her hands. "I don't want to go home."

Maureen paced, steeling herself against the tears. Was that all this lady did? She cried at the mention of Vespasian. She cried at the mention of her husband. Maureen wanted to grab her by the shoulders and shake her silly.

She'd planned to keep an eye on Suzette while she lived under her roof. Yet, she and Vespasian had managed to sneak about under her watchful eye. Suzette wasn't the dumb one. She was.

She glanced at her guest—*still weeping*. Damn, she thought, but didn't say it. She couldn't let this go on for another moment. If she kept tramping from one end of the parlor to the other, she'd wear a hole in her mother's Persian carpet. Stopping directly in front of Suzette's chair, she repeated: "You must go back to your own home."

Suzette raised her head. "I hate my house. Claude Leveque will be back soon. The maids will tell him I stayed at your house and he'll tell Monsieur St. Aubin."

"He said you could see your cousin Vespasian, have him escort you about town."

She wailed again but cut it short when she saw Maureen's fierce look. "He never … actually said that," she whispered. "He forbade me to see almost anyone … most especially my cousin

Vespasian. St. Aubin knew Vespasian had called on me. Leveque told him."

Maureen put her hands on her hips and leaned forward, meeting Suzette's eyes. "Is there no end to your deception? You lied to me. I trusted you. How could you?" She was practically shouting.

"I knew if I said Monsieur St. Aubin approved, you would arrange another meeting. I'm sorry ... I'm sorry."

Maureen threw her hands up in exasperation. "What can I do with you?" She lowered her voice, not wanting Luz or Julia to hear. "I can't trust you to stay here." There, she'd said it. The meeting she'd set up at Desselle's Millinery, the lunch at Antoine's. All of this was her fault. What's more, Ben Merritt had witnessed the lovers in each other's arms. She, Maureen, had allowed that to happen.

"Vespasian started it when he came to call on me claiming to be my cousin."

That was the first honest sentence from Suzette's mouth since they'd become re-acquainted weeks ago. Maureen faced her again. "We've discussed the consequences of your feelings for Vespasian more than once. Surely I don't need to enumerate them again."

"We didn't make love last night." Suzette shook her head and—oh Lord—tears streamed down her cheeks again. "I asked him to," she whispered. "But he said I wasn't ready ..."

Maureen let out the breath she'd been holding for what seemed like a century.

"I'm grateful to you," Suzette went on softly. "Thank you for allowing Vespasian and me to see each other in your home. I understand you owed him a favor?"

Maureen wanted to grab her throat and choke her. Could Vespasian have told her she had helped the couple see each other in return for his silence about their night in his library? Surely not.

Suzette looked down, finding her hands suddenly fascinating. "I'll never breathe a word of it."

So Vespasian had told Suzette he had blackmailed her! Of all the nerve! "I owe Vespasian nothing," she hissed. "And I owe you nothing."

Sinking into a chair, Maureen took a deep breath and tried to think rationally. Suzette rarely left her house. She had no friends so she probably hadn't spoken to anyone about Maureen's night with Vespasian.

She closed her eyes for a moment. She had to get this woman out of her house, away from her, away from any opportunity to tell Ben or anyone he knew about her past.

The country.

"You have family you enjoy visiting. Why not go upriver to see them for a few days?"

Suzette's face brightened. "I could ... I could talk to my mother ..."

"Excellent." Maureen clapped her hands. "There's a boat going north every afternoon around three, I think. Noah can drive us to the dock. I'll pay your fare and Alice's, get the two of you on the boat, then send a telegram to notify your mother of your arrival time."

Maureen paused and swallowed, attempting to temper her enthusiasm. "I can also send a note to your household staff here telling them where you are."

"You'll do all that for me?"

"With pleasure." Maureen answered a bit too quickly, but Suzette didn't seem to notice.

But again, the lady's face turned solemn. "It's just ... well, Monsieur St. Aubin doesn't like me to go upriver to visit my family."

"Good God!" Maureen shouted. "He forbids that, too?"

Suzette's eyes squinted. Tears overflowed down her cheeks. *Again.*

"Then you must bribe Claude Leveque and your other servants to keep quiet about your activities while your husband is gone. Surely their loyalty is to you and your family, not to a foreigner."

"Leveque came from Martinique with Monsieur St. Aubin."

Maureen almost said *damn* out loud for the second time this morning. "What about the others?"

"I'd be afraid to try it. If my husband ever found out I paid the servants extra, he'd … I think he'd hurt me." Her voice dropped to a whisper. "I'm afraid of him."

Maureen sucked in her breath while Suzette clamped her hand over her own mouth. Her tears became torrential, like a New Orleans thunderstorm in August.

"Dear God," Maureen said out loud. She jumped from her chair, sat down beside Suzette and wrapped her arms around her shoulders. While Suzette wept, Maureen rocked her gently as Renee had taught her to do with the twins when they were fussy. She patted her hair and rubbed her back, all the while cooing softly that it'd be all right, that she'd think of a way to help her.

Suzette sputtered between her tears that sometimes Monsieur St. Aubin whipped her with a leather belt; that he slapped her now and then across the face; that he had made her nose bleed once or twice. That sometimes he tied her to the bedposts.

Nauseated, her head spinning, Maureen suggested they concentrate on getting her and Alice packed. The faster she put her on a steamer north, the better. She forced Suzette to hurry and, thank heavens, they just made the three o'clock boat. Never did Maureen feel better than when she gave Suzette a hug and promised to go to her house for her clothes and send them on the steamer tomorrow.

She spent the rest of the afternoon, trying to imagine Suzette's position. She couldn't picture what sort of terror a woman experienced when she feared her own husband, when the man who was supposed to protect her, harmed her.

How many men treated their wives this way? She'd never heard any gossip about such a thing in New Orleans or in Atlanta. Now that she was an adult and thinking of marriage to Ben Merritt every minute of every day, she decided to ask her father about such marriages when he returned home.

You wouldn't know you'd married such a cruel husband until you were under his protection, essentially owned by him. He could command you to do as he pleased. Was there a cruel streak in either of her suitors? The one she no longer wanted to marry or the one she did?

Vespasian loved women. He enjoyed spending time with females and he'd never hurt a woman. Of that, she was sure.

Ben? She shuddered. Did opium addicts turn violent after they smoked? She'd not seen him angry, except last night and she understood that seeing Vespasian's shoulders and her skirt together infuriated him.

She heard the door knocker slam. Vespasian and Guy talked in the front hall. She waited for Guy to summon her.

Vespasian jumped up from his chair when she entered the back parlor and took her hand. "Are you ill? This glum face is how you greet your betrothed?"

She glared at him. "It's no joking matter."

Vespasian led her to the sofa and suggested she sit at the end closest to the fire. "I came for supper per your father's orders that I'm to dine with you nightly, to court you. He left me a note on my desk." His unsaid words were written on his face. *And see Suzette.* At least he had the decency to not ask for her with his first words.

"Meanwhile, Ben's forbidden to be here per Papa Tyrant's orders to me."

Vespasian poured them two drinks. She watched him standing at the cellarette and spoke to his back. "Suzette has gone upriver to visit her family."

He whirled around at her words, disappointment clouding his face.

"I'll pour a double then."

He handed her a drink, stood in front of the fire and gulped his whiskey. "I know you were angry," he said, "but did you have to send her away?"

"Let's go to the greenhouse where we can talk."

The moment they sat down at the table there, Vespasian unfolded his tale. "Ben didn't interrupt actually." He put his glass down and ran a hand through his hair. "Suzette trembled in my arms—but not with excitement. She was terrified. She asked me to get it over with."

She bit her lower lip. "I know why."

"Not exactly what I'm used to hearing from ladies. She actually told me to do anything I wished to her. Not *with* her, *to* her," he went on. Then stopped. "What? You do?"

She hesitated because she'd never spoken of such things. She glanced behind her at the sunroom, leaned closer and lowered her voice. "Listen."

Her stern command got his attention. He stared at her, his eyes widening with every word she spoke. She ended with the worst. "Sometimes her husband ties her to the bedposts and whips her."

"Oh, my God!" The color drained from his face and he covered it for a moment with shaking hands. "My sweet Suzette," he choked. "What a horrible bastard."

"I guess her fear of him extends to all men, including you. And you'd be a fool not to tread carefully where this St. Aubin is concerned."

He stood and paced. "Now I understand why she lay on the floor like a ragdoll."

"Knowing what her husband does, I couldn't send her back to her house." Still hurt that the two had tricked her last night,

Maureen turned her head away from him and concentrated on taking a ladylike sip of her drink. "She can't be in that house with him again."

Vespasian sighed. "I'll find witnesses who'll testify at a divorce hearing. She'll stay in the country with her own family until an attorney files for divorce."

"Then you'll marry her?"

"That would solve our problem, wouldn't it?" A brief smile crossed his face. "Unfortunately, it may take several months." His hands dropped in resignation and despair. "If I can't orchestrate it by May 1st, I'll leave the country and your father will have no groom for you."

"Which will leave me broken-hearted, but free to marry the man I choose." She grabbed his hand, stood and met his eyes. "Suzette told me she knew I owed you a favor. I hope you didn't reveal ..."

He tightened his grip. "Surely you know me better than that. I told her you'd stolen liquor from your father's cellarette when you were a child and I threatened to tell him."

"I don't know whether I believe you or not, but it doesn't matter. I will never ..." She paused to get his full attention. "...be involved in another clandestine meeting between the two of you again. I don't care if you tell Ben you and I spent a night together in your library."

Chapter Twenty-Seven

A young maid swung open the front door of the St. Aubin home.

"Madame St. Aubin's not home," she snapped. "She's upriver, in the country."

Maureen nodded politely. "Yes, I know. I'm Miss Maureen Collins, a friend of Madame St. Aubin. This is Luz Bichet, my companion. I've been to call previously—Monsieur Leveque, the butler, may remember me."

Pausing, Maureen locked eyes with the young Negro servant, who continued to frown at the two women at her door.

"Monsieur Leveque is out, Miss."

"May we come in?"

"Yes'm, I suppose." She stepped aside and ushered them into the hall.

Maureen asked her name and addressed her. "Danielle, as you probably know, Madame St. Aubin was my houseguest earlier this week."

"Yes'm." The wary servant eyed them, clearly not sure she'd been wise to let them in.

"Madame Suzette's father is ill and her mother asked that she come. She left in a hurry from my house. She asked that I stop by, pick up some of her clothes and ship them to her."

"Yes'm, I know." She lowered her voice. "Just so you know. Monsieur Leveque is expected back within the hour."

Maureen took a deep breath and suggested she'd just run up to Suzette's room and gather a few items. Danielle hesitated, even longer than she had in admitting them to the house, but then said it was fine with her. That permission granted, Maureen had the temerity to go a step further.

"Is there a washwoman?"

The girl shot her a look and Luz filled in quickly. "Madame Suzette's maid Alice said she needs some items from the laundry."

"Just off the kitchen."

Maureen smiled apologetically. "I feel awkward being here, but I'm trying to help Madame Suzette. Perhaps Luz could fetch those items while I go upstairs."

"Madame's bedroom is the first door to the right at the top of the stairs.

"Thank you."

Danielle nodded toward Maureen, then spoke to Luz. "Follow me."

Maureen started up the stairs slowly, but the moment she heard Danielle and Luz leave the hall, she lifted her skirts and took the steps two at a time. Her actions would have horrified her dead mother.

There wasn't a lady in New Orleans who wouldn't love Suzette's bedroom. Maureen's eyes flew from the pink roses decorating the wallpaper to two windows hung with heavy damask curtains in a shade that matched the wall covering. A Persian carpet with rose and blue medallions covered the floor. Above the mantel hung a pastoral scene featuring a blonde, blue-eyed shepherdess in a pink dress amid her flock. A chair, upholstered to match the curtains and bedspread, sat close to the hearth, a sewing table beside it. A rosewood four-poster bed dominated the room. A large wardrobe, a bonnet cabinet and a marble-topped dresser belied Suzette's words. If these were even half-filled, her husband wasn't stingy.

Maureen crossed the room fast and yanked open the wardrobe's double doors. *Yes, he was.* Four dresses hung there: the plaid wool Suzette wore the day they met Vespasian at Desselle's; the green wool she wore when Maureen called on her; the pink silk with ruched bodice she wore to the tea party; one other formal dress, a dark green velvet, her Christmas dress, perhaps. Two skirts, four shirtwaists, two ball gowns—one she remembered from the Twelfth Night Revelers—completed her collection. Maureen grabbed the two dresses suitable for day wear, the two skirts and selected two shirtwaists, which she put on the bed.

Behind the second door, mostly empty shelves. This side housed only three pairs of shoes, two handbags, several pairs of gloves, a parasol and a tapestry valise. She selected a black pair of shoes and white gloves. Placing these on the bed with the valise, she hurried to the bonnet cabinet. Three hats. All from Desselle's. All beautiful and expensive. But for the wife of a wealthy planter, a decidedly paltry collection. She selected the blue hat Suzette had worn with the plaid dress, found a hatbox in the lower cabinet, and put it safely inside.

The lingerie in Suzette's dresser told a different story. The lace trim on her camisoles, nightgowns and even on her drawers spoke of large sums of money spent at the modiste. And the colors! Maureen had never seen red or black silk drawers with matching corsets! Why would a man want his wife to wear a red or black corset? Was it more alluring than white or pink? Did Monsieur St. Aubin purchase these undergarments in Jamaica or in France? She'd never seen such items for sale in New Orleans—at least not in the fine stores where she shopped. Perhaps in shops on Gallatine Street, which catered to prostitutes.

Not quite sure why, Maureen took black drawers and a black corset and placed them in the valise. A moment later, she withdrew the corset and held it up to her own body in the mirror. What would Ben think of her in this? She moved her hips from side to side until her face became quite red.

Maureen Collins, what are you doing going through another lady's undergarments? Suzette had asked for a few *dresses.* This truly was the craziest thing she'd ever done. It was far more serious than sneaking off with Vespasian to his house last year. She would have a very hard time explaining what business it was of hers to be in Suzette's underwear drawer.

The case packed, Maureen stood for a moment, unsure of her next move. She tiptoed to the hall threshold and heard no noise from downstairs. Luz was doing a superb job keeping Danielle occupied. The bedroom's other door, too large for a closet, probably opened to a bathroom or perhaps to her husband's room. Did she dare?

She turned the doorknob slowly, prayed the door wouldn't squeak as she pushed it, and found herself in a spacious bathroom with a tub, commode and sink. For sure, the door opposite led to his bedroom.

The master's room was the mirror image of Suzette's, but while every inch of hers spoke to a feminine sensibility, the decor of his was unabashedly masculine. From his red and gold striped wallpaper to red velvet curtains to a red leather chair in front of the fireplace to the painting over the mantel depicting hunting dogs and men on horseback, the room belonged to a man. She glanced at the four-poster bed, a dresser with a shaving stand, a wardrobe for his clothes. And just as in Suzette's room, every item was in place. No books lay open on the bedside table, no hairbrush was out of line on the dresser. No shoes or socks on the floor.

Maureen's nerves began to fail her. She shivered in the cold and then reminded herself that January in New Orleans made old houses damp and cold, particularly when no fire glowed in the grate. But her uneasiness went beyond temperature. She felt as if she were wandering through a stage set before the play began. Did anyone really live in these rooms?

She ran back through the bathroom, through Suzette's room to the hall doorway. She peered out and listened again. Absolute silence. No one cared what she did up here. Reassured, she hurried back into Monsieur St. Aubin's room and checked his belongings. In his wardrobe, her eyes swept across suit coats, starched shirts, waistcoats and trousers, dozens of them. Shoes lined his shelves. In his dresser, cotton union suits filled one drawer, socks another, dozens of cravats carefully folded in the next. How odd that he had more than enough clothes and Suzette—except for lingerie—owned almost none.

Furious with the man, Maureen swirled and glanced around the room one more time. His room contained a desk; his wife's didn't. She opened the drawer on the right and pulled out four pieces of rope, each about three feet long.

Oh, my God. Rope. Bedposts. Her mouth went dry. Still holding the rope, she stepped to the foot of the bed. Friction had rubbed the finish away down low on the bedposts. Indentations in the wood indicated repeated use. She glanced at the headboard and the posts on each side. Identical marks. *God help Suzette.*

Her hands shook; her lips trembled. She put the ropes back and slammed the drawer. She had no business in Monsieur St. Aubin's home, in his bedroom, and most especially in his desk drawers. Even so, she yanked open the left drawer, which contained only two black leather ledgers, about three-by-five inches each. She lifted one, opened to the first page and read:

December 1884
The Training of Suzette St. Aubin

She flipped back, close to the center:

Dec. 10, 1885

After a year under my tutelage, my dear Suzette becomes more docile by the day. Last week, I believe she enjoyed the ropes. She used to struggle and even run from me. But now she knows it's best to obey. I demand obedience. She stretches out her hands and feet and allows me to tie her without a whimper.

She dropped the book into the drawer and clutched her stomach as a wave of nausea swept her. She must go quickly and send a note to Vespasian. The man kept a journal of his atrocities.

With trembling hands, she picked up the second book. It contained dates and numbers, going back more than a year. A date, a number of pounds, and a total figure. Something to do with shipping. It might be valuable in assessing his wealth, in finding his weaknesses.

She heard voices and laughter from below. Clutching the account book to her chest, she shut the drawer with her hip and ran into Suzette's room. She knew she'd been upstairs way too long. She tossed the ledger in the valise and zipped it. She just made it down the stairs before Luz and Danielle appeared.

"There ya'll are." Her voice sounded somewhat normal, so she continued. "I've gathered just what Madame Suzette needs for another week or two in the country. Luz, did you get the other items Alice asked us to fetch?

"Yes, Miss Maureen, I did." She pointed to the basket over her arm, which contained folded underclothes and nightgowns. "I'll return the basket later."

"Thank you, Danielle," Maureen said as she put five nickels in her hand. "Madame St. Aubin asked me to give you something for your trouble."

The maid's mouth dropped in surprise, but she recovered quickly, closed her hand over the coins and pocketed them just as the front door opened.

Claude Leveque, in the formal clothing of an on-duty butler, scowled at Maureen. She did her best to nod and smile and explained quickly that Madame St. Aubin's father was taken suddenly ill; she'd seen her to the steamer yesterday and had come to retrieve the items of clothing she needed.

"So very sad Madame's father is ill." His expression and tone indicated he didn't believe the story for a second.

Maureen could scarcely breathe. Her upper lip trembled slightly. Did he notice? She offered him another smile and spoke as calmly as she could. "We must all do our best to help Madame Suzette."

"Yes, we must. Now if you have what you came for, we can say good afternoon, Miss."

He started toward her and she shrank back, fearing he'd take the valise away. But he gestured to the carriage outside. He offered his arm to escort her down the front steps, then handed her up. Were his hands icy cold or did she merely imagine feeling Monsieur Leveque's frigid hands through the leather of her gloves? Maureen thanked him, sat back against the cushions and shivered.

Luz climbed in without assistance and plunked down opposite her.

The moment the carriage pulled away from the banquette, Luz peppered Maureen with questions. "Did you get her clothes? You were upstairs a long, long time. I thought I'd never see you again. You got down just in the nick of time. What would Leveque have done if he'd found you upstairs?

What would he have done if he'd opened the valise and found the ledger? Tied her to the bed and left her there until Monsieur St. Aubin came home to punish her properly?

She trembled and bit her bottom lip.

"I tell you this, Miz Maureen. They scared to death of that man, Leveque. He writes down every word Madame say and every move she make. Danielle say the poor lady cries most of the day and night."

"That's good to know."

Luz shook her head. "Not for Madame Suzette!"

"I meant it's good others in the household know how cruel her husband is. It will help her obtain a divorce."

"Lots of men like that."

Not like this, I hope. She bit her lower lip.

Chapter Twenty-Eight

e'd not called on Maureen since the disastrous evening when he'd—when they'd—been caught with Maureen dressed in only a nightgown and robe. Following what Ben privately called *every young man's worst nightmare,* he'd be damned if he went anywhere within a thousand yards of the lady.

The only positive thing that his lonely evenings offered were endless hours to pursue his mission. After work Wednesday through Friday, he'd hired a horse, ridden to the last nurseries north of the city he needed to visit, bought plants and dug them up. No opium.

Three nights had passed since he'd seen her, and though he'd purposely exhausted himself, sleep eluded him. Friday night found him pacing a circle around his living room like a caged animal. Finally, he resorted to the whiskey bottle, hoping to banish the image of Maureen's luscious bare breasts from his mind.

It didn't work. His dreams were a torment—an image of Maureen slowly slipping her nightgown off her shoulders—revealing those perfectly creamy breasts with their tiny pink buds—alternated with an image of Captain Kwan, the red slit across his throat. Sometimes he had the sense there were people in the next room; he heard dim whisperings about kidnapping the Collins lass. He ran from door to door, opening one after another. Fifty doors, one hundred doors, and no people behind them.

Ben woke with a start. The knocking on his front door persisted. His mouth dry, his head pounding, he climbed from bed, and grabbed his robe. Combing his hair back with his hand, he tightened the sash and opened the door.

Letitia's worried face peered at him. "My God, you look like death itself."

He stepped aside and motioned her in. "A little early to be calling, even on your brother, isn't it? It's only eight. And Saturday. I don't work today."

She shook her head mournfully. "You're in no condition to do much of anything."

He hugged her and kissed her cheek. "Welcome back. Did you have a good trip?"

"Wonderful trip! I have a briefcase full of recipes and other notes. Rebecca's quite amazing at the helm of a donkey cart on a country lane. We visited cabins in the swamps and called on ladies at plantations. Everyone we met shared at least one family recipe. I can't wait to start writing."

Ben threw a few logs on the fire and slumped into a chair. "Did you get a recipe for coffee?"

"I can take a hint." Smiling, she trotted off to the kitchen, calling back to him. "Even upriver, Captain Kwan's murder was on everyone's mind. Newspapers were vague. They reported a thug murdered the Chinese captain on his ship in New Orleans. The police have no suspects. But I bet you do."

"I do, but Captain McCorkle, the local constable, doesn't want to hear a word. It's his murder investigation."

"I want to know," she said, raising her voice so he'd hear her over the sounds of boiling water poured into a drip pot. She appeared in the doorway, her arms folded across her chest. "Tell me. It'll be a minute before the coffee's ready. You have cream?"

"In the icebox. And rolls and butter. Excuse me while I dress."

He went to the bathroom, washed his face, brushed his teeth, combed his hair. He stared at his reflection in the mirror. *He did look like hell.*

He returned to find coffee and warm rolls on a table beside the fire.

"Thank heavens. You look better." She motioned to his chair, then sat opposite him and took a sip from her own cup. "New Orleans coffee is the best I've ever tasted. I picked up a few chicory and coffee recipes."

"The world will be grateful when you tell readers how it's blended." In between bites of a roll and gulps of coffee, Ben said he believed the captain was murdered by a rival group of smugglers, but that was for her ears only. "That's all I'm going to say. I want to hear about Maureen's tea party. We never discussed it before you left town."

"I'll start by saying Maureen's pretty—as you well know. She's also extremely intelligent, a charming hostess, and has at least one friend—Carine—who's her match in wit."

Looking away from his sister's face, Ben stared at the fire and imagined Maureen's dancing eyes, the tilt of her head and move of her hand when she flipped her curls off her bodice to her back. He wanted to see her, hold her, ask her to be his wife. A real proposal on his knees. He wanted to tell her he loved her. But he'd never said that to a woman in his life.

"You didn't hear a word past 'pretty.'" Letitia paused and sighed. "You're sick with love, aren't you? I didn't so much as mention her name and your face took on a faraway stare."

He flung his hands up in a hopeless gesture. "I care for her more than I've ever cared for a young lady, but I'm not thinking of marriage." Ben stood and paced in front of the fire, pausing on one pass to unclasp his hands and hold them above the fire screen. "Heavens, no. I'm not thinking of that yet." Why was he denying it? That's exactly what he was thinking. He'd told her father he'd proposed and she'd accepted.

Letitia took her time drinking her coffee. "We had tea in her greenhouse. Maureen seems quite serious about botany. She seems content tending to her plants. Would she be as content tending your offspring?"

Ben felt himself grow warm. There was nothing he wanted to do more than take Maureen into his bed and spill himself inside her. Did Letitia have an inkling of his passion? Had she ever felt such physical attraction?

"More coffee?" she asked. She filled her cup, then his. As she handed it to him, he asked if she'd noticed Maureen's blue eyes.

She took a sip. "I've not seen their equal on three continents."

"Did you see how they dance when the light hits them?"

Letitia put her cup down and raised an eyebrow. "I see you're smitten, all right. Maureen's young. She wants to go into the nursery business. She showed us the grafts she's done with the red camellia you gave her." She took a roll off the tray. "One of the guests—Aisling Moreau—made a rather lewd comment about them."

He chuckled. "Really? Ladies having tea discuss the phallus?"

"Aisling did." She shrugged. "Maureen put her firmly in her place—reminding her that her grafts were a science experiment."

"Good for her. So men were a topic of conversation?

Letitia smirked. "I suppose you'd like to think you were discussed?" She shook her head slowly. "Perhaps my presence made tales of your exploits about town *verboten*. Vespasian Colville—the man we met at Antoine's—seemed to be the major interest."

Tensing, Ben kept quiet, waiting for Letitia to share every word the ladies had spoken. His sister talked a great deal and from the youngest age she felt everyone was entitled to her opinion.

"Aisling mentioned him first. Then Suzette St. Aubin—remember her?

He wished he didn't.

"She'd like to have an affair with this Vespasian. I think Aisling already has."

Ben leaned toward her. "What was Maureen's reaction when the young man's name came up?"

Letitia patted his knee, "Believe me, she's not interested. Maureen mentioned they were childhood friends. Aisling said she'd heard it was an adult attachment, with great emphasis on the word *adult.*"

"Damn him," Ben muttered between clenched teeth. Then he took a deep breath and explained Maureen's predicament— the mothers' agreement, her father's insistence that she marry Vespasian on May first.

Letitia's eyes narrowed. "That's medieval. Do fathers still think they can arrange marriages?

He shrugged. "You haven't met her father. He's used to getting his way in *everything.*

"But Maureen's in love with you. I see it in her eyes when she looks at me."

Ben's pulse jumped. "At *you?*"

"When she looks at me, she sees you—there's so much that's similar. Our skin tone, hair color, eyes."

Ben stood and stretched his legs. "I think she loves me, but she doesn't trust me. Tuesday night, she accused me of being an opium addict."

Letitia grinned at him. "Oh, dear. But I can see why she wonders. All your trips to the docks. You have to admit it's odd."

He slammed his fist on the mantel. "I'll tell her the truth— that I'm a plant inspector for the customs office. You know, they even gave me an official badge that says that's what I do. It's supposed to give me access to ships. I look for infested and diseased plants."

She laughed. "Smart to give you identification that can explain your strange behavior. But why did you tell me the truth?"

"You know the Secretary of the Treasury." He shrugged. "I suspected you might be doing government work yourself in London."

"I'm not," she said quickly. "I do carry a pistol, but that's at mother's insistence."

He shook his head in wonderment. "I had no idea you were armed."

She rolled her eyes. "A lady traveling alone, you know." She rose to clear the table. "So Maureen thinks she's falling in love with an addict at best."

He sighed, "I guess that about sums it up."

"If I were in her position, I'd be nervous." She must have read the pleading in his eyes because she went on. "She's a lady who enjoys her independence. Her nursery, her grafting experiments. She's not ready for marriage with Vespasian or you, if you ask me."

Ben ran his hand through his hair. "I thought that's what women wanted. Can't she have both?"

She took her time responding. "Women today want to develop as human beings first—do something with their minds and their talents. They have to figure out if they want to tie themselves to one man forever. Doesn't a lifetime with one woman scare you even a little?"

"Not with Maureen."

Letitia tilted her head sideways. "Not the slightest doubt in the world?"

Swiveling, he faced her and a smile spread across his face. He chuckled at the humor in the situation. "I'm in love with a woman who thinks I'm an opium fiend. I think her father may be the mastermind in an opium-smuggling operation. Maureen might even be involved herself.

The opium in the roots of plants might have been her idea. Who knows more about plants than she does?"

"Are you going to marry her *after* she does her prison time?"

"Don't joke about it," he snapped. "I'd like to believe the Collins family is innocent. But then there's Colville." He collapsed into his chair once again. "I have to convince her father that I'm a better match than he'll ever be."

Sitting up straighter in her chair, Letitia assumed an air of confidence. She pointed a finger at him. "I'm positive Maureen's not in love with him. And I doubt she's the kind of young woman who would allow her father to marry her off so easily. Marriage is a lady's choice."

Maureen had made a mad dash into his arms at midnight. That night she was running from someone, probably Colville. Maureen would rush from the church, hop in a carriage and flee if it came to it. She wouldn't marry Colville. "I'm jealous. I can't help it. He's an important part of her past."

"Almost a sibling," Letitia added.

"I heard Colville tell her 'she owed him.' That haunts me."

Letitia glanced at the watch she wore on a chain around her neck. "He can't have bedded her. If he had, then he'd owe *her* a favor, seems to me."

His sister could make light of it, but it broke his heart to imagine Maureen and Colville together. "If Maureen's been intimate with him, I'd be upset. It would disappoint me."

Letitia reached over and patted his knee again. "Let me tell you something, Ben, about ladies today."

God help him, he needed to learn every secret his sister could impart. He leaned forward in his chair.

"Ladies nowadays—whether on the continent, in England or America—are more adventurous than our mother and the ladies of her generation. Ladies are more aware of their bodies and understand that sex isn't only for procreation. They enjoy their bodies; they enjoy men's bodies."

He arched an eyebrow. "And you know that firsthand?"

"I don't mind saying I do. Don't you?"

He didn't try to mask his reaction. His mouth dropped open. Was her partner in London? In New Orleans? She'd said it so casually.

Letitia didn't give him time to reply. Standing, she yanked him to his feet. "I need an escort back to the hotel, sir. I'm having dinner with George Hebert tonight. And tomorrow Maureen asked me to join her at the Bouchards to sort clothes donated to the Christian Women's Exchange."

"Sunday afternoon?" he asked as he held her coat. "Thank you for the chat. It's helped me think more clearly."

In the hotel lobby, she kissed him on both cheeks. "The most important person in a woman's life is her last love—not her first. Think about that, Ben."

Chapter Twenty-Nine

*B*en took the key from the ledge where he'd watched Maureen place it weeks ago. He unlocked the front door and then returned the key to its proper place.

He knew the rooms to the right. Front and back parlors and a sunroom, the greenhouse off that. On tiptoe, he glided down the main hall hugging the left wall. The master bedroom, a private sitting room and Collins' library mirrored the rooms on the opposite side. Beyond these the wide hallway opened to a massive dining room. He glanced inside. A stained glass bay window depicted unicorns and gryphons. At the far end of the room, four carved caryatids –draped female figures in the Grecian style—supported an alabaster mantelpiece. A silver, bronze and crystal gas-lit chandelier hung above a massive cypress table. A set of French doors opened to the terrace beyond and offered a view of Maureen's garden. The kitchen was somewhere behind the dining room as was the servants' staircase.

He started in the library, most likely to contain a man's business papers. He winced as the door creaked on its hinges. *A little oil might help, Patrick.* The sun shone brightly outside, but the room resembled a cave. Heavy deep green drapes covered a set of French doors. Dark oak paneling and floor-to-ceiling bookcases, chockfull of colorful leather volumes, covered three walls. On the fourth wall, a massive stone fireplace. Perpendicular to the French doors sat a large desk. The room smelled pleasantly male—a mix of leather, tobacco, brandy, and burned embers.

Ben went to work. The desk drawers contained the expected paraphernalia. Pencils, pens and ink, stationery, scissors, rulers. An account ledger for household expenses lay on top of the desk. Opening it, he chuckled at the marginalia. Beside monthly payments to Desselle Millinery and Frau Kohlmeyer, dressmaker: *Maureen looking more like her mother every day.* Three exclamation points next to gardening expenses, which were noted: azalea bushes, rose bushes, fertilizer, fencing, pagoda, gardener's salary. Two columns of numbers listed Greenhouse Materials and Greenhouse Wages. Beside the total: *Worth every penny.* Just before Christmas, an entry noted duty paid at the customs house on three cases of Collins whiskey. So Collins *wasn't* smuggling whiskey in from Ireland. Why smuggle opium and not whiskey?

His breathing quickened when he tried a drawer and found it locked. He pulled a felt pouch containing lock picks from his overcoat pocket and had it open in minutes. Damn it, nothing but personal letters. There was correspondence between Collins and his deceased wife, Bridget, during her trips to visit her sister in Atlanta, and his trips to Lowell and Boston to visit mills. A more recent packet tied with a ribbon contained letters from Maureen during the years she lived with her aunt in Atlanta. Interesting that Collins, who lacked anything resembling sentimentality in his business dealings, treasured a cache of letters. Ben longed to sit down and spend hours with Maureen's letters, but his stomach twisted at the very idea. Being here, in her house, in her father's desk, troubled him enough. He'd feel uncomfortable looking over anyone's personal papers, but his feelings for Maureen made his task twice as difficult.

"Nothing here," he muttered, moving on to Collins' bedroom. His own father kept his private papers in a safe in his bedroom. Perhaps Maureen's father had a similar habit. Warmer than the library, the bedroom and its adjoining sitting room contained banked coals in their fireplaces. He wasted little time on the dresser. Quickly, he realized it contained nothing of interest. He opened the gentleman's walnut wardrobe. In the left side hung trousers and coats. A safe occupied the right. Taking a deep breath, he knelt beside it and put his ear to the dial.

Listening for the tiniest click, he turned the dial to the left, then right, left again. It seemed to take hours, but his training and patience paid off. With sweating palms, he turned the crank, swallowed hard and swung open the door. His eyes landed on a sheaf of documents, but again, nothing illegal. The deed to the St. Charles property, deeds to his office and warehouses, a last will and testament.

He took his time examining bankbooks showing deposits and withdrawals for Collins Factorage for several years back. Nothing unusual caught his eye. The largest deposits occurred just after harvest when the factorage sold cotton to mills in England and New England. The withdrawals paid bills for planters for everything from seed to food to their wives' dresses and their children's school tuition. Deposits and withdrawals rose with remarkable consistency from 1881 through the first half of 1885. Indeed, Collins ran a very profitable—and legal—business as his personal bank account showed.

He closed the safe and stood. Could the man be innocent? So many threads pointed to him. He signed Imperial Shipping's contract without a thought. And the *Hailong Hao* was registered to Imperial. If he were a smuggler, it made sense that Collins hoped to expand the shipping line's access to New Orleans. For the fiftieth time, he wondered if Captain Kwan ran the smuggling operation without his superiors' knowledge or if the entire company dealt in smuggled goods. Collins' innocence or guilt lay in the answer.

But why would anyone with bankbooks this flush risk imprisonment for smuggling? Sure he could amass more money smuggling opium than he made at the factorage each year. But why? Was he that greedy?

His mouth went dry as he thought of Maureen. Was she involved, too? She read about opium in the Tulane library, but spoke only of camellia texts when he questioned her. She found the captain's body. Could it have been her idea to hide the tins in the roots of plants? Wouldn't that be the irony of ironies? Did he bring her a camellia with a tin of opium in its roots—the drug smuggled into port by her father's minions?

Absurd. Absurd. He fell back on his training. He focused on his goal. Patrick and possibly Maureen smuggled opium. If so, there would be evidence hidden somewhere in this house. In the dining room, he looked in the drawers of the sideboard, the silver chest, and behind paintings for another safe. Nothing. Next, he tackled the sunroom, looking in the large pine cabinet there. He even pulled up the sofa cushions and returned them to their places.

In the greenhouse, he searched the drawers of Maureen's workbench. Wrapped in a piece of striped fabric, tucked beneath several notebooks, he found the original tin of opium and one he supposed she pulled from the white azalea. She'd made a point to hide these, but from whom? Her father? Why not just throw the tins out?

He returned to the front hall and the staircase beckoned to him. Maureen had talked of a ladies sitting room on the second floor where she and her mother spent many hours together in her last months of life. While her mother did needlework, Maureen read to her. He wanted to get a glimpse of it. What was the harm in that? The stair treads creaked, just like the library door, but he didn't worry about it.

The room's décor screamed of Maureen. Clumps of purple and lavender flowers colored the wallpaper. Delicate lace curtains hung at the two windows. A dark green rug, and a sofa and two chairs upholstered in a fabric embroidered with purple tulips gave him the sense he'd stepped into a garden. It smelled like one, too. Vases on each side of the mantel held cut roses. He paused and breathed in the scent of her.

Turning slowly, he took in a bookcase, two side tables, two crystal lamps, a tray holding decanter and glasses, and a high shelf of very old dolls, some probably belonging to her grandmothers. A mahogany ladies writing desk sat on the floor beside the chair nearest the fireplace. He reached for it, sat, and placed it on his lap. Essentially a miniature desk, it had a hinged top opening downward rather than upward as real desks did.

Damn it, locked. He used precious minutes to get it open. Several small cubicles held stamps, a bottle of ink, and pens. Printed felt, white flowers with green leaves on a brown background, covered the writing surface, which measured roughly eight by ten inches. Under this, he found the inner compartment.

His own letters filled most of the space along with stationery and envelopes. He reached a hand in and picked up a letter. Beneath it, the corner of a black leather ledger protruded.

Holding his breath, his hands shaking, he grasped it and flipped it open. A date topped each page. Under it, notations in black ink recorded pounds of *Goods* imported, pounds sold, and profit made.

"My, God. What a bastard," he hissed. What kind of father would incriminate his own daughter by hiding his ledger in her desk? His second thought sickened him. Nobody would hide this book in his daughter's belongings. Maureen hid it there herself. His mind racing, he walked to the window and examined the book in the light. The handwriting matched on every page.

But it wasn't Maureen's.

He didn't think it was Collins' handwriting either. Holding the book, he bounded back down the steps and ran into the library. He lay the small ledger next to the big one on the desk. Different handwriting. If Maureen didn't record these numbers and her father didn't, then who in the hell did? He knew William's writing, too. It wasn't his.

Colville? Was Vespasian Colville the mastermind of the operation?

He heard horses' hooves on the brick drive. He left the household expense ledger open on the desk, snatched the small ledger up and slammed the library door behind him. Taking the steps two at a time back up to Maureen's sitting room, he dropped the book in her lap desk, covered it with his own notes to her, and placed it exactly where he'd found it on the floor beside the chair.

The front door opened as he descended the back staircase into the kitchen. He left by the back door, cut through the side yard and out to the street.

Maureen hung up her coat and hat, went into the sunroom and poured herself a glass of sherry from the decanter there. She straightened a lopsided cushion, and sat. Slipping off her shoes, she curled her feet under her and mulled over Letitia's parting words. Maureen and Letitia shared a cab back from the Bouchards to her hotel where they hugged good-bye and promised to meet again soon.

Ben's sister had said she wanted to leave her with one thought, but actually she left her with two. First: "Ben is not exactly what he seems." She had corrected that notion immediately. "I mean he's more than what he seems. He's a fine, fine gentleman."

Next she had pronounced: "Ben loves you," which made Maureen's heart beat faster than she believed it ever had.

He loves you. Maureen replayed the words in her mind again and again. Although she'd never had a brother and therefore couldn't say for sure, she didn't think sisters said *He loves you* to ladies without knowing it to be true. What in the world did

Letitia's other remark mean? Was she trying to say she knew Ben was an opium addict, but he was still a fine, fine gentleman? Or was she hinting he was not an opium addict, but acted like one for a reason she couldn't reveal to Maureen?

Maureen's week of self-imposed separation from Ben would end Tuesday. That evening she intended to plead with her father to release her from her betrothal to Vespasian. This would be the most important conversation she'd ever had with him—far more serious than her request to go into business selling camellias. That had gone nowhere. She needed to write out a speech and memorize it. She hurried to her sitting room, grabbed her lap desk and returned to the sunroom. She took the key from her pocket.

Unlocked?

She'd locked it when she hid the ledger there. Surely she had.

Opening the box, she found the ledger exactly where she'd left it, half buried beneath Ben's notes. *Actually, not so.* She had hidden it completely beneath Ben's letters and clearly someone had moved it.

She couldn't get Monsieur Leveque out of her mind. His piercing eyes had seemed to peer deep into her soul when he helped her into the carriage. She told herself she suffered from a guilty conscience so she imagined he could read her mind. He didn't know she'd stolen the ledger when he met her in Suzette's house. But he *did* know she'd been upstairs. Of course, the odd man might not even know the ledger existed. She'd taken it from Monsieur St. Aubin's desk. In his bedroom.

Feeling cold, she shifted on the sofa, and rubbed her upper arms with her hands. She didn't like being in this big house all alone. The servants were off from ten o'clock Saturday night until ten Sunday night. The clock on the mantel chimed five. Five more hours before Luz would bounce in and share all the gossip she'd heard that day.

She put a log on the fire and went into the kitchen to make tea. Julia always left soup and fried chicken, fresh bread, and cookies, but she'd eaten cake at the Bouchards so wasn't hungry. As she bent over the sink to fill the kettle, the back door slammed. She jumped and whirled around.

No one. Julia hadn't locked the screen door. It banged each time the wind caught it. She went to latch it and stopped dead. The kitchen door, glass on top, paneled wood on the bottom, was unlocked, too. Surely Julia hadn't forgotten to lock the main door.

Back in the sunroom, she settled in front of the fire. Her eyes fell on the pine cupboard, which once housed her gardening tools. The door was ajar. Pulling it open, she glanced inside. She kept vases there now and nothing seemed to be disturbed. She went quickly into the dining room and noticed an open door on the sideboard. The tablecloths and napkins had been handled. She opened the silver chest and counted—a set of twelve knives, forks, spoons, salad forks and soup spoons. She didn't count the serving pieces. In fact, she didn't know how many pieces of silver the family owned. The lopsided paintings over the mantels added to her suspicions.

Curiosity drove her to look further. In her father's library, the household ledger lay open on the desk. Her father always closed it. Icy dread spread over her: Someone had been in the house while she was out. Monsieur Leveque looking for Monsieur St. Aubin's ledger? Ben stealing something he could sell to support his habit?

Her heart beating wildly, she wanted to run out the front door, flag a cab on St. Charles Avenue and go to William and Renee's house. But to do that, she'd have to go outside and walk through the property in the dark. Sending a note to William to come to her also meant going outside and walking along St. Charles until she found a messenger. Perhaps she shouldn't have sent Suzette away.

Oh, hell, if she were here, she'd be crying. She wasn't help-less like Suzette. Maureen Collins didn't need anyone to tell her what to do or how to protect herself. The intruder had left by the kitchen door. She had relocked it. All the doors were locked, downstairs windows, too. She'd go upstairs; she'd feel safer there. In the kitchen, she put a chicken leg, a piece of bread, a little cheese and some cookies on a tray in case she got hungry. She threw water on the fire in the sunroom, reducing it to a safe smolder.

In the ladies sitting room, she locked the door and tried to make herself comfortable in front of the fire. No one could get through the solid oak door. No balcony offered access. The win-dows, in front of which no vines or trees grew, were at least thirty feet off the ground and locked. Yes, Monsieur Leveque might know she'd taken the ledger, but he wouldn't dare break into the Collins home on a Sunday evening.

Was it Ben who broke into her house? But why? What did he hope to find?

Chapter Thirty

*A*t breakfast the next morning, a letter from Vespasian sat beside her plate. Suzette, he reported, was a bundle of nerves, weeping at both the idea of returning to her husband and at the idea of defying him by staying away.

Poor man. He must be losing his mind.

It continued with the news that Suzette knew nothing about her husband's business dealings, which Vespasian believed to be true. She read the last sentence twice: *I am developing a plan I believe will persuade your father to choose Ben to be your husband rather than me.*

Vespasian had devised excellent schemes to get what he wanted from his earliest days. He invented excuses—plausible or not—with ease. When hungover, he'd eaten bad oysters (it wasn't oyster season); when he stopped for a card game or two, he'd been waylaid by a streetcar accident (they didn't run after ten at night); or his favorite, he'd gotten lost in the woods (there were no woods in New Orleans). People tended to swallow his outrageous lies because of his infectious good nature, sincere remorse and, of course, his good looks. If anyone could engineer what they both wanted—a broken engagement—Vespasian could do it.

Emboldened by his words, Maureen decided to see Monsignor Valdois at St. Louis Cathedral today. Although the Collins family went to the Irish church, St. Patrick's on Camp Street, her father, as a wealthy prominent Catholic, was involved in raising money for the restoration of the cathedral. The monsignor had become a frequent dinner guest at the Collins house.

Maureen felt sure he'd have a solution to Suzette's problem. No one, even the Catholic Church, could expect a woman to stay with a husband who beat her. Who did more than beat her. Shuddering, she wasn't sure she'd have the courage to tell the monsignor *everything*, but she would try.

Noah drove the carriage and Luz accompanied her. In the church office, a young priest said the monsignor was hearing confessions for the next two hours. Maureen returned to the carriage and almost let her fears stop her. But thoughts of Ben gave her courage. Telling Luz and Noah she was going into the church, she marched straight across the square and through the main doors.

A line of six penitents waited at the monsignor's confessional, tucked in an alcove in the back of the church. Selecting an empty pew four from the rear, Maureen genuflected, placed her handbag on the oak bench, knelt, lowered her head and tried to organize her thoughts. What in the world should she say? She thought if she prayed, she might have the courage to go through with this, but as she turned to retrieve her rosary beads from her purse, she caught sight of Monsieur Leveque in a pew on the side aisle, two pews behind her.

Facing the altar, she lowered her head. The beads shook in her hands. Did the man follow her in? She told herself he did not. He was French, no doubt a Catholic. He had every right to drop in for a visit or to go to confession. *The way he treated Suzette, he needed to.* She felt his eyes boring into her back. She tried to assure herself that he might not have seen her. It didn't work. She fingered the beads one after another, but for the life of her, couldn't say a full Hail Mary. *Hail Mary, full of grace. Blessed art thou* .... The words she knew by rote jumbled in her mind. *The Lord is with thee.* Perhaps the butler had searched the Collins house yesterday, remained there all night and had come in a cab following her carriage to the church.

No. She reined in her imagination. Ben had been in the house. She'd decided that yesterday. Leveque probably saw her cross the square and followed her into the church. It'd been pure coincidence that he'd walked through the square just as she did.

She willed herself to move. Holding her breath, she stood and slipped from the pew, not stopping to genuflect and not glancing in Leveque's direction until she took her place. Third in line. Her position offered a good view of the man, but he couldn't see her without turning his head almost completely around. For the moment, she felt safe from his beady eyes. The two people in front of her were quick. Not much to confess. *Practically saints.*

Her turn. With a shaking hand, she pulled back the curtain and sank down on the kneeler in the wooden box. She heard murmuring, the voice of someone on the other side of the monsignor, who sat between two sliding wooden panels, which provided privacy to the person telling his soul's secrets.

The door slid closed on the other side. Her side opened. She saw the white-haired man's profile, sitting sideways in a chair.

"Monsignor Valdois, this is Maureen Collins," she whispered.

"Ah, Miss Collins. Please give your father my regards." The voice sounded tired and old. But kind. "What can I do for you, my child?"

"I need help for a friend. A woman friend who's afraid for her life."

"Her eternal life? Her immortal soul?"

"No, Monsignor, her life on earth. Her husband ... hits her." Maureen caught her breath, swallowed and went on. "She's afraid. She's scared of him. She wants to annul her marriage."

"Are she and her husband Catholics?"

Maureen nodded, then realized she had to speak. "Yes, Monsignor," she said.

"Married by a priest?"

"Yes, a little more than a year ago."

"Do you know," he paused and cleared his throat. "Has the marriage been consummated?"

"Yes, Monsignor, it has."

He sighed heavily. "There is nothing I can do, Miss Collins. No annulment. She may divorce him in civil court, but she cannot remarry in the Church until his death."

Maureen's heart sank. This was exactly what she'd feared. Suzette could end the marriage, but she and Vespasian couldn't marry. "Monsignor, there must be some way ..."

"Go in peace, my child, and pray for her."

The wooden door slid back into place, closing him off. Maureen pushed herself to a standing position. She wanted to scream. Suzette was young and inexperienced. She had no idea what this man was like when she married him.

"*There is nothing I can do.*" The words slammed into her brain. "*Nothing I can do.*" "*Nothing.*" So harsh, so very harsh.

She emerged from the confessional, and turned to check on Monsieur Leveque, whose cold eyes met her own. Her legs shaking so badly she worried they might not hold her, she hobbled out, threw her weight against the heavy door at the rear of the church and hurried into the vestibule.

Monsieur Leveque had exited from the side-aisle door. He kept pace with her step by step. Conscious of the sound of her heels clicking against the marble floor—and the sound of his—she walked as fast as she could until she burst through the massive outer door.

Cold February air hit her face. The carriage waited a half block away. She turned in that direction. Leveque called her name, but she didn't look back. Not stopping, not slowing down, she hurried across the uneven slate in front of the cathedral, keeping her eyes on the stones at her feet.

A hand gripped her upper arm tightly, squeezing far harder than necessary. It brought her to a halt. She gasped, then turned on him, her eyes flashing, her hand slapping at his. "I beg your pardon, sir."

His hand remained in place. His black eyes bored into hers. "Stay away from Monsieur and Madame St. Aubin. Their lives don't concern you."

She stood in a public place in broad daylight. Dozens of people walked by them, several ladies giving them a second glance. Carriages moved slowly down the street on either side of the pedestrian area. Her own carriage, with Noah at the reins, Luz inside, waited within sight. She raised her voice. "Remove your hand, sir."

He didn't. She glared at him, but there was no way to hide the quiver in her voice. "Madame St. Aubin is my friend and I'll help her in any way I can."

He yanked her so close she got a whiff of garlic on his breath. "Stay away from her or I promise you, Miss Collins, you will regret it."

With those words, he let go and stalked away. Stumbling, Maureen regained her footing and moved as quickly as she could without running. Luz opened the carriage door, Noah jumped from his perch and helped her inside, then climbed back on the bench and took off at a breakneck speed.

Luz hugged her. "Lawd, child. What did he say?"

"He said if I don't ..." She had to stop a moment to catch her breath. "He said to stay away from Madame St. Aubin or I'd regret it."

Luz grabbed her hands. "I knew helping Miz Suzette was gonna mean trouble."

Shaking, Maureen sat back and folded her arms across her chest. Anger overcame fear. The nerve of Monsieur Leveque to accost her in front of St. Louis Cathedral! Did she realize who her father was? How dare he threaten her!

Luz's voice was grave. "He ain't dumb. He knows you's been snooping around in the house."

Maureen bit her lower lip. Luz was right. Danielle—the young maid, scared, worried for her job—probably told the butler Maureen had spent quite a bit of time alone on the second floor.

If Monsieur Leveque knew the ledger was missing, he knew exactly who had it. Then why not simply demand its return? On the other hand, maybe he *hadn't* noticed its absence. When Suzette's husband returned and found it missing, there would be hell to pay. But she had a little time yet, she hoped, and in any case, she refused to be intimidated. She sat up straighter. She was a Collins after all.

Just before midnight, her father's arms swallowed her in a big hug. He'd sent a telegram announcing his arrival a day earlier than planned. He kissed her on each cheek, then held her away from his body and looked at her face. "It's so good to see you, lass. I feel like I've been gone for years. I'm glad you waited up. Shall we share a brandy?"

She led him into the back parlor where a roaring fire and a plate of cheese straws and apple slices on a side table worked some magic, as she'd hoped they would. He relaxed immediately; a smile came to his face. "It's wonderful to be home. What would you like?"

Maureen sat on the sofa, leaving the chair closer to the fire for her father. "Collins whiskey and a little water, please."

He went to the cellarette to pour. "I'm bursting with news," he began. "Remember when Ben Merritt advised me *not* to sign a contract with Imperial Shipping?"

"What about it?" She tried to keep her voice casual; she remembered every aspect of the set-to over the shipping company. At the time, she'd admired Ben for standing up to her father. "Umm, as I recall, Mr. Merritt was against it, but you signed it anyway."

"Turns out he was absolutely right."

She arched an eyebrow.

"Mr. Merritt saw the contract's flaw and tried to warn me. Imperial Shipping fleeced a few Boston companies, charging them for entire cargoes they claimed were jettisoned at sea— exactly what Mr. Merritt said might happen. Imperial's owner and two managers are going to trial in London in a few weeks. The company is in bankruptcy and all contracts with it are void." He paused long enough to take a sip of brandy.

"So you're free to negotiate with another company to ship the fall harvest."

He nodded, clearly pleased by his narrow escape. Maureen picked up the plate and passed it to him. He took two cheese straws and turned to her. "What have you been up to? Is Madame St. Aubin still your guest or did she return home? And how are your camellia grafts doing?"

Would he like the truth?

Let's see. I haven't seen Ben Merritt because I gave you my word. Suzette's no longer here. She's terrified of her despotic husband, so I sent her to the country. I went to her house to pick up some dresses for her and examined everything in her bedroom. More horrifying still, I went through Monsieur St. Aubin's wardrobe and desk drawers, found ropes and a journal outlining his torture of her. I left the journal, but stole his account book.

She stalled, staring at the fire. "I haven't seen Ben Merritt because you asked me not to and I obeyed."

"I'm very pleased to hear that." He drained his brandy snifter and returned to the cellarette for a refill.

"I haven't seen much of Vespasian either. He's up the country with Suzette and her family. I think he loves her very much."

He waved his hand in the air, as if that action could brush aside her words and more importantly, the facts. "I'll have a talk with him. I'm convinced Colville is the right man for you, lass. Someday you'll thank me."

That's not likely. Before she lost her nerve, she launched into Suzette's full story. Her father clenched his hands so tightly on the arms of his chair his knuckles turned white. "Damn the man who treats his wife that way," he muttered several times while she described St. Aubin's behavior. Red in the face, he turned to her and began a lecture.

"Sadly, it's not uncommon, Maureen, particularly when a man's been drinking, to hit his wife." He reached his hand across from his chair to touch her arm. "I'm telling you this right now. If Vespasian Colville ever threatens you, throws something at you, or raises a hand to you, even a slap on your cheek, whether he's drunk or sober, leave him at once. Walk out the door and never go back."

Maureen nodded, waiting, building her courage for her assault.

"We've never discussed such things. Your cousin Sarah, I'm afraid ..." Sighing, he shook his head.

"William told me about his sister."

"It's a sad, sad tale. Married to a rake. Handsome, which I suppose attracted her, but the man is cruel. I understand from William he ..." His voice trailed off and he brought the glass to his mouth again. "There's no divorce in Ireland."

She could have hugged him for giving her the perfect opener. "There's none for Catholics in Louisiana either."

"True enough."

"I spoke with Monsignor Valdois today. If Suzette divorces her horrid husband, she cannot remarry in the Catholic Church."

Shocked, her father glared at her. "You discussed your friend's intimate relationship with her husband with a clergyman? That's overstepping all bonds of friendship."

"Suzette asked me to help her." She felt slightly ashamed she was using Suzette's plight to further her own cause, but she was desperate to reach an understanding with her father. In a rush, all the lady's secrets tumbled from her mouth. The ropes, the bed-posts, the whippings.

Her father's face turned ashen and he sputtered he was sorry she even knew such activities existed.

She sank to the floor at her father's feet. "Suzette's case makes me realize how very, very serious marriage is. It's forever."

He nodded solemnly.

She spoke her rehearsed lines calmly. "I don't want to marry Vespasian. He doesn't want to marry me. We'll not be good together. You and the Colvilles are condemning us both to a life of misery. Or if not misery, boredom. We don't love each other."

She held her breath for a moment while he put his glass on the table, and grasped her hands. "Don't you worry a moment about Vespasian. You and he will get along just fine. I don't want to hear another word about it. I've made my decision."

"But ..." She jumped to her feet. "I've made a decision, too. Isn't mine as important as yours? Isn't it more important actually? I'm the one who has to live with him. The man she marries should be a lady's choice."

"Enough!" he thundered.

She turned her back and walked slowly from the room, not glancing back.

Chapter Thirty-One

$\mathcal{M}$aureen did her best thinking while watering her plants. Can in hand, she tipped just the right amount of water onto the soil of each pot. Her eyes swept over the plants Ben had given her. The red *camellia,* quite a few of its limbs now gone, still covered in blooms. Nearby on the floor the four rose bushes, lovely to look at and so fragrant. The *polygonum orientale,* the *jasminum nudiflorum.* All beautiful gifts from a man who told his sister—who'd told her—he loved her. She took a deep breath and let it out in a sigh.

She hadn't seen him in almost a week and their separation left a pit in the center of her chest. Her father had returned, but some good her pleading had done. The *only* item she had going for her—and one of the few positive things she could think about the laws of the Church right now—was the rule forbidding marriage during Lent. No matter what her father wanted, she couldn't marry Vespasian before Easter.

Julia announced her luncheon was ready. As usual, Maureen ate alone. While she took a few bites of the chicken pot pie on her plate, she glanced at the *Daily Picayune* left on the table. She scanned the advertisements, particularly the want ads, for sales of plants or seeds. The words FLOWER SALE caught her eye.

GARDENERS, YOUR SHIP HAS COME IN
Lafitte Nursery
Bayou St. John at Esplanade Avenue
Exotic Lilies, Flowering Vines, Seed Varieties
Today Only, 3 to 5 O'clock
NO CREDIT

Maureen glanced at her watch. It was almost two. She guessed it would take thirty to forty-five minutes to get to this address, which was beyond the French Quarter. Could she make it before the sale ended? Perhaps this was just the thing to take her mind off Ben Merritt, respectable attorney and *housebreaker*. She couldn't think *housebreaker* without the perennial question why.

Whatever Ben did, whatever he was, whether he broke her heart or not, she would not marry Vespasian. She didn't love him. If she disobeyed her father, refused to marry his selected candidate, would he disown her? Would she have to support herself with her cultivations? The very thing he forbade her to do.

She finished the pie on her plate, swallowed down her cup of tea and hurried to her room. She took two five dollar gold coins and some other change from her top dresser drawer and tucked it in the zippered inner pocket of her black leather handbag. She selected her blue velvet hat with velvet flower appliqués from her bonnet cabinet, and her dark blue coat from her closet, tiptoed down the stairs and stashed these articles in the greenhouse.

Just as she'd done the day she went to the docks and discovered the dead captain, she told Julia and Luz she was spending the afternoon in the greenhouse and wasn't to be disturbed. Then she left by the greenhouse door and hurried out the side gate to hail a cab.

When she neared her destination, she peered out the window and saw a number of horses and carts blocking Esplanade Avenue.

On her right, a group of at least twenty men milled about in some semblance of a line in front of a dilapidated wooden building with peeling paint and a few cracked windows on its upper floors. The shabbiness of the establishment surprised her, but a rectangular wooden sign above the front door announced FLOWERS FOR SALE in purple lettering.

The men in line wore work clothes, boots and peaked caps, gardeners' attire. Some women, all dressed in calico with only shawls to keep them warm, talked and laughed as if on holiday. She'd stumbled upon a wholesale market, a place where nursery-men and flower-stall girls bought their wares. Her heart pounded. Like the rest of the group, she couldn't wait to get inside. The doors opened and the crowd surged forward.

The cab driver eyed her coat and hat. "I ain't believing this is the place you intended, is it, Miss?"

Maureen assumed an air of confidence she didn't quite feel. "I'm in the gardening business." She nodded toward the building. "Will you wait, please? I won't be long."

"For a half dollar extra."

Outrageous. She handed over the money. "I won't be long," she repeated.

He grunted, turned his back, and she strode toward the entrance where a large man with a swarthy complexion and untamed black hair thrust market baskets into shoppers' hands as they entered. "Stuff it full," he shouted to no one in particular. He looked familiar, but she couldn't place him.

She stepped past him into the warehouse, then glanced over her shoulder for a second look. He was the man she'd seen walking away from the *Hailong Hao* the day she found the dead captain. She hadn't actually seen him leave the ship; it could have been a coincidence that he hurried along the dock. But she was sure of him.

Determined to enjoy herself despite the man's presence, she breathed in the heady mix of fragrances. The perfume of many flowers, fertilizers and peat intoxicated her. This place in no way resembled the refined sort of nursery that sold to genteel ladies. Intrigued by the volume of bulbs, seed packs and potted plants, Maureen slowed her pace down the main aisle to examine everything.

Wooden bins, the type used to display vegetables at the French Market, contained many varieties of bulbs: iris, tiger lily, milk and wine crinum, amaryllis, double tuberose. She scooped a handful of each into bags and labeled these with one of several pencils tied with twine to an adjacent table. Three women gathered around smaller crates containing seeds in brightly illustrated paper packages. Her eyes scanned hollyhocks, sunflowers, dahlias, pinks, petunias, phlox and verbena in a huge variety of colors. And the price! So inexpensive.

She skipped the vegetable seeds and moved toward the back of the building where potted plants sat on rough pine plank tables. She selected a bleeding heart. *How perfect for a lady forced to marry against her will.*

Next, she cogitated at length between a yellow or pink angel's trumpet before deciding to buy both. A vast assortment of geraniums attracted her attention. The most popular bedding plant in America, they flourished in every New Orleans garden. They grew well in the climate here and would act as fillers among more exotic plants when she laid out this spring's garden. She picked out a dozen: four red, four white, four deep pink. The large man approached and carried each plant she chose upfront to a clerk at the cash register.

Her clothing set her apart from the other shoppers, so she made a point of doing nothing to call attention to herself. When she handed the clerk two five-dollar gold pieces and received two bills in change, she noticed quite a few eyes on her. Snapping her handbag closed, she put it securely over her arm, bent her arm so the purse rested safely in the crook of her elbow and loaded her plants into one of the wooden wagons on hand for patrons to transport their goods to the street.

The sun was fast sinking over the bayou when she emerged from the warehouse. Her mood sank with it. She'd given the driver the cost of a dozen seed packs to wait for her. He was nowhere to be seen.

Ben left his office a little after three o'clock and took a cab uptown to the livery stable on Jackson Avenue to take possession of his new cabriolet. From its black leather seats and bonnet top to its well-sprung chassis, the carriage offered good looks and a smooth ride despite the horrid condition of New Orleans streets. He wrote a check to the proprietor for the carriage and a horse, a lively black stallion named Mephistopheles, Mephy for short.

Yes, he lacked a beautiful woman riding beside him, but if all went well, he'd remedy the shortcoming in the next day or two. In the last twenty-four hours, he'd wrestled with the evidence he'd found yesterday and was convinced that no one in the Collins family had written the notations in the ledger book.

So where did Maureen get it? She'd hidden it as a favor to whom? Colville? Suzette? One of the Bouchards? He smiled at the third prospect. Elise Bouchard batting her eyelashes and smuggling opium? *Ludicrous.* But he couldn't rule out Suzette or Colville.

He guided Mephy to Lafitte Nursery. The ad in the paper had piqued his curiosity. What was Vito Mendoza doing? Was he selling all his plants without opium in the roots at a steep discount? Surely he wasn't getting out of the opium trade. That made no sense unless Mendoza had not murdered Captain Kwan. Had another smuggling ring entered the trade here and eliminated Kwan? Could Mendoza be selling in a panic?

Today, he hoped to learn who owned the ledger. He would call on Maureen tonight—in the greenhouse—with a gift of flowers. Surely, she'd tell him where it came from. With that knowledge, he would be a big step closer to telegraphing Carleton with the smugglers' identities.

Then he could concentrate on the task closer to his heart: convincing Patrick Collins he was a worthy suitor for his daughter. He hadn't seen him since he returned from Boston, but he'd heard from William that Imperial Shipping faced charges for fraud in London. Collins had even said he should have listened to Ben. So he'd impressed the man with his brains—at least.

Thinking of Maureen's black curls, her giggle, her deep blue eyes—and her warm, lush body lying against his on the sofa—he urged his horse to hurry, hoping to arrive in time to secure a few prized plants for her. Perhaps if he were very lucky, he would even see her. If she had seen the ad, she would have sneaked out to the flower sale.

Turning his eyes away from the carriage directly in front of him, he scanned the lawn in front of the warehouse, just ahead on his right. He spotted a young lady—his favorite young lady in all the world—standing at the curb. A hand cart beside her overflowed with flowers.

His pulse raced as he reined Mephy in, threw back the leather top, stood and waved.

"Mau ... Miss Collins," he shouted.

She didn't hear him, didn't acknowledge him. She turned her head toward a man standing quite close behind her.

Tall, thin. Hellfire. Leveque.

At that moment, the man's arm chopped down on Maureen's, knocking her purse to the ground. He snatched it up and ran. She swiveled and gave chase.

Leaping from his carriage, Ben sprinted toward them.

Maureen grabbed for the thief's jacket, missed it, and nearly fell. She regained her footing and shouted. "Stop, thief! Stop."

The man headed down the muddy path beside the bayou. A hand on each side of her coat holding her skirt above her ankles, Maureen kept pace with him. His mind flashed to their first meeting. A fast runner, not a stroller, after all.

He wasn't sure if Leveque tripped or if Maureen brought him down with a tackle to his legs, but the pair hit the ground. Maureen landed awkwardly on top of him. She punched at the man's shoulders, shouting, "Give it back!"

Unable to slow his own speed, Ben angled his landing to avoid Maureen, and splashed down into a mud puddle a foot away from them. Just as he landed, the villain flipped Maureen's body off his, jumped to his feet and raced away, leaving the handbag. He itched to give chase, but Maureen concerned him more. She'd landed hard.

He pulled himself to his knees, reached a hand out and helped her to a sitting position. Her beautiful eyes widened in surprise.

"What are you doing here?"

"Kneeling in a rather large mud puddle."

She put a hand to her mouth and began to laugh convulsively. "I'm ... sorry," she choked out. "You look ridiculous."

His clothing, from his cravat to his overcoat to his trousers, wore a slick black coat of Louisiana mud. Maureen, on the other hand, had made it through the debacle with only a few splashes of mud on her coat. She looked beautiful as always, but she'd taken quite a fall.

"Are you hurt? Are you all right?"

It took her a while to answer. Every time she attempted to speak she dissolved into spasms of laughter. It delighted him to see her laugh—he couldn't help smiling along with her—but it also worried him. Was it shock from the ordeal she'd just been through?

"I don't think so," she finally managed, still chuckling and catching her breath. "But I can do without that butler, Monsieur Leveque"—she tossed her head in the direction of the fugitive—"harassing me."

He sobered instantly. He turned to see the man's form fade into the distance. "You know him?"

She wiped the tears of laughter from her eyes. "Monsieur Leveque. Suzette St. Aubin's butler, of all people."

He reached for her purse to hide his surprise. Show no emotion, he'd been told for six months. Using his handkerchief, he cleaned the leather as best he could and handed it to her. "Suzette's butler, a purse snatcher? How odd! Are you sure you're quite all right?"

She slipped the handbag on her arm. "I'm not hurt, but I do need an escort home."

Watching her adjust her hat, he admired her lovely face, which now had a smudge of mud on the left cheek.

"Glad you wasn't hurt, Miss," said a voice Ben recognized. "The ruffian won't be here again, I promise you that." He nodded to Maureen, then recognized Ben. "Oh, Mr. Franklin! Good to see you, sir. I'm betting this is the lady you've been buying all them flowers for."

Ben introduced Maureen to Vito Mendoza. She bowed her head slightly. A few people had gathered to gawk at the sight of a lady on the grass, a gentlemen kneeling in a mud puddle beside her. Mendoza waved the bystanders away. Ben stood and helped Maureen to her feet. He offered her his arm, which she took with a grimace.

He raised his eyebrows in mock horror. "I don't recall ever having that reaction from a young lady."

She exhaled loudly. "I believe I've hurt my wrist."

"My vehicle isn't far. I'll have a look at it there. Hold your wrist at your waist." With a hand at the small of her back, he guided her slowly through the wagons, leading her back to the street.

She smiled until her dimples showed. "I'm so glad you're here."

He wanted to lean down and kiss her right there, but he controlled his urge. "You have plants to transport, I'm guessing?"

"Quite a few …" She pointed out her wagon, which hadn't been disturbed.

He laughed out loud. "Yes, quite a few."

Chapter Thirty-Two

$\mathcal{M}$aureen's breath caught when Ben's hands squeezed her waist gently to help her onto the bench seat.

"You're my first passenger. I bought the vehicle and horse just this afternoon. Mephy is his name." He nodded at the coal black stallion.

She rubbed her gloved hand across the leather seat. "It's lovely. No, I suppose that's what women say about a new dress or new curtains. What do men say?"

"It's handsome."

"A very good word." She knew little about carriages. The seat was pleasantly firm. "I suspect I'll enjoy riding in this." She almost added "for many years to come," but how could she say such a thing when her father had other plans for her? She licked her lower lip, sat back and cradled her left wrist in her right hand. If she kept it very still, the throbbing lessened.

Ben moved her handcart alongside his vehicle. She focused on his strong, broad shoulders as he lifted her purchases, one by one. He placed the big bag containing all the seed packets and the smaller bags of spring bulbs at her feet. Then, two at a time, he moved the geraniums to the floorboard, asking her to slide toward the center to allow more space. "You'll have to hold this one beside you," he said as he placed the largest plant, the bleeding heart vine, on the leather bench.

She moved to the center, quite aware that their bodies would be very close when Ben boarded. *Mr. Franklin, was it?* Whatever his real name—Merritt, Franklin, or maybe half a dozen other names—she felt safe with him. Claude Leveque wouldn't dare come near her while this man sat beside her.

Ben swung himself into the driver's seat, but didn't pick up the reins. She breathed in his lime scent and warmth flooded her body. She murmured again how glad she was to see him.

He put his lips on her earlobe. "I'd like a kiss—kisses—one for each day I haven't seen you. That would be ..."

She interrupted him in a normal voice. "I don't believe it would be proper. We've made a spectacle of ourselves, as it is."

"I have at any rate." With a grin, he gestured to his clothes. "You must give me your hand. I'll have a look at your wrist before we start for home. If it's broken, I'll take you straight to your doctor or to a hospital."

She leaned close, nearly putting her lips to his ear. "It's sore, but do I trust myself to an attorney who uses a false name when he purchases plants and now pretends to be a physician?" She slid a little to her right, looked up, her eyelashes fluttering, her voice teasing.

Her wrist likely broken, Maureen flirted with him. Once again, he admired her pluck. He wanted to scold her for coming out alone to the warehouse. She'd been in real danger, but she didn't know Mendoza and Leveque were suspects in Captain Kwan's murder. And she didn't know they were partners in a lucrative opium smuggling ring that almost certainly involved Francois St. Aubin. And Suzette?

Shrugging, he motioned to her wrist. "I use the name Mr. Franklin at the docks."

She raised an eyebrow. "I see. And at nurseries?"

"It's not unusual for businessmen to use an alias," he said breezily, then continued. "I can't claim to be a physician, but I speak from experience on the matter of broken bones. I had my share as a child. You?"

"None." She leaned toward him again and rested her wrist gingerly on his trousers, palm up. "Do what you will."

Gently, he pushed the sleeves of her coat and shirtwaist up and peeled her leather glove down. She inhaled sharply at her wrist's swollen, blue-black appearance. It looked ghastly.

"Can you move your fingers?"

Maureen wiggled each one in turn.

"Good. Real test. Can you bend it? At the wrist? Up and down and side to side?"

Maureen made a face, and he took the opportunity to put his arm around her shoulders and hold her tight. "Try it."

Lifting her hand, she bent it downward. "It hurts a little, but I can do it." She moved it from side to side and even pushed it backwards with the fingers of her right hand. "What do you think?"

"May I?"

Releasing her shoulder, he brought both hands to her wrist and ran his fingers lightly along the left side, the right side, the top and underside. Touching her intoxicated him. It was all he could do to keep his hands from cradling her face and bringing his lips to hers. He couldn't here, not in a carriage with just a leather covering over the seat. She'd made that clear. "I see and feel no jagged bone protruding. Wrist looks straight to me. I think it's sprained."

She sighed with relief. "Thank you for sharing your expertise."

"Shall we head for home now?" Just sitting here beside her made him happier than he'd been in a week.

"Please." She turned her head up and smiled, but the dimple on her left cheek was hidden by mud. "One more item first."

Did she expect a kiss? Her lips parted for a moment until she saw his unfurled handkerchief. He wet it with his tongue and carefully wiped her frowning face. "A glob of mud on your cheek might cause your father to wonder where you've been."

He guided Mephistopheles into the stream of carriages and focused on his role as a driver on the crowded, dark street. Neither spoke for several moments.

"I believe he's working late tonight. No one at the house will ask what I've been up to."

"Not Luz or Julia?"

"They think I spent the afternoon in the greenhouse."

His hand clenched on the reins. If her passion were needle-work, she might sneak away to a shop and buy embroidery floss. But ships on the river, warehouses on the bayou? "You should tell someone where you're going when you leave the house."

"You sound just like Papa! Do you?"

"What?"

"Tell someone every time you leave your lodging."

He smiled. "I've no one to tell. Besides, men and women are different."

"How astute of you to notice."

He chuckled and drove on without remarking.

"I'm not an idiot, you know. I asked the cab driver to wait, even paid him extra to do so."

"You probably told him you wouldn't be long, didn't you?"

They glanced sideways at each other, their eyes met and they laughed. "The first time I went in there, I spent twice the time I intended. You must have been enthralled."

Maureen looked at her watch and admitted she'd been in the building well over an hour and a half.

"And if I'd not arrived—to buy you a plant—which I failed to accomplish, you might have had difficulty getting home. No one would have known where to start looking for you."

"It was a plant sale on dry land—not a ship."

"You have no idea how vicious these people ... these men are."

She laughed. "Vicious? Nurserymen? Mr. Mendoza? He seemed quite pleas ..."

He interrupted. "I think he killed Captain Kwan."

Her face paled. For a moment, he wished he hadn't told her, but they were discussing a murder she had come close to witnessing. And he owed her the truth.

"Ben!" She clutched his arm. "When I went to the ship that afternoon, Mendoza was the man I saw walking away."

"You're certain?"

"Yes! I never saw his face and I never actually saw him *leave* the ship. But his shoulders, his height, the way he walked. I'm positive."

His mind spun. Maureen had just confirmed his suspicions. He wouldn't pretend for one moment that it was a coincidence that Mendoza wandered along the dock the afternoon Kwan died. He'd been on the ship later with the crew who dug up opium that night. Ben had followed Leveque until he'd disappeared down an alley between two houses on Chartres Street. Suzette's house, no doubt.

Maureen poked his shoulder hard. "Don't do that to me. We're talking about murder. You can't just clam up. What makes you say it was Vito Mendoza?"

He steered the carriage around a cart stopped dead still in front of them for no apparent reason. "I went to the *Hailong Hao* the night you found the dead captain. I was certain his murderer would come back for the plants."

"Because they had opium tins in the soil?"

He couldn't admit that. "Because, as you know, the ship contained hundreds of valuable plants. Plants Mendoza would love to steal and sell himself." He jerked his head in the direction of Lafitte Nursery.

"Please don't lie to me. I stole an azalea bush the afternoon I found the body. It had opium in the roots just like the camellia you bought from him."

"Do you still have it?"

"The bush?"

"The opium."

"Do you want to smoke it?"

"No, I don't want to smoke it."

"It's all right," she said soothingly. "I understand it's easy to become addicted and I'd like to help you. I've read about opium addiction. You can get better. It won't be easy, but there's a doctor who has a successful cure."

Her kindness stabbed his heart. She meant it. She wanted to help him beat the addiction she thought he struggled with. He turned his body to face her. "I'm not an addict, but I'm flattered that you would still care for me if I were."

She sighed, licked her bottom lip and seemed to take a great deal of interest in the geraniums at her feet. Did she believe him? Plants worth a fortune? Some were, but very little compared with the opium in the roots. Her lip—still moist—drove him mad. Despite the mud that was quickly drying into a stiff coating on his clothes, he was aroused by her nearness, her scent, and her incessant licking of that lovely lower lip.

He forced himself to concentrate on the smugglers. Suzette St. Aubin's butler had been on the ship with Mendoza. He needed to know more. "What's your connection with Leveque, the butler? Why on earth would he try to steal your handbag?"

She whispered and he had to lean toward her to hear. "He wants to frighten me."

"Why?"

"I … it's a long story."

"I want to hear every word."

Maureen shuddered a few times as she told Suzette's sad tale. He guided Mephy with one hand and put his other arm around her shoulders. "The poor woman. I felt there was something odd about her. I just didn't know what."

"It was the same with me. She seemed to behave strangely and make inappropriate comments. I didn't understand why."

He rubbed Maureen's upper arm and she snuggled closer to him.

"There's more, Ben. Don't be angry."

His pulse raced with anxiety when she told him she'd visited the house to get Suzette's clothes. The rest came out in a jumble: The red and black corsets, the worn ridges on the bedposts, the ropes. All details turned his stomach. When she said she'd gone through Monsieur St. Aubin's desk, he held his breath and prayed the ledger belonged to Suzette's husband. At last she said she'd found a book. "A black journal."

He exhaled. *Thank God. The ledger in Maureen's lap desk belonged to St. Aubin.*

Her next words crushed his hopes, then disgusted him. "The book outlined the 'Training of Suzette St. Aubin.' That was written on the first page."

Ben's mouth went so dry, he couldn't speak. Monsieur St. Aubin kept an account of the torture of his wife.

"I shouldn't have seen that," she said softly. "I wish I'd never gone in his bedroom."

He pulled her closer to him, wanting to shield her from the world's horrors.

"I left the journal, but I found something else—and—I took it."

Chapter Thirty-Three

"I stole Monsieur St. Aubin's account ledger."

"You!" he shouted with a mixture of relief and jubilation. He dropped the reins for a second and hugged her. Her father wasn't a smuggler. Neither was she. His dear Maureen didn't suggest hiding opium in the roots of plants. "You'll never know how glad I am to know you're a thief."

She glanced up at him, a frown wrinkling her forehead. "I know I shouldn't have. Honestly, I don't know what came over me. I saw it and just grabbed it."

"I'm so happy you did."

"Please don't tease me."

"I'm not." Although he believed he knew what was in the book, he asked her to tell him anyway.

"He's a coffee importer, you know. It's a list of pounds he imports per week, with the profits totaled for each month. And he makes a fortune."

"I didn't realize he imported coffee. I thought his money came from his sugar plantation."

"Coffee and sugar both, Suzette said. That's why he travels to Jamaica so often. Jamaican coffee."

So that was his story. Coffee, not opium.

"The profits were huge. I wonder if Suzette knows."

She lost him there. Hadn't she just said Suzette told her about the coffee? "Knows what?"

"How rich he is."

Given the way her husband treated her, he doubted it, and said so, then asked her to try to remember everything she could about Leveque.

Maureen said she thought Monsieur St. Aubin was hiding more than the fact that he beat his wife. "Unfortunately, beating your wife is not illegal."

Maureen's words tested him. He guessed she knew what Monsieur St. Aubin imported, but he forced himself not to tell her. He kept his voice even. "Leveque must know you're the one who took the ledger. St. Aubin wouldn't want his personal finances revealed. Maybe he thought you had the ledger in your purse." He shrugged. "Where is it?"

"It's safe. But I think Leveque was in the house Sunday looking for it while I was working at the Bouchards." He acknowledged her thought with a nod, then a frown. "That'd be very bold of him."

"Somebody was there, I'm sure of it." She proceeded to tell him all the mistakes the intruder had made—from leaving the kitchen door unlatched to disturbing the linens in the sideboard to leaving paintings crooked and sofa cushions out of place.

He was damn glad Carleton wasn't around to hear her summary. He moved closer to her so their legs touched. Despite the cool night air, he grew warm from the motion of his thigh against hers. He wanted to turn into an alley, stop his horse and kiss her. Block by block, their legs pressed as he leaned toward her, making a turn or executing a pass of another carriage. Her sore wrist slid from her lap to his coat, resting on his thigh, where she left it. He drew in a sharp breath. He felt as if his blood were boiling beneath the surface of his skin.

At the corner of Canal Street and St. Charles, Ben pulled on the reins and stopped, jumped down, and lit the lanterns on each side of the carriage. When he climbed in the seat again, he asked if she were warm enough and was pleased when she said no. He lifted her sore wrist onto his thigh again, then put an arm tightly around her shoulders. His physical longing intense, he hardly trusted himself not to slide his hand down her side until it reached her hip, her bottom.

He turned into the side street that marked the edge of the Collins property and helped Maureen down. He watched her go into her side yard and walk into the garden. As agreed, Ben gave her a ten-minute head start, then he and Mephistopheles trotted right up the drive to the front door. He unloaded all the plants on the porch, then knocked.

Julia gaped at the sight of him. Ben wasn't sure if her reaction resulted from the mud covering him or from the array of colorful plants surrounding him. Whichever, she recovered quickly.

"Heavens to Betsy, Mr. Ben, come in, sir." She stepped aside and gestured him into the front hall. Then she peered out at the porch again and chuckled. "Miss Maureen's gonna be excited to see you! Hand me your coat. Make yourself at home in the parlor, sir."

"I'm afraid I better stay right here." He gestured to his muddy feet.

Julia eyed his boots. "You're a mess, that's for sure."

If Maureen had been an actress on stage, she couldn't have played her part better. She came down the hall and greeted him as if she hadn't seen him in a week. She had tidied her hair with more pins and changed her shoes and skirt. Her high-collared shirtwaist was the same he'd seen peeking from the top of her coat earlier. Her skirt was bright blue wool and slim cut, fitting closely to her waist and hips. Lord knew where she'd hidden her mud-splashed coat.

He bowed to her and announced he had a few gifts for her. He signaled Julia, who opened the front door. Bringing her hands to her cheeks, Maureen shrieked. "My goodness, Mr. Merritt, what have you done?"

"Beautiful flowers for a beautiful lady," he said with a bow and broad smile. "Julia, is Guy available to help me get them into the greenhouse?"

"He's off on errands. I'll get the hand cart, sir, and bring 'em around to the back door. That sho is a lot of plants."

"Thank you, Julia," Maureen said.

Maureen and Ben helped load the cart with plants. The minute Julia turned her back, Ben grabbed her hand and led her halfway down the hall.

"How long for Julia to get around back?"

"Not long enough."

He didn't have the mastery of his senses to be delicate in his kisses. The memory of her nightgown and robe mingled with the desire gnawing at him during the drive produced a raging hunger. Spreading his legs, he put his hands on her hips and pulled her tightly against him. The smell of her ignited a fire.

Maureen circled his neck with her hands, pressed her breasts against his chest and met his tongue with hers. Mad with desire, he wanted her to touch him. He moved her hand to the hard length of him and groaned with pleasure when she grasped him.

The greenhouse door banged as Julia came in. Maureen, her face flushed, stepped out of his arms, turned and hurried away from him. He couldn't face the cook in his present condition so he remained in the sunroom and listened to the women discussing where certain plants should go.

When he joined them, he dutifully carried the bleeding heart from the cart and placed it on the floor very close to the back door. The bag of bulbs and seeds went on the workbench. He lined the geraniums on a shelf where they'd get plenty of sunlight, per Maureen's instructions. The plants arranged, Ben sat on a stool at the workbench and motioned toward his feet. "If you'll excuse me, I best clean my boots before I join you in the parlor."

In her sink, he scrubbed the mud from the soles and dried them with the rags he found beside it. Minutes later, he stood in front of the fire, hands clasped behind his back, while Maureen sat demurely on the sofa. Julia placed a silver tray of sandwiches on the end table, went to the cellarette and poured their drinks. She served Maureen a glass of sherry, then gave Ben a large glass of whiskey, saying that a gentleman who brought that many flowers and destroyed his clothes in the process deserved a solid bit of refreshment. Ben laughed heartily and took a good gulp.

The moment Julia left the room, Maureen pulled a ledger from the sofa cushion.

"I ran upstairs for it. I want you to see it. Perhaps you should take it to your lodging."

"I think it's safer here, now that your father's back."

He sat on the floor, long legs outstretched, and leaned against the sofa's back. He read the first three or four pages slowly, then flipped through the rest. Monsieur St. Aubin and his butler, Leveque, had been bringing in large amounts of opium for more than a year. The product was referred to as *Goods* in the ledger, but the pounds imported and the profits earned spoke volumes. They weren't importing coffee.

He closed his eyes for a moment and breathed slowly. He would telegraph Carleton tonight. He'd completed his mission and could now follow his dream. He knelt up on one knee, not caring if he left mud on the rug.

"I have two points to make before you're allowed to speak one word, Maureen Collins."

Her eyes shone.

"One, I'm a man who lives in two worlds. I work as an agricultural inspector for the Department of the Treasury as Mr.

Andrew Franklin. My job is examining plants that come into port on ships."

"Plants?" Her mouth dropped open and she simply stared. "Plants?" she repeated. "You don't know a geranium from a rose, a camellia from an azalea. How could you possibly ..."

"I know pests—wooly apple aphids, cottony cushion scale, citrus mealybug, San Jose scale—when I see them." Her eyes widened as he continued. "And fungal diseases like phytophthora. California's fruit orchards have been devastated by some of these. The U.S. government is trying to prevent the spread of pests and diseases by inspecting imports."

She shook her head in disbelief. She questioned him in a small voice. "You board ships and look at their plants?"

"It's a long story—a favor to a friend. The U.S. government doesn't allow plants and trees to be imported that might affect our native plants."

"I know that. It could be disastrous."

"Exactly. It's what I do. I'm protecting the very plants you love from disease and pests." He paused for a moment. "We're both plant people."

His recital of horticultural pests hadn't impressed her as much as he thought it would. He tried again. "I know when you found opium, you thought the captain was a smuggler—and you thought I was. I think he hid some tins in flower pots for his personal consumption. More important is this. The lemon trees on board the *Hailong Hao* have cottony cushion scale. If they're allowed in the country, it'll spread through Florida and devastate the orchards there. No offense to you because I'm sure you're careful, but some plant sellers and buyers aren't as aware as they should be. Plant collectors want exotic plants from Japan, Australia and Europe. Diseases are cruising from one continent to another on the leaves of plants."

"I'm impressed with your knowledge. I am." She held up her hand. "Very well done. Now perhaps you can answer a question for me. Why didn't you just tell me this? Why keep it a secret that you work for the U.S. government?"

Ben sighed and thought quickly. This wasn't going according to plan. "I'm following orders, you know," he said. "One of those orders was not to reveal my mission to anyone. I really am a maritime lawyer."

Maureen tilted her head to one side and studied him for a moment through slightly narrowed eyes. Then she seemed to come to a decision. "Fine. No more of that. You said two things and you're bogged down on point one."

He laughed. "You don't mind calling me to task. Two, Miss Collins, I don't care what your relationship has been with Vespasian Colville in the past. And three"—he paused for a moment.

"You said only two," she interrupted.

"Three, I love you." He lifted her hand and rested it on his heart. "I've missed seeing you so much this week, I realized I can't live without you. Will you marry me, Maureen?"

Maureen felt her face flush at his declarations, a little deeper red with each. When he said he loved her, she sucked in a breath and held it while her heart thumped more quickly than it ever had in her life. A shiver climbed up her spine. "Tell me more about the last point, number three," she said hoarsely.

He bent forward. He let go of her hand and placed his just above her left knee—far more improper and intimate than her placing her limp wrist on his coat earlier—and squeezed her thigh through the fabric of her skirt and petticoat. She felt the pressure on her leg and enjoyed an ache higher up, a very pleasant ache, between her legs.

"I want to marry you."

She stared into his eyes, dark and intense with desire. "I love you, Ben, but my father ...'"

"We'll find a way around him. Say yes."

"I ..." Maureen tried to answer, but she couldn't breathe. Every five or six seconds, he tightened, then loosened, his grip on her leg. The ache was growing into a pain so acute Maureen wasn't sure she could sit still another moment. "Yes, Ben, yes."

The left side of his mouth rose in the quirky grin she'd loved the first night she saw him. "You weren't quick about it, but you've made me the happiest man on earth."

Keeping her hands off his body took all her willpower. He continued to play with her thigh and she wanted—well, she wanted to reach out and feel his arousal—and not through his clothes. If she could only unbutton his trousers and touch him. So hot she was sure her face was on fire, Maureen looked away from his pants to her shoes.

"I'm mad with desire for you," he whispered. "Do you understand what I'm saying?"

"Yes," she answered. "I do. I am for you."

"May I call later—at your bedroom balcony?"

She shook her head. "Not here. My father ..." Her voice trailed off. "If he caught us together again, I'd be sent to a convent for life. I'll think of some other way."

Chapter Thirty-Four

On Friday afternoon, William coerced Ben into inspecting a warehouse three blocks back from the river. The owner had offered it to Patrick Collins for a good price. Ben pleaded ignorance of real estate values in New Orleans, but William persuaded him: He'd be another pair of eyes.

Ben's mind on Maureen, he struggled to keep his attention on the cavernous frame building. Dutifully, he asked about dimensions, the number of bales of cotton it could hold, its distance from the barges where cotton was unloaded from the plantations, its distance to the cotton press they used, and finally, the distance from the press to the wharves where the ocean-going vessels bound for Liverpool and Lowell docked.

"It's a little out of the way, I'll admit," William answered to every one of those questions, "but it's inexpensive per square foot."

"I would advise against it. Labor will only increase in cost as time goes on. If you look at the extra hours taken in transporting cotton in and out of this place, you'll spend the difference you save in cost per square foot on the cost of labor. And then some, by the end of the century."

William gave him a shrewdly approving glance. "Exactly my thoughts."

"And your uncle thinks you should snap it up?"

"He does."

"I'd do some calculations based on double the current wages."

"I'd like you to look at another building, more expensive to purchase, but much closer to the river. Then I'll quote your objections to Patrick if you don't mind."

"Please do." The sun shone and the thermometer registered the mid-sixties, comfortable for February, compared with weather in Philadelphia or New York. A warm, gentle breeze blew off the river. For the moment, he felt content just to be out of the office, walking with William. He supposed the man knew of his banishment from the Collins home, and he wondered what he and Renee thought of it.

"Are you and Renee going to the Proteus ball Tuesday night?"

"We are. Renee thinks it's the best ball of the season." William glanced at him. "You're one of the krewe, aren't you?"

Ben nodded. "I'll be there. I invited Maureen and her friends Elise and Carine. Since I'll be in costume and mask, I intend to dance with her as often as I like. I presume you know I'm forbidden to see her."

William pursed his lips. "I've heard my uncle's set the date for Maureen's marriage to Colville. Renee and I hope he'll change his mind." He sighed heavily. "He values the sacrament of marriage too much to force Maureen to marry someone she doesn't love."

"I've proposed to Maureen and she's accepted."

William slapped him on the back and shook his hand. "Congratulations and welcome to the family."

"Thank you." The thought of marrying his love buoyed his spirits. "Maureen and I aren't going to give up. And Colville doesn't want to marry her either."

"How about a drink to celebrate? I owe you one for looking at these properties. There's a tavern up ahead. It's a sleazy place—I hate to admit I even know of its existence."

Peeling paint rendered the wooden sign, *Sugar Park Tavern*, which jutted out from the building over its alley entrance, almost unreadable. The name seemed vaguely familiar to Ben; perhaps he'd heard it mentioned by sailors on one of the ships.

Not much more than a tumbling down wooden shed, the place held no appeal. "We're going in here?" he joked. "Or better question, will we get out of here alive?"

He missed William's response, blending as it did with the bartender's shout, "Afternoon, Guvs."

William chose the booth and the bench closest to the front door. Ben slid onto the opposite bench. A pine table carved with names divided them. The barmaid's large breasts bursting from the top of her bodice, her wild red hair, the sign outside, these wooden booths, and even the smell of the river mixed with spilled beer jogged his memory. Ben glanced at the dark barge-board walls, and heard voices and laughter from the booth behind them.

"It's a hangout for cutthroats, no question," William said in a lower voice. He signaled the barmaid and ordered two beers.

Ben's mouth was so dry he couldn't open his lips to respond. He hadn't felt this thirsty since the evening he smoked opium with Captain Kwan. The barmaid set the mugs of beer on the table and winked at him. "Good to see you again, Guvner."

Ben took a gulp and felt some relief as the cold liquid flowed down his throat.

William smiled slyly. "Seems you're well-known for someone who's never been in here."

Ben shook his head. "I've never ..." He lifted his mug an inch or two off the table, then put it down again. He looked toward the front door, took in the bar at the far end and the serving girl leaning against it. "I *have* been here."

"It's not a sin." William chuckled. "The beer's actually not bad. So you've had a drink here. What of it?"

Ben felt feverish. Wet with perspiration, his hair stuck to his forehead, and he pushed it away with a trembling hand.

William frowned at him. "You look sick, Merritt. Do you need some air?"

"I thought I dreamed I was in this bar. But I think I *have* been here."

William's eyebrows arched upward. "So?"

Ben took a deep breath and exhaled loudly. "One afternoon, I smoked a pipe of opium with Captain Kwan."

"I tried it once in Paris," William shrugged. "Once was enough; it made me sick."

Ben raised his hand to his head. "It made me sick, too, but I had an incredible dream. And, William, I was here. Right here." He ran his hand across the table. "I drank a beer. Several beers. Many beers, I think."

William jerked his head in the barmaid's direction. "You must have left her a big tip. She remembers you well."

"There's more." Ben's voice cracked when he spoke. "While I was here, I overheard two men plotting a kidnapping. One man said he was making a lot of gold to kidnap ..."

Instantly, William sat up straight. "Who, Merritt?"

Ben formed each syllable slowly, having difficulty thinking it, much less saying it. "A ... Collins ... lass."

William's eyes went wide with incredulity. "Are you sure? Could it have been an opium fantasy? And why haven't you mentioned it until now? What's wrong with you, man?"

The noise around them ceased. It seemed everybody in the place wanted to hear what the gents were discussing. The barmaid sidled over. "More beer, gentlemen?"

"No," William snapped. When she moved away, William leaned across the table and grabbed Ben's arm. "What do you mean a Collins lass? Maureen or Renee?"

"Maureen." Just saying it out loud caused cramps in his stomach. "One of the fellows said her father would pay a lot for her and he needed help to do the job. The other man refused, said they'd be caught and hanged."

William shot him a look of disgust. "I don't suppose you got a good look at them?"

"No, and I have no idea what their names were. I don't know. I had the red camellia for Maureen. I put it on the bench beside me. I remember that."

William ran his hands through his hair. "Good God, you must remember something else."

"I don't," Ben locked eyes with him. "All I know is it wasn't a dream. Someone's planning to kidnap Maureen."

William stood. "We have to get back to the office and tell her father. He'll contact Captain McCorkle."

It was all Ben could do to keep from sprinting to Maureen's side. Captain McCorkle? He didn't expect much protection from that fine public servant. But, no question, they must warn her father.

William and Ben burst into Collins' office to find the man at his desk. Without any preamble, Ben reported what he'd overheard at the Sugar Park Tavern some weeks ago. Embarrassed, he explained he'd had a long day and night and thought the conversation was a bizarre nightmare. Until he returned to the tavern this afternoon.

Collins' emotions escalated rapidly from disbelief to outright rage that someone would dare to even think about injuring his daughter. Just as quickly, he turned to logical plans. Within minutes, he had a messenger on his way to the police station to hire off-duty officers to watch his house and guard his daughter. "I know she's safe for the time being. She's planting seeds in the sandbox in the greenhouse today." He looked at Ben and chuckled softly. "Merritt, you bought her enough seeds and plants to beautify the whole city of New Orleans."

Ben and William exchanged a glance. So she'd told her father she was spending the day in the greenhouse? *Which probably meant the exact opposite.* His heart pounded as his mind flew to the places Maureen might be. A shop? A nursery? Renee's? Suzette's? Yesterday, she had sneaked out to Lafitte Nursery alone. Leveque had grabbed her purse, but he could have done far worse. He could have rushed her into a carriage as dusk fell.

"Where the hell is Colville?" Collins asked.

William lifted a shoulder. "I haven't seen him in days. He seems to have vanished in thin air."

Shaking his head, Collins turned to William. "I'm going to see Maureen. You handle matters here. I'll grab a cab and head straight to the house."

That's exactly what Ben wanted to do. He stepped forward. "I'm happy to be of service. My carriage is right outside. Please, let me take you to her. I only want to know that she's safe."

Collins met his eyes. "I caution you, Merritt. I've not changed my opinion of you in relation to my daughter. This is a business matter. I expect you to bill the factorage for your time."

Ben replied, "No, sir. With all respect, this isn't a business matter."

Shifting his eyes from Ben to William, Collins pursed his lips and put his hands on his hips. "I'm not sure how much I want Maureen to know. I don't want her living in fear."

Ben had to speak up. Not informing a potential victim of danger made no sense. "I believe the more she knows the better she'll be able to protect herself."

Collins narrowed his eyes. "She's my daughter, Merritt. We'll tell her *I've* received a kidnapping threat from Imperial Shipping because the factorage joined the lawsuit against it."

Driving at break-neck speed down St. Charles Avenue, his knuckles white on the reins, Ben hoped to heaven that Maureen was in the greenhouse planting seeds, just as her father said.

So Colville had disappeared? He didn't need to strain his mind to know he was in the country with Suzette, and the factorage be damned. And this was the gentleman her father wanted Maureen to marry!

Thank God William had taken him to the Sugar Park and that his memory—though vague—was keen enough to recall some of the conversation and know Maureen was in danger. From whom? Dozens of ruffians might want to kidnap her for a ransom. Her father was one of the wealthiest men in the city.

But did it go beyond money? Did Patrick Collins have particular enemies who wanted to cause him the anguish of losing his daughter?

Chapter Thirty-Five

What on earth? Maureen heard footsteps racing down the hall in her direction. She looked up from the sand bed to see her father moving toward her through the elephant ears and ferns. Circling her one palm tree, his arms extended toward her, he called, "Thank God, Maureen. You're safe."

Even more startling, Ben followed right behind him. Ben and her father together?

Swallowing her in a big bear hug, her father held her long enough for her to feel the tension in his body ease. He stepped back, then gestured toward Ben, who bowed his head in her direction. "Ben offered me a ride to be certain you were here planting seeds and safe."

Frowning and locking eyes with Ben, she asked, "Is there a reason why I might not be?"

"I've some distressing news to share. Let's go in the back parlor and talk."

Instantly nervous about what she might hear, she removed her gloves, untied her apron and tossed both to the workbench. Going up the steps ahead of the men, she glanced back at Ben. He nodded. "There's no serious cause for worry. Everything is going to be all right."

"Yes, thank you, Merritt, for reassuring her. We didn't mean to alarm you, Maureen. We're just being cautious."

Once seated, with Ben in a chair across the room, she studied her father as he paced. He explained quickly that he'd been told this afternoon of a rumor circulating at the docks that he was to be kidnapped sometime in the next few weeks. "I'm guessing the threat comes from Imperial Shipping because our firm has joined a lawsuit against them." On the one hand, he dismissed the idea as not likely to occur. On the other, his brow furrowed in genuine worry.

Maureen was terrified that he might be in danger, but she marveled at the possibility that this company would plan something so preposterous. "Are they planning to kidnap the heads of all the companies they do business with? That must be half the shippers in North America."

He agreed she had a good point, but reiterated this was very serious. He explained he'd hired guards—likely to arrive within the hour—to protect the Collins house.

"But why are guards coming here to protect you, Papa, when you're at the office most of the day? Why not protect the factorage?"

At that moment, the door opened and Guy rushed in, a letter in his outstretched hand. "Messenger said it was urgent, Mr. Patrick."

Taking the envelope, her father ripped it open. "Dear Lord." His face reddened. "There's a fire at the Calliope warehouse." He shot across the room to the door.

Maureen jumped up. "A fire?" she shrieked. "How bad is it?"

"Fire's under control, but William's worried some of the workers may be injured. I have to go right his minute." He put his head in the hallway. "Guy, will you ask Noah to ready the carriage?"

Ben followed on his heels. "Shall I come, too, sir? There could be legal ramifications."

"Stay here with Maureen until the guards arrive."

Maureen rushed forward, caught her father at the door and kissed him on the cheek. "Please let me know what's happening. And be careful."

The door shut behind him. She wrung her hands for a moment and nearly collapsed from a mix of emotions. She'd been peacefully planting seeds when the men burst into her calm. Her voice sounded willowy to her own ears. "A kidnapping threat, a fire, workers injured? It's all too much for one day."

Ben came up behind her, gently took her arm and led her back to the sofa. "Would you like tea?"

"No. Sherry, please. You have a drink, too." She motioned to the cellarette.

He handed a sherry to Maureen, but he took nothing. "May I sit?"

She nodded and patted the cushion beside her. He sat very close and circled her shoulder with his arm.

"Thank you," she murmured. "I'm glad … you're here." Tears tumbled from her eyes. Next came wrenching sobs. Ben took her glass, put it carefully on the side table and wrapped her in his arms. He settled her head against his chest and gave her his handkerchief. He rubbed his hand up and down her back. "Calm down, my love. The fire sounds like it's under control. And someone probably panicked and sent word about injuries without actually taking a count of the workers. Happens all the time."

His words soothed her, but it took her quite a while to get control. The word kidnapping hammered in her ears. "What about the kidnapping? Is Papa really in danger?"

"I doubt it. A rumor like that? There may be no truth to it at all. Your father's smart and he's seeing to it that guards are protecting you and him. He's not going to take any chances." He held the glass to her lips and she took another sip of sherry. "And while I'm on the subject, Miss Maureen, I was terrified as we raced over here that you weren't really in the greenhouse."

"But I was."

"Today, yes, but you're not always where you say you're going to be. Please don't tell Julia and Luz one thing and do something else until this issue is resolved."

Could she promise something and stick to it? She side-stepped. "I'll be careful."

Standing, he stretched out his hand and grasped hers. "Why don't you show me around the garden and tell me where you intend to plant some of your new acquisitions."

Maureen sprang to her feet. "I'll get a wrap."

She returned with a plum wool shawl over her arm. Handing it to him, she swept up her hair and turned her back to him. He placed the shawl on her shoulders with a gentle caress of her upper arms. She sighed and leaned back against him. "I like the feel of your lips there."

Maureen's plans for the garden were on the table in the greenhouse. She began to explain the positions of various flowerbeds, but she saw he was distracted. She wasn't surprised when he suggested they go outside.

She gestured to a bare spot where she'd asked her father to have an arbor built. "The four rose bushes you gave me will be the first of many climbers to grow on, under or beside the arbor. I'm a little worried about bees, but you can't blame them for loving roses as much as I do."

"Do you suppose when your father allows me to call on you— *and he will eventually*—I'm sure of it, I could kiss you under the arbor?"

She faced him, wrapped her arms around his neck, closed her eyes, and tilted her mouth up for a kiss. "You can kiss me where the arbor's going to be."

Ben teased her lips and trailed kisses down her neck. He traced the contours of her earlobes, and her eyebrows with his lips.

Laughing now, Maureen laced her fingers in his and hurried them down another path and through a break in the yaupon hedge that ran beside it.

"I love you, Ben. It's been way too long since we've had a moment alone."

He crushed her body to his. With the tip of his tongue, he circled, he advanced, he retreated, savoring the sensations of her lips. While his tongue delved deeply into the heat of her mouth, he brought his hands to roam over her waist and hips. He cupped her bottom and pressed her into his hard member, sending a shock of pleasure through her. "I love you, Maureen, more than anyone in the world."

She tugged his shirt and undershirt from his trousers and slowly slid her hand up his bare chest. Her fingers played with his chest hair and flitted over his nipples. Dropping her hand to the waistband of his trousers, her fingertips played in the hair on his lower stomach. He gasped and she delved lower, grazing his stiff penis with her fingers.

Ben pulled her hand from his pants. "I love what you're doing to me, but I think it'd be safer if we went indoors."

Embarrassed, she stepped back.

He lifted her chin and stared into her eyes. "Your father asked me to protect you, not make love to you."

Hurt, she lashed out at him. "You know what? I'm no fool. It's an absurd story, this kidnapping. It's Papa's way of watching me day and night until I marry Vespasian in May."

He didn't answer right away. Unfortunately the kidnapping threat was against her, not her father. And it was real. Very real.

"The guards will be here soon. And I want you safe until then. We're in the garden in daylight. If we continued ..." He motioned to his crotch. "I'd be so distracted, I might miss a movement behind the hedge or the sound of footsteps approaching."

She allowed him a small smile. He circled her waist with a firm arm and led her toward the greenhouse. The only sound was the crunching of their shoes on the oyster shells. Once inside, he made a show of locking the door and cautioned her that she mustn't be in here without locking up. She poured him a whiskey and herself a sherry. They sat at her table.

There was no point in talking about the two subjects most on their minds—the kidnapping and the fire. They had no information and idle speculation would likely distress her.

She brought up Suzette. "When she returns, I'd like to show her the ledger. She needs to know how much her stingy husband earns on his coffee imports. It may help her with her divorce." They talked briefly about Maureen's visit to the monsignor and a civil divorce being Suzette's only recourse.

Maureen shuddered and he lay a hand atop hers. He didn't know whether an imprisoned spouse, which was surely St. Aubin's destiny, was grounds for divorce in Louisiana, but he soothed Maureen by saying he thought it would all work out for her friend.

"Will you keep the ledger, please? I don't want anything the man touched anywhere near me. It's in the workbench, first drawer on the left." He rose, grabbed the book and put it in his inside coat pocket. He patted his jacket and volunteered to help Suzette any way he could.

She took a few sips of sherry and studied him closely as she spoke. "Your job sounds fascinating. Inspecting plants. I'd like a job like that myself. What would Papa say if I told him that was my ambition?"

"He'd be horrified, I believe."

"It's terrible that something as beautiful and calming as plants led to murder. What exactly was the motive again?"

"I'm looking into it," he said, his voice stiff.

"Hmm. Does that happen often in your experience, plants leading to murder?"

"New Orleans is my first assignment so I have no idea. You know, though, that these plants are worth hundreds of dollars, some of them." He shrugged. "When there's a lot of money involved, the value of human life diminishes, I suppose."

"How will you ever prove Mendoza murdered Captain Kwan? It could have been anybody who knew he had a deck full of exotic plants."

"I have some ideas." He didn't elaborate and he knew she was disappointed.

She leaned in and whispered. "Who are you, Ben? *Honestly*, who are you?"

"An attorney who does plant inspections at the port as a favor for a friend."

"Letitia told me you weren't what you seemed." Her bottom lip protruded in a pout.

Damn Letitia. She knew much more than Maureen did, but he thought she had the sense to remain quiet.

"It hurts my feelings that you lead a double life and you don't trust me enough to tell me what I can do to help. I'm going to be your wife."

He caressed both her hands with his, careful to be gentle with her sprained wrist. "And I can't wait for you to be my wife. I think you can help me. May I pick your brain?"

She quirked an eyebrow. "Sounds unpleasant."

"You know everybody in the city, don't you?"

She nodded enthusiastically. "A bit of an exaggeration, but there aren't many people I don't know ... or know of."

He smiled at the triumphant look on her face.

"All right. Here's a question. I saw Claude Leveque and Vito Mendoza on the ship the night the captain died. You took the ledger from St. Aubin's desk, so we know he's involved. There was a third man aboard the *Hailong Hao*. A man the others called Benoit. Do you know any Benoits?"

"It's an old New Orleans name. Can you describe him?"

"Tall and thin, white hair. Looks a lot like Leveque except he has a mustache and short beard. Not physically strong. Injured. A war injury, probably. Walked with a pronounced limp in his right leg. Used a cane."

"Dark eyes?"

"I couldn't see well enough to say for sure."

He imagined wheels turning in her brain as a frown tightened her forehead. "Some of the Benoits are French with dark eyes. Some of them have some German blood in them. They're fairer with blond or light brown hair and blue eyes."

"If I say I think he's part of the French branch, does that give you any ideas?"

"Eyes just like Madame Soniat's," she murmured and tilted away from him, her own eyes glazed over in thought. Then she frowned again and looked back toward him. "Let me tell you the story. Therese Benoit Soniat was Renee's mother-in-law during her brief first marriage. She had eyes dark as night." Maureen shivered. "Thank heavens, she's deceased.

"Maureen! What a terrible thing to say."

"She was a terrible woman."

Ben's heart pounded. He probed. "This Madame Soniat? She had a brother? A cousin?"

"A brother named Alphonse, supposedly killed at Shiloh." She leaned forward and whispered. "They never found his body." She paused a moment. "People said he deserted. I heard a rumor a few months ago that he's nearby, that he lives on a houseboat on Lake Pontchartrain."

Ben's breath caught as he voiced his last question: "And he'd be how old?"

She fixed her eyes on the greenhouse's glass ceiling for a moment as if that would help her mathematical calculations. "He was among some of the last gentlemen in the area who signed up. He was in his forties when he joined the army. I'd say, sixty to sixty-five. Papa bought the factorage from his mother," she added, just as Julia came in to announce the arrival of the guards.

"Ahhh. Makes sense." That was the piece of the puzzle that had confused him. Benoit and his cronies weren't just opium smugglers. They'd planned Maureen's kidnapping as revenge because her father had taken over the Benoit family's business.

He jumped to his feet. "Thank you, my love. I'm off to find Benoit."

Maureen's mouth dropped open at his abrupt change of tone. He bent and kissed her on the lips, then turned to Julia. "Maureen and I are betrothed."

The cook put her hands on her hips. "Mr. Vesp ..."

Ben cut her off. "Please watch this young lady like a hawk, will you?" He grasped both Julia's shoulders. "Maureen means more to me than any person in the world. I need you and Luz to keep her safe in this house."

Chapter Thirty-Six

Monsieur Gaudet, proprietor of Belle Fleur, refused to meet Ben's eyes when he came through the door. He couldn't blame the man for being wary. He'd nearly strangled him on his previous visit. As he approached the counter, Ben held both hands up in a gesture of peace. "I promise I'll not harm you. I'd like to buy a flowerpot."

Gaudet hesitated a moment, but then seemed to decide to be polite and probably make a sale. "I have many beautiful hand-painted pots, as you can see. What size do you need?"

"I'm looking for a plain white pot. About a foot high, about a foot in diameter." Ben indicated the size with his hands.

The man shook his head. "It's not the fashion at all."

Ben shrugged. "My lady friend believes a white pot shows off the flowering shrub planted in it to better advantage." Ben grinned. "You know, no competition with the flowers painted on the pot. That's her idea. Do you have anything in the back room?"

Gaudet mumbled that he'd look and disappeared. Five minutes passed, then ten. Perhaps he'd gone to find a police officer whom he'd drag in to arrest Ben for assault on his previous visit. If a blue-coated officer emerged from the curtained room, Ben thought to make a run for it. If he were arrested, he knew Captain McCorkle would side with Monsieur Gaudet rather than a Yankee lawyer and plant inspector.

The last thing he needed was a night or two in jail. That would give Patrick Collins another ace in his hand in betting against him as husband material. In truth, Ben was annoyed with himself for his heavy-handed approach with Monsieur Gaudet. He seemed a simple sort who most likely would have told Ben everything he knew without a hand laid on him.

The sound of footsteps signaled the man's return—carrying nothing. "I'm afraid I couldn't find anything, sir."

Ben exhaled. "That's a shame. I'll pay double what it's worth." He paused for emphasis. "I'll pay triple what it's worth because it's her birthday. Do you mind looking again?"

A minute behind the curtain and Gaudet returned with exactly what Ben wanted—a white clay pot with a matte finish. He didn't care that the man's delays were a ploy to up the price. He played the fool and raved over the pot. "And what do I owe you?"

"Eight dollars, sir." Smirking, Ben removed his wallet and counted out the bills. If Maureen were standing beside him, she'd say the pot wasn't worth more than a half-dollar. At the outside, a dollar.

"Shall I wrap it?"

"Yes. Please just wipe it clean first." He squinted. "I see a cob-web or two inside."

Gaudet put on gardening gloves and cleaned the pot thoroughly inside and out with a wet rag. Ben nodded graciously, thanked him for his help and was off.

At Lafitte Nursery, he spotted Vito Mendoza unloading a mule-drawn cart at the side of the building while a helper unhitched the animal. Mendoza yelled a greeting as Ben crossed the yard toward him. "Mr. Franklin, good to see you. I hope the lady has recovered from the mishap a few days ago."

"She's perfectly fine. I'm sure she'll be back next time you advertise a big sale. I think she'd walk through fire and brimstone to acquire an exotic plant."

Mendoza chuckled. "She has an eye. She bought some fine flowers." He glanced toward the spot where Ben and Maureen had landed on the ground. "I try to keep the ruffians away, but there's a lot of pirogue traffic on the bayou." He shifted his feet restlessly. "There's only so much I can do."

Nothing more he could do? Ruffians? No. A butler in a French Quarter home. In his employ or vice versa? Ben stared blankly at the plants in the cart, hoping Mendoza believed Mr. Andrew Franklin was nothing more than an idle rich man who doted on a young woman. "I'm looking for something truly outstanding for the lady. And I brought my own pot today."

Motioning to the fifty or so small-leafed green bushes, half in the cart, half at his feet, Mendoza asked, "Don't suppose I could interest you in an English boxwood?"

Ben shook his head. "She likes flowers."

"So she does," he agreed. Mendoza shouted to the man leading the mule toward the barn at the back of the lot. "Finish up here, Timmie." He faced Ben. "Let's see what I can find for you, Mr. Franklin."

Mendoza tossed his work gloves on the counter beside the cash register as they entered the warehouse. He led the way up the rickety staircase, where each tread creaked and each riser squeaked. Ben was a big man, tall and broad, but he had no desire to challenge the plant seller in a fight. Captain Kwan's body, his head nearly severed, came to mind. He swallowed hard to steady himself.

"My shrubs with sweet roots are in the back here." Mendoza waved a hand toward the far end of the room. He started into a path through a maze of plants, but Ben didn't follow. "I have camellias, azaleas, one more blooming *polygonum orientale*," Mendoza called over his shoulder.

"I've given her all those," Ben answered, raising his voice. "Do you have something a little different that'll fit in my pot?"

Mendoza nodded and continued his stroll among the plants. The man bent over now and then to touch a leaf, smell a flower. He had murdered Captain Kwan and maybe a half-dozen others for all Ben knew, yet he seemed to genuinely love his plants. Probably talked to them when he was alone in here.

Stopping and turning around, Mendoza held up a plant with lavender blooms falling from its stems like lush bunches of grapes. "Here's a wisteria. What do you think?"

He hadn't known the flower's name, but Maureen's sitting room had wallpaper printed with these blooms. She would be pleased with it, he was sure. "I'll take it! I believe the young lady will love it."

When Mendoza drew close, Ben held up his pot. "I'd kill it if I tried to transplant it myself. Do you mind?"

"It's not part of our typical services, but you're a good customer, Mr. Franklin."

Mendoza braced the wisteria against his chest with one hand while he hooked his thumb in the white pot, his fingers on the outside, and carried both to a workbench on the left wall.

Ben began pacing at the top of the steps, giving the man the privacy he needed to transfer the opium with the soil. They both knew opium was in the plant's roots; they both knew Mendoza would charge a fragrant-root price and Ben would happily pay it.

The repotting completed, Mendoza brought the plant down the stairs to the counter, Ben right behind him. His wallet in his hand, he asked the price, handed over five dollars and shook Mendoza's hand. Eight dollars for the pot, five for the wisteria. Quite a bit of money, but he was sure Maureen wouldn't think it too high a price to pay for the evidence he would gather with this pot.

Trying very hard to look relaxed, Ben slowly removed his gloves from his coat pocket and put them on. He picked up the pot and walked as calmly as he could from the warehouse back across the yard to his carriage. Taking a deep breath for the first time in more than thirty minutes, Ben took the reins and directed Mephy back up Esplanade Avenue. Heavy traffic, the result of tourists flocking to the city for Mardi Gras, slowed his travel. No matter. He'd done it.

At his lodgings, Ben placed the wisteria carefully on his desk and turned the gaslight up as high as he could. He dusted the pot with charcoal he'd scraped from the bricks in his chimney. The results couldn't have been better. There were two crisp thumbprints on the front of the pot and three perfect fingerprints from each hand on the back.

He ate cold ham and cornbread, drank three cups of coffee and donned the rough clothes he wore when he went to the docks at night. Into his jacket's pockets, he loaded everything he might need: a pair of leather gloves, a large envelope, a hack saw, a short length of rope, a handkerchief for a blindfold, a kerchief for a gag. In an ankle holster strapped to his right leg, he placed his 38-caliber pistol. He slipped his knife into his left boot.

At ten o'clock Ben sauntered down the levee. The wind blew hard, nearly taking his hat, waves broke against the dock, but he felt no rain yet. A lantern on the *Hailong Hao*'s deck surprised him, so he took cover behind a sugar barrel and watched. McCorkle, as brilliant as a farmer who shuts the barn door after the cows escape, had stationed a guard on the deck.

Ben timed the man's trek from bow to stern and back until he had a consistent timetable.

He put on his gloves. On the officer's next trip to the stern, he dashed up the gangplank and dove behind two barrels beside the cabin door. He held his breath when the man came near him.

The instant he turned his back, Ben sprang. He struck the butt of his gun against the man's skull, making far more noise than he imagined it should. The body slumped to the deck. Dropping to his own knees, he pulled the man close and checked his pulse.

Relieved he hadn't killed him, he tied him up. Hands first, then feet, then blindfold, and finally the gag in his mouth.

Taking the one lantern on the deck with him, he walked through the first room, opened the door to the second, and gagged at the stench of dried blood. His boots stuck to the gummy substance on the floor. Groping in his pocket, he found his handkerchief, held it over his nose and mouth for a moment, then tied it securely in place.

What kind of operation did Captain McCorkle run? It unnerved him that no one had cleaned up. He hadn't expected to re-live the crime tonight. He swallowed hard, fighting nausea. Maureen, too, had seen the dead man, the blood. He imagined she'd have nightmares off and on for years. Very soon, though, he'd be beside her in bed to comfort her when she dreamed of Captain Kwan's slashed throat.

Standing on the threshold between the rooms, he held the lantern high and surveyed the smaller room, taking in the bed where he'd smoked a pipe with the captain, He looked to the larger room, specifically to the desk where Captain Kwan had tucked Ben's payment for the camellia into a drawer. The laziness of the locals worked in his favor. It appeared nothing had been touched since he and Captain McCorkle had left here. Leveque, Benoit and Mendoza had been here for hours digging up tins in the roots of plants, but the desk looked untouched.

Ben worked quickly. No money remained in the shallow drawers. In the dim light, he strained to see fingerprints on the desk, but the dark mahogany hid them. He shuffled through the papers. Receipts for goods purchased in Jamaica—bananas, rum, coffee—nothing more than for the crew's consumption.

How long did he have before the officer woke? He had no idea. Carleton, who'd taught him to knock someone out, had failed to mention that important fact. My God, he was thinking too much. He riffled through unused envelopes in a cubby. His eyes fell on a bloody thumbprint emblazoned on the paper as clearly as a seal in wax. He exhaled slowly as he turned the envelope over. On the back were four clear fingerprints. How fortunate the murderer didn't wipe his hands before searching through the desk. Retrieving the larger envelope from his jacket, he placed the evidence inside and put it safely away.

He turned to exit and caught sight of another print. On the pine-planked door, just at waist height, was another thumbprint. On the door's opposite side, four finger prints were sharper than a printer's proof. Did he really need these?

The plank door looked none too sturdy. A crossed piece of wood at the door's top and another at the bottom was all that held the board he wanted in place. He kicked swiftly and the lower part of the plank came loose. A few jabs of his elbow released the top. Squinting at the prints, he braced the board on a chair and split the lower half away with his foot.

For the first time, he became aware of rain hitting the roof. Heavy rain. Damn it, the plank had to remain dry. He removed his jacket and carefully rolled the board inside it. He left it and the lantern inside the outer room and stumbled outside in the darkness. The wind had turned violent; the rain lashed at his face and quickly soaked his clothes. The guard lay on his stomach where he'd left him, but he thrashed his feet, attempting to wiggle the rope free. Ben dragged him the few feet into the cabin, turned his face toward the wall and issued a stern warming. "If you turn around, I'll kill you."

"No, please. Jesus, I won't move."

Ben tucked the jacket that protected both the plank and evidence envelope under his arm, snatched the blindfold off the guard and dashed from the room, across the deck and down the gangplank. Holding his coat against his body, he ran the two blocks to his carriage. He placed the jacket under the seat in a small box designed for just the purpose of keeping important items. Then he took the time to greet Mephy, pat his head and slip him some sugar cubes. His horse eyed him with disdain, but accepted the treat.

"I suppose you don't like a mission in the rain." Mephy's head bobbed up and down and Ben laughed out loud. "I don't either, but I have exactly what I need. I'll have you home and dry in no time."

At the livery stable, a boy greeted him enthusiastically, saying he'd take good care of the beautiful horse. Ben tipped him, retrieved his jacket from the box and watched as the boy led Mephy away. The sight jarred his memory.

Timmie leading the mule away. *Timmie. Timmie was the man's name at Sugar Park Tavern who'd asked for help with the kidnapping! Smiley was the man who'd refused.* He remembered, on Twelfth Night, hearing the name Smiley, the leader of the group who attacked him. As he suspected, he'd not been a random victim.

Chapter Thirty-Seven

The knocking on the door began just as Ben finished dressing. *Not Letitia. She had returned to Philadelphia.* He wondered who thought he'd like to be disturbed on a Saturday morning.

The pounding continued. His cottage's defenses consisted of one door. He tiptoed to it and flung it open.

"It's about time," Maureen scolded. "I've been standing in this courtyard feeling like a fool for some time."

"What a pleasant surprise!" He stepped aside, ushered her in and wrapped her in his arms. His mouth on her lips, his eyes caught sight of her rough wool cape. He drew back. "What on earth?"

"Do you think I can walk out the front door as Maureen Collins?" Smiling, she twirled in a circle, almost a dance move. "Luz's clothes and bonnet."

"Ingenious!" He laughed in spite of her recklessness. He almost reprimanded her for sneaking out when there was a plot in place to kidnap her, but she didn't know that, so he had to admire her for finding a way to see him. He supposed the disguise she wore to deceive her guards would thwart kidnappers, too. "You're brilliant. Let me look at you."

She removed the cape. The red and white striped cotton dress with long sleeves and a slightly gathered skirt fell just a little long over her shoes. Its square bodice molded to her breasts and accentuated her hips in a most alluring fashion. The bonnet, black felt with red flowers appliquéd to it, and ribbon ties under her chin, shielded her face under its brim. She untied the ribbons and dropped the bonnet on a chair. "I hope I'm welcome."

"Welcome? Does the most beautiful woman in the world— my betrothed—have doubts I'm pleased to have her visit my lodging?"

Eyes bright, cheeks dimpling, she sent her curls from her bodice to her back with a quick movement of her hand. "None," she said softly. She licked her bottom lip. God, he loved her bottom lip.

The memory of yesterday in her garden heated his blood. Today they were alone in a safe place with a locked door. He considered the opportunities this presented, but wondered if hers and his were the same thoughts. He studied her smiling eyes. They looked mischievous.

Maureen turned away from him, circled the room, murmuring about his books, the coals smoldering in the hearth, his comfortable chairs.

"Let me add a little wood to the fire." As he spoke, he gestured to a chair for her. In minutes, he had a warming blaze. She wasn't here to see his lodgings. He knew she wanted him. God knows he wanted her.

The wisteria in the white pot caught her eye. "How lovely."

No one knew she was here. If this wasn't an invitation to make love to her, he didn't know what it was. Fighting his arousal, he took a deep breath and decided to play to her whims. Perhaps she regretted coming alone to his rooms. Could being alone with him make her nervous? Was that why she now acted like a stranger politely admiring a plant?

He was happy just seeing her and flirting with her. He didn't need to do more than that if she didn't want to. He bent close to the base of the pot and pointed. "Look closely," he said. "Do you see the fingerprints on the surface?"

She brought her face close to his to see what he saw, then gazed into his eyes. "I see distinct swirls."

"It's a perfect match with prints from the *Hailong Hao*. Sit down over there and I'll show you more."

She sat in his desk chair. He went to the bedroom and returned in seconds with the envelope containing papers from the desk and the blood-stained board. He laid both on the desk beside the flowerpot. "I examined them when I returned home last night. But I'd like your opinion. It seems clear to me Mendoza's the murderer."

She recoiled a moment at the sight of the bloodied envelope, but she accepted the magnifying glass and compared the prints. Standing beside her, he breathed in her scent.

"This is amazing. It's so obvious that these are from the same person. You're sure no two people have the same print?"

"Positive. Each person's prints are unique."

"What are you going to do, now that you know this?"

"Without prints on the knife, I don't have conclusive proof. All I know is Mendoza, with blood on his hands, was in the captain's cabin. I believe it'll be enough to convict him."

This time she bit her lip instead of licking it. "Ben, please tell me the truth. What are you doing in New Orleans?"

He had been an actor from the moment he arrived in this city. He'd pretended to be a customs official inspecting plants, pretended to be an opium smoker, pretended to be a rich man interested in buying plants with sweet roots or fragrant roots depending on the merchant. He'd pretended an interest in Maureen Collins to get inside her father's house.

No, the last wasn't true. From the moment he saw her, he felt a fierce attraction. He'd kissed her on the street in front of her house, stunning himself with that action. He was in love. She would be his wife. If he couldn't trust his own wife, then what did love really mean to him?

Saying he had much to tell her, he took her hand, guided her to one of his comfortable leather chairs by the fire, and sat on the floor at her feet. He began his story with his discovery of his great-grandfather's journal when he was twelve. He explained his research on the Opium War of 1840, his guilt over his family's ill-gotten wealth, his recruitment by the Secretary of the Treasury, his training in lock picking, breaking and entering. His expertise with guns and criminal detection methods. He told her everything.

Hands folded in her lap, Maureen listened, nodding now and then. When he began his description of his work in New Orleans, she raised an eyebrow and interrupted. "You were in my house last Sunday, weren't you?"

He admitted it all—his suspicions concerning her father because he was the port's biggest shipper, his surveillance of her house the night they met, and his break-in at her house.

"When I found St. Aubin's ledger in your lap desk, I knew it wasn't your hand-writing. I knew it wasn't William's. I ran downstairs to the library and compared your father's in his ledger. I knew it wasn't his." He shrugged. "I thought it might be Colville's. I didn't care that I had to begin my investigations all over again. I was so relieved the Collins family wasn't involved. After I knew you'd stolen the ledger yourself and from whom, I asked you to marry me. Remember?"

She protested. "How could you possibly suspect my father or me of smuggling?"

He met her eyes and spoke the absolute truth. "I didn't want to believe it was possible, but I'd been trained to suspect everyone until I could prove otherwise.

She sighed softly. "Thank heavens I'm no longer a suspect—or my father. When will you arrest the smugglers?"

"I won't actually be involved. When Monsieur St. Aubin returns to town, my colleagues will arrest him at his home. They'll surprise Mendoza at the nursery and confiscate the plants with opium in the roots. When they are questioned, I'm sure these two will implicate the others—Leveque and Benoit."

Maureen's heart swelled. Her instincts about him had been correct: He was a good man, a kind, intelligent person working for the U.S. government. Knowing the truth, she felt ashamed she'd ever doubted him.

"Ben, your trips to the docks. Your gifts of dozens of plants. I really thought you were an opium fiend who smoked what was in the tins and then gave me the plants." Her voice dropped to a whisper. "I tried to get you to admit it the night you found Vespasian and Suzette because I wanted you to know I loved you even if you were an opium addict."

He reached up to touch her hair, pushing it behind her ear, then stroked her cheek softly. "You're so sweet and kind. If I'd smoked that much opium, I wouldn't have gotten out of bed for days at a time."

She laughed softly. "If you recall, I didn't see you for days at a time. I read a book on addiction that Vespasian bought for me. You met all the criteria—like lying and being late and disappearing for days."

He ran his hands through his hair. "All my actions reinforced your suspicion."

She began to giggle at the absurdity of their misjudgments. "And that story about being an inspector who boarded ships looking for diseased plants simply wasn't credible, even if you could rattle off a dozen fancy terms."

He showed her his identification card from his back pocket and she admitted it looked authentic. "I'd prefer no secrets from this moment on just the same," she whispered, sliding off the chair and kneeling beside him, pressing his face into her breasts.

"Never, my love, never."

A twinge of conscience gripped her. Would she lose him if she told? She cleared her throat. "I have a confession of my own. The reason I owed Vespasian a favor ..."

He leaned toward her. "I'm sure it wasn't losing a horse race."

"Last year when I thought I loved him, I sneaked out and we spent the night at his house, alone in his library. We drank a lot of wine. Nothing more." She rushed through the story, ending with her departure at dawn in a cab. "I asked him not to tell a soul—especially you—because I thought you wouldn't love me if you knew."

As she spoke, a smile spread across his face, making his mouth all the more inviting to her.

"You and Vespasian didn't have your stories straight," he said. "He told me you beat him in swimming matches." He laughed. "It didn't matter. I loved you. Whatever you and Vespasian shared in the past wasn't important."

He brought his lips to hers in soft, tingling kisses. He moved to her jaw, her earlobes, her eyelids and back to her lips. Feeling his warm breath on her neck, smelling his lime and bay leaf scent, she thought she might catch fire herself from the heat of him so near. Still, she pulled back. "I love you with all my heart and soul. Our only problem is my father." She paused.

"Something tells me you didn't come here to talk about him."

Chapter Thirty-Eight

"*I* didn't."

Her words unleashed Ben's passion. He deepened the kiss with his tongue. She opened her mouth to him while he gently laid her on the floor and moved on top of her. Ben felt so hard, so strong against her. She wanted to see him, to touch him. From the minute he proposed, she'd thought of little other than making love. She knew the gist of the sexual act from a book Renee had lent her more than a year ago, but in practice—in the moment—all scientific thoughts flew from her mind.

"I love the way you feel against me. Am I wanton?"

"I think you're a passionate woman who's in love." He kissed her again and again, slow lingering kisses. In a few moments, he pulled back and asked when she knew she loved him.

"You must tell me first."

"All right." He whispered in her ear. "I loved you from the moment you said my mirror needed a little dusting."

"You deserved that, you know. You seemed awfully arrogant, telling me you had a friendly smile. I loved you the minute I slammed into your chest. And I've wanted you to make love to me ever since." The words tumbled from her lips. She'd never spoken more honestly. "Make love to me," she repeated.

"There's nothing I want more. Are you sure? We'll be married soon."

She lowered her eyes to the floor. "If only that were so. I don't want to wait."

He tilted her chin up to meet her eyes. "I'll win your hand if it's the last thing I do." Then he stood, helped her to her feet, and scooped her up in his arms. Laughing, she twined her arms around him and nuzzled her face against his neck. He put her on his bed and sat next to her. Faster than she thought it possible for a man to undress, Ben cast his coat and shoes on the floor. While he loosened his cravat and tossed it aside, she boldly and swiftly undid the buttons of his waistcoat and linen shirt. He pulled his undershirt over his head.

"Oh, my." She reached her trembling hands up, ran them across his muscled shoulders and down his arms to his wrists, then back up his torso where she pulled playfully at his chest hair.

It wasn't enough. What she really wanted was to feel his hot skin against hers. His chest hair tickling her nipples, his manhood ...

She wasn't sure about the rest of it and whispered her anxiety. "I don't know much. I'm nervous."

He put fingers to her lips. "Shh. You're thinking too much. We'll go slowly. We'll do what feels good to us, that's all. I love you, and I want to make you happy—forever."

Unable to speak, she nodded.

Kissing her hungrily, he unbuttoned her dress. She helped by pulling the shoulders down and slipping her arms from the long sleeves. His hands at her waist, he bunched the cloth and lifted it over her head. She wore no corset and, as his eyes devoured her breasts through her thin chemise, she felt herself quiver with the desire to share all of herself.

He raised his hands, cupped a palm around each breast and rubbed his thumbs over her nipples. The pleasure surprised her. A sudden thought of her father's reaction to what they were doing, what they were going to do, made her hesitate a moment.

He seemed to read her mind. "Tell me if you don't like something."

"And if I do? Should I tell you that?"

"Absolutely, so I can do it again."

She squeaked when her nipples went stiff. Her whole body tingled while she untied her chemise with trembling fingers. Her breasts exposed, she raised her eyes to see the hot admiration in his gaze. His breath came shallow and fast.

When he dropped his mouth to her breasts, his tongue played with the soft areola of one breast while his fingers played with the tip of the other. Her breasts swelled; her nipples grew harder still. He eased her from sitting to lying on her side. He lay facing her.

For a moment she closed her eyes. Was she in a trance? She felt an ache in her core that demanded his attention. She couldn't ask him to touch her, could she?

He seemed to read her mind. He reached the hem of her chemise, and lifted it as he ran his hand up the inside of her calf to her knee. She squeezed her knees together, and the ache between her legs grew more intense. His hands found the tops of her stockings and he slowly rolled each down her leg.

His hands moving up her calves to her thighs sent shivers through her body. The skin of her face, her neck, her torso and legs warmed to the burn of a fever. He stoked the flames with a soft brush of her hair that concealed the deep source of her ache.

Ben lifted her chemise up and over her head. He put a strong arm around her shoulders and settled her on her back.

She turned again on her side and put a hand on his trousers.

With a grin, he gestured to his arousal. "I see where your interest lies," he whispered.

"I want to touch you. Your skin."

"Ahhhh." He laughed softly. "I want that, too."

She unbuttoned him slowly. One, two, three, four, five. His manhood pressed against his underclothes. He raised his hips from the bed, pushed his trousers off and kicked them to the floor.

His ridge strained against the soft cloth. She crawled her fingertips under the waistband and touched him. Soft skin covered a hard, hot shaft. She stroked him and it seemed to harden further.

"It moves on its own? Are you doing that?"

He grinned. "You are. Keep touching me."

He slid off his underclothes. He shot straight up.

She gasped at the sight. "Oh, dear."

In the next few moments, she studied him curiously. This body part enjoyed a life of its own. If he didn't desire her intensely, it wouldn't be behaving like this. She knew that much. She circled the burning staff with her hand, squeezed gently and felt it pulse. She ran her fingers along the length of him to the base and a bed of downy hair. His thighs tightened around her hand. She played with the sack at the base, causing his manhood to strain.

In the next moment, he sat up and slipped off her drawers. There was nothing left between them and she instinctively reached for the bedcover in embarrassment. She was certain she blushed red.

Ben smiled and pulled the cover from her hands. "Your body is magnificent. Don't be shy." His eyes scanned her tenderly, then he dropped his head to hers and kissed her.

When he moved a hand to her knee, she parted her legs. She felt ready for this—for whatever he wanted. He slid his fingers up the soft flesh of her inner thigh. Her legs began to shake; her muscles tightened involuntarily. She hungered for more. With the tips of his fingers, he began to play with the tendrils of her soft floss.

That, she didn't like. She rasped. "You're teasing me. Touch me, please."

"Be patient," he commanded softly. For what seemed like an eternity, he brushed her thighs and her maiden hair. She closed her eyes and stroked her own nipples as waves of pleasure washed over her. This was beyond imaginable. They were the only two people in the world and nothing else mattered. Ben was her handsome prince awakening her to exquisite delights.

"Ahh," she nearly screamed, when the tips of his fingers finally brushed the core of her passion. She arched her back and pushed her hips up to meet his hand. Her legs strained to relieve the tension.

"Do you want me to stop?"

In answer, she raised her knees and hips, and pushed harder against his hand. As his thumb massaged her, she fell into a dreamy state she'd never known. Was she conscious or not? She wished this one moment with this one man could last forever. She had never felt so fully alive.

Ben covered her with his body and she spread her legs wider. He moved his wet shaft across the cleft of her womanhood. Bigger waves of pleasure wracked her body. She couldn't catch her breath. Wrapping her legs around his waist and lifting her hips off the bed, she rocked against him. Panting, she clutched his shoulders, pulling him to her, as she rode on surges of ecstasy that grew higher and higher. All at once, she felt she was breaking apart and traveling to another place she'd never experienced. Could this be heaven? Every muscle in her body stiffened. She shuddered, shut her eyes and screamed out in joy.

He held her tight. "Shsh."

A moment later, she opened her eyes and saw a huge grin on his face. "I'm guessing you enjoyed that?"

She waited for her heartbeat to slow. "I did. I had no idea...."

Half-lying, half-kneeling between her legs, Ben's left elbow balanced his body above hers. She watched him inch forward, guiding his erection with a steady right hand.

"Tell me how this feels. I don't want to hurt you." He came inside her slowly, not more than an inch, maybe two, she couldn't tell.

"Oh." She tensed around him. He pulled out quickly.

"You're too big. Is this possible? I can't believe it's possible."

"It's possible, but we don't have to." He lay beside her and kissed her tenderly.

She knew he wanted to possess her. She'd read the book from Renee. Men sought a release. She wanted him to enjoy her.

"Let's try again. Let me help you," she suggested.

This time she guided him with her own hand. When he was in position, she braced herself, grabbed his buttocks and pushed him in. She stifled a cry from the sharp pain and dug her fingernails into his back. He didn't move, and in a moment, it no longer hurt. He filled the space inside her in the most natural way.

She reassured him immediately. "It feels all right." He lay still, his body covering hers, his warm skin against hers from torso to toes, his head buried against her neck. She was momentarily confused. "Is that it?"

"No." Nibbling her ear, he whispered, "Now I move."

After the surprise of his first thrust, she lifted her hips to meet him. He groaned, his eyes fluttered closed as he increased his pace. She wrapped her legs about his waist, grasping him tighter to her. In another instant, he pulled out, shouted more loudly than she had and released his seed on her stomach.

Tears of happiness coursed down her cheeks.

Rising on an elbow, he dried her face with a gentle touch of the corner of the sheet. "I'm so very happy you came for a visit, Miss Collins." He tilted her chin up playfully. "Are you? Are you all right?"

"That was … It was like we were one person."

"We are. I'm yours and you're mine. Forever."

Chapter Thirty-Nine

That evening Maureen murmured all the right pleasantries to Sophie and her father, who settled down to play chess in the back parlor. It pleased her to see them together tonight. Sophie had been noticeably absent since her father returned from Boston. She didn't dare ask him if they'd had a spat of some kind. It was, she constantly told herself, none of her concern. She hoped her father loved Sophie. If he did, perhaps he might be more understanding of her situation. Would a man in love force his daughter to marry a man she didn't love?

She wondered if the couple detected her happiness. She felt a lightness in her whole being. Her feet seemed to float across the carpets. In love—her love and Ben's declared and consummated—she was the happiest young lady in the city.

She and Ben belonged together forever. She would never change her mind—no matter what her father thought or said or did. This morning after they made love, Ben had asked if she would run away with him to Philadelphia if her father refused to relent by May 1st. She hadn't hesitated for one moment. Yes, she would. If her father disowned his only child, she'd be sad. But it was a risk she was willing to take.

Vespasian arrived at eight o'clock. Dashingly handsome as always, he greeted her with a kiss on the cheek, then shook her father's hand and gave Sophie a polite bow. Maureen poured them both a drink at the cellarette, while her father addressed Vespasian.

"We've missed you at the office, Colville, but I well know that Mardi Gras revelries can lead to a lapse of duties. We'll talk on Wednesday—after Carnival's over."

In the front parlor, Maureen took a chair by the fire. "I hope I'm mollifying Papa by spending time with you. And I hope he recognizes the fact that I'm not the least in love with you."

"You aren't?" Vespasian smiled between sips of whiskey. "I'm horrified that you'd say it to my face. You know you adore me— always will."

"Adore, yes." She batted her eyelashes over the rim of her sherry glass.

He placed his hand over his heart. "You're as good at flirting as ever. And as lovely. But there's something different about you tonight. You're positively glowing. Is a certain Ben Merritt responsible for the change?"

She felt her skin flush to the roots of her hair.

He winked. "I suppose I have my answer."

Putting her glass down, she folded her hands demurely in her lap. "Tell me about Suzette. How were things up country? I think about her often. I've written twice, but received no reply. What do her parents think of your attentions?"

Vespasian sighed. "Madame Juneau accepted me. Once Suzette confessed everything to her and I assured her that I could support Suzette more than comfortably after her divorce and marriage to me, she was on our side."

"Her father arranged the marriage to Monsieur St. Aubin. What does he think?"

Vespasian stood and paced. "Headstrong just like yours," he whispered. "And adamantly opposed to divorce. Fathers get certain ideas in their heads when it comes to daughters and acceptable husbands." He gulped his whiskey. He looked away from her, gazing for some moments into the fire, his expression troubled. "It's tortuous not having an outlet for my passion. It's gotten so bad I've started writing Suzette lengthy love letters, which are quite good if I do say so myself."

Maureen raised an eyebrow. "All you ever did for me was scrawl on a scrap of paper."

"I'm sorry. I truly am." He grimaced. "I never meant to cause you any pain."

Maureen reached out, grasped his hand and squeezed. "You're forgiven, Vespie. I'm glad you've found someone you truly love."

He sat down again and she went on. "I do worry that you two may have a difficult road ahead."

He shrugged. "I realize it's unlike me to wait for a woman. I'll never have you. But I'm willing to wait forever for Suzette."

"I hope you'll be happy you did."

"I don't use the word *tortuous* lightly. You don't know, it actually hurts to be so aroused—you have no idea."

She did. She was tortured—that was a good description of the ache between her legs—by her desire for Ben. Her mind flooded with images of their tryst this morning. She still couldn't believe she'd been so driven by physical desire she'd sneaked out and showed up at Ben's door. How bold she'd been! How absolutely wonderful he'd been!

Another sip of sherry brought her mind to her adventure with Vespasian last year. When he had spread a blanket in front of the fire, she had realized she didn't want to make love to a gentleman rumored to have more partners in bed than he had at the card tables. And he played cards weekly! She knew in her heart Ben's lovemaking today was more beautiful and precious because of her innocence.

With a poke on her arm, Vespasian snapped her to the present. "Lost in reverie, are you?"

"I'm sorry." Again, she felt her face grow hot and changed the subject. "How is your mother reacting to you and Suzette?"

"I've been chipping away at her resolve to pair you with me. She's weakening."

Maureen jabbed a finger in her father's direction. "That's not likely here."

"I've sworn my love for the lady to my mother. I've talked incessantly about our future together after Suzette divorces her husband. And I've reminded her constantly that you've set your sights on another."

Maureen felt tears sting her eyes. "I've done all those things, too." Her voice caught. "I've told Papa about Suzette. I've said you and I aren't suited and will be miserable. But he's immovable. He clings to the idea of May 1st."

Vespasian stood. "Shall I help myself to more whiskey? And you?" He took her glass and returned with stronger spirits for her. "It's whiskey. Better for you."

She thanked him and swallowed almost as much as he did.

"Everyone at the factorage is whispering about the kidnapping threat to your father." He gestured toward the window and the guard visible on the porch.

"I wish none of us had ever heard of Imperial Shipping Company."

"Not too fast, Miss." He returned to his chair and lowered his voice. "I have an idea. Your father has been singing the praises of Ben Merritt since he returned from Boston. He gets telegrams from London daily giving more details about the shipping line's theft of cargo, the arrests of its principal partners and so forth. He speaks glowingly of Ben's prescience. And just the other day I heard Ben had advised against the purchase of a warehouse that's quite a distance from the river." He leaned closer. "Your father agreed with Ben."

"That's all well and good." Maureen shook her head. "But that's business, not personal."

"It's a start. He thinks Ben's a good businessman whereas I ..."

She interrupted. "Papa has been very upset that you've not been at work much this week. I've told him I guessed you were with Suzette. He said her problems weren't your concern."

"Good. He's thinking I'm not dependable while he's thinking Ben is trustworthy and intelligent."

Vespasian put his drink down and motioned for her to do the same. He took both her hands in his. "I know we'll always love each other as friends. Hell, we're practically brother and sister."

She raised her eyes to his, wondering what might come next.

"As the older brother you don't have, I must ask. Are you sure Ben's the man for you? Are you sure he's not an opium smuggler or an opium addict?"

"I love him." She smiled and Vespasian grinned back at her. "And he loves me. As for the opium business, he's not involved. I can't go into all of it, but I trust him."

"I wanted to hear it from your own lips because I've been mulling over a plan to ensure Ben a firm place in your father's heart."

Maureen's mouth dropped open at Vespasian's suggestion. She said no. She repeated that word three more times.

But as Vespasian continued to talk, his idea sounded less and less outrageous.

Maureen bit her lip, hesitating a moment. "And do you promise that by the end of Mardi Gras day, Papa's going to give Ben and me his blessing?"

He patted her hand. "You can count on it."

"In that case, I'll do whatever you say."

Chapter Forty

On Mardi Gras afternoon, Maureen strode down Royal Street in her black woolen trousers, a white cotton shirt-waist with full sleeves, a scarlet and yellow paisley waistcoat, and a scarlet jacket, all made by Frau Kohlmeyer. Luz had braided her hair and wound it around her head. A black patch over her left eye, a black mustache glued to her upper lip, a flimsy tin knife tucked in her belt, black boots and a black hat with an ostrich plume completed her look. A swashbuckling pirate she was.

She imagined a huge grin on Ben's face when he saw her in men's clothes. He'd love the way the pants fit tightly across her hips, how they nipped in at her waist, accentuating her shape. When they kissed later this afternoon, he'd feel her nipples against his shirt because she wore no corset. He would certainly like that.

The crowd moved as one giant serpent, spilling off the banquettes and into Royal Street. Her group stayed together, thanks to William's diligence, as they made their way to the Boston Club on Canal Street where they planned to watch the Proteus parade. The throngs of pedestrians made the roads close to impassable for carriages. Most revelers preferred to walk the street in costume and mask greeting those they knew and those they thought they knew.

Leading, Sophie looked beautiful as a shepherdess in a blue and white gingham dress and straw bonnet, the mate to her father, a simple shepherd boy in woolen britches to his knee, a rough-woven jacket, and a brown wig that took ten years off his age. In his hand, he carried a shepherd's crook. They looked happy today. Whatever had troubled them no longer did.

Renee, dressed as Juliette Capulet, came next. William, her Romeo, in tights, tunic and very short pants, held her hand.

The sherry she'd drunk at William and Renee's party earlier in the afternoon did nothing to calm Maureen's nerves. She worried that Vespasian's plan was too risky, but every time she let her mind drift in that direction, she decided she'd do anything to change her father's mind.

The Boston Club, festooned with tinsel in green, yellow and purple, welcomed the onslaught of guests. The second floor's iron balcony was reinforced with a wooden structure beneath it so the weight of shouting, drinking revelers didn't bring it crashing to the ground. Just to one side of the club's front door, a set of wooden bleachers provided seating for those who wished to be at street level.

Inside, costumed men and women mingled in the parlors, spilled out into the back courtyard and into the street out front. Waiters passed champagne, milk punch and a selection of wines to St. Peter, Marie Antoinette, St. Joan of Arc, a parrot, a jester, Pope Leo, two Cleopatras, two George Washingtons in federal blue and at least three Napoleons. A mermaid, a merman, a satyr, and a clown came in as a group. At the bar Maureen was amused to see two Robert E. Lees in Confederate gray throwing back shots of rum with an Abraham Lincoln.

The bar staff turned out drinks with both skill and speed. William handed Maureen and Renee sazeracs, powerful concoctions of rye whiskey, bitters, Herbsaint and sugar syrup with a twist of lemon. Her own father, in a lively mood, gave her a second sazerac not long after. She thought it something of a peace offering when he murmured he thought she looked fantastic in her costume.

Feeling a little dizzy, Maureen guided Carine—dressed as Jane Austen in Regency clothes—to the buffet table. She noticed a gentleman standing to their left watching them and jerked her head in his direction. "Don't look now, but the man there— Charles Dickens, I believe he is—seems to be taken with you."

Carine blushed and leaned closer. "He's one of the editors of the *Daily Picayune*. Someone here told him I'm a writer. And he's asked me to come by the office next week to discuss ideas."

Maureen hugged her. "That's so exciting. I want to hear about it the minute you talk to him."

Wondering out loud what sort of writing the man had in mind, Carine served herself fried chicken, tomato aspic and asparagus in addition to ham biscuits. Maureen took two biscuits. They settled into chairs at a tiny table for two. Carine eyed her quizzically. "You're not eating?"

"I had luncheon with William and Renee." Maureen popped most of a biscuit in her mouth and enjoyed the taste of the salty ham flavored with cloves and honey. "They have good cooks at the club, don't they?"

"Is that what passes for conversation between best friends?" Carine didn't give her time to reply. "You seem restless. Can't you relax and enjoy yourself?"

"I'm nervous," Maureen admitted. "I invited Ben here after the parade. I hope to have some time with him without my father knowing."

Carine squeezed her arm. "I so hope it works out between you. And I'll keep an eye out for him. What's his costume?"

"He's on the thirteenth float, titled Ceres. He said he'd be dressed as some kind of fruit."

"Mother Earth," Carine remarked. "Goddess of agriculture. And he knows you're a pirate?"

Maureen nodded, took a few more sips of sazerac and suggested they go out to watch the parade. The pleasant beat of drums floated toward her on the early evening breeze. In the distance, glimmering flambeaux lit the dusk. More nervous than she'd ever been in her life, she climbed onto the top rung of the bleachers and sat between Elise and Carine. She told herself to concentrate, count to thirteen, and blow Ben a kiss when his float passed her.

Leading the parade, a Negro man carried a torch-lit placard announcing: "Visions of Other Worlds." The elaborate floats moved by. The Sun, Mercury, Comet, Saturn, Mars, each pulled by mules, rumbled past. Made of wood and papier-mâché, each cart portrayed a different landscape. The maskers, as the riders were called, cavorted in elaborate costumes of satin and sequins. On Saturn, six-armed creatures dancing amid cacti left the crowd awestruck.

Maureen stood to see every detail. She shouted and clapped. At least on Mardi Gras, ladies were allowed to show some enthusiasm with raised voices. Finally, Ceres came into view. Maskers dressed as strawberries, raspberries, grapes, lemons, limes, and grapefruit waved from a landscape created of giant pineapples. She'd not worn a mask today per Vespasian's instructions. Ben should have no trouble recognizing her as he passed. But how would she know him?

As soon as she had the thought, her eyes locked on a banana who threw her three bags of roasted peanuts. She caught two; the third sailed over her head. She assumed a pirate's stance, hands on her hips, and looked straight at the tall banana man. She heard a whoop. *He liked her figure in a man's outfit.* She waved and blew him a kiss.

The moment the parade ended, her stomach dropped. It was time to put Vespasian's scheme into action. She made an excuse to Carine that she'd like to stay outside awhile to enjoy the beautiful weather. She walked about, examining each masked face at it approached her. Was that clown coming right toward her? How about the owl with the elaborate feathers?

She felt a distinct tap on her shoulder, not an accidental nudge in the crowd, and turned to see a tiger mask of black and orange fur and a gaping mouth complete with fangs above a tiger-printed tunic.

He whispered curses in her ear, swore he had a knife at her back, and yanked her through the crowd moving between the club and the adjacent building. She didn't raise a complaint. He opened the door of a waiting carriage, picked her up and tossed her inside. She braced her fall with her hands, but they stung from the impact on the floor. So did her knees.

"Lie down, face down, bitch." The rug smelled of grass, topsoil, whiskey and sour milk.

What was Vespasian thinking? This was disgusting, not what she'd expected at all.

With a knee on the small of her back to hold her down, the tiger yanked her hat off and covered her eyes with a kerchief.

Reeling with confusion, she mustered her most authoritative voice. "See here, sir, that's not necessary. Antoine, I believe your name is. I have one eye covered as it is."

"Shut the hell up. I do what I'm told."

He tied the cloth so tightly, she expected to have a headache in minutes. "I don't believe you were told to do that!"

"Give me your hands. In front."

Obedient, Maureen turned around and held her hands in front of her, but the rough rope cut into her skin. "That hurts my wrists. You're not supposed to hurt me."

His raucous laugh filled the carriage. "I weren't told nothin' about hurtin' you or not. Shut yo mouth."

Maureen swallowed hard and followed his advice. The tiger played his part well. He tied her ankles tighter than he'd tied her hands. Then he issued a warning: "Don't move. I'm lockin' the carriage doors. If you scream, I'll kill you."

This was not the picture Vespasian had painted. He'd said she shouldn't scream or make any sort of fuss that might attract a policeman or the rare sober gentleman who might turn heroic and try to save her. The last thing she and Vespasian wanted was an *interrupted* kidnapping.

The tiger left her lying on her side. She curled into a ball, her mind racing. She supposed the man enjoyed playing a real kidnapper. Vespasian hadn't mentioned rope. She tried to move her wrists, but she couldn't without a lot of pain. There was no slack and with every movement, the rope bit into her. Wiggling loose was impossible so she lay there, trying to figure out how long it would take to travel down St. Charles Avenue from Canal Street. She'd pass her own house, pass the Cotton Exposition site to Riverbend. An hour? More?

Not too long to gain a lifetime of happiness. She took a deep breath and occupied herself with memories of Ben. His strong arms and lime scent when she ran smack into him on St. Charles Avenue, his amused expression when he walked into Renee and William's parlor and saw her there. His black eye at the Twelfth Night ball. The night in her bed when he came to comfort her. And best of all, their lovemaking Saturday morning. His beautiful strong body, his obvious joy in bringing her pleasure.

She tried to run through her memories chronologically, but she kept losing her place. The main thing she remembered was his tenderness. Was there a more wonderful man on earth?

Church chimes startled her. The clanging bells couldn't be more than a block or two away. *Good heavens. St. Louis Cathedral!* She counted seven. Seven o'clock. The carriage poked along cobblestone streets in the French Quarter. Maureen pulled herself to a sitting position, her legs in front of her, her back resting against the forward-facing carriage seat. She supposed there had been a change of strategy. That was so like Vespasian. He never pulled a prank halfway. The kidnapping was intended to fool her father, Sophie, William and Renee, but this wasn't going according to plan. She was sure of it: Her kidnapper wasn't going uptown.

She'd grown impatient with this masquerade some time ago. She could use a warm bath and dinner. She needed time at home to dress for the Proteus ball that began at nine o'clock. She had a gorgeous new blue velvet dress she couldn't wait to wear. What had she done? What she'd agreed to was very, very selfish. Why hadn't she confided in Carine when she'd had the chance?

Fear drove her guilt away. Could she count on Vespasian to tell Ben where she was? On Mardi Gras, Vespasian drank from dawn to dusk. He might forget where he'd asked tiger man to take her. She thought of Vespasian's favorite haunts. Bars and dance halls on Gallatine Street.

"The Absinthe House," she said out loud.

"Shut up," growled a voice through the roof hatch. "I'll knock you out if you make another sound."

"Sir, I don't think we're going the right way." Drunken laughter answered her. The driver had enjoyed some Mardi Gras spirits himself. Maureen raised her voice. "Sir, I was told I'd be taken to a house in Riverbend in Carrollton. Was there a change in the plans?"

"You were told?"

She jumped at his loud voice coming from the roof window. She nearly gagged from the smell of sour liquor hitting her nostrils. She shivered. Laughter bounced off the carriage walls.

"You don't need to be rude," she shouted back. "I'm sure you're being paid well for your efforts."

"Your father's sure as hell goin' to pay if he wants to lay eyes on you again."

Refusing to accept what he said, Maureen took a deep breath and tried to come to an understanding with the man. "You're playing your role well, sir. I'll tell Mr. Colville what a fine job you did. I'm sure he'll pay you extra. Now if you'll just turn the carriage around and take me to the house in Riverbend, Mr. Merritt will rescue me and everything will be fine."

"I don't know no Colville or what in blazes you're talkin' about. Just shut up, lady."

A chill ran up her spine. She admitted to herself what she'd realized some time ago. *Tiger man wasn't Vespasian's hired hand.*

She'd actually been kidnapped. She'd been kidnapped in her pirate costume on Mardi Gras day, right in front of the Boston Club. She should have realized it the minute he cursed. Vespasian had promised her kidnapper would be gentlemanly.

Tiger Man works for Monsieur Leveque and the murderer Mendoza.

Tears stung her eyes and wet her blindfold. She couldn't catch her breath. Her teeth chattered, her body trembled. Her feet would be shaking the carriage floor if they hadn't been tied. And she'd played along. She'd made her abduction simple. The most cooperative victim in kidnapping history.

Think, think. She guessed the carriage traveled down Esplanade Avenue straight to Bayou St. John—to Lafitte Nursery.

Ben would know to look for her there. When he didn't find her at the house in Riverbend, he'd come to the nursery. But in the Mardi Gras traffic, how long would it take him to get to her? Would it be too late?

Chapter Forty-One

*B*en's float came to a final stop where Canal Street met the river. Climbing into the crowd, he felt ridiculous in his satiny, tight-fitting banana costume, but when he saw Colville he laughed out loud. The poor man was in a gauzy fringed pink skirt, with some sort of wings protruding from his shoulders. The two walked as fast as the crowd allowed toward the Boston Club. Ben was surprised by Colville's sober demeanor. "Not drinking?"

"Tonight at the ball."

Ben's mood lightened with every step as they neared the club and Maureen. He readjusted his hat to cover his dark hair. His face, hidden behind his buckram mask, was unrecognizable. A banana in bright yellow, skin-tight satin pants, a long-sleeved satin and sequined tunic that buttoned at the crotch and a satin hat, he could slip past Patrick Collins without a worry. A banana on the loose in New Orleans, he would enjoy every moment with Maureen.

Ben scanned the club's lobby quickly, looking for a pirate's plumed black hat. "Do you see a gorgeous lady dressed as a pirate? Do you see her, Colville?"

His companion gazed about. "Let's find Patrick Collins. He'll know where she is."

Miss Carine Bouchard in a high-waisted brocade dress and spectacles rushed toward him. "Are you Mr. Merritt?"

One look at her ashen face stalled his heartbeat. He greeted her by name and admitted who he was.

"I'm so glad you're here. Maureen asked me to look for a fruit."

"Is something wrong? Will you lead me to her?"

"She's missing," the young lady choked out. "No one's seen her since the parade passed."

"My God!" Ben turned to Colville, still a few paces away. He struggled to get any words out. If only he'd arranged to sneak her onto the float with him as she'd suggested. The kidnappers wanted the Collins lass. "Maureen's missing," he shouted over his shoulder.

"Good evening, Miss Bouchard," Colville said with a polite nod. "I'm sure Maureen's here in the mob somewhere," he went on. "We all know she's hard to keep tract of."

Maureen's friend pointed to a corner of the front parlor, where William, Patrick, Madame Renee Collins and Madame Sophie O'Brien stood in a knot together. Colville took her arm and began a slow stroll in that direction.

What was wrong with this man? Ben spun once, looking in every direction. No pirates; no Maureen. He rushed past Colville, feeling his pulse accelerating by the second.

"Ladies," he bowed, but didn't try to doff his banana stem hat. "William, Mr. Collins, I understand Maureen's missing."

"Is that you, Merritt?" Patrick asked.

"Yes, sir. Let me help find her."

"Please, we need everyone looking."

"Who saw her last?" Ben asked. "And how long ago?"

William put a reassuring hand on his shoulder. "Elise and Carine left her when the parade passed here—about six o'clock. She wanted to stay outside for a bit."

"We'll send messengers to the house, to William and Renee's, Sophie's," Patrick said. "She might have left if she'd felt ill." He stopped, glaring at Ben. "Did you have plans to meet her here, Merritt?"

Lying didn't occur to him. "Yes, sir, I did. And I can't imagine she left the club willingly." He removed his mask, met Patrick's eyes, then William's. They understood his unspoken message.

Collins' usual ruddy complexion paled, his eyebrows rose, he started to speak, but Miss Bouchard interrupted. "He's right, Mr. Collins. Maureen asked me to look out for Mr. Merritt and find her the minute I saw him. She wouldn't have left here on her own."

Collins' eyes widened and his mouth opened slightly. He glanced at Sophie who grasped his forearm. He took a deep breath and took charge. "We know for certain she was taken against her will. The police will be powerless to help us. They're stretched thin today."

Thin in numbers and in skills, too. Ben knew it was up to the men who loved her to find her—he, her father, her cousin and Colville.

Patrick continued with instructions. "You ladies stay here where you'll be safe. William, go north, I'll go south. Merritt, east; Colville, west. She's probably on foot with her abductor. If she's in a carriage, she can't have gone far in the traffic, so waylay any vehicle that has closed curtains. Each of us will send a messenger back to Sophie and Renee every thirty minutes."

Colville made excuses. "I wish I could help out, sir, but I have an engagement at the Absinthe House in a very few minutes." He pulled a watch from a pocket at the waist of his short fringed costume skirt. "I'll certainly keep an eye out for Maureen as I walk that way."

Patrick whirled around. "My God, man, my daughter's been kidnapped! This isn't a joking matter."

Speechless, Ben couldn't believe even the hedonist Colville could place a social meeting above a search for Maureen. He grabbed the man's arm. "What's wrong with you?" he exploded. "It's Maureen! Maureen is missing!"

Ben realized that Colville didn't know Maureen, rather than her father, was the intended kidnapping victim. Patrick had told all the factorage staff that Imperial Shipping had threatened *him*. But this was the gentleman who'd once professed his love! Ben didn't believe he'd ever heard a less concerned statement. The Absinthe House, for God's sake!

"I'll find her, sir," Ben said, struggling to steady his voice. "If I die trying."

Colville gave him an appreciative nod. "That's good of you, Ben."

Ben charged through the crowd, Colville at his heels. On the sidewalk, he turned. "Get out of my way. Go meet your friends and drink."

"Wait, Merritt." Colville gripped Ben's sequined tunic. "I'm going to help you." He waved a hand back toward the club. "That was all an act."

In the next minute, as they moved through the crowd, walking as rapidly as the throng allowed, Colville explained that Maureen's kidnapping was a ruse, concocted by him. "You'll rescue her and be a hero. I'm a selfish idiot, don't you see? Not husband material."

Ben swore. "Are you out of your mind? Maureen agreed to this?"

Colville nodded.

"Dear God. The threat to Patrick Collins isn't real. Maureen's the intended victim. Patrick didn't want her to be scared, so he didn't tell her the truth."

Horrified, Colville stopped dead. Several revelers ran into his back, then stepped around him. "I didn't know that," he said slowly. "But she'll be fine, I promise."

"I overheard some ruffians planning it a month ago."

Colville brightened. "All the better. Patrick Collins will be sufficiently frightened."

"You're a lunatic."

"She's safe, Ben. I paid someone to take her off. I know exactly where she is."

"You do?" Every taut muscle in his body began to ease as Colville explained. "I can't believe Maureen actually agreed to this."

"She loves you. Her father will be so thrilled when you return her to him—while I'm drinking at the Absinthe House—he'll allow you to marry her."

"Lead me to her fast. How long do you intend to keep her father in the dark?"

"Let him think about what Maureen wants for another hour or two. Do him good, in fact. My carriage's at a livery stable a block away. Let's go."

Colville took the reins and drove recklessly around other carriages, velocipedes and pedestrians in his path. Once they passed the Exposition site uptown, he increased his speed on the dirt road. At Riverbend, he pulled up in front of a small pink shotgun house with green shutters. Colville bounded up the stairs, across the porch to the door, Ben right behind him.

A young Negro man answered on the first knock. "Antoine, this is Mr. Merritt." Colville waved a hand in Ben's direction. "Ben, Antoine Granier." The two shook hands. "We've come to retrieve Miss Collins."

The man shook his head, a loud sigh escaping his lips. "I ain't got her, Mr. Colville. I never saw a lady who matched her picture in front of the Boston Club."

Ben stopped breathing.

Colville staggered back and leaned against the porch banister. "That's impossible. You saw no lady dressed in a pirate costume?"

Antoine shook his head again. "She weren't there."

"She expected you, Antoine. She wouldn't have gone off with just anybody."

"I was there. She weren't." Antoine shrugged, removed a photograph of Maureen from his shirt pocket and held it out to Colville. "I'm sorry, sir."

Ben took the photo, a beautiful shot of Maureen in a ball gown.

Colville, his face white, sank onto the top step of the porch, his head in his hands. "Dear Lord, now what?" He mumbled something about the perfect plan. "I even told her not to scream or struggle, to go peacefully with Antoine when he tapped her arm."

Ben fisted his right hand, ready to slam Antoine's jaw. But it wasn't Antoine's fault. It was Colville's and Maureen's. How could they have thought this was a good idea? Actually it was Patrick Collins' fault that neither his daughter nor Colville knew real kidnappers were after her.

Carleton's words came to him: *Never waste time assigning blame. Keep your eyes and ears open. Learn everything you can. Think before you act.*

Ben questioned Antoine and learned he'd walked up to the reviewing stand at exactly ten minutes after the last float passed—just as he'd been told to do by Colville. He'd waited nearly an hour before giving up.

"Did you see anything unusual?" Ben asked. "Did anything strike you as odd?

Antoine's forehead wrinkled as he gave it some thought. "I saw an old carriage, sheddin' paint and so forth, two nags pullin' it, comin' out the alley beside the club. Odd for a fancy place."

"Which way did it go?"

"Turned toward the Quarter."

"Thank you. Thank you, Antoine." Ben grabbed Colville, who still sat immobile on the steps. "I know who has her and I'm sure they've gone to Bayou St. John. I'm driving."

Ben picked up the reins. Colville directed him down the unpaved roads of Carrolton, far quicker, he said, than going back

downtown and through the French Quarter. During the harrow-
ing drive, the men remained silent. Colville's pallor didn't improve.

They arrived at the warehouse on the bayou quicker than Ben
imagined possible. Not a light shone in the warehouse, in the barn,
on the dock. His body tense for a fight, he led Colville to the large
building first. He turned: "We're going in. Are you armed?"

"In this outfit?" His hands waved over his skirt, then motioned
to the wings protruding from his back. "Only a knife in my boot."

"Same for me. A knife."

He cursed under his breath and put a shoulder to the door.
The wood splintered. Night had fallen and the room was pitch
dark. He shouted her name a half-dozen times, hoping to hear a
whimper, a scrap against a floorboard, something. "There's a counter to our right. A lantern maybe."

Colville felt around, found a candle and matches. They
searched the downstairs, then went up the steps.

Ben's eyes lit on a hairpin on the floor. He dropped to his
knees. "It's Maureen's, I think. Look, does that belong to Maureen?"

"She orders hers from France."

Ben turned it over and saw a hallmark: *Jacquet.* He shoved it
under Colville's eyes. He nodded.

"Thank God," he said. "She's left us a trail."

Colville found another hairpin near the front door. They tried
the barn next, where they found a mule, two horses and a carriage
that certainly fit Antoine's description of *shedding paint.*

Colville scurried up a ladder to a loft. "All the saints be
praised," he shouted down.

His heart in his throat, Ben called out: "What?"

"Guns. Two rifles and a pistol. All loaded."

Not Maureen. But still a great find. Colville handed down the
guns to Ben one at a time and scrambled back down the ladder.
Ben slapped him on the back. "Well done, Colville. She must be
on the lake. Let's go."

They found two more hairpins on the dock. They climbed in a rowboat tied to a piling.

Ben whirled at the sound of limbs rustling. A young Negro boy jumped from a tree to the ground and called to them. "You lookin' for a lady?"

"Yes," Ben answered. "Do you know where she is?"

The boy shrugged. "I seen her before at Captain Kwan's ship."

"Yes, that's the lady. Have you seen her tonight?"

"They took her. She's tied up. Mister Claude and Mister Alphonse. They's goin' to the house boat on the lake."

"Thank you. What's your name, son?"

"Percy, sir."

"Stay hidden and be careful, Percy. These men are mean. When I get back I'll have something for you. Give us some help, will you?"

The boy gave them a good push out into the calm waters. Ben picked up an oar and handed one to Colville. "I hope you know how to get to the lake from here. I certainly don't."

"I do. I'm a swamp rat. I grew up fishing around here with my father and brother. I'm your man."

Ben glared at him. "You better be. You've gotten Maureen into one hell of a mess and you're going to help me get her out of it."

Chapter Forty-Two

Maureen shook so badly she had to bite her lower lip to keep her mouth from quivering. Tied to a chair on Boss Benoit's houseboat, she was soaking wet from the ride in a pirogue, cold, hungry and terrified. At least they'd removed her blindfold.

Alphonse Benoit, white-haired and bearded with black beady eyes, paced in circles around her, his cane tapping a grotesque rhythm as he moved. "I'm going to send your father a ransom note." He laughed, a strangled guffaw, which sent shivers from the base of her spine to the nape of her neck. "I expect he'll be mighty surprised to hear from a Benoit after all these years. Twenty-one years since your father robbed my mother of the cotton factorage."

Anger gave her courage. She shouted. "Robbed?"

He flinched in surprise. She supposed he didn't expect a woman to contradict him, but she'd been outspoken since she learned to talk. She wasn't going to let Benoit get away with a lie. She turned her head to the man in the corner.

"Monsieur Leveque, don't believe a word this man says. Just so you know, my father paid a fortune for the factorage and the warehouses. He felt sorry for Madame Benoit and gave her much more than the business was worth. The warehouses were falling down, holes in the roofs, rats and raccoons living inside." She shuddered.

Benoit stood still. The incessant tapping stopped for a moment. "Your father's going to pay if he ever wants to see you again." He moved again. Tap. Tap. "Lots and lots of money."

Her father had lots of money. He'd worked tirelessly to provide for his family *and* his employees. Tears pricked at the back of her eyes, but damn it, she wasn't going to cry in front of these men.

Benoit continued. "All the partners are meeting here to get a look at you." Benoit walked. Tap, tap, tap. "Someone will take the note back to town. I want that scheming thief Patrick Collins to know I have his daughter when he comes to his breakfast table in the morning."

"And just how will my father know you have me?" She regretted it the moment she said it. Her mouth went dry. She'd read of kidnappers cutting off their victim's ear or finger as proof. *Please, God, no.* She swallowed. "I'd like a glass of water." Her voice squeaked. "I'll do you no good if I faint."

"You think we have running water here? Leveque, some brandy."

Suzette's butler poured a glass from a bottle kept in a cabinet on one side of the room—what she supposed served on the boat as a parlor or sitting room. How absurd to be served by her friend's butler. Sneering at her, Leveque pushed the glass under her nose.

"Thank you, but I'd prefer to drink it myself. I'm not going to run away. I ... I can't swim."

Benoit's face creased into a smile. "I suspected as much, a lady like you." He resumed his circular pacing.

The tapping was driving her mad.

He gave an order. "Leave her feet bound, but untie her arms. She'll drown if she makes a move."

When the butler cut the rope, she raised her hands above her head for a moment, then laid them in her lap. Her hands stung with the increased flow of blood into her palms and fingers. She flexed them carefully, then slowly bent her wrists. Pain shot up her arms. They'd been immobile for several hours. That's all it was. She was all right, so far, and she'd gained a measure of freedom. She examined the skin on her wrists. Red bands like bracelets marked her flesh where she'd given herself rope burns trying to loosen the bonds. Her arms and shoulders ached, too, and she worried she'd lost all feeling in her feet.

Putting on a polite smile, she looked up at Leveque. "I'd love that brandy now." She forced herself to take dainty sips. She was thirsty and scared, both conditions the brandy would help. But she hadn't eaten in hours. No doubt her captors would love to see her drink too much. But she knew better.

She could swim, she could dive. Most ladies could do neither. The houseboat was anchored offshore, but in the dark she'd not been able to judge the distance. If she dove in at night, she wouldn't be able to move fast on shore, assuming she made it there. It would be too easy to get lost in the dark. She relaxed a little, knowing she would not try to escape until daylight. But escape she would. No one kept Maureen Collins against her will.

With her hands untied, all she needed was a few moments to undo the rope binding her ankles. She took a good look at her captors. Her guards resembled skeletons, not men. She could fell Benoit by sticking her leg out to trip him, followed by a few kicks in the chest or head. She'd outrun Leveque and tackled him at Lafitte Nursery and could do it again. But outrun him where? Around and around the deck of the houseboat?

"I'm asking your father for a half-million dollars if he wants to see you again."

Benoit's words snapped her out of her reverie. With great drama, she gasped and brought one hand to her neck. "My father doesn't have that sort of money."

"Then he'll have to sell some of his property, won't he? Or just sign the factorage over to me. It belongs to my family."

Maureen thought it'd be smart to laugh at that. Both men bristled, so she laughed a little louder.

She'd been a horrible daughter. Against her father's wishes, she'd allowed Ben into her room. She'd accepted his marriage proposal. Her father had forbidden her to speak to the man and yet she'd gone to his lodging. They'd made love. As if all that duplicity weren't bad enough, she'd agreed to Vespasian's plan to fake a kidnapping. Here she was, kidnapped. It served her right. Her father loved her. He only wanted the best for her. She'd truly been an awful daughter.

Which gave her a brilliant idea. She pulled a handkerchief from her pocket and blew her nose. "You must not be aware that my father and I are estranged."

Benoit's head snapped in her direction. His eyes flashed. He tapped his way closer to her.

"Ah, Monsieur Benoit." She dabbed at her eyes. "You didn't know that, did you?"

He paced away from her. Tap, tap. She jabbed a little deeper. "My father and I rarely speak. I don't think he'll think I'm worth any amount of money at this moment. Certainly not a half million dollars, even if he had it, which, as I said, I'm sure he doesn't."

Benoit circled around her chair once, then twice before he stood in front of her, staring down, a deep frown wrinkling his forehead. She shrugged. "Not even a hundred thousand. Probably not ten thousand. Probably not five thousand, or five hun ..."

"Shut up," Benoit snapped. He turned his back, made his way slowly to the cabinet and poured himself a brandy. He handed the bottle to Leveque, who poured a glass for himself.

Maureen asked for more brandy and Leveque served her a full glass.

Giggling a little, pretending to be more intoxicated than she was, she batted her eyelashes at the old men. "Here we are together with a very good bottle of brandy! It is very good, don't you think? We should all drink a toast to Mardi Gras." She held her glass up and the men did likewise. "It's such a cheerful time in Louisiana, isn't it? To Mardi Gras!"

The men looked at her as if she were insane, but each drained his glass.

The bayou opened up into the lake more quickly than Ben expected. He began to hope they might get to Maureen soon. They doused the lantern and followed the shoreline. The moon had risen, but the weather had been unseasonably warm and a fog began to rise as the air cooled.

Barely dipping the oars, Ben moved the boat slowly. "It's soupy. I can hardly see where we're going."

"I'll be the lookout." Colville climbed into the bow of the boat, sat on his heels, the rifle beside him, and peered into the gloom. "I'm betting we'll see the boat soon. If they travel back and forth to the nursery, it'll be on this side of the lake. She can't be far."

"They're not going to kill her because they want the ransom money," Ben said, voicing the thought he'd been repeating to himself silently for the last hour.

Colville took up his positive talk. "Patrick Collins would give every penny he has to get his daughter back and I'm sure these men know it."

They fell silent and Ben's mind sorted through what the smugglers knew about him and his connection to Maureen. As Andrew Franklin, he'd bought plants from Captain Kwan—which they might not know. But he'd bought numerous plants from Mendoza beginning with the roses. He'd made it clear to the man that Maureen was his lady friend. He'd rescued her at the plant sale and loaded her and her purchases in his cabriolet. And Claude Leveque knew Maureen had stolen the ledger.

What the smugglers didn't know, he hoped, was that he worked for the U.S. Customs Service. If they knew, kidnapping Maureen served a dual purpose. They were using her to capture him. He might be walking straight into an ambush with only Colville as his ally. Unfair not to tell Maureen's former beau what he was getting into.

In the next few minutes, Ben explained that the men who kidnapped Maureen were opium smugglers, that Leveque, none other than Suzette's butler, and the old deserter Alphonse Benoit were the men Percy mentioned. Their partners, Mendoza and St. Aubin himself, might be on the boat, too. If so, it'd be a serious fire fight.

"Suzette's husband? I can't wait." He turned and grinned at Ben. "I see the boat. Do you have a plan?"

Straining to see in the fog, Ben barely made out a shape in the water ahead. "Get Maureen off the boat."

"She swims, you know. Quite well. And she can shoot better than most men."

Ben chuckled in spite of the knot in his stomach. "I never believed your story of swimming races with her."

"She beat me many times. And she's dressed as a man. Swimming is an option. How about you?"

Ben revealed his prowess as a swimmer. "How good a shot are you, Colville?"

"I've been practicing for years, expecting to be called out in a duel."

He quickly told Colville what role each would take. Then he slipped off his shoes, tucked his knife in the waistband of his banana suit and wished the other man good luck. Slipping noiselessly over the side of the boat, he swam toward the houseboat. They'd come daringly close, not thirty yards from it. The swim was easy, the water warmer than he'd expected.

His fingers touched the boat's wooden hull. It rode close to the water making his access easy. He reached one hand up, then

another, pulled his weight up and peered over the side. Seeing
and hearing nothing, he swung a leg up and climbed aboard. He
crawled across the deck toward a lighted window. He heard talking, a man—Benoit's reedy tones.

And Maureen's voice. *Thank God.* She was alive and sounded
like herself. Then her laughter. Then another male voice—
Leveque's. Listening beneath the window, he heard the men slur-
ring their words. They were foxed! How bizarre. Maureen giggled.
Was this a party or a kidnapping?

Crouching beneath the window, he removed his knife from
his banana pants—which, ridiculous as they were, had helped
him glide through the water with ease—while Maureen related
a lengthy story. Amused, he listened to Maureen's tale that she'd
acted on Suzette's orders when she'd gone in the house and taken
Monsieur St. Aubin's account book.

"Madame St. Aubin wanted to know how much money her
husband earned every month. He was so stingy with her clothes
budget. She thought perhaps—and you gentlemen can imagine
the horror of this—well, she worried she'd married a pauper."

Maureen sounded like she'd had quite a bit to drink, too. She
went on. "Generally an older man gives a young wife anything—
and I mean anything, gentlemen, she wants. It's the only way to
keep her happy. But not Monsieur St. Aubin."

Leveque interrupted to say she'd meet Monsieur St. Aubin
later tonight and she could tell him anything she wished about
his wife.

St. Aubin. Perfect. He'd returned from Jamaica, then. Ben had
telegraphed Carleton yesterday, suggesting he and his team arrive
tomorrow.

Would St. Aubin be alone tonight or with Mendoza? Or a
dozen others? Raising his eyes just above the window's ledge, Ben
surveyed the room. Maureen, in a straight back chair, hands untied,
drank a dark liquid from a water glass. Brandy? Leveque, with a

rifle slung over his left shoulder, slumped half-in, half-out of an upholstered chair near the doorway leading to the right deck. In his right hand, he, too, held a glass. Benoit stood near Maureen, but he swayed precariously.

Three sheets to the wind, her two guards looked ready to pass out any minute. Maureen began another tirade against Monsieur St. Aubin while both men took hefty swallows of their liquor. "I can't wait to meet the gentleman. I can't say I've had the pleasure. I'll tell him straight out if he expects to keep Suzette happy, he'd better buy her more gowns and hats. Shoes. The lady doesn't have many pairs. Furs and diamonds wouldn't hurt either."

Benoit turned away for a moment. Maureen spilled most of her drink on her black trousers before bringing the glass to her lips.

Good for you, my love.

Benoit faced her again and took a few tentative steps closer to her. "We have a two-fold plan for you, Miss Collins." He leaned heavily on his cane. "We know you're sweet on Ben Merritt, who also calls himself Andrew Franklin. And we don't like the way he's been snooping around Lafitte Nursery."

"You mean buying plants, Monsieur Benoit? Do you think a gentleman shouldn't buy plants for a young lady?" she demanded. "Beautiful perennials are a sign of everlasting love!"

Leveque croaked from the corner. "Merritt works for the U.S. Customs Service."

She laughed again, peals of drunken giggles. "That's the most ridiculous thing I've ever heard. He's an attorney. Works for Collins Cotton Factorage. The man pores over contracts day and night. He's practically blind; his sister told me he wears spectacles to read. He doesn't know whether my eyes are blue, green, or brown."

He did so. Blue. What had Letitia said? She'd not seen their equal on three continents. Spectacles? Practically blind? Her act almost convinced him his sight was poor.

Benoit came closer. Tap, tap, tap. "He bought you some very expensive plants," he said in an accusing tone. "Plants with opium in the roots."

"Opium!" She gasped and patted her chest with her free hand. "What are you talking about? I never saw any opium. You mean the substance people smoke?"

"How daft are you?" Benoit sneered. "I see you didn't inherit your father's brains. The tins, lady, the tins in the roots."

"Mr. Merritt gave me plants with *fertilizer* in the roots." She entertained them with another tale of Ben checking out books at the library for her. Her exaggerated gestures, typical of someone in a drunken state, seemed to fascinate her audience. "I spread the fertilizer carefully. Grafting isn't easy to do, you know. Most grafts fail, but the ones with this fertilizer on them did well. I think you're quite mistaken. There was no opium in those tins."

She stuck her lower lip out in a pout. "This rope is cutting off the circulation. I really do wish you gentlemen would untie my feet." She lifted her shoes, then stomped on the floor for emphasis.

Ben's mouth dropped open in surprise as Leveque rose, left his rifle on his chair, and staggered toward her. He retrieved a long-bladed knife from his waistband, bent and cut the ropes. Maureen raised her feet, wiggled her ankles a little, flexing them, making circles to the right and then to the left. "Oh, my, that does feel better. Thank you, Monsieur Leveque."

The man's knife clattered to the floor and slid under her chair. He looked around for a moment, but didn't see it. Tottering, he made his way back to his chair and sat, balancing the rifle in his lap.

Chapter Forty-Three

Colville's voice rang out across the lake: "Ahoy, there. Anyone aboard? I'm taking on water. Anyone there who can throw me a rope?"

A fleeting smile swept across Maureen's face. She tried to stand, but Benoit stepped forward and swung his cane into her back. *What a bastard!* She moaned and sank back down, her hand rubbing her shoulder.

Colville shouted again: "I've got plenty of Mardi Gras whiskey. I'll share!"

Benoit jerked his head toward the bow. "Shoot him. That'll shut him up."

Leveque, rifle raised, lurched through the door to the starboard deck. Shots came toward the boat, not from it. Leveque's scream rent the air.

Ben charged through the door. With a step and a leap, he tackled Benoit. They crashed to the floor, the man's cane landing at Maureen's feet.

For a split second, Ben's eyes met hers. "Run," he mouthed.

But she didn't. Leaning over, she picked up the cane and shoved it into his hands. He slammed Benoit in the ribs, hoping his blows had killed him or come close to it.

Maureen stood, put one foot out and fell forward, hitting the floor hard.

Benoit gripped her ankle with one hand. In the other, he clutched the blade he'd found under her chair. Kneeling, he lifted the knife, poised to slash the back of Maureen's neck.

No, no. Not Maureen.

"Dodge right," Ben screamed. Her body moved at his command. He lunged for the man's torso and thrust his own knife into Benoit's heart.

Maureen scrambled to her knees, tried to stand again, but couldn't. "I have no feeling in my feet," she shouted.

"You won't need them when you're dead," Leveque hissed from the doorway. Maureen, crouched on the floor halfway between the two men, impeded Ben's angles of attack. He could easily leap over her to tackle Leveque, but only if she remained still. If she tried to stand …

A pistol tucked in Leveque's belt, his only visible weapon, looked to be out of his reach. Blood streamed from his useless right arm. His midsection, too, bled profusely and he held his left arm against it. His body trembled with effort as he stepped toward Maureen. He spoke haltingly: "I'll kill you both."

"No you won't," Maureen shouted as she threw herself at his ankles and brought him crashing to the floor. Ben leaped at the same moment, just missing Maureen and landing with his knees on the butler's legs, pinning him down.

Ben grabbed the gun with one hand and Maureen's waist with the other. He wrapped an arm around her, pulled her to her feet and hugged her tightly against his side. "Thank God, you're safe."

"Here's his rifle." Colville entered wearing a huge grin, carrying two rifles—his and Leveque's.

"Great job, Colville." Ben slapped him on the back.

Maureen kissed his cheek and thanked him. Her eyes traveled from her former beau to Ben. She crossed her arms and sighed heavily. "It's about time, gentlemen. That's the longest kidnapping I've ever endured."

Ben couldn't help himself and laughed with relief. Colville joined in.

Maureen, pretending to be annoyed, began to lecture Colville. "It wasn't quite what I expected. Treated gently? No cursing? A comfortable coach? No ropes?"

"Antoine would have been very pleasant to you."

Leaving them to their lively discussion, Ben crossed the room and knelt beside Leveque. "Benoit's dead. What time do you expect St. Aubin tonight? And who's coming with him?"

Leveque tried to sit up, grimaced, and lay back, nearly lifeless. "I don't know," he sputtered.

"Leave him," Colville called. "Let's get Maureen back to town."

"Don't leave me here." Leveque's weak voice pleaded.

Ben threatened him in a hoarse whisper. "I'm going to ask you once more, Leveque. What time is St. Aubin coming?"

"I don't know."

"Like hell, you don't." Ben put the pistol against his temple. "I'll give you more brandy for pain and get you a short jail term if you cooperate. Or I'll kill you. It's all the same to me."

Shaking, Leveque narrowed his eyes. "All I did was ... the account book ..."

Ben cocked the gun and pushed it harder against Leveque's skull. "You choose. A short prison sentence or eternity in hell. Beginning right now. Five, four, three ..."

"Eight o'clock," he whispered.

Ben feared Leveque might pass out any minute. He softened his voice. "With others?"

"Mendo ..."

"Mendoza? That's all?"

Leveque struggled to talk. Between pants, he said they didn't trust Timmie. Believable. He had not seen Timmie on Captain Kwan's boat digging up opium tins.

"Mendoza killed Captain Kwan, didn't he?"

Leveque nodded.

"Is there a signal for tonight's meeting?"

He nodded again. "A lantern …"

"Where, damn it?" He wanted to shake him, but he had to soothe, not bully. "You're going to be all right, Leveque. I'll have you to a hospital soon. Where is the lantern supposed to be?"

"On the bow."

Ben looked up. Colville sat on the floor beside Maureen coaxing her to drink some brandy. And thank God, he'd covered Benoit's face and half his body with a small blanket, which sopped up some of the blood. Angry as he'd been with the man earlier, he was a good shot. He'd been a huge help. He wasn't sure he could have saved Maureen without him.

He turned his attentions back to Leveque. "One last question. Which way are they coming?"

"From the Gulf. Through the Rigolets."

Turning around, he asked, "His friends are coming through the Rigolets. What's that?"

"A deep-water pass connecting the lake here to the Gulf of Mexico," Colville answered. "We can pick them off as they approach us."

Thank God Colville was confident. He leaned toward Leveque's ear. "If one word of this isn't true, I'll kill you first. Colville, give him some brandy, please. Lots of it. I want him to pass out."

"Maureen, can you find some sort of bandage?"

She left the room for a minute and returned with a sheet, which Ben tore in strips and wrapped around the butler's upper arm. The wound in his stomach bled a great deal, but he thought Leveque would live if they could get him help soon. He bound his wrists, his ankles and then tied him to the upholstered chair. Not long after, Leveque fell into a fitful sleep.

While Colville reloaded the weapons, he suggested again they leave Leveque and return to town. Ben shook his head. Mendoza and St. Aubin would be here soon. One a murderer, the other the leader of an immense smuggling operation. And on board right now, he expected there were thousands of dollars' worth of opium, which he wanted to take with him when they left.

He had a job to do. He asked Colville to take Maureen and Leveque in the rowboat, but Maureen refused to leave. Then Colville refused to leave. As much as Ben hated having Maureen on board, he needed Colville's help.

In the valuable time they had left, he prepared his defense—better yet, his offense. A center closet off the galley offered a safe hideaway for Maureen, no matter how fierce the gun battle on deck proved to be. At ten minutes to eight, Ben put the lighted lantern in the bow, led her to the pantry and handed her a pistol.

"I know how to shoot," she said.

"Colville told me. I'm sure you can handle anyone who comes your way. I don't know another person in the world who could have talked her kidnappers into untying her." He chuckled. "We'll take care of St. Aubin and Mendoza quickly and get you home." He leaned into the small space and kissed her.

Holding the pistol, she wrapped both hands around his neck, and murmured that she loved him. They held each other for a few minutes until Colville shouted an alarm. Ben gave her one last directive: "Don't leave the pantry until you hear me or Colville say it's safe. If anyone else opens the door, fire right at his chest."

Every muscle taut, Ben listened to voices and laughter floating toward them on the dark water. Only the two—St. Aubin and Mendoza—in a rowboat lit by a lantern in the bow. Loud and vulgar, they came across the lake just as Leveque said they would. In place on the bow of the houseboat, the signal—one lantern—cast an eerie glow on the water. He and Colville crouched at two open windows in the dark room.

They waited until both men's feet were on the deck. Two rifles at close range. They fired at the same instant. Four, five, six shots. Mendoza went down first, hollering that his leg was hit. He yelled a second time and gripped his shoulder.

Ben put a bullet in St. Aubin's stomach. The man dropped to his knees and rolled on his back.

Colville held a gun on them while Ben took their rifles from the deck and their knives from their belts and threw them in the lake. Together, they dragged the men into the main room where Ben tied Mendoza up, securing his hands behind his back and his ankles together.

"Mr. Franklin, I'm surprised," Mendoza taunted between groans of pain. "Who'd have thought you knew how to fire a gun?" Blood pooled underneath his leg. Ben couldn't tell how seriously he was hurt, but he figured he would probably live to serve time. "You had me fooled. I thought you were like every other dope fiend with a yen for good opium."

Ignoring Mendoza's words, Ben checked St. Aubin's pulse. It was faint, so faint he thought him harmless, only minutes from death.

Maureen held her breath as the sound of guns split the silence. It seemed to her they lasted longer than they should have. How many shots did it take to disable two men? Or were there more? Before it began, she'd planned to count the shots, but that proved impossible. They were simultaneous and far louder than she'd imagined. Was it five, six, eight?

Screams and footsteps came from the main room. She couldn't see the face of her watch in the pitch black of the closet. She forced herself to count to sixty. Maybe she was a little faster than a real clock, but she did it five or six times. How long did it take to shoot someone? Certainly not more than five minutes.

If the men had all killed each other, she could sit in this pantry forever and no one would find her. Leveque would die without treatment. Ben or Vespasian might be hurt and need their wounds tended. She might have to row them back down the bayou to Lafitte Nursery. If one of them were conscious, she could do it with their directions. Damn it, she could do it *without* their directions. Even on Mardi Gras night there might be some traffic on the bayou. Someone to help her.

She couldn't sit here while Ben and Vespasian battled the smugglers alone. She could shoot. She could help. The pistol in her hand, she tiptoed from the galley down the short hallway toward Benoit's sitting room. Slinking along the wall, she listened, then peered inside. Vespasian knelt beside Mendoza who lay on his side—ankles tied, hands tied—and poured brandy in the murderer's mouth.

Ben methodically knotted the rope securing St. Aubin's ankles. She shuddered at the sight of Suzette's husband. A huge round red face, bug eyes, fat cheeks, a sunken chin and high forehead topped a short, stocky body.

Staring at him, she saw St. Aubin's hand move slightly, then reach into his jacket.

"Ben," she shouted, "Look out."

Diving sideways, Ben fired his own pistol at the body on the floor. More gunshots exploded around him. Maureen screamed.

Had Maureen been shot? She'd screamed. My God, it couldn't be. She'd warned him. She'd saved his life.

Trembling, he turned to where he'd seen her last. Maureen crawled toward him, moving one hand, one knee, one hand, one knee. Ben rushed to her, scooped her off the floor and cradled her in his arms. "Are you hurt? Were you hit?"

Burying her face in his shoulder for a moment, she wiped away tears. "I'm fine."

He closed his eyes and breathed her rose scent. "Thank God, you're safe."

She raised her face and smiled at him until her cheeks dimpled. He kissed her, put her feet on the floor, but kept an arm wound tightly around her.

Ben turned to check on Colville.

"I've never been better, Merritt," he said, a grin spreading across his face. He slapped an arm on each of their shoulders, forming a circle. "You both have to admit my scheme wasn't a bad one. I expect Patrick Collins will give you two his blessing before the evening is out."

He nodded toward St. Aubin's body. "And I have an unexpected benefit: Suzette's a widow. I can't say I'm sorry about that."

"Neither are we," Maureen said as Ben nodded.

Pulling out the watch from her pocket, Maureen waved it in the men's faces. "You know, gentlemen, it's just nine o'clock. We have a Mardi Gras ball to attend tonight. Don't you think we should celebrate?"

Historical Note

As writers of historical fiction, we strive to be accurate in all details from the cut of a gentleman's coat to the shape of a lady's shoe.

Opium smuggling, a serious issue in America in the late 1800s, plays a central role in *The Devious Debutante*. Opium usage increased four-fold from the 1840s to the 1890s. More than 77,000 pounds of opium, taxed at $6 a pound, entered the country legally in 1880. Three years later, still weighed down by Civil War debt, the government raised the tariff on the popular drug from $6 to $10 a pound. Legal opium imports plummeted while illegal imports skyrocketed as did the number of opium users and dens.

We gave our hero Benjamin Merritt the task of uncovering smuggling rings in New Orleans and reporting back to the U.S. Customs Department, under the Department of the Treasury. By 1885 when he arrives in the city and meets Maureen Collins, smugglers are bringing in more than 25,000 pounds of opium annually, most of it through the ports of New Orleans, New York, and San Francisco.

Merritt's mentor, Samuel Carleton, is based loosely on the life of Henry Ossian Flipper, the first African-American to graduate from West Point in 1877. Flipper was commissioned a second lieutenant and was the first black officer to command white troops during his service in the Indian Territory. Later, he worked as an assistant to the Secretary of the Interior for many years.

We admit to playing a little loose with dates to improve our story. Merritt uses fingerprints to identify a murderer, pre-dating Scotland Yard's use. But it's not much of a stretch that a well-trained investigator would have been aware of the technique. It had been long established by scientists that every person's prints were unique. Mark Twain's 1883 book, *Life on the Mississippi*, contains a scene in which fingerprints are used to catch a criminal.

Finally, Mardi Gras, a moveable feast depending on the date of Easter, was celebrated on March 9, 1886, but we moved it up a month to February 9 to give Maureen and Ben fewer days to fall in love. Painstaking research enabled us to be accurate in placing the Proteus parade on Mardi Gras evening (not Monday night as it is today), and to put Merritt on the Ceres float dressed as a banana.

Author's Note
on Language

New Orleans from its earliest days blended cultures: French, Native American, Spanish, African and French Canadian. After the Louisiana Purchase in 1803, Americans of largely English descent arrived. Many Free People of Color lived in the city before the Civil War. After the war, many former slaves resided there as well.

By the 1880s, immigrants from Western Europe, Eastern Europe as well as South America and the West Indies had settled in the city. In such a cosmopolitan seaport, a businessman might converse in French, Spanish, German and Italian in the course of an afternoon.

In this book, we have given our characters the wildly different speech patterns of New Orleans citizens, whether they are African-American, Irish, French or Cajun—of all classes—while still making them understandable to contemporary readers.

Acknowledgements

We want to thank our agent, Claudia Cross, whose enthusiasm for the Love in New Orleans Series kept us hard at work on Book 3, *The Devious Debutante*.

Many thanks, too, to the members of the Valley Forge Chapter of the Romance Writers of America who kept us believing in the dream.

Invaluable to us in our study of the 1880s were: the Louisiana Division, City Archives and Special Collections at the New Orleans Public Library; the Williams Research Center of the Historic New Orleans Collection; and the Louisiana Collection at the Earl K. Long Library, University of New Orleans.

We learned grafting techniques for camellias from Robert J. Halliday's book, *Practical Camellia Culture: A Treatise on the Propagation and Culture of the Camellia Japonica*, published in Baltimore, Maryland, in 1880. (Reprinted by Applewood Books, Bedford, MA)

To familiarize ourselves with opium and the historical understanding of its effects as well as the treatment for addiction, we referred to Dr. Harry Hubbell Kane's *Opium Smoking in America and China* (G.P. Putnam & Sons, 1882).

Author Bio

Ursula LeCoeur is the pen name for a mother-daughter writing team, Mary and Helen Scully, who set their Love in New Orleans Series in the 1880s, during the Gilded Age in America.

Helen rescued Ursula, the family cat, from the streets as a kitten, post-Katrina. LeCoeur, a common name in New Orleans, meaning *heart* in French, is perfect for a romance writer.

Mary and Helen's ancestors settled in New Orleans in the 1830s. Through the years, the family spread out along the Gulf Coast as far as Mobile, where Mary was born.

They love to hear from readers. Email them at ursulalecoeur@gmail.com. Visit their website, www.ursulalecoeur, for blogposts on New Orleans history and family recipes for traditional Southern food. Follow their Facebook page (UrsulaLeCoeur) and keep up with them on Twitter (@ursulalecoeur).

Don't miss the next novel in Ursula LeCoeur's Love in New Orleans Series. Enjoy this excerpt from *Miss Carine's Love Lessons*

Chapter One

New Orleans
May 1887

"You *can't* be serious, Mr. Swenson! I'm to work with him?" Carine Bouchard stabbed a finger in the direction of the young man standing in the doorway, then leaned forward over her editor's desk and lowered her voice. "Perhaps you don't know Mr. Colville's reputation. His advice will be the same, no matter what our readers ask: 'Have a drink or two and bed the lady. That's what she needs.'"

"Miss Bouchard!" Swenson bellowed. "Show some respect!"

Vespasian Colville, a jaunty grin on his face, sauntered into the office and shook the editor's hand. "Her remarks don't offend me, sir." He turned to her and bowed. "I'll soon prove myself worthy to work with Miss Bouchard. I have no doubt I'm up to the challenge."

Carine's heart sank. It was insulting enough that Mr. Swenson thought it imperative to add a male's point of view to her popular column, *Dear Jacqueline*. But to saddle her with this man! Her stomach roiled. Perhaps she could make him so miserable, he'd decide not to work with her. "I doubt you're up to it, Mr. Colville."

Swenson cleared his throat. "Sit down, Mr. Colville. A little tension between writing partners will add some spice. *The Daily*

353

Picayune will be ahead of every newspaper in the country. I'm going to call the new column *Dear Jacques and Jacqueline* and run it three times a week. The readers will love it."

He paused to knock ash from his cigarette into the crystal bowl on his desk. "I envision you agreeing on a suitable response to most letters. If you cannot—agree, that is—you'll each write your advice. Readers will take sides. Men against women and so on. It'll sell newspapers."

Did Mr. Swenson really think they'd ever agree on answers? *Not likely.*

Carine had known Vespasian for years. It seemed whenever she spent the day with her best friend, Maureen Collins, he showed up, too. The pesky boy had interrupted their dolls' tea parties, pulled their hair, put frogs down the backs of their dresses. When Maureen made her debut two years ago, Vespasian had courted her, which caused a huge riff between the friends.

Feeling certain Maureen would suffer from a ruined reputation and a broken heart, Carine told her so. They didn't speak for many months—until Maureen saw the rake for what he was, threw him over, and married another. As Carine recalled, Vespasian then made a foolhardy play for a married lady.

"Miss Bouchard?" Swenson repeated.

She'd not heard her name. Vespasian jabbed her arm and jerked his head toward their boss. She looked up in time to see Mr. Swenson pull a fistful of correspondence from his desk drawer.

"As I was saying, Miss Bouchard ..." His piercing eyes fixed on her, then on her new partner. "Mr. Colville. I have more than a dozen letters here. All these came in yesterday. I suggest the two of you go into the room next door and determine how you're going to proceed. I need five hundred words before five o'clock." With a smirk on his face, Vespasian accepted the letters from Mr. Swenson.

Oh, dear heavens, he handed them to him, not her. Carine stood, yanked her skirt into place, and snapped: "You shall have an excellent column, Mr. Swenson, as always."

They entered a room furnished with eight straight-back chairs, and a long oak table on which sat a pitcher of water, two glasses, a writing tablet, two pencils, a typewriter and paper for it.

Taking charge, Carine issued an order: "Sit down, divide the bundle and start reading. When you find something interesting, set it aside. I'll do the same. If we're lucky, we'll find three or four letters that are usable. Dictate them to me and I'll type. She shoved the letters in his direction and straightened the typewriter. "A modern writer who doesn't know how to type. Imagine that!"

"Actually I do."

She raised her eyes to his.

"I suspect there's quite a bit you don't know about me," he said.

Her breath caught, but for just a moment. She motioned him toward a chair. "I know more than enough to last a lifetime, so please, don't make conversation."

He quirked an eyebrow. "I taught myself to type in the last two months. Practiced daily. I quit my job as a clerk at Collins Factorage the minute I was hired here."

"Perhaps you shouldn't have." She glared at him. "Sit. And start reading."

He gestured toward her. "You're standing. A gentleman doesn't sit while a lady—"

"Oh, hush. This is the working world. And as far as I'm concerned, you're not a gentleman."

He covered his mouth to hide a smile. "Perhaps not. But we're writing an advice column on etiquette and social interactions, are we not?"

She yanked a chair out, sat and scooted the chair up to the table. Vespasian sat beside her. He sorted the letters as he might deal cards. One for her, one for him and so on until all fifteen were divided, leaving her with eight.

"Have you been reading the column, sir?" She asked without looking up.

"Monday and Thursday." He paused. "Religiously."

She couldn't tell if he were making fun of her and rushed on. "It started as a weekly, you know, but it's so popular that___"

"I'm here." He leaned back in his chair and turned his palms up, grinning.

His smile showed off his remarkably straight teeth. The skin around his eyes crinkled and his green eyes sparkled. He was enjoying himself. Sparring with her was his day's entertainment. He could joke, but she needed this job. Her family wasn't in the poorhouse, but since her father's death nearly a year ago, her mother had curtailed all luxuries. Carine had to make this partnership work if it killed her. And it just might.

As if he read her mind, he spoke with quiet conviction. "I know I've not impressed you in the past, Miss Bouchard, but I'm a changed man. If you give me a chance, I think you'll be surprised."

Sighing heavily. "I'm sure I won't be. That's the problem. *Read.*"

The words of her first letter were in the tiniest script she'd ever seen. She removed her spectacles, cleaned them with a handkerchief from her purse and replaced them. From the corner of her eye, she saw he noticed the gesture for what it was—a nervous habit—but she ignored him. She certainly wasn't going to turn and let him see her full face without her glasses. She'd worn them for the last five years; she'd become "the young lady in glasses."

Maureen often told her she hid behind them. Perhaps she did, because, in fact, she could survive a Mardi Gras ball or a night at the opera without them. She needed them to read, but not for her daily existence: a staircase's uneven treads, the actors on a stage, the face of a handsome male dancing partner.

They both read silently for a few minutes. Much to her dismay, she grew hot sitting this close to the man who thought himself the handsomest in Louisiana—or New Orleans—at the very least. Such arrogance. And such a rakehell.

She gritted her teeth and forced her attention back to the letter. But before she made it through the first few lines, he began to laugh. "Listen: 'I think we should use this one. It's from a young lady who wants to let a certain young man know she's interested in him. Listen:"

I made my debut in January and he danced with me at quite a few Mardi Gras balls, but he's not called on me. What can I do to let him know that I'd like to become better acquainted?

Young Lady Hoping for a Caller.

Carine took a deep breath, praying for patience. "Are you familiar with the language of the fan, sir? At a house party or garden party, she should carry the fan open in her right hand, signaling she's desirous of acquaintance."

Vespasian's forehead creased in a frown, but she continued.

"And when she knows he's watching her, she closes it, indicating she wishes to speak with him."

He shook his head. "I see why I've been called in to help," he muttered. "I hate to tell you, dear writing partner, but men don't know what all that fan business means. Do you honestly think the Jesuits make a mission of tutoring young boys in the language of the fan?"

She tilted her head a moment. Indeed, she'd long suspected men didn't know about fans. "That may be a valid point," she said slowly. "Suppose she drops a handkerchief so he must pick it up? She thanks him and a conversation begins."

He sighed loudly. "I will tell you exactly what she should do. Please type, Miss Bouchard. I'll dictate:

Dear Young Lady Hoping for a Caller:

"*I*—or are we saying *we*? I like *we*.*"

We suggest the next time you meet the gentleman who interests you, contrive to move close and stand beside him. If we have to tell you how to manage this maneuver, you should still be in the schoolroom.

"Are you with me so far?"

She sat up straighter in her chair. "I type very fast, sir."

While smiling brightly, angle your body to thrust your chest forward, preferably in a gown that shows some décolletage.

"I'm not typing that line. If a young lady behaved like that, it would ruin her reputation."

He raised both eyebrows. "Hear me out. I'm not finished." He cleared his throat.

You must glance at his trousers. Again, if we have to explain what part of his trousers your eyes should find, go back to the schoolroom.

"Mr. Colville!" Her hand slapped the table beside the typewriter. "I will *not* type that."

Ignoring her, he continued.

If you do not see evidence of his interest in you, move on to another gentleman.

"You—Dear Jacques—cannot write that!"

"Miss Bouchard, I believe you're blushing."

She cleared her throat. Indeed, her face felt very hot and her mouth had gone dry. "I can't believe you're suggesting such a charade to her. She might do best to just ask him if he has room in his bed for her." She stood to reach for a glass of water, but Mr. Colville gallantly leaned across the table and retrieved the pitcher and a glass. As he did, the back vent of his coat opened and she had a view of the seat of his trousers, pulled taut across firm thighs.

She was certain as certain could be, she was blushing now. She accepted the water glass from him and took several rapid swallows. "Thank you," she murmured.

Vespasian's eyes fixed on her hair, moved downward to her face, her neck and her bosom. Smiling, his eyes returned to her face. Did she—her physical person—please him or repel him? She knew very little about men, but she would not let him take control here. It was *her column*, after all.

"I'm afraid the two of us must be honest with each other, Miss Bouchard, if we're to write together." He leaned closer, his lips nearly on her ear and lowered his voice. "If a gentleman is not aroused by the sight of a young lady's breasts at close proximity, nothing she does or says will induce him to call on her."

Startled by his frankness, Carine sat perfectly still, her hands poised above the keys, her body keenly aware of the warmth of his beside her. Her rational thoughts, which had momentarily abandoned her, now swung into action. She'd never had a man speak of such things with her. She managed to say three words. "Is that so?"

"I assure you, it is."

"It's not the same with women."

He patted her wrist, surprising her with such familiarity. "Of course it is. She may not admit it, but there's a little thrill low in her belly, a queasiness when she sees a certain gentleman across the room. If there's not, she doesn't want *him* to call on *her*."

"But he might find her fascinating if only he paid a call ...."

He waved his hand in a dismissive gesture. "She can drop a thousand handkerchiefs if she likes. He'll pick them up and be polite, but he won't call on her if he's not interested in her body."

"You're impossible! Is that what love is all about? For men?"

He nodded. "I believe so. And there's no point in this young lady thinking she can attract him if he's not interested."

"Perhaps her father has a huge bank account."

He threw his hands up. "Ahh, that's a different story. I'm sure we'll have a letter about marriages of convenience before long. Meanwhile, this lady needs to hear the truth."

Carine sighed. "All right. I like your idea of moving close to stand beside him, but I'll alter the wording to say—if he shows no *interest* in you." She typed.

He shrugged. "I don't suppose Mr. Swenson would permit my wording."

"I'm quite sure he would not. One finished. Let's move on." She opened the next letter, scanned it and shook her head.

"Distasteful, I presume?"

Carine read aloud:

Dear Jacqueline,

Is there any chance a man will marry me when his parents are against our union?

Loved by Him, Not Them.

"A Romeo and Juliet." Vespasian sighed. "How romantic."

Startled by his sentiment, Carine bit out. "I can only hope you're employing sarcasm, sir." She shook the letter in her hand. "We have Shakespeare to blame for scores of young ladies thinking this type of situation is romantic."

Vespasian grimaced. "I suppose you'll say it's hopeless."

"Because it is."

"Let's each write an answer, Miss Bouchard. You may choose your instrument." He gestured toward the tablets and pencils, then to the typewriter.

"I'll type."

He leaned across the table again to grab paper and pencil, giving her a second view of his long legs and a peek at his bottom as his coat slid sideways. She felt a queasiness low in her belly. No, not so. She must have imagined it. She concentrated on putting a new sheet of paper in the typewriter and wrote:

Dear Loved by Him,

Are you prettier, more intelligent, better educated, better dressed or better off financially than your future mother-in-law? Any of these could inspire jealousy and disapproval.

Or is it the reverse? If it's your lack of social standing, family background or large bank account that offends your intended's parents, these are nearly impossible to overcome. It could take many years of exemplary living and a houseful of adorable children before they accept you. And to be blunt, there's absolutely no guarantee—none—that your actions will ever change their opinion of you.

I advise both of you to think this through very carefully before you run off together. If he gives up an inheritance for you—which I suspect will be the outcome—you must be certain deep in your hearts that love will endure without the trappings money buys.

Vespasian asked her to read her reply first. He rose and began pacing, rubbing his chin as he went up one side of the table, turned and strolled back on the other side. When she finished, he turned to face her. "Miss Bouchard, the last thing this couple should do is *think this through.*"

Carine squeezed the skin of her forehead into tight lines to make her eyes narrow and fierce, a technique that always sent her sister Elise scurrying from the room. "Is everything a joke to you? I—we—might alter the course of someone's life with our advice. We have a serious responsibility."

He didn't flinch. "How often does one find real love? If these two are in love, they should follow their passion and live happily ever after."

She gestured toward his tablet. "I suppose that's what you advised?"

Picking it up, his voice hoarse with emotion, he read: *Tell this man your sun rises in him each morning. If he were to abandon you, you would have no warmth, no light, no love.*

A shiver ran down Carine's spine. What a beautiful declaration. No one had ever expressed such a sentiment to her. She supposed no one ever would. She was a full twenty years of age and had never had a proposal, much less a serious suitor. It was lovely, what

Vespasian had written, but it was utter foolishness. She swallowed before she spoke. "I refuse to offer this woman the expectation of happiness in a marriage that begins with his parents' antagonism."

"Romeo and Juliet ..."

"Died. Remember? Shakespeare didn't write of the myriad problems likely to beset such a couple."

A smile crossed his face. "Let's either use both answers or leave this letter out."

She shook her head. "We can't. We're running out of time and we have to fill the designated space."

He began pacing again. "Mr. Swenson suggested if there came a time when we couldn't agree, we could offer two answers. People will talk about it on the streetcar and in the coffee shops. Can't you hear them? 'Did you read what Jacqueline said to *Loved By Him, Not Them?* She's absolutely right. Poor way to start out.' To which her friend will answer: 'I hope they follow Jacques' advice.'"

His eyes glittered with excitement. "It'll draw readers to us."

"I already have plenty of readers," She snapped.

"Apparently not as many as Mr. Swenson would like."

She scowled. Always had to have the last word, didn't he?

"I'll type." Her hands flew across the keys. She yanked the paper out and handed it to him. "Anything else you'd like to add to Jacques' ridiculous answer."

He motioned for her to put the paper back in the machine. He continued: *If your intended won't run away with you, he's either a lying hypocrite playing with your affections or he's a spineless bastard who will never stand up for you against his family. If either proves true, end this relationship immediately."*

Carine held up a hand. "We can't write *bastard* in a family newspaper."

"It's how men talk."

"Perhaps, but—"

"Fine, fine," he conceded. "Whelp. A spineless whelp."

She typed and once again handed him the page to read.

"Good. Done. I think we did an exceptional job, if I do say so myself."

She scowled for the second—or was it the hundredth time—this afternoon?

He shook his head, a big grin on his face. "Oh, Miss Bouchard, admit it. It's a good column."

"Mr. Swenson will be the judge," she said in a crisp voice. She stood. "In the future, I think we should work separately. I'll take all the letters from women. You take the men's letters. We'll each work at home, but we'll sign them from Jacques and Jacqueline together. Mr. Swenson will never know whether we agree or not."

Vespasian shook his head, his grin widening. "I believe the whole point is to disagree."

Carine understood that, but the fact remained: She didn't want to write with Vespasian Colville. What's more, she didn't want to be in the same room with him. How could she say it kindly? And why did she wish to be kind? "It's unpleasant to ... to argue with you."

"It's challenging."

She spoke in her practiced business voice. "I will collect all the letters on Monday, sort male and female, and send them by messenger to your lodgings. Are you on Esplanade in your family's home?" She knew he didn't reside there any longer, but she didn't want him to know she knew. He gave her his address.

"If you wish to work alone, Miss Bouchard, just say so. It won't offend me. That's the problem with women. They never say what they think."

That did it. She could be direct—as direct as any man. "You find it strange that I don't want to work with you? Are you really that obtuse?"

He shrugged.

"I created this column. My answers attracted attention and the number of letters increased. Mr. Swenson added a second column per week, and now a third. If the situation were reversed, I expect you would have quit without blinking an eye. The great Colville must write with a woman? You would have walked out."

His eyebrows arched, his face flushed. "Forgive me, Miss Bouchard." He bowed his full head of curly hair for just a moment. "I admire you for sticking with the task. I expect I will learn a great deal from you. You've done a wonderful job."

She stared into his green eyes and swallowed hard. Had he actually apologized for his attitude, given her a compliment? She didn't know how to respond.

He continued. "I appreciate your honesty, Miss Bouchard. If you wish, we'll work independently and see if the columns have the same liveliness, shall we?"

She nodded crisply. She'd won. But the victory felt hollow. When would she see Vespasian again?

34920891R00221

Made in the USA
Middletown, DE
11 September 2016